# FANGS

## PRODIGIUM ACADEMY BOOK FOUR

KATIE MAY

EXPRESSO PUBLISHING, LLC

*To all of you who grew up and now realize that you no longer want a Prince Charming but a monster who fucks you until you're seeing stars. Don't get me wrong. A knight in shining armor is great and all, but a villain who's willing to burn the world to the ground just so you can live? Or...even better...a monster who hands you the matches and stands by your side with a proud smile on his face while you light everything on fire? Yum.*

# CONTENTS

# FOREWORD

This is a paranormal academy reverse harem romance and is not suitable for anyone under the age of 18. There is strong language throughout the book, as well as sexual situations and graphic violence. This series also contains MM themes. Put this book down if such material offends you. Or if you're related to me. I'm not even joking about the last part. Grandma, if you're reading this...I love you, but please, please don't torture us both like that. Put the book down and read your newspaper. I'm not even kidding.

Previously on Prodigium Academy...

Violet Dracula and her men compete to win the Roaring, a series of dangerous games that put monsters in life or death situations. During the second game, Violet is transported to a room with her father, Vladimir Dracula, and Dimitri Gray. She is told that she is actually the daughter of Lucifer Morningstar and Hera, but Hera begged Dracula to look after Violet when she was born in order to hide her from Lucifer, who believes her to be dead. The room explodes, Dracula is stabbed in the heart, and Medusa, Mason's mother, kidnaps Violet.

Medusa brings Violet to Mount Olympus where she tells her about two prophecies. One states that a woman named Violet will rise from the ashes and claim her rightful throne. Another states that Dracula's daughter will murder Mason. While in Mount Olympus, Violet also meets the eccentric king of the gods, Zeus.

After returning to the academy, Violet discovers that Hux and Jack's body has been taken over by a murderous monster named Balor. Violet can't figure out Balor's purpose, but he seems to hold a violent grudge against vampires.

During a race through a deadly maze, Cal reveals himself as one of Violet's mates. They have sex, and upon discovering them, Barret appears to be jealous.

Violet and her mates make it through the maze, winning the Roaring, and they are taken to meet Lucifer, who requested to meet the winners. During the meeting, the group is attacked by vampire hunters and Violet is taken captive.

Violet is tortured by Stefan Van Helsing, Vin's father, and some of his followers. Cheryl Ness attempts to free Violet, but she's killed in the process. Violet, struck by grief and rage, loses control of her powers. When she returns to herself, everyone in the room has been brutally murdered.

The professors of Prodigium Academy, including Dimitri Gray, arrive and sentence Violet to detention for the next one thousand years, where she'll be forced to pay for her crimes.

**Characters:**

**Violet Dracula** - Dracula's clumsy, eccentric daughter. She is revealed to be the mate of Frankie, Mason, Vin, Cal, Hux, and Jack. At the end of book two, you discover she's actually the biological daughter of Hera and Lucifer. She is arrested for murder and taken to detention at the end of book three.

**Vin** - a Van Helsing, sworn to protect humanity from monsters (particularly vampires) at all costs. He's originally rude and an asshole to Violet before he repents. His twin sister is Vanessa. He's one of Violet's mates.

**Mason** - the son of Medusa and a Fairy Blossom addict. He becomes Violet's first friend at the academy. A prophecy states that Dracula's daughter will eventually kill him.

Because of that, Medusa wants to eliminate Violet once and for all to protect her son. He's one of Violet's mates.

**Frankie** - a cold man who is only passionate about his work...until he meets Violet. He is one of Frankenstein's experiments and also one of Violet's mates.

**Hux** - the alter-ego of Jack. He's slightly psychotic and already desperately in love with Violet. At the end of book three, it's revealed that he and Jack are trapped inside of their head and that Balor is in control of their body. Hux is one of Violet's mates.

**Jack** - the kinder alter-ego of Hux. He is more level-headed than his brother and refuses to use swear words or resort to violence. At the end of book three, it's revealed that he and Hux are trapped inside of their head and that Balor is in control of their body. Jack is one of Violet's mates.

**Dimitri Gray** - once a professor but now the headmaster of Prodigium Academy. He's a stone-cold assassin who has been looking after Violet since she first arrived at the academy. He knows the truth about her lineage. Despite his surly attitude, he appears to have genuine feelings for her, and she for him. However, they're both too stubborn to admit the truth.

**Cal** - otherwise known as Cupid. He's half-fairy and half-incubus. After helping supernaturals find their fated mates, the monster council forced him into detention, where he developed a relationship with Barret. He's revealed to be one of Violet's fated mates in book three.

**Barret** - otherwise known as the Boogeyman. He's forced to remain in the upper levels of the school for a crime he committed. He's currently in a relationship with Cal and is close friends with Violet. He confesses to being in love with Violet in book three.

**Cheryl** - Vin's ex-girlfriend, who's desperate to win him back. She cheated on him with Mason, which broke off their relationship. She is the daughter of the Loch Ness Monster and also Violet's sworn enemy. She's killed at the end of book three trying to protect Violet.

**Vanessa** - Vin's twin sister and a fellow hunter. She's Violet's best friend.

**Cynthia** - Violet's old roommate who found her fated mate, Pete the Pumpkin. She's a banshee and the Woman in White.

**Dracula** - Violet's father and the leader of all vampires. He is the most hated and feared monster in the entire world. At the end of book two, he was stabbed in the heart with a god-blessed dagger. He's still recovering throughout book three.

**Alex** - a transfer to the school and a necromancer. He hates vampires with a passion and seeks to make Violet's life a living hell. However, he sacrifices himself to save her life in book three. When we last saw him, he was broken and bleeding but still alive.

**Stefan Van Helsing** - Vin's father and a feared monster hunter who targets vampires. Violet kills him, along with a handful of other vampire hunters, at the end of book three.

**Balor** - a Formorian who has taken up residence in Hux and Jack's head. Violet can't figure out his intentions, but it's hinted that he's trying to free his people from their prison in Hell.

**Diedre Stevens** - a vampire teacher at the school who committed murders in order to frame Violet. Revealed herself to be Violet's "sister" and Dracula's biological daughter. Murdered by Violet at the end of book one.

# CHAPTER 1

VIOLET

One of my favorite pastimes when I was an innocent, little vampire student was sneaking into detention to visit Cal and Barret. Or Cupid and Boogeyman, respectively. Callie Poo and Boo Bear.

Okay. Maybe I didn't refer to them as Callie Poo and Boo Bear *often*, but those nicknames totally fit the terrifying, psychopathic monsters I befriended. Both of them have soft, gooey centers underneath layers of rippling muscles and gorgeous façades.

*Anyway*…back to what's important—my favorite pastime. Chilling with my dudes. My bros. My amigos. Though can I call Cal a "bro" after he made me come so hard, I saw stars? Yeah, probably not. Ew.

My stomach flutters madly at just the memory of his tan hands on my skin, his pink hair wildly tousled, his eyes glazed with pleasure, his huge, erect dick pistoning in and out of my tight channel.

*Anyway...again...* Over time, the decrepit walls of the upper level of the academy have become almost comforting. Peaceful, even. A reminder of the men I've grown to care for and the bond we all share, one fabricated out of mutual respect and friendship before blossoming into something inherently more.

But weeks relegated to detention by myself really ruins whatever warm fuzzies I might've previously felt about the place. Even my boredom can't completely eclipse the mounting terror whenever I think about the reasoning *for* my detention...and the fact that I'm technically on trial for murder. And not just any murder, but the murder of super important and super scary and super powerful monsters.

I'm sure I would've been able to get away with *normal* murder if the circumstances had been different, but this wasn't just a simple killing. It was a goddamn slaughter.

And I don't remember a single second of it.

One moment, I was being tortured by a bunch of vamp-hating assholes, and the next, they were all dead and I was standing in the remains of their bodies. And there was blood...so much fucking blood. It stained the walls, splashed across the floor, painted my skin and clothes in dark-red pigments. I couldn't look anywhere without being bombarded by the pungent, copper-smelling substance.

When I was first shoved into detention by Prodigium Academy's professors, I made an immediate beeline towards the bathroom. My hands shook as I gripped the countertop, my vision slightly blurred as I stared at my reflection in the dirty mirror.

I didn't recognize myself, no matter how hard I tried to.

Matted blonde and white hair colored red with blood.

Skin coated in slimy guts.

Clothing ripped and stained.

Bruises and cuts littering my naturally alabaster skin.

My face was ashen, the color seeming to have drained from it, and my eyes glimmered with unshed tears. There was something so haunted about my expression, so desolate, that I couldn't tear my gaze away.

What the fuck happened in that room? How did I...?

A knot manifested in my stomach and crawled up my throat like a spider, and a shaky exhale blew through my slightly parted lips.

I desperately wanted my mates. No, I didn't just want them. I *needed* them. Their embraces and soothing touches. Their love. Their steadfast loyalty and unconditional acceptance.

But I was alone.

I'm *still* alone.

I lost track of how long I've been trapped up here, but if I have to hazard a guess, I would say weeks, maybe months. Time moves sluggishly with no natural sunlight to announce the arrival and departure of morning. I only know when it's night because the dim red lights overhead will turn off for exactly one hour right at midnight. At least, I think it's midnight. It could be five thirty-seven p.m. or something equally as annoying. I wouldn't put it past the monsters to mess with me like that.

Loneliness creeps in unbidden as I stare at the rusty can of soda resting on the desk opposite me. My new best friend.

Ms. Soda Pop.

"So...what's shakin', bacon?" I drawl casually, my attention riveted to Ms. Soda Pop as if I honestly expect a reply.

Spoiler alert—she doesn't talk.

Second spoiler alert—even though she doesn't technically talk...she still communicates with me. Kind of.

My lips dip into a frown the longer I stare at her wide, robust frame. Seriously, Ms. Soda Pop has curves to die for. I'm actually a little jealous.

"I'm sorry. I didn't realize it was offensive for me to call you bacon." I pause, canting my head to the side as if listening to her berate me, and then continue on. "I promise you, I didn't intend to be rude. How was I supposed to know it was an insult in your culture?"

I swear, Ms. Soda Pop gets more and more dramatic every time I talk to her. That bitch has some major issues. Even more issues than I currently have, trapped in detention and waiting to be shipped off to Revenant, our monster prison. Nobody knows much about the elusive prison that houses the most dangerous of monsters—hell, most people don't even know the *location* of it—but a tiny, nagging voice in the back of my head warns me that if I'm forced to go there, I'll never see my mates again. I doubt I'll even live past the first few hours as an inmate.

Vampires are the most feared and hated monsters in the world right now. And me being Dracula's infamous daughter is only vomit icing on the shitty cake.

God, how did everything go so wrong? I don't know what the fuck I'm supposed to do with this mess I've found myself in.

Problem number one—Balor, the third soul inhabiting the body Jack and Hux share. Their third brother, triplet, whatever the fuck he is. I still don't know exactly what his endgame is or anything about him…except for the fact he's a sadistic bastard who tried to blow me up during the Roaring. Low-key still salty about that, if you can't tell.

Problem number two—my mates. Vin, Mason, Frankie, Hux, Jack, and apparently Cal. The cupid's claiming honestly took me by surprise, mainly because we've been best friends for weeks before he made his move and I thought him to be in a relationship with Barret. Still, my body heats deliciously when I think about his hard cock pounding inside of me as we both careened over the edge.

They're probably worried sick about me, and I fear what they'll do to set me free. I know innately that Vin won't shed a tear over the death of his father, but will a tiny piece of him blame me for the bastard's death? Will he resent me? What about Cheryl, his ex-girlfriend? I didn't kill her, but will he think I did? Will he be upset by her death? Grieve her? I won't fault him for that, not at all, but I abhor the thought of him hating me for something I didn't even do.

Problem number three—Barret. Cal's sort-of boyfriend… and my secret crush. Sort-of crush? Maybe? I don't necessarily know how I feel about the sweet boogeyman with rich, ebony skin, soulful eyes, and bright green hair. But I can't help but remember the way he looked at me when we ran into each other in the maze…shortly after my coupling with Cal. Was the jealousy emitting from his eyes because *I* slept with *Cal* or because *Cal* slept with *me*? Both? Fuck.

Problem number four—Dimitri fucking Gray. Headmaster of the school. Sexy-as-fuck assassin. Asshole extraordinaire. He brought me to ruin with nothing but his touch and then ditched me like yesterday's trash. I can never tell if he hates me, wants me, or something in between. The last time I saw him, he was staring at me with wide blue eyes, those cerulean depths swimming with violence and maybe even a little fear. He saw me standing in a pool of blood, mutilated body parts scattered around my frozen form. And then he brought me here, to detention, without so much as a word of reassurance. He has to know that this won't end well for me, so why didn't he stop it? Why didn't he save me?

And finally, problem numero cinco—Alex. Just Alex. Do I really need to say more? The surly, irritating, dangerous necromancer who made me shit my pants one day and then saved my life the next. Guilt can't help but percolate in my stomach when I think about his bruised and broken body being lugged through the maze. He sacrificed himself to save my life, and I still don't understand *why*.

Oh...and I suppose you can say there are problems six, seven, eight, and nine too.

Lucifer, my bio dad, who apparently wants to kill me.

Hera, my bio mom, who hid me with Dracula to save my life.

Dracula, my adopted dad, who was stabbed with a god-blessed dagger by Medusa and is lying in a hospital bed, dying.

And then the she-bitch, snake woman herself, who believes I'll be responsible for killing her son and my mate, Mason.

I just can't win, can I?

My life is a steaming pile of shit collecting sunlight and flies as the smell threatens to knock you out. And when you're knocked out, a horse will come out of nowhere, sniff at you for a few seconds, and then let loose a few turds on your unconscious face. And *then*, when you're drowning in feces, a meteorite will fall from the sky and crush you beneath its immense weight. You'll die alone and covered in shit.

That... *That* is my life currently.

"What the fuck am I going to do?" I murmur, dropping my face into my hands. I don't cry, but I also don't pull my palms away as my body shakes with silent sobs, my tumultuous emotions determined to drag me in an undertow of pain I can't escape from.

Maybe I don't *want* to escape from it.

"Violet Dracula?" The soft voice jerks me upright, my eyes instinctively darting towards the pop can.

"You can talk?" Incredulity bleeds into my voice, and a rough, almost brittle laugh emanates from...behind me? The fuck?

I spin around so fast, I fear my head will fall clean off my shoulders and splatter on the ground at my feet.

Bright red eyes peer back at me through the inky darkness, though the rest of the stranger's face is obscured in shadow. Fear balls up into a tight knot in my throat as I take an automatic step backwards.

"Who are you?" I'm grateful when my voice doesn't shake, doesn't bely the fear cascading through me in crushing, icy waves. But fear, I've come to realize, is a wide ocean full of dark currents that I can't begin to fathom. When you give in to the crippling emotion, when you stop fighting to breach the surface and allow the waves to cart you off to sea, you can never be free of it. You'll lose yourself to the great expanse of the ocean.

And I'm goddamn determined not to drown in my fear.

"My name doesn't matter." A bright yellow grin materializes in the darkness, reminding me eerily of the Cheshire cat. A...Cheshire cat with bad hygiene and poor dental practices.

"Are you a student in detention too?" Fuck. There was definitely a quiver in that question, one I quickly try to mask with a tentative smile.

If he *is* a student in detention, then that means he did something bad. Really bad. And now, I'm trapped with him.

Fuck. Fuck. Fuck.

Oh...and *fuck*. You can never have too many fucks to give. At this point, I'm passing my fucks out like candy.

*You get a fuck, and you get a fuck, and you* definitely *get a fuck.*

That yellow grin of his widens, and I swear on closer inspection, his teeth are almost triangular in appearance, the sharp, pointy tips covered in an indefinable substance.

Canines.

No, *fangs*.

"Violet Dracula, I'm your savior." Amusement rings through each of his words as he takes a step closer.

I counter it with an instinctive step backwards. "What?"

*Yup. Real coherent, Violet.*

"I'm breaking you out, of course." A hand coalesced of shadows extends towards me, its fingers crooked. "What would you say to a little jailbreak?"

# CHAPTER 2

For all intents and purposes, "jail" and "break" are two of my favorite words when they're together. Separate, however, is an entirely different story. I really, really don't like jail, and I really, really don't like things breaking. Like… me. I don't like *me* breaking.

So why does my pulse skitter in trepidation and fear at the unknown monster's words? Why do I continue venturing backwards, a malignant tumor the size of Texas resting in the center of my chest, directly over my heart? Why do I feel a little pee trickle down my leg?

The monster's grin quite literally crawls across his face. Literally. One second, it's below his pure red eyes, and the next, it's shifting a few inches to the right. Are those…tiny legs I see sprouting from the edges of his lips? It's too hard to tell with his face still shrouded in darkness, but that little pang of fear inside of me only intensifies as I swallow convulsively.

"Don't be scared."

I'm sure he means for his voice to be soothing, almost coaxing, but with that perpetual grin still fixated on his face and his sparking red eyes, it comes across as eerie and shit-inducing. As in, I kind of want to shit my pants right here, right now, in the middle of the abandoned classroom.

"I was sent to free you, little vampire."

I can no longer swallow, no longer breathe, my attention riveted by the strange creature directly in front of me. He doesn't take a step closer to me, but then again, he doesn't need to. Even from this distance, the raw power he exudes in slimy waves practically incapacitates me, scuttling across my skin like a thousand beetles. My knees quite literally shake despite my feigned bravado.

"Who sent you?" I fire back.

"That"—his hand extends towards me once more—"will be answered in time."

"No," I growl. "I'm not leaving with you until I know who sent you. Was it one of my guys? Dimitri Gray? Dracula?" I continue to spit out names as his right eye begins to twitch in irritation. That's a common emotion I evoke in my friends and enemies alike.

"I'm done asking," he finally snarls out, stalking out of the shadows and down the aisle of the classroom.

The flickering red light finally illuminates his features, and a sharp gasp of surprise escapes me.

He's...hideous.

I don't use that word often, considering ninety-nine percent of the people I converse with are monsters, but that's the only descriptor that truly encapsulates the large man striding towards me.

I was right when I thought the smile on his face was made out of tiny legs. It almost appears to be a motherfucking pink centipede pasted on his face, the thin, hairy legs skittering across his skin and moving his lips with it. He has no nose that I can see, but his glowing red eyes easily take up most of his small, pinball-sized face.

And though his body appears somewhat normal, it doesn't change the fact that he has honest-to-fuck crab claws as arms, each one the size of my body.

Is this a descendant of the Crab Man? I didn't even know such a creature existed.

As he steps closer, stopping directly in front of me, his ears begin to wiggle and shake. It's only then I notice they're *not* ears but spiders. Gross, slimy, gray, hairy spiders.

Bile burns a scorching pathway up my throat as the monster's clawed hand snakes out and touches my collarbone.

"This won't hurt..." His macabre lips twist and distort once more, becoming something I would almost describe as a smirk. "Much." And then he pierces me with the tip of his claw hard enough for blood to well.

"Ow! Ow! Fucking hell!" I cry out, my hand instinctively closing over the wound. It stings like a bitch, but other than that initial stab of pain, it doesn't hurt all that bad.

I narrow my eyes at the fucker as that demented smile of his grows. I swear it looks as if the centipede-like creature glued to his face cleaves itself in half, and its insides are nothing but jagged, rotting, serrated yellow teeth.

"What did you do?" I breathe, blinking up at him rapidly.

"Wait for it." He lifts his claw in the air in the universal "don't get your panties in a twist" gesture as I continue to stare at him owlishly.

And then...

Explosion.

Pain.

Agony.

It feels as if my skin melts clean off my bones and becomes a puddle of goop on the floor. My gut burns as writhing, twisting fire eats away at it, gnawing on my tender flesh.

Is this it? My death?

I always thought it would be…more.

Sure, dying of acid or whatever this is is a painful way to go. But I kind of assumed my execution would be flashier. Perhaps a public hanging? Guillotine? Stoning? I was nearly certain it would have a crowd of spectators throwing tomatoes at my face and booing my mere existence.

Fuck, this hurts like a bitch.

I can feel my body wash away, becoming nothing but liquid. My eyelids squeeze shut instinctively.

Pain.

That's all I know, all I'm aware of, the only word that defines me. It pokes and prods at the edges of my mind, whispering words that I can't quite make out.

As abruptly as it began, the pain stops. It's so sudden that I half wonder if my body has just turned numb, if it's attempting to protect itself from the agony coursing through my veins.

I also appear to be…smaller?

*The fuck?*

I try to speak, try to scream, but all that manages to escape me is a tiny sound of distress. A squeaky, high-pitched sound.

I move backwards instinctively, but my body feels weird, leaden, metallic, as if I'm on all fours and there's an immense weight pressing down on my spine.

Wait…

My tiny head swivels from side to side, horror inflating me like helium in a balloon when I realize I no longer have two legs. I have eight, and each one is dark and spindly.

Almost like…

A bug.

Holy shit. Holy shit. Holy shit.

It's then that I realize my surroundings have changed and morphed, the muted red light now a dull shade of gray. *Everything* is now painted in blacks and whites, including the monster grinning down at me. I want to say that without his eerie red eyes, he looks almost friendly, but that would be a lie. The monochromatic gray sparks with malice as his centipede lips stretch into an amused smirk.

"Ahhh. I love silence," the now-giant man murmurs, bending down to pick my tiny bug body up.

I attempt to run, but it's quite literally impossible as his crab claws close around me hard enough to squeeze out my internal organs like toothpaste in a tube.

*What the fuck did you do to me?!*

Of course, I can't actually say those words in this form, so another string of incoherent cries, squeaks, and chirps fill the air instead. That only makes the monster's smile broaden, though he doesn't respond, placing me in the pocket of his shirt.

And then…

All I can see is cloying, fathomless darkness.

I sway uncerimoniously from side to side, each sudden movement jarring my poor little bug body. All I can think of is how close I am to death. If this monster were to, say, run into a wall…I'd be crushed. If he decided to do the Pledge of Allegiance and place his hand over his heart…crushed. If he wanted to give a buddy a chest bump…crushed.

I never really thought about how often people touch their chests until that moment. And here I am, an innocent, teeny bug-creature, and I have no doubt the slightest pressure will make my guts spray in every direction.

Oh god.

What do my guts even look like in this form? Are they red? Pink? Black?

Do I have black guts?

Do bugs even *have* guts?

Terror orchestrates a song inside of my chest—the ominous screech of violins, the clang of organ keys being banged on, the thump of a drum. I'm sure if I were in vampire form, I'd be hyperventilating. Probably rambling.

I don't know how long my kidnapper walks for, but it feels like hours. I half wonder if I'm going to run out of oxygen where I'm placed inside of his shirt pocket. Do I even need oxygen?

Oh fuck. Oh fuck. Oh fuck.

After what feels like an eternity later, clawed hands grip my slimy body in an iron vise and pull me out. Panic tightens up my disgusting insides, and I feel slightly light-headed... slightly bug-headed? I'm still working on the logistics of my condition, even in my own brain. If I *have* a brain, that is...

The monster sets me on the ground, but before I can scuttle my disgusting ass away, he pierces my back once more.

Pain sears my veins and lights a fire in every single one of my nerve endings. I half wonder if he crushed my bug shell. It feels as if my body is caving in, my skin and bones deteriorating until I'm nothing but flaky ash that can be swept away in the breeze. A scream lodges in my throat, but I don't bother to allow it to escape. I know I won't be able to make coherent noise, not in my current form. Spots freckle my vision, and I feel myself falling, falling, falling...

And then growing, growing, growing.

It's a slow and gradual process, as if all of my limbs are being tugged in every direction. I feel like I'm made out of Play-Doh, and some little kid is attempting to make a person out of the sticky blob, twisting and distorting the clay to do her bidding.

My arms expand, and then my legs, and then my head, and then my torso. Pain burns a fiery pathway down my spine as tears get locked behind my eyelids.

Fuck. Fuck. Fuck!

As abruptly as it began, the pain diminishes, leaving me panting and gasping for air.

But hey, on the bright side, at least I didn't blow up. When Cal and Barret were put in detention years and years ago, they had a device implanted inside of them that would make them go *boom* if they were to try and escape. Apparently, good old Headmaster Gray forgot to inject me with it. Or maybe… Maybe he did it on purpose. After all, I doubt anything happens within the walls of the academy that escapes the meticulous Dimitri Gray's notice.

I'm naked, something that becomes painfully obvious when I reopen my eyes and the crab monster gives me a lewd grin. I awkwardly cross my arms over my chest, trying to hide my nudity from his prying gaze.

"Where am I?" I demand briskly, once it becomes clear that I'm no longer in detention.

To be completely honest, I don't recognize my surroundings. It appears to be…an apartment? Maybe?

Everything is decorated in dizzying shades of white and black. The stark white tiles contrast with the black leather couch, black armchair, and black, granite-like coffee table. The living room bleeds into the kitchen, where an obsidian stone countertop dominates the majority of the space. Surrounding it are black, wooden shelves, kitchen appliances, and an apron that reads Kiss This Cook's Fine Ass.

But all of this isn't what freezes me to the spot. It isn't what siphons the breath straight from my lungs and fills my brain with nothing but fluffy cotton balls.

It's the view from the living room window that has me reeling. Spiraling. Gasping.

Patches of craggy black rocks are visible from where I stand, rivulets of red liquid seeping from their surfaces like streams of lava. On closer inspection, I decide that's what the strange liquid is—lava. Brilliant red lava that blazes like fire in the red sun. Yes…the *red* sun, hovering in the center of an inky-black sky and canvasing the world in shades of garnet and orange. Volcanoes dot the horizon, and lakes of what appear to be fire stretch across the landscape.

The clawed, unnamed monster hands something to me, and it takes me a long moment to realize it's a bathrobe. Quickly, I shrug the fabric over my shoulders and tie it, still struggling to adjust to what I'm seeing.

"Where the fuck am I?" I breathe, horror infusing every syllable.

The answer, surprisingly, doesn't come from my mysterious kidnapper. Instead, the low, rough voice sounds from directly behind me, causing me to jump about a foot in the air.

"You're in my home, my dear Violet." The poignant, unmistakable clap of Lucifer's shoes against the marble flooring sounds as he moves to stand directly beside me. His eyes, however, don't stray from the window. He seems just as riveted as I am by the horrifying and enticing sight laid out before us. "Welcome to Hell."

## CHAPTER 3

"**L**ucifer."

My heart pounds erratically within the confines of my rib cage, threatening to break free at any moment and splatter across the meticulously polished white tiles. Seriously, those fuckers are so clean, I can see my reflection in them—a sight for sore eyes, I'm afraid, considering the fact that my blonde hair is ratty and matted and that dirt stains my cheeks.

Lucifer doesn't drag his attention off the horizon as he clasps his hands behind his back. Everything about this tall, powerful man exudes danger and violence. He's practically brimming with it. Raw, malevolent power radiates off of him in tangible waves.

This...

*This* is my father.

The man who tried to kill me when I was a baby. The man who thought I was dead for all of these years, after my birth mother, Hera, hid me in the safekeeping of Dracula.

What is he doing here?

Okay. Stupid question. A better one would be what am *I* doing here? I have no doubt that this apartment belongs to him, so why am I here? He couldn't possibly know the truth about me, could he?

Fear skates down my spine like a hairy spider, and I resist the urge to shudder at the strange, prickling sensation.

"You probably have a lot of questions, Violet," Lucifer begins in a soft voice.

A strong part of me wants to stare at him shamelessly, to search for any and all similarities between the two of us, but the rest of me knows that wouldn't be wise. Instead, I focus on the demented scenery spread out before me, just as he is doing. Still, I can't help but flick my gaze in his direction every few seconds, swallowing convulsively around the dry lump in my throat.

Lucifer is tall, almost abnormally so, with broad shoulders leading down to a tapered waist. The hard angles of his face are emphasized by a dark beard and mustache, a shade or two darker than the hair on his head and a startling contrast to my own golden curls. Like the last time I saw him, he wears a pure white suit, similar in color to the floor and walls, and a bright red tie.

Wait…

What did Lucifer say?

Shit. Something about having questions, right?

Curse my thoughts for running away from me.

"You could say that." I try to act nonchalant, but inside, I'm screaming. Maybe whining would be a better descriptor, but fuck me in the ass with a dildo made out of barbed wire, poisonous darts, and lemon juice. This man wants to *kill* me, for fuck's sake. The only thing that might save my miserable excuse of a life is if he doesn't know the truth about my lineage.

I suppose my story has always been fated to end in death. I'm a vampire, a species that is universally hated because of things we can't control, and my father is the infamous Vladimir Dracula. If any story were going to end in bloodshed, it would be mine. I survived the Roaring by the skin of my teeth...errr, fangs, murdered a bunch of powerful supernatural creatures, and then got tossed away like trash. The monster council would've either decided to execute me or send me to prison because of my crimes, both of which would've seen me dead within days.

And now?

Now, Grim Reaper is wearing a new face, one that looks eerily similar to my own. I just have to pray I'll survive the downward swoop of the scythe as it impales me.

"Why don't you shower and change?" Lucifer jerks his chin towards a doorway, where the monster who kidnapped me stands, his huge, clawed arms folded over his chest. "Memphis," Lucifer addresses the ugly beast, "come with me."

The monster, Memphis, dips his head in acknowledgment before pushing away from the wall and sauntering to where we stand.

Before he can reach us, however, I mutter, "What the fuck is he?"

I'm not really expecting an answer, so I jump about a foot in the air when Lucifer replies, "He's a bugbear."

"A...what now?" Surely, I heard him wrong. A fucking bugbear? I've never heard of that species before, and I consider myself pretty smart when it comes to the monster community.

Okay...kind of smart. But still.

"He's actually related to that boogeyman of yours," Lucifer continues in a low, almost conspiratorial voice.

"Barret's related to...him?" My widening eyes must betray my disbelief because Lucifer chuckles. Barret's a sexy mountain of solid muscle, while this creature is...something else entirely.

"A cousin, actually," the bugbear, Memphis, responds with a twist of his centipede lips. "But I'm considered the handsome one in our circles."

"...the fuck?" I blink. And then blink again, sure I heard him wrong and the only way to get my ears to work properly is to open and shut my eyes like I'm having a seizure.

I make a mental note to research everything I can find on bugbears. Maybe I'll ask Barret...if I see him again, that is. The thought that I won't fills me with so much melancholy that tears actually prick my eyes.

*Don't think like that, Violet.*

"We'll be back shortly," Lucifer tells me, finally dragging his attention off the landscape to face me.

It's unnerving to be the sole focus of his attention, and I shuffle from foot to foot uncomfortably. My skin suddenly feels too tight, too itchy, and I rub at a spot on my upper arm where I swear the skin is rippling and flexing with every passing second.

"The front door to my apartment will be locked for your own protection." He lowers his voice ominously, and I bristle before I can stop myself.

Is that a warning or a threat?

A *thrarning*? Yeah, that sounds right.

A Zeus-damned *thrarning*.

With that statement, Lucifer stalks out of the room, Memphis trailing a few steps behind him.

"Nice meeting you, little vampire." The bugbear gives me a lewd grin and tips an imaginary hat in my direction.

I decide immediately I don't like that monster, regardless of the fact he broke me free from my prison. The only question is... What new fucking hell did he bring me into?

Quite literally.

Despite Lucifer's warning, I still try the front door, not surprised in the least to find it locked. Fucker. I then snoop through the rest of the apartment, searching for anything I may be able to use as a weapon. Aside from a tiny steak knife, there's nothing of substance. Still, I shove that knife into the waistband of my pants...before remembering I'm naked under my robe, so I effectively nick my skin and drop the knife on the ground instead.

Deciding that there's truly no escape from this apartment of horrors, I head into the room Lucifer indicated and find it to be a spare bedroom and bathroom. Everything smells clean—like rose-scented laundry detergent—so I conclude that no one has used this room in a while. At least, I think that until I open up one of the drawers and see a collection of clothes. Skirts, shirts, bras, and panties. There are even a few pairs of socks. *Matching* socks.

What fucker has matching socks?

A satanist, that's who.

Or...a Luciferist.

Does Lucifer have female company over who spends the night in this room?

Ew. Yuck. Gross.

I definitely do *not* want that visual in my head.

I bypass the underwear and bras—because there's no way in hell I'm putting some random woman's panties on—and then grab a pair of pants and the largest sweater I can find. Normally, I wear short skirts, but I don't feel comfortable wearing something so revealing without any underwear on, especially around a man who is my bio dad. There's so much "ick" in that statement, I don't even know where to begin unraveling it.

I shower as fast as vampirely possible, even as my mind reels with everything that has happened. I got kidnapped—a-fucking-gain—and now, I'm in the belly of the beast. Or the apartment of the devil, as the case may be.

Does this have something to do with winning the Roaring?

My trial?

Surely, he doesn't know that I'm his daughter, right?

Right!?

After toweling off, I throw on the pants and sweatshirt, startled to realize that both pieces of clothing are my size. It wasn't something I had noticed earlier, but now that I think about it...

I quickly rush back inside the bedroom, skirting around the queen-sized bed, and open up the drawer once more.

On closer inspection, everything folded inside is something I would wear. That black skirt with the bats on it? Yup, would definitely wear it. That pink corset? Yup. That leather jacket? Hell fucking yes.

I finger one of the tags, my wariness growing when I see that it's in my size.

Because of course it is.

It's just my luck that I would get kidnapped by a creepy, disgusting monster, arrive in the secret lair of my murderous birth father, and then find a ton of clothes that are specifically tailored for me. Great. Is this the part where I'm trapped inside the bedroom until the end of time as Daddy's little puppet?

And...

That sounded gross, even in my own head.

"Violet?" Lucifer's dogmatic voice echoes through the apartment, and I jump about a foot in the air, slamming the drawer closed as if I have been caught snooping through his personal belongings.

I take a few deep breaths to steady myself, dragging lung-fuls of oxygen back into a body that seems to be starved for it, and then run a hand down my baggy sweatshirt, grateful it's not entirely visible I've forgone panties and a bra.

Attempting to emulate a confidence I don't truly feel, I exit the bedroom and pad on bare feet back into the living room-kitchen combination.

Lucifer and Memphis have returned, speaking in hushed tones to one another, but what shocks the ever-loving shit out of me is that they're not alone. They're joined by a third man—a very familiar, very sexy man that I hate with the entirety of my pathetic vampire being.

"Alex?" I gape in disbelief, blinking rapidly at the necromancer.

The last time I saw him had been in the maze during round three of the Roaring. He had been badly injured trying to protect me, so my guys had been forced to carry him to the finish line.

"You're... You've healed," I murmur dumbly, unable to tear my eyes away from the striking man with black tourmaline-colored hair, dark tattoos, and that distracting lip piercing. His eyes—chips of russet woven with inky black—snag my own as that familiar scowl twists down his lips.

"So are you." He gives me an unreadable look before focusing once more on Lucifer and Memphis.

Wait...

Is he working with them?

With the asshole who wants me dead and the asshole who kidnapped me?

"What the fuck is going on here? Where are my mates?" I demand, my voice loud enough to garner all three of their attentions.

Memphis's strange lips purse, Lucifer frowns, and Alex just appears annoyed. But then again, that seems to be Alex's standard expression. I doubt his facial muscles know how to display anything else.

"Sit down, Violet." Lucifer waves a hand lazily at one of the barstools in the kitchen. "There's a lot we need to talk about with you."

I shake my head adamantly, taking an immediate step backwards. "Not until you tell me where my mates are," I insist.

This is the hill I will die on. Yes, the hill may be insignificant and small, but I claimed it as my own, dammit. And I'll happily shed blood on it too. Even if that blood *is* mine.

If it were even possible, Alex's scowl deepens, his russet-black eyes once more flashing with an unnamed emotion. He holds my stare for a solid ten seconds, the twitch in his jaw commandeering my attention, before he whirls around to face Lucifer.

"The dungeons," he murmurs to my bio dad, his voice so low, I wouldn't have heard him if it weren't for my enhanced vampire hearing.

Lucifer's features twist and distort, the frown on his face giving way to smooth indifference. He seems to consider Alex's words for a moment, churning them around and around in his mind, before he nods sharply.

"She won't be happy," he responds quietly.

"*She* is standing right here," I hiss, my fingers curling into fists by my sides. "And *she* doesn't like being talked about as if *she's* not in the room."

Am I going too far with the pettiness? Maybe, but if I'm being completely honest, I don't think I'm going far enough. Lucifer may be the supreme ruler of Hell, but I'm the Zeus-damn Queen of Drama. If my one weapon against these fuckers is pettiness, then I'll use it to my advantage.

I don't know where this bravado is coming from, but I suppose it stems from the fact that they're already going to kill me. Why not go down swinging, even if it's only with words?

"You're right." Lucifer's lips twitch, though I can't quite tell if it's in irritation or the makings of a tentative smile. Probably irritation, because that tends to be the reaction most people feel when they're in my presence. "I apologize." He extends his hand and nods once, a single dip of his chin. "Come. Let me bring you to your mate."

# CHAPTER 4

I bite my lower lip to hold in the cough that wants to escape. Fumes tickle my nostrils as I crawl forward like a damn worm, my arms slightly in front of me and my legs swiveling back and forth, back and forth. My elbows press against the cold vent as I push myself forward—that's the only word I can think of. Forward.

I just need to move forward.

Dust particles sting my eyes, and I release a curse, tears streaming down my face.

"Fucking shit," I growl at the intercom shoved into my ear. "Remind me again why I'm stuck doing all of the hard work?"

Vin's sardonic, dry laugh echoes through the speaker, so loud and deafening that it sounds as if he's directly beside me and not miles away in the van we bought.

"Because you're the...smallest," he decides on at last, and my lips twist into a caustic scowl.

"Smallest?" I repeat. Now I know he's full of shit. I am

most definitely *not* the smallest. I'm six foot one of solid muscle, and yeah, I may not be as broad as him or Barret...or have the wing span of Cal...or have the dad bod of Frankie...

Well, fuck. I suppose I am the smallest. Violet certainly keeps the company of big, scary fuckers, doesn't she?

My heart flutters in my chest at the thought of my girl. I wonder what she's doing right now, what she's thinking about. *Whom* she's thinking about. It's been weeks since I last saw her. All I want to do is drag her into my arms and fuse my lips to hers, remind her all over again who owns her, heart, body, and soul. Does she think that we've forgotten about her? That we won't come for her?

Guilt seeps into my veins at the thought, and it takes every ounce of effort I possess to keep the slow and steady pace we decided on as I crawl through the academy's vents.

How can Violet remain so oblivious to how loved she truly is?

Even Cynthia and Vanessa wanted to help us free Violet from detention. They were as terrified as we were when the truth about Violet's predicament came to light. However, Cynthia's halfway across the world on her mating honeymoon with Pete the Pumpkin and Vanessa is doing damage control with the remaining Van Helsing members. We had to assure them repeatedly that we had this handled to get them to back the fuck up and stop incessantly blowing up our phones to demand updates.

"Wait!" Frankie exclaims suddenly, and I freeze where I am, one of my arms slightly raised as I prepare to drag my body forward. Over the com, a flurry of keys click, there's a muffled curse, and then... "Okay, you can move now. Just had to take down a contingency the school put in place. I'm ninety percent sure I got it shut down, at least for a few minutes."

"What does this contingency do?" I ask warily as I

continue to crawl forward…though much more tentatively than I did before. I really, really don't like the sound of that.

"It's supposed to burn the skin straight off your body," Frankie supplies candidly. When I freeze, terror gripping my heart in an iron vise, he quickly adds, "Don't worry. I turned it off. Well…I'm, like, eighty percent certain I did."

"Eighty percent?" I choke out. Yup. Don't like that. Not one fucking bit.

"Fine." Frankie heaves out a heavy breath. "Fifty percent."

*Fifty percent?!*

"But there's going to be a one-hundred-percent chance it'll turn back on if you don't move your tiny ass."

"Really? More tiny jokes?" I continue to propel myself forward, army crawling through the small-as-fuck shaft—no pun intended—as poisonous fear burns a fiery pathway through my veins.

"Just move," Frankie urges curtly. "You have…ten seconds to get past the piece of yellow tape stuck to the side of the vent. Do you see it?"

"Ten fucking seconds? I don't see any…" I trail off as my gaze snags on a tiny sliver of yellow tape stuck to the vent in front of me.

Nearly ten feet away. And at the rate I'm going…

"Oh…shit. Shit. Shit. Shit." I continue my flurry of incessant curses as I crawl forward as fast as my tiny—I roll my eyes—body can carry me.

The yellow tape grows closer and closer, so close I would be able to reach out and touch it if I had use of my arms beyond the two inches I'm able to wiggle them.

"Two. One." Frankie's voice is practically deadpanned as I throw my body past the yellow tape and lower my head to the cold, metallic floor.

Behind me, nothing happens—no ominous green mist or

acid seeping from the walls—but then again, I'm no longer there to set off any booby traps.

I'll never be more grateful in my life for being so-called *tiny*. Tiny bitches can move faster than heavier ones, thank you very much.

"You need to take a left at the next fork," Dimitri instructs crisply, and I can practically picture the pretentious fucker stalking back and forth in the secret cabin we bought, his hands clasped behind his back and that perpetual scowl of his tugging down his lips.

"Yes, boss," I drawl lazily, despite the fact I already knew that. I have these vents practically memorized at this point. If I were to take a right, I would circle back to the classrooms and eventually the teachers' lounge. But by going left…

I begin to move even faster, knowing the end is in sight. It won't be long until Violet is in my arms where she belongs and no one can ever take her away from me again.

A delicate tremor reverberates through my entire body, and I wouldn't be surprised if the entire vent shakes with the force of it. Excitement thrums within me, a palpable entity, and I can practically taste Violet on my tongue.

*I'm coming, Pinkie.*

Almost there.

We've been working on this plan since Dimitri first came to us and explained what happened…and how Violet will be put to death for her crimes. The icy asshole may hate the world as a whole, but Violet? I don't think he ever truly hated Violet, despite his claims. He was just as frantic as the rest of us when she was sentenced to detention.

The plan to free her is quite simple, actually. Brilliant but simple.

Dimitri, as the headmaster of Prodigium Academy, supplied us with blueprints for the ventilation system, as well as all the traps and securities in place to keep this exact thing from happening. We studied the diagrams extensively before deciding that I would be the one crawling through the shafts. Not because I'm small, obviously, but because I'm fearless.

Yup. That's definitely the reason.

I'm motherfucking fearless. The bravest fucker we all know.

Vin's waiting in the getaway van a few blocks away from the academy, and Frankie and Dimitri are at the secret apartment we purchased halfway across the world to hide Violet from the monster council.

Cal and Barret are the only two not connected to the coms, and for good reason—they're staying on campus as the distraction. I have no idea what the fuck they're doing, but whatever it is seems to be working. No teachers or security guards have discovered anything's amiss. If they were to get caught, however, they're under strict instruction to escape as fast as they can. Cal will fly away, and Barret will turn into a tiny bug that can fit into his pocket.

Easy peasy.

Right?

Why did my "easy peasy" feel more like a "lemon squeezy," as in my heart is a lemon and it's being squeezed to death by outside forces?

"You should be there soon," Dimitri tells me, and I twist my head to the side, spotting the vent that'll lead me to my destination.

Detention.

"Sir, yes, sir," I deadpan as I continue to crawl forward.

Now comes the tricky part.

The vent in front of me—iron bars each the size of my very, very large pinkie fingers—is secured by strong magic. I have the elixir to break the spell and the tools to then break the bars apart...but it's extremely hard to grab anything out of my back pocket with how small the vent is. Seriously, if I were a bigger man—not that I'm not huge naturally, because I totally am—I wouldn't be able to even wiggle my toe. I don't know how I'm going to reach behind me, grab the elixir and screwdriver out of my pocket, and then use those fuckers on the vent.

Unless…

An idea occurs to me, and I have to stop myself from grinning like a maniac.

I shove my head back down flush against the vent and rub my forehead back and forth across the cold metal until my beanie becomes askew. When it gets low enough on my face, I grab at it with my teeth, pulling it the rest of the way off my head. For a moment, I'm blinded, the dark gray fabric of the beanie obscuring my vision, but soon, it's off, and my snakes hiss eagerly.

"What the fuck are you doing, Mase?" Vin growls into my ear.

"Improvising," I respond, flashing a cheeky smile that he sure as shit can't see but can most definitely hear in my voice.

"Don't you dare," Dimitri snaps.

I laugh eagerly as the snakes on my head all stand at attention like hair that has been electrocuted. "Too late."

It happens instantaneously. One second, there's a metal grate in front of me prohibiting me from getting to my girl, and the next, the metal is nothing but stone. My snakes continue to writhe and hiss, and before my very eyes, the stone begins to crumble, turning into fine particles of dust.

"Fuck yeah!" I try to fist pump before remembering I'm pretty much stuck like this, so I settle on wiggling my butt in the air instead.

"Stop messing around and get our girl," Dimitri bites out.

"Our girl?" Vin snorts derisively.

Dimitri growls, the noise low and threatening, and I bite down on my laugh. Who would've thought the headmaster with a stick the size of Kansas up his sculpted ass would be head over heels in love with Violet Dracula, the epitome of everything he hates? Chaos. Rebellion. Disorder.

"Enough bickering," Frankie snaps in his no-nonsense voice. "Mason, go in and extract the target."

"Are you fucking with me? The target? Don't you mean our mate?" I drawl lazily as I push myself forward until my head is out of the vent and then my arms. I wish there were a way I could twist my body so my legs leave the vent first, but beggars can't be choosers and all that shit. "This is going to hurt," I grumble at the same time I dive out of the vent.

I attempt to twist my body in the air to land on my ass instead of my neck, but the drop isn't quite tall enough for me to do more than awkwardly roll to the side. Pain explodes through my shoulder where it crashes against the linoleum flooring, and I curse up a fucking storm as I stumble to my feet.

"You okay?" my best friend demands, concern lacing his voice.

"Just peachy," I tell Vin as I attempt to roll my shoulder back. Yup. Dislocated that fucker.

Shit.

"Do you see her?" Dimitri breaks in, and his cold, stoic voice is like thunder in my ears.

"Give me a damn second," I gripe just as Vin snaps, "Give him a bit."

I appear to have landed in the main hallway of detention, where a few classrooms lie to the right of me and the break-room and bathrooms sit to the left. The faint red glow of the emergency exit sign up above provides the only light. Fuck. I hate the thought of my pinkie living in such darkness.

And then I think about Cal and Barret—and how they've been trapped up here for decades—and my heart pinches uncomfortably. I try to ignore the sudden tightness in my chest at the thought.

"Pinkie?" I cup my hands around my mouth, not bothering to be quiet. Only forgotten souls live up here. No one will think to check on Violet. It wouldn't surprise me if she's already been forgotten by the majority of monsters. "Pinkie! Where is your cute butt?"

Silence.

Pressing and cloying silence.

"Violet Dracula! Get your ass out here!" I bellow again.

Again, no answer.

Something akin to panic begins to thrum through me and lights a fire in my belly. I ignore the voices in my ear as I run forward, checking each room for a glimpse of her familiar golden hair.

"Where the fuck is she?" Vin demands, his voice momentarily managing to eclipse the terror pressing down on me.

"She's not... She's not here."

"What?" That roar definitely belongs to Dimitri. The assassin is a scary motherfucker when he wants to be. "What do you mean by that? She's not scheduled to be moved to Revenant for months!"

"I mean that she's not here!" I insist, finishing my sweep of every room before leaning against the wall. "Violet Dracula is gone."

# CHAPTER 5

"So...when you say 'dungeon,' do you mean an actual dungeon? Like, with prisoners, chains, and whips? Or is it the name of a cool club? Maybe a strip joint or something? Is it a sex dungeon?" I ramble as I follow Lucifer and Alex down a winding staircase located at the back of the apartment.

Alex throws me a withering look over his shoulder that suggests he's sincerely questioning my sanity while Lucifer just chuckles lightly.

Neither of them answer.

Of course, that means I have to babble even *more* in a desperate bid to fill the silence.

Incessant chatter—good.

Quiet—bad. Very, very bad.

"There was a really awesome club near Dad's home in Romania called the Dungeon. It was created to look like something plucked straight out of nineteenth-century Europe. Cinder blocks. Chains. The whole shebang. Very classy place. Ohhh. That rhymed! Kind of. I mean, I suppose if you say both words really, really fast you can claim they rhyme. Chains…shebang. Chains. Shebang. Chains. Shebang. See? They kind of rhyme. Kind of. I'm a poet, and I didn't even know it. But I don't want to blow it, so I'm just going to mow it."

Alex gives me another narrow-eyed glare, one I return with an added middle finger.

Lucifer, on the other hand, goes rigid, but I have no idea what caused that reaction. Is it simply my voice, which I've heard from more than one person is high-pitched and annoying? Is it the mention of my home in Romania?

My use of the word Dad?

He doesn't acknowledge my chatter with a response, so I press my lips together in a futile attempt to keep my word vomit under control. The last thing I want to do is piss off the super scary and super powerful King of Hell. He's the type of man to skin me alive and then wear my flesh as a nice and cozy coat.

Though if I'm being completely honest, he would look *awful* in my skin. Totally not his color. Maybe if I were a little paler…

I don't know how far we descend, but soon, we reach a nondescript metal door at the bottom landing. Lucifer procures a heavy-looking key out of his back pocket and twists it in the lock. I watch him return the key to his pants with a calculating frown.

I just *know* I'll need to snag it from him later.

I've been called petty on more than one occasion. But a petty thief? I suppose if anyone can make that leap, it'll be me. I won't hesitate to steal from him if that's what it takes to free my men and stay alive.

Lucifer gestures for me to enter ahead of him, but trepidation keeps my feet rooted to the ground. Enter through a dark, spooky doorway before my murderous father and the asshole necromancer who stares at me like he wants to mount my head on a pike? No thanks. I rather like my head firmly on my shoulders, thank you very much, and I wouldn't put it past either of them to stab a knife through my back while I'm unaware.

I'm Violet motherfucking Dracula, and I *always* pay attention to my surroundings and the threats lurking nearby. I always—

*Ohhh. What's that?*

My gaze snags on a flickering light inside the darkened doorway, and I take a step closer instinctively.

*Shiny. So shiny.*

Dammit. I'm weak.

Alex pinches the bridge of his nose, almost as if he read my mind and found my thoughts lacking any and all intelligence, and I swivel my head around to give him my best glare.

"Got something to say, butt muncher?"

The ire in his expression momentarily fades to be replaced by confusion, and he blinks at me. "Butt muncher?"

"Cum stain dipshit," I correct with a decisive head nod, as if I took his confusion to heart and worked tirelessly to come up with a solution.

That tiny crease between his dark brows only deepens. "Are you…insulting me?"

He sounds so incredulous that I have to bite down on the smirk that wants to escape.

*Keep up, goth boy. This ain't rocket science.*

"*Am* I insulting you?" I counter…because yeah, I'm totally into mind games. I'm an expert on all things mind fuckery.

"You called me a butt muncher. And then you randomly blurted out cum stain dipshit." Those russet-black eyes of his blink repeatedly down at me. For once, that combative glint

I've come to associate with the angry necromancer is nowhere to be seen.

"Did I? Or did you call *yourself* a butt muncher and a cum stain dipshit?"

Alex flicks his gaze from me to Lucifer and then back to me again. He seems at a loss for words, which I take as a win.

When he's not talking, he's actually sort of attractive. Stupidly attractive. Ugh. I want to pour acid all over his face just to make him a little uglier. Or maybe euthanize the poor fuck to save women everywhere from falling prey to his charms—or lack thereof. Because who am I kidding? Alex has the appeal of a snake. Not a snake *charmer* but the serpent itself. I half expect him to lunge forward and take a bite out of my flesh, infecting me with his venom in the process.

I may be the vampire, but Alex sure as fuck has the fangs in this fucked-up relationship we share.

Or don't share.

Definitely *don't* share.

Ugh.

With my chin held high—so high I can see the dome-like roof of the ceiling above us—I stalk forward, purposely ramming my shoulder into Alex's side as I go. It doesn't actually hurt the bastard, but his frown *does* deepen, so I call that another win.

Violet…two.

Alex…probably five hundred, but I'd like to believe it's zero.

My amusement fades pretty damn quickly when I see who Lucifer has imprisoned beneath his hellish apartment.

A startled gasp rips from my throat before I can contain my reaction, and I bring my hands to my mouth instinctively in horror.

Hux-slash-Jack sits on a wooden chair in the center of the

dark, barren room, his hands tied behind his back. Wait. No. On closer inspection, I see that it's not one of my mates.

It's Balor.

The cocky grin curling up the corner of his lips can only belong to the asshole who is currently inhabiting the body of my lovers.

Jack and Hux are brothers and the offspring of Jekyll and Hyde. As such, their two souls share one body. Despite both men having long, opal-colored hair and lightly tanned skin, I could never mistake them. Jack always wears a pair of dark glasses and has hair brushed forward, obscuring most of his features from view. Hux, on the other hand, keeps his hair tucked behind his ears to reveal the jagged scar carving the skin of his cheek. Jack exudes kindness and compassion; Hux emanates unwavering loyalty and fierce devotion and possession.

And Balor?

He just looks like he wants to take a nasty shit on a child's face, that sadistic fucker. What man shits on children?

Balor, that's who.

His black hair is pulled into a messy man bun at the top of his head, a few loose strands framing his sharp cheekbones and smooth jawline. The grin on his face is decidedly psychotic, and his eyes glimmer with some unnamed emotion. Whatever that emotion is doesn't bode well for me. It makes me want to run in the opposite direction, screaming at the top of my lungs.

Correction. It makes me want to charge at him as fast as I can with a blade poised over his heart, ready to swoop down and kill him.

"Balor," I say stiffly, though I hate dignifying the bastard with a greeting at all. Not after everything he did to me, my mates, and my fellow vampires.

"Little vampire." He cants his head to the side in a way

that feels almost mocking, like he's studying and dismissing me all within a second.

He may be the one tied to a chair, but I'm not fooled in the slightest. Balor still has all the goddamn power between the two of us, and that prospect terrifies me.

A growl pushes its way past my clenched teeth even as a desperate, aching need opens a hole in my chest. Fuck, I miss Jack and Hux with everything that I am. I would give my right tit just to hear Hux purr "Precious Treasure" in my ear one more time. His silky, British accent always managed to caress my lobe like the hot, languid flick of a tongue.

I whirl towards Lucifer and Alex angrily—well, I start whirling towards them angrily before remembering that Lucifer is an evil asshole who will probably kill me if I so much as look at his shoes the wrong way. Instead, I aim all of my ire and fury at Alex, who simply scowls in response.

"This isn't my mate." I jab my finger over my shoulder at a cackling Balor.

"He's in the body of your mates. Isn't that close enough?" Though Lucifer's voice is an indolent drawl, I can hear the distinct lilt of amusement ringing through his words.

It only serves to infuriate me.

Is this some sort of psychological torture? Putting every-thing I want within my reach yet creating an indestructible barrier I have no hope of getting around?

"Not close enough." My nails dig into my palms hard enough to draw blood. "Where are my other mates?"

Alex's tongue snakes out to fiddle with his lip ring, and for a brief moment, I'm transfixed, watching his pink tongue circle the metal bud the way I imagine he'll do to my clit—

What the fuck?

Where did that revolting idea come from?

Yuck. Ew. Yuck.

Alex, oblivious to my internal turmoil, folds his thick

arms over his chest and aims another one of his patented scowls in my direction. "Probably running around like chickens with their heads cut off, trying to save you."

"Trying to save me?" My poor, abused heart actually gains tiny butterfly wings that begin to flap erratically at his words. Warmth spreads through my body in blissful waves.

The guys…are trying to save me? I don't know why I'm surprised, but there's no denying that a tiny piece of me wondered if they planned to leave me to rot. I stayed holed up in detention for *weeks* without hearing a single peep from the men I loved.

The knowledge that they're trying to free me, that they haven't given up on my broken soul, has my heart hammering somewhere in the vicinity of my throat. A tension I haven't realized I'd been carrying leaks out of me like water in a wrung-out sponge.

Alex's upper lip pulls away from his teeth. "Did you really think they would leave you to be put to death?"

"No." I think over my next words carefully. "But I suppose they don't need to save me anymore…because you guys saved me. Why is that?" I punctuate my question with a lot of pauses, gauging both of their reactions carefully.

Lucifer's lazy grin remains firmly in place, and Alex doesn't even bat an eye. They're like books written in foreign languages—utterly unreadable without accurate translations. Unfortunately for me, I don't think anyone here speaks Devil and Crazy Necromancer. And if anyone does, I would like to meet them pronto.

"So many questions, Miss Violet." Lucifer tsks his tongue disapprovingly.

"So many secrets, Mr. Lucifer," I retort immediately, and I swear his grin broadens, though I convince myself that the flickering dungeon lights are playing tricks on me.

The devil scowling is scary enough as it is; the devil

smiling makes me want to curl into a tiny ball in the corner of this room and rock back and forth incessantly.

"You're the one who demanded we take you to your mate," Alex barks.

Zeus, he is such a dick. Which monster pissed on his Cheerios this morning?

"We took you to him. Happy now?"

"Why is Balor here?" I direct my question at Lucifer, knowing that Alex won't be able to answer unless the big bad gives him permission.

I'm beginning to believe that Alex is nothing but a little bitch.

Lucifer's smile turns cold—cruel, almost. It's nothing but a calculating twist of his lips. And though he directs that sneer in Balor's direction, I still feel gooseflesh pebble all across my skin.

"Extortion tends to make me...angry." He flicks his gaze off of Balor for a brief moment to stare at me. "He told me something I already knew in a futile attempt to free his...people."

Balor's entire countenance seems to change at Lucifer's dismissive words, his shoulders tensing and a vein in his neck throbbing. Still, he doesn't refute Lucifer's claim, and I have half a mind to wonder what Balor tried to extort Lucifer with before deciding I really, really don't want to know. Ignorance is bliss and all that shit.

"I want to talk to him." I narrow my gaze at the tied-up man even as I direct my words at the two bigger threats. At least, I think they're bigger threats, despite the fact they haven't actually, you know, threatened me.

Lucifer and Alex are both silent for a long moment, and I twist my head to stare at them over my shoulder, finding that they've exchanged unreadable looks.

"Why the fuck would you want to do that?" Alex peels his gaze away from Lucifer to shoot me an incredulous glare.

"Ohhh. You're so terrifying," I mock, placing a taunting hand to my chest. "I'm quaking in my boots when you give me those scary eyes."

He growls, low and sharp, and takes a step in my direction. Lucifer's hand immediately clamps down on the necromancer's shoulder, stopping his advance.

"We'll give you time with your mate," Lucifer relents, giving Alex a pointed—yet still unreadable—look.

"Balor is not my mate," I counter, though I feel as if I'm beginning to sound like a broken record at this point.

"But Violet," Lucifer continues, ignoring my interruption. He pierces me with a dark look, one I feel all the way to my toes. Fear skirts down my spine, and I fist the end of my sweatshirt, gripping the material like a lifeline. "Do not let Balor go. Am I clear?"

And am *I* such a lost cause that he would have to state such a seemingly obvious fact? Why in the world would I let the murderous asshole go when he's trapping my mates in the prison of their own minds?

Then I think about all of the other stupid decisions I've made in my twenty-something years on this earth…and yeah. I see why Lucifer would warn me.

Damn.

That's sad.

I give Lucifer a salute, Alex my middle finger, and then twist to face Balor once more. I don't even turn to watch Alex and Lucifer leave. Instead, I merely listen to the poignant, deafening slap of their shoes against the cement floor a second before the door slams shut, signifying they've left. My attention is fully consumed by the striking man tied up before me.

"Balor," I growl out, shocking even myself with my

sudden burst of courage. I take a step closer, content in the knowledge that he won't be able to harm me tied up the way he is. This asshole stole my mates from me, and I'll be damned if I leave this room without getting them back. "We need to talk."

# CHAPTER 6

BALOR

The little vampire fascinates me.

She's so angry, so volatile, so full of life and death and a thousand different emotions I can't even begin to name, let alone understand. Even now as she glares down at me, her arms crossed over her chest, I feel my cock jump to attention as need pulsates through my bloodstream.

I give her a slow, salacious look, one that makes her lip peel away from her teeth in a snarl, before meeting her eyes.

"You seem upset," I muse in a purposeful, nonchalant tone that has her bristling. It's a tone I've perfected over the years, one that suggests I have no shits to give and nothing is capable of penetrating the walls I've erected around myself. "Is this prison not to your liking?" I tilt my head to the side as she continues to glare at me, seemingly too angry to speak. That's okay, though. I like her anger. It tastes decadent on my tongue—like chocolate and coppery blood combined. "Because make no mistake, Violet Dracula. That's exactly where you are—a prison. You may not be in chains like I am, but do you really think Lucifer will allow you to leave this place alive, knowing what you are to him?" I bite down on my lower lip to hide my smirk as her face drains of color.

"He knows?" she manages to bite out, something dark manifesting in her glittery blue gaze. When I don't immediately respond, content to let her stew in her myriad of questions, she adds, "That I'm his biological daughter?"

Does she deem me stupid? Does she truly believe I need clarification?

I heave out a breath as she meets my stare unblinkingly.

Even in her frumpy, oversized sweatshirt and sweatpants, she's beautiful, something I resent with my entire being. It isn't fair that my idiot brothers get to claim her as a mate while I get cast aside. It's not as if I even *want* her as my mate, not with that vampiric blood coursing through her veins, tainting her, but still. I would at least like the option of rejecting her.

"What?" Violet's voice takes on a distinct, mocking lilt. "Cat got your tongue? You're awfully quiet for someone who usually can't shut up."

I attempt to shrug my shoulders, something that proves difficult to do with my hands tied behind my back. Of course, I'm capable of breaking free at any time, but she doesn't need to know that. I like my prey to believe they're the strongest, fiercest, baddest monsters in the room. It makes them lower their defenses just enough for me to sneak in and strike. And trust me when I say that I always, *always* go for the kill.

That kill always tastes sweeter when it's unexpected.

And of course, I'll never admit this to anybody—certainly not the petite female glowering down at me—but a tiny seed of fear has taken root in my stomach. That fear… It's caustic, poisonous, acidic. I've heard rumors about the way Violet destroyed those vampire hunters a few weeks ago—the way she tore them apart and bathed in their blood—and a tinny, mechanical voice in the back of my mind warns me against getting on her bad side. She won't kill me, mainly because this body houses the souls of two men she loves, but she'll damn well try if I piss her off.

"I have some questions for you." Violet takes more steps closer, and I allow my grin to widen with each slap of her feet against the cement floor. By the time she's directly in front of me, my face actually hurts from smiling so broadly. "And you're going to answer."

"What makes you think I'll do that?" I ask in a lazy drawl designed to infuriate.

"Don't you like hearing yourself speak?" She widens her eyes mockingly, and I throw my head back in hearty laughter.

"I would rather hear *you* speak," I tease. "Or maybe scream. I imagine you would scream nice and loud if I fucked your tight little cunt—" My head jerks to the side, pain splintering from where her open palm connected with my cheek.

Well…

Damn.

That hurt like a bitch.

A cold, malevolent grin tugs up my lips, exacerbating the pain in my abused cheek.

"You little whore—" I hiss.

Her laughter cuts off my words, and she absently shakes out her hand where it rests by her side, as if that slap hurt her more than me. "Ahhh. There's the Balor I know and hate. Knew you couldn't keep up the flirty act for longer than a minute. Once a murderous asshole, always a murderous asshole."

Zeus dammit.

This girl just fucking played me.

I allow the smile to slip from my face, revealing the

monster I've kept hidden under lock and key. It's the same monster that craves her flesh and blood, the way zombies and vampires do their prey. I suppose it's only on the metaphorical scale, though. I don't actually want to eat Violet Dracula. I just…want to destroy her. Kill her. Wrap my hands around her tiny throat as her breasts bounce in my face and her pussy squeezes my cock in a choke hold.

"There's a lot you want to know, little vampire whore," I singsong. "And there's not a lot I'm willing to tell you."

"Why the fuck not?" she demands, sounding almost like a petulant child. Is she going to start stomping her foot like a toddler who doesn't get her way? "What do you have to gain from keeping your secrets? You're tied up, for fuck's sake, so obviously the man you thought you could trust didn't extend you the same courtesy."

This time, my smile is sharp enough to cut her perfect little neck until the ground is red with her spilled blood.

"I guess I overestimated how badly Lucifer would want to kill you." A severe oversight on my part, if I'm being completely honest. It makes me question everything I thought I knew about him.

Violet inhales sharply and then frowns, as if she's pissed at herself for revealing any emotion except anger. Her hands ball into fists by her sides, and she lifts one to aim it at my face. Thank God she's not pointing at me. I fucking hate that shit. If she were to jab a finger in my face, I would have no choice but to break free of my bindings and snap it.

"Tell me what I want to know," she demands.

"Can't do that." A loose strand of black hair tumbles free from the bun on my head, and I blow it away with a huff of irritation. If I had my choice, I would shave it all off. What's even the fucking point of long hair on a guy?

"Why the fuck not?"

"You swear a lot for a female," I point out, and she bristles, her back straightening and her eyes spewing venom. I continue on before she can scream at me some more. "And I can't do that because you never told me what you wanted to know."

"Why did you make an appearance now?" she fires off, not bothering to beat around the bush. "Why did you take over their body now, after all this time?"

"I made a ton of appearances," I counter instinctively, remembering all the times I shoved Jack and Hux to the dark corner of our shared mind and took our body on a fun little joyride.

"But never this long. And you never allowed them to know that you were there to begin with," she points out.

"You know...I could be feeding you a bunch of lies right now. You'll have no idea what's real and what's fake." I offer her a cocky smile, one that'll surely get her blood boiling. Simmering. Scalding.

"You could...but you're not. At least, not yet." She leans forward until her blonde hair falls in front of her face, nearly touching the top of my thigh, and my attention snags on her pouty pink lips. "Want to know how I know that?"

Those lips would look damn good wrapped around my cock—

"How?" I lean in close enough to taste her on my tongue, to share her breath. She smells vaguely like strawberries and something else. Something sweeter. Honey, perhaps?

"Because I'm a vampire, motherfucker." She leans in even closer, and my heart gives a traitorous thump. I have to swallow down the dry lump in my throat. "And I can hear your heartbeat."

She pulls away before I can do something idiotic, and it takes me a solid minute to comprehend what she just said. When I do, a surprised, startled laugh bursts from my lips.

"So you can tell when I'm lying," I muse in understanding.

"Clever girl. I suppose you're more than just a tight pussy and a juicy ass to fuck."

She makes a face at my crude assessment of her, and that only makes my grin widen.

"You're disgusting." She gives me a look like I'm the shit beneath her feet.

I'm not going to lie—it does stuff to me. I swear my cock has never been so hard in my entire existence.

I've been many things throughout my long life, but I can proudly say I've never been stepped-on poop before. Why the fuck am I getting so turned on by being it now?

"Well, what exactly do you want to know, darling?" I ask with a taunting smirk. "I'm an open book."

Her full lips purse together, and I watch in fascination as her tiny pink tongue sneaks out to lick her lower lip. If only she weren't a gross vampire...

"I said it before, and I'll say it again—why now? Why are you here? What do you want?" Her no-nonsense stare sears my flesh, alighting my skin in a dozen tiny fires.

"I want to free my people." I decide there's no harm in telling her that truth. It's not one that can destroy me. Besides, it feels good to trust someone else with that secret. For years—for goddamn centuries—I've been holding that truth close to my chest, refusing to allow it to see the light of day. Most monsters have no idea what I mean when I claim I want to free the Formorians, and the gods...

The gods will destroy me if they get an inkling of my intentions.

"Your people..." Violet repeats slowly, carefully, testing the words out. She nibbles on her lower lip as a deep indent manifests between her brows. "You mean Jack and Hux?"

A bitter laugh escapes me. "They're not my people."

"No?"

I debate what to say next, wondering how much I'm

going to tell her, if anything. And then I decide…fuck it. I'm already a prisoner to Lucifer. What harm will it be telling his eccentric, ridiculous, idiotic daughter the truth? Not the entire truth, of course, but just enough to satisfy her curious, tiny brain.

One would think that the feared and malevolent Lucifer and the great and powerful Hera would've produced an offspring who…well…to be frank…had more brain cells. I suppose something got lost in translation when it came to the creation of Violet Dracula.

"Have you ever heard of the Formorians?" I ask candidly, watching her face carefully, gauging her reaction.

She blinks, and that crease between her brows deepens, becoming more pronounced. As if she can feel the blemish on her skin, she lifts a hand to rub at the spot absently.

"Was I supposed to?"

"No." Another low, foreboding chuckle leaves me. "We're nothing but ancient history, my dear Violet. Forgotten souls."

Her hands tangle in the fabric of her oversized sweatshirt, tugging at the material as her glistening blue eyes ensnare my own.

"Is that what you are? A forgotten soul?" She stares at me as if I'm a piece of a puzzle she yearns to assemble, a cog that she wants to see turn.

Good luck trying to understand me, girl.

I don't even understand myself.

"Aren't we all forgotten souls?" I muse, tilting my head to the side as I pretend to ponder this grand epiphany.

She growls sharply, her disdain for me dripping like acid over an eroding rock. "Are you incapable of answering a question? I'm sick of all your half-truths and philosophical musings."

Philosophical musings? I rather like that. Perhaps once all of this is said and done—when my people are freed and the world is destroyed—I'll go to college and get my degree in philosophy. That's assuming, of course, all of the colleges haven't been decimated.

"In the beginning…" I begin in an over-the-top, dramatic voice.

She rolls her eyes so high, I'm surprised they don't get stuck in the back of her head. "Here we fucking go."

I ignore her quip and continue with a wry smirk. "In the beginning, there were no monsters. No humans. Only gods and Formorians."

"You keep saying Formorians like I'm supposed to under-stand what they are," Violet points out.

"I suppose you can say they were Earth's first monsters… before monsters became a goddamn fad and trope." I roll my eyes at the sheer ridiculousness of that, and Violet bristles.

"Don't knock monsters until you try them," she snaps.

"Do you mean…try their bodies? Try their flesh? Try their—"

"That is most definitely not what I meant." Her nose wrinkles with disgust, and she gives me a look that clearly and eloquently states, *What the hell is wrong with you?*

I smile sharply. The pure, venomous rage I harbor at just the thought of what happened to my people claws its way to the surface. "Formorians were what you got when you crossed a monster and a god…though at the time, there were no monsters. We were like you guys, though, but…better."

"Better," she repeats dryly.

"Taller, stronger, faster, smarter." I shrug my shoulders as best as I can with my hands still tied behind my back. I like bondage just as much as the next chap, but this is a little too extreme, even for me. "It's in that way we took after your precious gods and goddesses."

"Okay." Her eyes practically cross as she attempts to piece together this information, to organize my words in carefully placed boxes. "So giant-sized monsters. Got it. What happened?"

Darkness seeps into my system and obscures my vision. My anger is like a huge-ass storm cloud descending on my fate and blotting out what little sunlight once managed to penetrate my defenses. The rage… It coils inside of me like a hungry beast, and I know the only remedy would be allowing it to have its pound of flesh.

I feel like the motherfucking reaper of death right now, and if anyone touches me, they'll fall dead at my feet.

"The gods started getting greedy," I confess through gritted teeth. "Zeus wanted more. Because isn't that word the epitome of human nature? More? He wasn't happy with just the other gods and goddesses. He wanted to be loved and worshiped. Revered and feared. So he created—"

"Humans," Violet fills in, and I nod once.

"Humans. And of course, Lucifer couldn't have that. Even back then, he was a jealous bastard who needed to be the center of attention. He couldn't handle the fact that his big bro Zeus had an entire species devoted solely to him, so Lucifer gave up portions of his soul to create—"

"The first monsters."

"The first vampires," I correct with a pointed look in Violet's direction. "Vampires are actually the closest subspecies to gods that this world has. Even more so than humans, because while Zeus crafted his creations from the earth itself, Lucifer used his soul. More and more monsters popped into existence after that—a natural facet of evolution, I believe. The world needed a balance between humans and monsters."

"This doesn't explain what happened to your people," Violet points out, this faraway glint in her eyes suggesting she still hasn't stitched everything together.

Stupid vampire.

"What happened was that greedy humans and monsters decided to take over a world that didn't belong to them," I growl out, remembering those days with vivid clarity. The violence. The bloodshed. Lucifer's mocking face. Zeus's haughty one. "Zeus had Olympus to rule, and Lucifer claimed Hell as his own, but my people? We weren't even allowed to stay on Earth, our home."

Violet's expression pinched, her eyes shadowing. "What do you mean?"

"I mean, we tried. Oh, we tried to live peacefully with Zeus's and Lucifer's creations, but it's sort of hard to do when you're monstrous in appearance and the size of a small house." They actually still have statues made of us, especially in Egypt where we lived for centuries. But that's a story for another time. "We made a deal with the gods and Lucifer. They could control the living, their precious humans and monsters, but *we* would control the afterlife. Our job was simple. We would hunt the world every night, corralling lost and broken souls and leading them to either peace or eternal torment, depending on their sins. They called us—"

"The Wild Hunt." Violet's voice is both fearful and reverent at once. Shock momentarily breaks through the anger marring her face before her mask settles back into place. She blinks myopically down at me.

"I suppose you have some brain cells after all," I muse, which earns me a scowl from her. I pretend not to see it, however, and continue on with my history lesson. "Hundreds of years ago, the gods decided they wanted dominion over both life and death. They couldn't be happy with what they were given. There was a battle—a battle that the gods and your dear old dad wish to erase from history. We tried to fight for our home and lost. Lucifer locked us away." My jaw clenches so tightly, I can feel pain reverberating down my neck.

"And you want to free them," Violet breathes, and I can't quite detect if her tone is one of horror or understanding. Perhaps it's a mixture of both.

"I want to liberate them," I correct. "This was their home first, after all. Monsters and humans are the interlopers."

"And that's why you hate vampires so much…" She taps a finger to her chin before pointing it accusatorially at me. The damn, fucking finger… "But one thing doesn't make sense."

"Which is?"

"This." She gestures towards my body with a sneer of disgust. "Jack and Hux. I know my guys have been around for a while, but they definitely haven't lived from the beginning of time itself."

Ahh. Maybe she's not as dumb as she looks. Though I have no doubt that if I were to glue a mirror to the bottom of a swimming pool, Violet Dracula would drown trying to stare at her reflection. She may not be a complete and utter imbecile, but I would never go as far as to refer to her as smart.

"All Formorians have special gifts, similar to the way monsters do. Usually these gifts have to do with the afterlife. It's what made us the best at capturing souls. My gift just happened to be…transcendence."

"Transcendence." Her right eye begins to twitch.

"My soul could leave my body for an indeterminate amount of time." I swallow thickly, my throat feeling as if it's been scraped raw with sandpaper. "When my people were taken against their will, locked away…" I lick my upper lip. "I was away. My soul was, at the very least. Lucifer captured my body, but he hadn't managed to claim the piece of me that actually mattered."

"So you hijacked my mates' body?" Her voice is heady with distaste, and she gives me an unimpressed once-over.

"I've tried to join many bodies over the years," I reply with an unrepentant shrug. I refuse to feel ashamed for the things I've done in order to survive. "But most were only able to house one soul, and I was weak being away from my body for so long. I couldn't fight the soul already present inside the body. Couldn't claim my place in the world."

"Until Jack and Hux."

I quirk my lips in a grin. "Their body was quite literally meant to hold more than one soul. What was one more houseguest? Though I'm not going to lie... I did grow fond of the two of them over the years. Even saw them as brothers."

"But that didn't stop you from destroying their lives," she points out with a scowl.

My heart feels heavy in my chest, weighing me down.

"How about I grant you a gift, little vampire?" The words leave my mouth before I can take them back, before I can consider the ramifications of my actions.

*What are you doing, Balor? What the fuck are you doing?* The words are a scream inside of my head, but even my internal voice doesn't have an answer.

"A gift?" Her voice holds wariness but a tiny bit of hope too. It's almost as if she senses the offer I'm going to make before I actually say anything.

"Your mates." I tsk my tongue before that flare of hope can burn even brighter—because I have a feeling that if it does, it'll burn a hole straight through my rib cage and destroy the measly heart hidden there. "Not forever, but... just for a little bit."

"You'll do that?" Her voice is a breath of air, scarcely above a whisper.

"Believe it or not, Violet Dracula," I murmur as I retreat farther into my mind, calling Hux and Jack to the surface, gripping their essences in an iron hold and tugging sharply. "I'm not the monster here."

# CHAPTER 7

HUX

I blink obsessively, trying to pull myself out of the cloying darkness that has been my constant for way too fucking long. It's like being submerged under water and attempting to swim to the surface. The tides and currents batter at my skin, dragging me farther and farther out to sea.

*Jack?* I ask groggily, feeling for my brother, for the warm caress of his soul.

*I'm here,* he tells me, but he sounds just as confused as I feel. Sluggish, almost.

I blink once more, and this time, I'm able to focus on the woman leaning over me with tears in her eyes. The most perfect fucking woman to ever exist.

"Precious Treasure," I pant as my eyes scour her heart-shaped face, taking note of the unnatural flush in her cheeks and the glimmer in her sea-blue eyes. Irrational anger fills me to the brim, until I'm practically bursting at the seams. "Why the fuck are you crying? Who do I have to kill?"

There's rope securing me to the chair, but it's so flimsy

that it's almost laughable. It only takes a flick of my wrist for me to break free and pull my precious treasure onto my lap. I band my arms around her immediately, trapping her to me.

I vow to never let her go again.

She sobs into my neck, her thin arms winding around me until she's gripping at the few loose strands of hair cascading around me. Wait a minute.

Why the fuck am I wearing a man bun?

What fuckwad wears a goddamn man bun?

*Balor,* Jack answers, his tone practically a hiss inside of my head.

*Did he hurt my precious treasure?* I roar as Violet continues to cling to me desperately. Her tears burn where they touch my skin, a physical manifestation of my failure.

*I don't think so.* Jack's inner voice has softened considerably as he considers the girl in our arms. *Her cries almost seem...relieved.*

*How the fuck can cries be relieved?* I demand. *You're either crying because your spleen has been ripped from your body or because someone just murdered everyone you loved while forcing you to watch. There's no other reason to cry.*

I swear, sometimes it feels as if I'm the only mature member of our little duo.

*Let me touch her,* Jack practically begs, and I can sense him pushing against my awareness, attempting to shove himself into the metaphorical driver's seat. *Please, Hux.*

*I can't let her go.* I shake my head adamantly. *I can't, Jack.*

*Please, brother.* Jack's desperation intermingles with my own, and I relent with a heavy exhale, allowing him control over our shared left hand.

Immediately, he begins to caress her back, decorating her skin in soothing circles meant to calm and soothe, while the right hand I still control digs into her hip.

"You're okay, sweetheart," he consoles, our shared voice a low murmur. "You're okay."

"Jack?" She sniffles and tilts her head to meet our gaze.

"I'm here," he assures her softly. "I'm here."

*What the bloody fuck happened?* I demand, struggling to orient myself and remember how we ended up in this… prison cell. *And why the fuck is Violet in this cell with us?*

Horror squeezes my heart and gives it a painful twist, and my right hand immediately flexes against Violet's hip.

*Obviously Balor did something, but I have no idea what. That… That poop head,* Jack hisses vehemently.

*If the three of us didn't share a body, I would rip off Balor's toes one by one and then shove them up his asshole. And then I would grab each one of his ass cheeks like they're pages in a book and rip until his rectum is revealed to the room at large. And then I would take the two halves of his ass and slap him silly, one cheek after the other, and say, 'Why do you keep slapping your cheeks with your cheeks?' And he'll sob and sob and sob, and it'll be really fucking funny.*

There's a beat of silence, and then Jack asks seriously, *What the hell is wrong with you?*

*A lot, my dear brother.*

"Violet," Jack says gently, using his hand to grip Violet's shoulder and push her back until she's staring up at us. "What happened? How did we get here? Where's Balor—"

Violet closes the distance between us and stamps her mouth to his. Ours. I can taste that kiss as surely as he can, and tremors of pleasure dance through my body as he kisses her back.

It's slow at first. Lazy, almost. A brushing of lips as his hand turns into a clamp on her shoulder.

But I know my brother, and slow and easy aren't two words in his vocabulary.

Most would believe that I would be the dominant one of

us two, and I suppose in some ways, I am. But not in the bedroom. I'm too inexperienced for that. Jack, on the other hand, is not. He knows what he wants and won't hesitate to take it.

Their kisses turn frantic as the hand he controls lowers to her breast, pawing at it through the fabric of the sweatshirt. But that's not enough. For either of us.

He pulls away, breaking their kiss despite Violet's whimper of protest, and the two of us work in tandem to pull the sweatshirt over her head. My cock hardens instantly at the glimpse of her full breasts and hard, pink nipples.

Everything disappears except for her, except for her perfect body and hooded eyes. My breathing is a ragged sound, distant through the thrumming of blood between my ears.

"Crap, Vi..." Jack murmurs reverently as he lowers his head to pull one of the tight buds between his teeth.

She gasps instinctively, her back arching to grant him better access, and I can feel the taste of her nipple as if I'm the one sucking on it. As if I'm the one rolling the nub back and forth with my tongue and then tugging it between my teeth.

Almost hesitantly, I lift my hand and begin to knead the tender flesh of her neglected breast, testing the weight of it in my palm and pinching her tight nipple. I make sure not to hurt her, applying just enough pressure so she'll know I'm here but not enough to cause her any pain.

Jack doesn't seem to have the same hang-ups as he sucks and licks at her nipple, wetting it with his saliva. She groans, raking her fingers through our hair until it falls free of the disgusting man bun and tumbles around our shoulders.

"I missed you both so much," she whispers as Jack brings her lips back to ours and kisses her fiercely.

My precious treasure shouldn't have to miss us.

We should be with her always. If only Balor hadn't—

I cut off that thought before it can fester, refusing to give Balor even a second more of my time. He's a goddamn parasite, and I have a feeling if I think about him, he'll make an unwanted appearance like Bloody Mary in the mirror. And the last thing I want is for him to see my precious treasure like this—half naked and moaning in pleasure, with her hips straddling mine as she rolls against my hardened length.

Jack reaches between our bodies and tugs at the waistband of her pants, shoving them down just enough to reveal she's not wearing panties. Both of us groan in unison—though my groan is internal, since Jack still has control of our lips—and I don't waste a single second spearing her on my finger. She's slick, already wet with arousal, and her head falls back as I begin to fuck her with my finger. Jack's digit joins my own, and he pumps it in and out of her as she gasps our names incoherently.

"You're so wet already, baby. So wet. Do you like when we play with your little pussy?" Jack growls.

*Damn, brother. Who knew you were so good at dirty talk?* I praise as Violet continues to ride our fingers, her breasts bouncing in a way that captures my eyes.

I swear Jack's cheeks turn red, though I'm unable to see them myself. However, I *can* feel the sudden surge of heat that zooms up my neck and to my face.

*Is this really the time to praise my performance?* he asks, flustered.

*I would definitely give you a gold star.* I nod sagely. *Maybe even two gold stars. Give me use of our mouth. I want to try my hand at dirty talk.*

Jack seems doubtful—his wariness permeating our shared mind—but he relents control easily.

Mason gifted me a lot of romance novels in preparation for this day. He told me Violet loves men who are rough, domineering, and possessive. He actually gave me a script to say if I were to ever get Violet in bed.

*Oh, I don't think this is a good idea,* Jack begins, obviously catching my train of thought.

Too late.

"You filthy fucking whore. I'm gonna pound my Little Engine That Could into your caboose until smoke emanates from your chimney. All aboard the cock-a-doodle express, destination—your sopping pussy, you little ho."

*Oh dear god,* Jack laments, and Violet freezes where she's writhing against our hands, her lips popping open.

"Did you just say—?"

I steal a kiss from her perfect lips, infusing all of my love for her in it. I want her to feel it in the marrow of her bones, in the blood that courses through her veins, in the way her body arches on top of mine. I want her to know that every inch of me loves every inch of her. Her imperfections only make me love her more.

She melts against me, her hands drifting to my shoulders. When she pulls away, her eyes are glimmering with tears, and I remember what Jack said before, about how people can cry for reasons that have nothing to do with pain or heartache. Tears are a response to feeling something so deeply, your body needs a physical outlet.

"I love you, Hux," she whispers. "I love you, Jack."

"We love you," I growl out, feeling the sincerity of that in my soul.

I don't even need to communicate with Jack to know he feels the exact same way. Violet's our sun, the light breaking up the monotony of darkness that has been our constant for so long, and we're the planets that will never stop orbiting her ethereal being. There's not a piece of me that doesn't worship the ground Violet Dracula, my precious treasure, walks on.

Jack and I both take a side of Violet's pants and shove them down the rest of the way, so there's no obstacle in our way. I move my hand to my fly and wiggle my jeans down my legs until my hard cock springs free, the tip already beaded with precum.

Violet watches us hungrily, her eyes dilated with lust, and Jack swallows heavily inside of our shared mind.

*Frick, man. She's...*

*Perfect? A goddess come to life? Light incarnate?*

*Everything,* Jack supplies as Violet's hand wraps around our dick and gives it an experimental tug. We both groan as her thumb swipes over the tip before inching downwards, towards the base.

"I want to taste you," she whispers with lust-filled eyes as she continues to stroke us.

I'm so fucking hard right now, I'm surprised I don't self-combust.

"Later, sweetheart," Jack promises with a gentle smile. I haven't even realized he regained control of our shared lips. "But we're not going to last long if we don't get inside of you. Do you want that, Violet?" He tenderly, almost reverently, brushes a strand of blonde hair behind her ear. "Do you want us to make love to you?"

Make love.

Not fuck.

"God, yes." Her voice is a breathy moan as she clamors farther up our lap until her pussy is inches above our hard, straining cock. "That's all I want."

"Good girl," Jack praises as he fists our length and lines it up with her entrance.

Slowly, keeping her hands on our shoulders, Violet lowers herself down until she's situated firmly on our lap, taking our entire cock like the perfect vampire she is. Her mouth drops open, and her lashes begin to flutter as she struggles to adjust to our length.

"You okay, Precious Treasure?" I growl out, somehow able to regain control of our mouth with only a little bit of nudging.

Jack and I… We're working in harmony, our sole purpose in life to please our girl and bring her to ruin. There's no push and pull. No strain. No pressure.

Just us and the girl we both love desperately…obsessively.

"I need to move." She gasps, using her heels to push herself up before dropping herself back down on our throbbing length.

"Fuck, yes. Fuck." I place my hand on her hip to help her move as she begins to ride us, her head falling backwards and inarticulate praises leaving her plush, pink lips.

Jack tugs at her bouncing breast, rolling her tiny nipple between his fingers.

"You guys feel so good. So, so good," she praises as she bounces on our cock.

I love how she doesn't differentiate between Jack and me. It's just…us. You guys. We.

Exactly the way it was always meant to be.

"You're beautiful, Violet." Jack tugs sharply at her nipple before releasing it, watching her breast bounce. "So freaking beautiful."

"You guys are," she pants as she digs her fingers into our shoulders and claims our lips in a bruising, possessive kiss. It's a kiss that states she owns it, owns us, and that she'll never let us go again. It's a kiss I feel in the center of my chest, pouring life into an organ I long thought dead.

This woman owns my body, my heart, and my soul. Before her, there was nothing but darkness, so thick and absolute I didn't see a future where I escaped it. But now, there's light, and it's so beautiful and brilliant that I can't imagine ever going back to the way I once was.

Jack's hand leaves her tit to rub at her clit, but I continue gripping her hip, holding her steady. She bucks wildly on top of us, golden hair streaming down her naked back. She's so captivating, so consuming, that I don't notice the door opening until someone inhales sharply.

I snap my gaze over Violet's shoulder, where Alex stands in the doorway, illuminated by the light of the staircase behind him. His eyes are wide, wild almost, as he fixates on a panting and gasping Violet, who's completely oblivious to his presence.

A growl of warning leaves my lips, but I find that I can't stop, that I don't *want* to stop despite the interloper. I continue pistoning in and out of Violet's wet pussy as she murmurs our names and begs us to keep going.

Alex's jeans tent with the evidence of his arousal, and his burnished black eyes burn with a thousand different emotions.

I can hear Jack's wicked intentions a second before his hand snaps down on Violet's ass cheek, causing the flesh to jiggle and her breath to sharpen. Alex's eyes grow wide, his pupils dilating, as he fixates on where Jack's hand now rubs away the sting.

*I don't want him looking at what doesn't belong to him*, I growl at Jack, even as I continue to fuck my perfect mate.

*Maybe that's not the case*, my brother muses as he brings his hand back to Violet's clit and begins to rub it incessantly.

*What do you mean?*

*Violet may not belong to him, but he sure as frick belongs to her.*

*Huh?*

But Jack doesn't answer—not that I blame him—as Violet shoots over the edge with a scream, milking our cock for all its worth. Her pussy clamps down on our length, and I feel my balls tighten a second before I shoot my load into her tight hole. Jack groans as we attempt to ride out the wave of such an earth-shattering orgasm, our bodies shaking and trembling with the aftershocks.

Jack lowers our head to Violet's shoulder, inhaling her sweat-soaked skin, and she scrapes her fingernails over our scalp.

"Fucking hell, guys. That was…"

"Incredible?" Jack suggests, and I quickly take over our mouth to voice my own opinion.

"Indescribable?"

"Perfect," Violet decides on at last, tugging at our long black hair until she can reclaim our lips with her own. Just before she kisses me, though, my gaze flits towards the now closed door.

Alex is gone, and I half wonder if I imagined him being there in the first place.

But I suppose that doesn't matter.

I have my precious treasure in my arms and my brother in my head. As long as they're with me, nothing else matters. I'll kill anyone who dares to try to take them from me.

VIOLET

My lips still tingle from Hux's and Jack's kisses as I lean against the door to the dungeon. I hate leaving them behind, but shortly after our...fun times, Balor reappeared with an indolent smirk on his stupidly perfect face. His eyes glazed over, turning hooded with lust, as he gave my naked body a dirty once-over.

"Have fun with your mates, little vampire?" he asked salaciously.

With a growl of rage at being separated from my mates again, I grabbed the rope off the floor and retied the bastard to the chair. I had no idea if it'd last, but I figured that even if he did break free of his bindings, I doubt he'd be able to escape the room.

I dressed quickly, still muttering under my breath and desperately missing my mates, before racing out of the room with my vampire speed.

Now...

Now, I rest my forehead against the closed door, pain

cinching my heart and tugging at the strings there. I bring my fingers up to my swollen lips and fight off my smile. Jack and Hux may share a single set of lips, but each man kisses so differently. Hux's kisses are tentative and unsure, and he acts as if I'm my nickname embodied—a precious treasure. He touches me as if I'm fine chinaware he yearns to purchase but fears will shatter beneath his fingers.

Jack, on the other hand, is the exact opposite of his brother, despite being the most even-tempered and gentlest of all my mates. He's normally so sweet, so shy, but when he touched me… My body felt alive with fire. He plucked, prodded, and tantalized me in a way that satiated something dark and twisted inside of me. He made me feel loved and possessed, his lips bruising and his hands hungry.

I'll find a way to bring them back to me, dammit, or my name isn't Violet Dracula. Or Violent, if you consider my birth certificate.

I see what I want, and I take it, no questions asked, no fucks given. Balor picked the wrong fucking body to hijack, that's for damn sure.

"Why the fuck do you look like you ran a marathon?" a snide voice retorts, the noise accompanied by the pounding of footsteps.

I lift my forehead away from the door and spin around to face Alex, who carefully avoids eye contact. What the fuck is his problem?

That scowl of his—the scowl I'm officially coining as Alex's scary face—twists his lips in a way that should be unappealing but has the exact opposite effect. Somehow, that scary face highlights the sharpness of his jawline and straight curve of his cheekbones. His obsidian hair falls forward, but he pushes it away with a huff of irritation, that scowl never dissipating.

"What's it to you?" I demand, folding my arms over my chest and matching his glare with one of my own.

He still refuses to meet my gaze, focusing firmly on my neck. His cheeks burn momentarily, and I have half a mind to wonder what the fuck that's about.

"Come on. You had enough time with your murderous mates." He turns towards the steep staircase without waiting to see if I'm following.

"I'll have you know that Balor is the only murderous one, and he's not my mate," I insist, stomping up the steps a few paces behind him. "Well...that's not entirely true. Hux is also pretty murderous. But Jack totally isn't. He's actually a sweetheart. I mean, I'm not saying he's never killed anyone before, because I'm sure he has, but I don't think he has the same murderous tendencies as...say...Hux. Hux is really murderous. Like, he has a shrine of all the people he killed in my honor in his bedroom. Not literally, of course. At least, I don't think so. I meant a metaphorical shrine and—"

Alex whirls towards me so quickly, I stagger back a few steps, my arms windmilling before I manage to right myself. His broad chest heaves as he narrows his strange, arresting, russet-black eyes at me. "Do you ever stop talking?"

I know he means the question rhetorically, but I can't resist answering him. My father—not my bio father, but my adopted one—once called me a shit stirrer, and I can't help but think that's an accurate description. Even now, all I can picture is me standing before a cauldron of disgusting brown poop, a malevolent grin on my face as I hold a huge metal spoon in my hand. Cackling like a maniac, I place the spoon inside the shit pot and give it a nice, juicy stir, swirling the contents around like a whirlpool.

Okay. Disgusting visual, even for me, but it brings a tiny smile to my face, one I immediately smother when Alex's piercing eyes fall to it.

"I don't believe in silence." I shrug absently, pushing past Alex to walk up the staircase in front of him. "Silence is so… boring, you know? Like, what's the point of it?"

"It allows you to think. To be alone with your thoughts." Alex hurries to move in front of me, but I purposely step to the side, blocking him. When he shifts to the opposite side, I throw my body that way as well, feeling oddly like I'm on a boat rocking back and forth.

"My thoughts are terrible company," I tell him seriously.

"So you decided to subject others to them too?"

I don't know if that's amusement or incredulity in his voice.

I shrug once more. "Why the fuck not? It's better than being alone with them."

He doesn't respond to my, admittedly, strange reasoning as we walk the rest of the way up the staircase. When we reach the door at the top, he shoulders past me, removes a key from his pocket—the same key Lucifer had, only a shade of gold instead of silver—and unlocks the door.

"After you," he drawls with a sardonic tilt to his lips and a mocking bow.

I pretend not to hear the obvious sarcasm in his voice and hurry past him.

"Where's Lucifer? I want to talk to him." I glance around the opulent living room, finding it empty. No Lucifer. No disgusting bug man.

Alex makes a strange noise in the back of his throat. "He'll talk to you tomorrow. He left for today already."

"He left? What the fuck do you mean by that?"

"Do you need me to give you a dictionary? 'He' usually means 'a male.' And in this case, I mean Lucifer. And 'left' means 'to go away' or 'leave' and—"

I throw my hand over his mouth, stopping him in mid sentence. His shrewd eyes narrow on the offending limb, but he doesn't lift his arm to push it away. And I'm too stubborn to remove it myself.

So…

We stand there, my hand half engulfing his face and his eyes on me with heated intensity. I lick my suddenly dry lips, and his gaze lowers, tracing the pattern of my tongue.

"I have questions I need Lucifer to answer." I swallow. "Can you answer them?"

He doesn't respond, and it takes me way too long to realize it's because my hand is still over his lips.

Oh. Duh.

Sheepishly, I drop my hand back to my side, surreptitiously wiping it on the bottom of my sweatshirt. I tell myself it's because Alex has cooties…and not because my palm is tingling from where we connected. Definitely not that. Nope. Not at all.

It takes me a moment to realize Alex is speaking, and I tune back into the conversation just in time to hear him say, "Tomorrow."

"Tomorrow?" It doesn't take a genius to figure out what I missed. "I won't get answers until *tomorrow*?"

I'm afraid my head will burst with the number of topics rattling around in there.

Topic one—what happened the night Stefan Van Helsing kidnapped me? I had been with Lucifer and my mates, then there was an explosion… Or something. The details are still fuzzy. What the fuck did I turn into when I murdered every monster in that room? And how can I make sure that doesn't happen again? The last thing I'll ever want to do is accidentally harm my mates.

Topic two—if Balor's telling the truth, then Lucifer knows he's my biological father. What is he waiting for? Why hasn't he killed me? What does he want?

And topic three—when can I see my mates again? Will he

let me say goodbye before he rips my head off? Or maybe Lucifer is a bloodless killer. Does he work with poisons? Perhaps he won't get his hands dirty but will send someone, like a surly necromancer, to do it for him.

We stop outside the bedroom Lucifer indicated earlier, and Alex gestures for me to enter ahead of him.

"Sleep, Violet," Alex instructs. "You won't find any answers here tonight."

"I can if I torture them out of you," I murmur sulkily, and Alex's lips twitch in the beginnings of a smile. Or maybe a grimace.

"Good luck with that," he drawls.

Before I can say anything else—argue, plead, beg—he places a hand on my chest and pushes me back a few steps. I stumble, just barely managing to stay on my feet, and my fangs descend as an icy, insidious rage encompasses my entire being.

"What the fuck, Alex?" I bellow, but the necromancer just gives me a bored look before slamming the door shut. I hear the very distinct sound of a lock being clicked, and I fist my hands into two tight balls, a low growl escaping me.

Fuck. Fuck. Fuck!

I suppose Balor's right.

I may have escaped Prodigium Academy, but I am very much still a prisoner. I doubt that will ever change.

I DON'T KNOW HOW I'M ABLE TO, BUT I FIND MYSELF DRIFTING off to sleep after hours of mindlessly banging on the door, attempting to break open the window, and crafting a weapon out of toiletries—I call it the hairbrush of death, if you were wondering. I still have my dinner knife from earlier, but I doubt either weapon will do me much good if I'm forced to fight Lucifer to the death.

I think I'm asleep. It's hard to say for certain, considering the fact that I'm standing in what appears to be a meadow with soft grass tickling my ankles and a cool breeze blowing back my curls.

I squint against the sun's blinding rays as a strange lump materializes in my chest. I'd almost equate it to a ball of coal, but that doesn't seem right. It's not necessarily heavy, though the way it sits inside of me draws all of my attention to its presence.

It almost feels like…hope.

"It worked!" a voice enthuses from deep within the forest surrounding me, and I spin quickly, my heart galloping up my throat.

Two familiar men stand where the trees meet the grass, tension thrumming through their large, muscular bodies.

"Cal. Barret," I breathe in awe, volleying my gaze between the two men.

It feels as if the walls I've erected around myself in the months following my imprisonment revert back to dust—prickly, annoying dust that I swat at impatiently even as it stings my eyes. The fortress I thought was impenetrable is apparently capable of being bested by the smiling faces of two of my guys.

Cal looks the same as he always does—perfection personified. His pink hair contrasts greatly with his lightly tan skin, and the white shirt he wears clings to his broad shoulders and flexing biceps. His brilliant red wings, now streaked with lines of obsidian, ruffle the longer he stares at me, though he doesn't make a move to step closer. He's…transfixed, and I half wonder if my face bested him, just as his did to me.

Cal the Cupid…brought down by the fanged smile of his vampire mate.

The thought broadens my smile, and that seems to shake him out of whatever spell held him captive. He stalks forward with sure strides, his attention never wavering, his piercing eyes never straying from my face. I feel as if he can see me, all of me. The good, the bad, and the ugly.

He sees it all, and he doesn't want to run or hide or leave me in the dust of my crumbled walls.

My heart bursts with love for this man as he wraps his arms around me and pulls me into his chest.

"Violet…" he practically purrs as he lowers his face into my hair and inhales deeply.

"Don't sniff me, you weirdo." I laugh giddily as I trace the muscles of his shoulders and biceps. His skin ripples beneath my caress, and heat explodes in my lower belly like errant fireworks.

"You smell divine," he growls hungrily into my hair a second before he pulls away and brings his lips down to mine.

I melt against his kiss, my arms twining around his neck and fingering the soft hair there.

If I smell divine—which I might, considering the fact that this is a dream—then Cal *tastes* diviner. Or is it supposed to be *more* divine? Fuck if I know, but his decadent flavor bursts on my tongue and wakes up every one of my nerve endings.

A throat clears behind Cal, and I pull my lips away from my cupid's to meet Barret's bashful stare.

This time, my heart twists for a completely different reason as I drag my gaze over the man I consider one of my closest friends.

And a man I secretly want to consider *more* than a friend.

His dark skin shines like onyx in the brilliant sunlight of the dream world. Green hair decorates the top of his head, the strands slightly longer than I remember them being. The stubble on his chin commandeers my attention, and I can't help but wonder what it'd feel like brushing against my lips. Against the inside of my thighs.

Most of my mates don't have beards or five o'clock shadows, which is a damn shame. Jack and Hux always keep themselves clean-shaven, and Mason… Well, I'm not even sure he's able to grow facial hair, considering his normal hair is made of nothing but snakes. Vin sometimes will have a tease of a beard on his face, but he'll usually shave it off before it can grow. I'm ninety percent positive Frankie—who was created in a lab—is incapable of having a beard as well, and Dimitri wouldn't be caught dead looking so disheveled.

Which leaves Barret.

A man who isn't my mate but who still makes my skin burn with flames. Languid, sweltering flames that kiss at my skin.

"Barret." I pull away from Cal, who surprisingly doesn't argue, and step towards the boogeyman. My cupid has been known to be a little…possessive of me, to put it mildly. "You came for me."

He clears his throat uncomfortably and shuffles from foot to foot. "Of course I did, Cheese Curd." My heart flutters at the ridiculous nickname he gifted me before I force myself to pay attention to his words. "I tried to visit your dreams in detention, too, but they were warded." Self-deprecation laces his tone, and he kicks at the ground with a guttural noise rising in the back of his throat. "Stupid, Barret," he murmurs to himself.

"Don't say that." I place my palms on either of his cheeks until he's forced to lift his head up and look at me. "I'm so happy you guys are here." Tears burn my eyes, but sheer stubbornness makes it so they don't fall. "I missed you both so much."

Barret's brows furrow, as if he's surprised I'm including him as well in that sentiment, when Cal sneaks up behind me and wraps a golden arm around my waist. He pulls me flush against his chest, and I can feel the evidence of his arousal poking against my backside. All I want to do is strip out of this frilly sundress Barret put me in, paw at Cal's clothes, and sink onto his cock, but there are things we need to discuss. Important things.

"...didn't forget about you," Cal is saying now, his voice a languid caress against the shell of my ear.

Oh wait. That's not his voice. That's his actual tongue, licking at my earlobe before pulling it into his mouth. His teeth bite down hard enough to elicit a shocked gasp from me.

"Wait. What?"

Words. Cal. Words. Violet. No understand. Words.

Barret's perpetual confused expression twists into a smirk. "She didn't hear a word you said, Cal."

Cal chuckles darkly and bites down again on my earlobe. Barret's eyes flare with a strange heat and some other emotion—an emotion I would almost describe as jealousy— before he turns away, focusing on the horizon. The tempo of my heart increases like it's in the crescendo of a song.

Before Cal discovered he was my mate, he was in a relationship with Barret. I know it must hurt the big man to see the man he loves wrapped around me. The last thing I ever wanted was to tear those two apart.

"I said..." Cal reaches around me and gives my nipple a twist through the fabric of my dress. I squeal instinctively, jumping about a foot in the air, and he laughs darkly. "That we didn't forget about you. We didn't stop trying to save you. We actually had a plan in place to free you from detention, but when we arrived, you were gone."

"We didn't arrive." Barret swivels back around to face us, his brows scrunched together. "We were the distraction. Mason arrived."

"I know, sweetie," Cal soothes, still tugging at my breast through the fabric. Not that Barret seems to notice. "I meant 'we' figuratively."

"Distraction?" Zeus-damn. It's hard to concentrate with Cal absentmindedly plucking at my nipple and then rubbing the sting away with his huge palm. "What did you guys do?"

I don't need to see Cal's face to know his eyes are emanating wicked amusement. It's evident in his voice. "Just started an orgy...or two."

"Five hundred and thirty-two orgies, to be precise," Barret butts in, and it's only then that his eyes lower to where Cal still touches me. He swallows heavily but doesn't look away. "We needed the staff to be preoccupied so Mason could sneak through the vents undetected."

A strange loneliness evades my system at his words. Because despite Cal and Barret being with me right now...I still miss my other mates. Fiercely.

"They came for me." I hate how soft and vulnerable my voice is.

"Of course they did, sweetheart." Cal presses a kiss to my temple. "They love you. Even that asshole Dimitri Gray."

"Headmaster Gray tried to save me?" I twist my head to stare at Cal in disbelief.

But can you blame me? Dimitri was the one who sent me away to begin with. Then again, he didn't really have a choice. He found me in the middle of a murder scene covered in blood...

"He loves you," Cal says simply, as if that answers everything.

But it doesn't.

Not even a little.

Dimitri loves pointy knives, mirrors, and making my life hell. He definitely doesn't love *me*.

"Where are you, Cheese Curd?" Barret ventures a tentative step closer to me. "We can't find you."

I growl sharply as the memory of the last day washes over me. Memphis. Lucifer. Alex. Hux. Jack. Balor.

"I'm in Lucifer's apartment," I explain, my earlier good mood at seeing the two of them dissipating. Because of fucking course. Every good thing in my life needs to be answered for, and this is no different. The devil has demanded his pound of flesh, quite literally, and now, I'm his unwilling prisoner waiting to atone for my sins. "In Hell."

"In Hell?" Cal screeches. Apparently, he wasn't expecting that answer.

Same, man. Same.

"I heard it's beautiful this time of year," Barret points out with a taut frown.

"Not the time, Bar." Cal rubs his nose in my hair, the repetitive motion almost soothing. "Okay. Okay. This isn't what we expected, but it's not impossible." He seems to be talking to himself more than me, and every hair on my body stands at attention.

"What do you have planned, Cal?" I spin in his arms until I'm able to see his painfully beautiful face. Resting my hands on his chest, I listen to the repetitive *thump-thump-thump* of his heart. I swear it picks up speed the longer I touch him as his glittering eyes devour every inch of my face.

"We're going to get you back, Violet. I already told you."

Horror squeezes me, shaking me from side to side like I'm nothing but a rag doll leaking stuffing. "What? No! You can't do that! You can't go to Hell!"

"I love you, Violet." Cal slants his mouth over mine before I can mount another protest, and I fall against him the way raindrops cascade from the sky and silently join the water in the ocean. His heat surrounds me, cocoons me, and it's so goddamn addicting, I'm terrified of what it'll be like to go cold again. "We'll be there soon."

"Wait!" I plead desperately, not daring to even acknowledge his declaration. Is this the first time he's confessed his love for me? I suppose I always knew he did—how could I not, when he stares at me like I'm the sun, the moon, and the stars combined?—but to hear it out loud…

"Wait for us, sweetheart. We'll be there soon." Cal gives me one last squeeze, infusing the love he feels for me in that single embrace, before releasing me and stepping back.

"Cal, Barret, wait!" I reach towards them desperately, ice-cold fear trickling down my spine and landing at my feet before hardening. I suddenly can't move, can't speak, can't turn away, my feet encased in layers of ice.

No. No. No.

My men can't come to Hell. Lucifer would kill them. I can handle a lot of things in life—my death being one of them—but I wouldn't survive it if anything happened to the men I love.

"No!" I'm not sure if I merely think that word or if I say it out loud, but when I wake up, it's a scream on my lips that rips apart the silence.

# CHAPTER 9

VIOLET

I'm bloodshot and tangry—that's tired, hungry, and angry, if you must know—when I wake up the next morning.

I shower and dress quickly, throwing on a pair of gray sweatpants and a black sweatshirt that reads I'm A Vampire, Hear Me Bite in bright pink letters. There's no hairbrush, so I use my fingers to comb through my tangled blonde curls. The white strands I added a few months prior are beginning to fade, so I make a mental note to buy more hair dye.

If, you know, I ever escape Lucifer.

Perhaps I'll be able to buy hair dye in the afterlife. Unless… Unless the afterlife is in Hell. With Lucifer.

How does that even work? If I die, will I just end up here again? Where did the souls go when the Formorians were in charge of the afterlife?

Wait. Am I already dead?

Can only dead people enter Hell? What about Mount Olympus? I'm assuming the good little souls go there.

I suppose it's pointless to even *think* about that. I'm the epitome of "naughty." Not evil, not bad, just…naughty, and not necessarily in a kinky way. I'm quite literally the devil's daughter, and if that doesn't tell you all you need to know, then I don't know what will.

"Focus, Violet," I chastise myself. "Keep your mind on the prize. Though…I don't really know what the prize is. Unless *I'm* the prize." I continue muttering to myself as I try the handle on the door, surprised to find it unlocked.

Surprised and a little fearful, if I'm being completely honest. This feels like one of those moments where the evil captor tests the beautiful, virgin victim to see if she's worthy. He'll leave the prison cell unlocked and study her intently. Will she run? Fight? Stay hidden in her cell?

The kitchen knife I stole yesterday burns a hole in my pocket.

As soon as I step out of the room, I flick my gaze towards the huge window overlooking Hell. Who would've thought that Hell would quite literally burn with fire? That's a cliché if I ever heard one, and I tend to avoid clichés like the plague.

The next thing I notice is a tall, domineering man standing before a chair in the dining room, his hands clasped behind his back and his eyes unreadable.

"Lucifer," I say stiffly, Balor's words from last night reverberating through my head. Twisting. Turning. Smoking. They goddamn *burn*.

He knows who I am.

This is it.

This is when he kills me.

"Come join me." Lucifer gestures towards the feast laid out before him. Pancakes. Bacon. Sausage. Eggs.

And goblets of what appears to be blood.

My mouth practically salivates—thirsty bitch—and I venture a tentative step forward before remembering myself.

This man, despite his nonchalant demeanor and carefree smile, is a threat, probably the biggest one I've faced. He'll kill me, of that I have no doubt, and the only question that remains is *when*. And how. And why.

Okay, three questions. Semantics.

Lucifer, no doubt sensing my trepidation, adopts a beguiling smile. "It's just breakfast, Violet. You like food, don't you?"

Who *doesn't* like food, especially breakfast food? Psychopaths, that's who.

Eyeing Lucifer cautiously—but seeing no reason not to enjoy the feast spread out before me while I'm already a prisoner here—I tiptoe forward and claim a chair opposite his at the huge table.

The decadent smell of maple syrup curls around me like smoke, and I feel my fangs prick my bottom lip as need arises within me.

"Splendid." Lucifer grins like the cat that ate the canary—or the devil who ate the sweet, innocent vampire—before sitting himself. He begins to scoop food onto his plate, and after a moment of indecision, I do as well.

"Where are Alex and Memphis?" I inquire, mainly to give my mouth something to do. I'm afraid if it's left up to its own devices, it will ramble incessantly about bio dads and schemes of mass murder. You know, the usual stuff people ramble about.

"I sent them away." Lucifer pours a generous amount of syrup on his pancakes before handing the container to me. "I wanted to talk to you. Alone."

"I didn't know Alex worked for you." I try to keep the accusation out of my voice but fail miserably.

Alex… He's an enigma I don't understand, a piece to the puzzle that doesn't quite fit right no matter how I arrange it.

"There's a lot you don't know yet, Violet." He clears his throat and moves to grab his fork and knife.

It's only then I see what's on his plate...and my blood runs cold.

Two pancakes. A spoonful of eggs. Two sausage links. Ten pieces of bacon.

I glance at my own plate, my brows furrowing when I see the *exact same fucking thing*.

Just to be a petty brat, I quickly grab a third sausage link and remove five pieces of my bacon. My heart aches, because bacon is life, but I refuse to be anything like that murderous fucker. Stubbornness has always been my default setting.

Lucifer's lips twitch once more, as if he has caught on to what I am doing and finds it amusing. That, of course, only makes my frown deepen. I don't want to be *amusing* to him.

I take a few tentative bites of the fluffy pancakes, hating that I find them delicious. They could be laced with poison for all I know, yet I'm hungry enough to devour them whole. Back in detention, I was lucky to receive one meal a day, and it was usually stale bread, tepid water, and some moldy piece of fruit. Poisoned pancakes are practically heaven at this point.

We eat in uncomfortable silence for a few moments before Lucifer clears his throat, dabs at his chin with a napkin, and turns towards me. "I wanted to apologize, Violet."

His words slam into me like a one-thousand-pound semi-truck. It quite literally knocks the air from my lungs and rattles my brain, until I'm blinking at him repeatedly, unsure if I heard him correctly.

"You...what now?"

Maybe I heard him wrong. Maybe what he actually said was, "I want to punch you in the face and stab your heart, Violet."

Lucifer continues as if I hadn't interrupted. "When you were taken by that Van Helsing scum…" Fierce indignation ripples across his face, and my blinking increases until I fear I'm having a seizure. Because it almost looked like that indignation was for *me*. Like he was angry on my behalf. He masks his expression quickly, though his eyes still encompass a dark, insidious emotion I can't quite name. "I should've done more to save you."

Wait…

The fuck?

No, seriously.

The fuckity fuck of a good fuck?

I try to remember what Stefan Van Helsing said during our friendly chat—read as, when he tortured and stabbed me before I turned crazy and murdered him.

Didn't he say that Lucifer attacked him? That it took thirty hunters to incapacitate him?

Why the fuck would Lucifer do that? It surely wasn't because of me, was it? He couldn't have wanted to protect me?

I feel as if I've just been shoved off the edge of a steep cliff and am currently rolling down a mountain, hitting every jagged rock along the way. Pain explodes behind my eyes, and I absently bring a hand up to my forehead and rub at it.

"They couldn't kill me." Lucifer chuckles wryly, the noise lacking any genuine humor. "But they definitely wanted to."

"Why would you want to save me?" I can't quite wrap my head around all of this. His heartfelt words. His earnest eyes.

Everything accumulates together to create one big pile of shit.

And then Lucifer says it. Right there, in the middle of his dining room in Hell, around a mouthful of pancakes drenched in syrup. He doesn't even flinch as he quite literally throws the monster equivalent of an atomic bomb at my head, awaiting the inevitable explosion.

"Because you're my daughter, Violet."

I'm out of my seat before he can blink, my hand clasped around the kitchen knife I stole yesterday. I pull it out of my pocket and raise it, prepared to fight with every ounce of strength I possess, when Lucifer's hand shoots up and captures my wrist.

Panic screams in my head like a banshee, and I feel something wet in my eyes. Tears.

I really, really don't want to die.

Slowly, never taking his eyes off of my face, Lucifer lowers my hand that is still holding the weapon. I fight against him, my limbs trembling from the exertion of fighting his godly strength, but it's futile. It isn't long before my hand is back by my side and the blade has clattered to the floor, bouncing directly in front of Lucifer's feet.

In my slightly hysterical state, I notice that his shoes have recently been polished. They're so shiny, I can see my reflection gleaming on the surface. I wonder who polished them for him. Alex? Nah. I can't see that asshole falling to his knees for anyone. Memphis? Maybe. He definitely seems like an ass kisser. But why would Lucifer even need such glossy shoes in Hell?

I don't know why I'm even surprised. Everything about Lucifer is meticulous, even first thing in the morning. I half wonder if he sleeps in that damn white suit.

I realize my brain has run away from me—is currently on freaking Jupiter while the rest of my body is caught in the gravity of Earth—and I work to focus on Lucifer once more.

"I won't let you kill me," I vow heatedly, staring into a pair of eyes so similar to my own. "I won't."

His brows touch. "I would never hurt you, Violet. *Ever.*"

The vehemence in his statement shrivels my lungs into raisins.

How the fuck can he sound so earnest, so sincere, when I know it's a lie?

"What the fuck do—"

My words are interrupted by a deafening bang. I only have a second to twist towards the doorway before the world is engulfed in chaos.

# CHAPTER 10

I f Violet wanted to see my declaration of love firsthand, then she got it. I'm pretty sure there's no saying "I love you" like blowing open the door of the devil's apartment in Hell with a machine gun strapped to my chest and two god-blessed katana swords on my back. I know none of my weapons will be able to kill Lucifer—I'm not an idiot and won't underestimate the asshole's power—but hopefully, they'll be able to stop him just long enough for us to save Violet.

Dimitri steps up beside me, a dark and deadly glint in his cold blue eyes. I've always thought he had dead eyes—vacant and unfeeling and impassive. I still believe that's true, but I've seen other emotions in the weeks Violet's been away.

Fear. Anger. Yearning.

Love.

The latter emotion practically knocks me onto my ass. The headmaster is known for a lot of things, but not one of them is good. So the knowledge that he's in love with my mate?

It's a sucker punch to the gut.

A part of me is grateful that such a powerful monster is on our side, will fight tooth and nail for the woman we all love, but another part fears what this means.

For us. For Violet. For the future of the monster world.

To have a single scary monster love you is one thing. To have several…

Worlds will burn if Violet has even a miniscule scratch marring her perfect flesh.

"Lucifer!" Dimitri bellows, for once not looking like a man made of ice but a creature crafted of flames. He looks like a predator, a creature so innately lethal that your only option is to run in the opposite direction or die. Fighting will just lead to your death.

Mason sidles up beside me, his beanie held loosely in his hand. The snakes on his head hiss and writhe as they search the room for any threats. It's not often my best friend will forgo his safety cushion—that damn hat—but for Violet, he'll do just about anything.

And that means becoming the very monster he fought so hard against.

Barret, Cal, and Frankie filter in behind me, and between the six of us, I know no one will be able to sneak past.

Barret has grown nearly three times the size that he is normally, his muscles expanding and contracting. His green hair floats with the force of his power as he steps in front of me and growls, low and feral.

"Guys?" a tentative voice questions, and a second later, Violet materializes in the doorway of the kitchen.

Her eyes widen, shock splaying across her face, before a choked sound escapes her. With a burst of her vampire speed, she propels herself across the room until she's able to barrel into the nearest man—which happens to be Barret.

The tension riding his body flees as soon as her soft curves press against him. And then it returns with a vengeance when he realizes that *Violet* is *hugging* him.

His arms hang limply by his sides, as if unsure what to do, but Violet doesn't seem to mind or even notice as she sobs into his chest.

Yeah.

That man has got it *bad*. He's almost as obsessed with Violet as I am.

As *we* are.

"Vi. Pinkie." Mason's voice is a breath of air as he gazes at her reverently. I swear even his snakes calm down, soothed by her presence.

But all of my relief at seeing her unharmed and alive dissipates when a tall, imperious man materializes in the doorway behind Violet.

"Lucifer," Cal growls, stalking forward with his red and black wings flexing.

Lucifer's eyes slowly drag across all of us in the room, his lips peeling back in disgust.

"There's more of you than I thought."

The strange words take me by surprise, but they're not enough to drop my guard. I'm in the presence of a predator, a beast, the creator of all monsters, and the man who can end us all with a flick of his fingers.

The only question is… Why hasn't he?

Dimitri charges forward like a man possessed, moving with a sleek agility I've come to admire in him. Unlike me and my assortment of weapons, Dimitri only carries a serrated blade. He says it allows him to move faster, and seeing him now, a blur of white hair and dark clothes, I can't even disagree.

One second he's beside me, and the next he has his blade pressed to Lucifer's throat.

"You know that won't kill me, Gray." Lucifer doesn't seem perturbed in the slightest. Not even when Dimitri applies a tiny amount of pressure and blood wells on the devil's pasty white throat.

"But it'll still hurt," Dimitri promises roughly. His gaze flicks to Violet, who now hides behind Barret's broad back, before focusing on the man before him. "You're going to let us go."

I swear Lucifer rolls his eyes as if the entire exchange is tiring to him. As if we're pesky flies he's been trying to swat away for hours now.

"You may be powerful, but are you really a match for all of us together?" I ask, punctuating my words with a single step forward.

I know the answer to that, and apparently, so does Lucifer.

Alone, all of us might get our asses handed to us.

But together? We'll stand a chance of defeating him once and for all. We're some of the most powerful monsters who have ever walked this Earth. If we want someone to bleed, to weep blood at Violet's shrine, then we'll find a way to make that happen.

"I'm not going to fight you," Lucifer says with another one of those annoyingly smug eye rolls.

Dimitri's arm tenses where it's still wrapped around the other male, and his blue eyes flare hotly—hotter than the fires of hell itself. He's been itching for a fight since Violet was first taken from us; we all have. The need for violence burns like poison in our blood. It's not just a yearning. We all might quite literally self-combust if we don't find a way to satiate the rage bubbling just beneath the surface.

"Don't be stupid, Headmaster Gray," Lucifer continues,

obviously sensing the same thing I am—the desperate, insatiable thirst for blood. Violet may be the only vampire present—or at least, the only being in this room who exhibits vampiric traits—but all of us yearn to taste the blood of this man. To bathe in it. "If you try to kill me, I'll try to kill you in return. And I don't think either of us wants that."

Violet pulls herself out of Barret's embrace, ignoring his growl of warning, and steps closer. Her hands ball into tight fists by her sides as she eyes the man who was partially responsible for her birth.

How can a man like Lucifer—a man so inherently evil, even I'm terrified of him—father a woman as jovial and vibrant as Violet? She's the flame that burns so hotly, you're liable to get burnt if you stand too close. However, you find yourself inexplicably drawn to her anyway like a damn moth. Closer and closer and closer, desperate to bask in her heat and light. You're no longer strong enough to face the darkness alone once you've had a single taste of her.

"Violet, stay back," Frankie barks, and if Frankie's ordering you around, you know you're in deep shit. The man is about as assertive as a damn teddy bear.

"I want answers." Her voice is practically a growl, and her eyes spew fire as she glares at her bio dad. "Why haven't you killed me?"

Dimitri, still not removing the knife from Lucifer's neck, straightens imperceptibly. "Yes, Violet. Let's ask the murderous psychopath why he hasn't killed you. Smart move." He accompanies his words with a dry look that makes Violet bristle.

Damn. No wonder Violet hates his guts. He's fucking horrible at showing his feelings. Every word that leaves his lips is said with indifference, as if he truly doesn't give a shit about what happens to her. As if he doesn't love her as fiercely as we all do. If I didn't see firsthand how rattled he was after Violet was arrested, I wouldn't have believed it myself.

Violet focuses her ire on Lucifer. "You know who I am. *What* I am. What I am to you."

Her emphatic words have all of us tensing.

Lucifer knows that Violet is his daughter?

Fuck. Fuck. Fuck.

Dimitri digs the blade in a little deeper, and more blood spills, cascading down Lucifer's neck and staining his suit collar. Lucifer's gaze follows the blood, but he doesn't immediately respond. I don't know if he's merely considering his words…or if he's waiting to pounce. I pray it's not the latter, but if it is, we'll be ready.

I meant what I said before.

Individually, we won't be able to harm a single hair on Lucifer's head, but together, we might stand a chance. A slim chance, but a chance all the same. That's all we need to get Violet out of here in one piece.

"I want to know the truth." Violet continues to advance on the deranged man, and I bite down on the venomous growl that wants to escape. Can my girl not sense the danger she's in? She should be running in the opposite direction, not slowly walking forward like she has every intention of reasoning with the bastard.

Mason, apparently on the same wavelength as me, rushes forward and grabs her arm. He's put his beanie back on his head—probably terrified of accidentally turning Violet to stone, despite my reassurances that he'll never hurt her. He's predisposed to protect her, just as I am. His brows pinch tightly together.

"Violet…" he warns.

She shakes him off and continues to venture forward. All of our gazes are riveted on her, on the girl who owns our hearts and souls. I want to stop her, want to beg her to run, but I don't.

I'm her mate, not her keeper. My duty is to stand beside her, not in front of her.

"I want to know the truth." Her voice shakes ever so slightly, and I can visibly see the way her shoulders tense.

"The truth?" Lucifer tilts his head to the side curiously, acting as if the blade digging into his skin doesn't exist. As if it isn't drawing blood with every passing second.

"The truth." She nods once, her lips pursing.

"The truth is...I will never harm you, Violet." His eyes ignite with a gleam that I can't quite comprehend. Sincerity, perhaps? Fucking ridiculous. I'd sooner believe that Lucifer eats babies for breakfast than that he gives a shit about Violet Dracula. Still, his voice is low and earnest as he continues on as if he's attempting to calm a skittish cat. Or...a skittish demon-goddess hybrid, as the case may be. "I told you that. You're my daughter."

Dimitri growls sharply and uses his free hand to grab at Lucifer's face. "Liar!" he roars, the noise so startling, especially coming from him, that I palm the hilt of my katana instinctively. "I know you tried to kill Violet as a baby. And I know Hera hid her from you with Dracula."

Shadows dance in Lucifer's eyes, and for the first time, I see exactly why every person in this world refers to him as the devil. Pure malice reflects back at me as darkness overtakes his face.

"Hera"—the name is practically a hiss—"is an evil, conniving bitch. She's the one who tried to murder Violet, not me. She's the one who told me that my daughter was dead."

"Lies!" Violet jabs a finger at him accusingly. "Hera tried to save me...from *you*. She asked Dracula to hide me."

"I can assure you that if she kept you alive, it wasn't intentional."

I've never seen a man so full of hatred as Lucifer is right at that moment. It radiates off of him in tangible waves, causing my arms to pebble with goose bumps. This time, I *do* grab my blade and hold it at the ready, waiting for the monster before me to pounce. To attack.

"She might not have been able to kill you as a baby, but I have no doubt she didn't try."

"I don't understand. That doesn't make any sense," Violet insists, and she looks so lost, so forlorn, that all I want to do is run forward, pull her into my arms, and hug her until all of her shattered pieces fit together again. "Why would Hera want me dead?"

"I think the question you need to be asking yourself is why did she keep you alive?" Lucifer's tone is grave. "And what does she plan to do next?"

# CHAPTER 11

VIOLET

I don't know how to wrap my head around all of this new information.

Is Lucifer insisting…that he's the good guy? I half want to scoff at such an absurd notion and half want to beg him for more information. My life feels like a giant jigsaw puzzle that has been assembled by a two-year-old. The pieces are covered in snot and drool, and nothing fits together correctly.

A dull ache begins to pound at my skull, and I have a feeling no amount of painkillers will alleviate it.

"I…I need a minute," I manage to choke out, not waiting for my mates to respond.

I spin on my heel and all but race into the bedroom I slept in the night before. I trust Dimitri and the others to handle Lucifer until I'm able to…well…I don't know what I need to do. Calm down? Try to decipher the validity of Lucifer's words? Freak the fuck out?

For so long, my world has been simple. Every monster

was shoved into a tiny, labeled box, and I knew immediately from looking at them if they were good or evil. And Lucifer? He was—and perhaps still is—the epitome of all things evil. But my time at Prodigium Academy has taught me that life isn't as easy as that. There are facets to every aspect of nature, and none more so than human nature. Evil and good. Pure and malicious. Is there really that big of a difference between the terms? Since when have the lines started to get so damn blurry?

"Vi?

I rub the sleeve of my sweatshirt against my eye, praying I'll be able to mop up all of the stray tears before Frankie can see them fall. Then I think, *Why the hell can't he see them?* and spin to face him, my eyes glimmering.

Frankie's stoic expression shatters, and he opens his arms for me to step into. A strangled sob lodges in my throat as I race across the room and all but throw myself at my mate. The arms that band around my waist are unfamiliar but definitely not unwelcoming. Frankie has never been the type to coddle me...or even cuddle me, for that matter. But he's always, always here for me when I need him.

"It's okay, sweetheart. It's okay. We'll figure this out," he coos in my ear, rubbing his hand up and down my back.

"Lucifer's lying, isn't he? Because if he's not lying, then that means Dracula was lying, and I don't know if I can—"

"Perhaps Dracula wasn't lying." Frankie places his hands on my shoulders and gently pulls me away so he can stare into my eyes. A thousand emotions swim in their gray depths, and I want to drown in them. Lose myself in the chaos that is Frankie. "Maybe he believed what Hera told him."

"But why would Hera want to kill me?" My voice betrays my incredulity. I can't quite wrap my head around golden-haired, petite, smiling Hera wanting me dead.

"We don't know that Lucifer was telling the truth, either," Frankie reminds me, giving my shoulders a reassuring squeeze.

So basically, we have no fucking idea who's a big fat liar and who we can trust. Wonderful.

"Do you have a potion we can use to determine if he is?" If anyone were to have a way, then it would be my Frankie.

"Do I…?" He snorts derisively, sounding a little offended I would even need to question him. "Of course I do." Leaning down, he presses his lips against my own. It's a chaste kiss—the merest brushing of skin against skin—but fireworks explode throughout my body in a kaleidoscope of brilliant colors and goose bumps pebble across my skin.

How can one simple kiss wake up every nerve ending in my body? How can spurts of electricity shoot through me in a way that's almost painful in its intensity yet still makes me crave more?

Frankie pulls away just enough so he can rest his forehead against my own. His hot, minty breath fans across my face, and I squeeze my eyelids shut.

"I can't believe you're here," I whisper. "I can't believe you came for me."

"I will always come for you, Violet. *We* will always come for you," he emphasizes, and the vehemence in his tone leaves no room for an argument. I can feel the depths of his words in my soul, knitting itself into my genetic makeup. "And do you know what we're going to do now?"

"Have hot sex and forget the rest of the world for a few hours?" I suggest hopefully, trailing a hand down his stomach and towards his rapidly hardening erection. I palm his dick through the material of his pants, and he hisses out a breath through clenched teeth. "You can do that thingy you did last time. You know…when you made your dick vibrate inside of me?"

Can you blame a girl for practically begging at this point? I'll get on my knees if that's what he wants—though now that I think about it, getting on my knees to suck him off doesn't sound too bad...

I had sex with Hux and Jack, but I need more. I need Frankie and Vin and Mason and Cal. And maybe...maybe some of the other assholes out there in the living room as well. I'm freaking insatiable.

Frankie gently, carefully, grabs my wrist and pulls my hand away from his erection. His eyes are pained as he drops my arm back to my side.

"As much as I wish I could say yes...that's not what I had in mind." He shakes his head once, and I have to resist the urge to pout. "You're going to go back out into the living room with your head held high because you, Violet Dracula, are a monster who deserves to be feared and respected. Even by the King of Hell himself." A tiny smile chisels itself onto his painfully handsome face.

Frankie may not be carved from granite like Vin or have rippling muscles like Cal and Barret...but there's no denying he's beautiful. While I once thought his features to be cold and calculating—hewn from blocks of ice—I now know them to be soft and ingenuous.

He's one of the best men I know, one of the best monsters in this whole damn world, and fate was smiling down upon me when it declared him as my fated mate.

"I love you," I whisper, the words almost shy. Tentative. Hesitant.

This time, the smile that rips across his face is breathtaking—the sun illuminating the horizon after days of swollen, gray storm clouds and zigzagging lightning strikes.

My heart, which has fallen to a repetitive and steady thump during our conversation, increases in tempo until it's all I can hear. All I'm aware of.

Or maybe that's just him.

Frankie.

His eyes ensnare my own, and I'm helpless to do anything but fall against him like a tree getting struck down by the fatal blade of an ax. My hands form tight little fists that I place on his chest, directly over his heart. He once told me that he doesn't have any organs, only machinery, but I swear I feel his heart pounding in sync with my own. Two bodies. One soul.

"I love you more than words can express, Violet Dracula." He places his hands underneath my chin and tilts my face up—

But before our lips can connect, a throat clears incessantly directly behind me. Even without turning to look over my shoulder, I would know that obnoxious throat clearing from anywhere. It's a very distinct cough-slash-gagging noise.

Dimitri fucking Gray.

"Fucking pussy blocker," I growl, keeping my lips a hair's breadth away from Frankie's. When he breathes in, I breathe out, and when I breathe in, he breathes out until we're quite literally sharing the same air.

The thought makes the butterflies in my stomach turn radioactive. No amount of pest repellant will be able to remove or kill them.

"Be that as it may, Miss Dracula,"—Dimitri's voice is like thunder that ripples through the night sky and pulsates through my body—"I need to know what you plan to do."

His strange words are enough for me to spin around, still in Frankie's arms. My mate's hands immediately lower to clamp down on my waist, and his huge erection digs into my ass. I can't help but wiggle against him, eliciting a pained grunt from his lips.

Dimitri watches the exchange with narrowed, icy-blue

eyes.

"What I plan to do?" I demand, frowning.

"With your father," Dimitri explains. "I have chains that should be able to contain a god…" He frowns, focusing on a water stain above my shoulder.

It's the only thing about the apartment that isn't immaculately clean and put together. I half wonder if it's an accurate depiction of Lucifer himself—suave and meticulous at first glance, but the closer you look, the more you notice tiny blemishes and flaws that had escaped your notice to begin with.

"But there are always risks doing something so—"

"Risky?" I finish for him, and his white eyebrow twitches.

"I would recommend for Lucifer to stay here. We can't kill him, but I also don't think it's wise to bring him with us." He folds his arms over his chest in a way that draws attention to the muscles of his biceps.

Dimitri is, and always will be, a chiseled god. He's the fairest out of all my men, with skin so pale I can see each individual vein and hair so white it reminds me of snow. And not that shitty snow you trounce around in either. Mountaintop snow—unblemished and untainted, a new layer constantly being added. Currently, those white strands are meticulously brushed into a low ponytail, but I know from experience that they hang just below his shoulders, softer than the fur of a cat—

Ugh.

Am I really waxing poetic about goddamn Dimitri Gray?

Vomit.

His words register to me then, and my lips tug downwards.

"I don't want to leave him behind." I don't even need to think about my decision before speaking. I know with unwavering certainty that Lucifer is a part of this whole mystery. I need answers first and foremost, and the devil is quite literally the only one capable of providing them for me. "He has information that I need."

Dimitri's right eye begins to twitch, as it always does when he's particularly irritated with me. "Are you purposefully being difficult and going against my wishes?" he demands, as if he truly believes me to be petty enough to argue with him just for the sake of arguing.

Though...

That may be not far off from the truth.

"Believe it or not, Headmaster Gray," I hiss, stepping out of Frankie's embrace and stomping towards the infuriatingly sexy and irritating professor, "the world doesn't revolve around you."

"Believe it or not, Miss Violet Dracula,"—he matches me step for step until he's directly in front of me and I'm forced to tilt my head back to stare into his eyes—"maybe my world revolves around *you*."

His declaration is a nocked arrow shot directly into my heart. He's the hunter, and I'm nothing but the helpless little bunny unable to escape the predator's death blow. But maybe, just maybe...

I don't want to escape Dimitri Gray.

His eyes widen imperceptibly, as if he's as stunned by his words as I am, but he doesn't take them back or refute them. Instead, he allows them to marinate in the air around us, to seep beneath my defenses like poisonous mist.

"Dimitri..." I don't know how to respond to him. I haven't a clue what to say. Words—which usually come so easily for me, even if it's in the form of inane chatter—fail me. I can't quite articulate the emotions percolating in my chest, fizzing and bubbling like water on a stovetop.

"I—"

"Did you guys decide what you're going to do?" Mason

pokes his head into the room, his eyes immediately locking on me as if no one else matters. As if the others don't even exist.

"Piss timing, Mase," Frankie drawls from behind me, and my gorgon frowns.

"Huh?" Mason glances between the three of us. "Did I miss something?"

"Nothing," Dimitri bites out, his tone scathing and probably the only thing capable of harming me right now. It's like a knife that jabs itself into my skin, poking and prodding and slicing until I'm bleeding profusely. "Absolutely nothing."

I try to swallow around the sudden stab of pain.

What is it about Dimitri Gray that's always able to hurt me? Why do I give him the power to do that in the first place? He makes me lower my defenses, open myself up to him, and then he uses my vulnerability against me, sneaking in for the attack.

The scowl carved into his harsh mouth is grim, and I can't help but wonder if the ire in his eyes is directed at me...or Mason.

What was he going to say to me?

Do I even want to know?

"We're taking Lucifer with us." Dimitri doesn't rip his eyes away from mine, even as he addresses Mason. "The damn girl refuses to listen to reason."

"This damn girl has ears," I hiss out. "And is standing right in front of you."

"If you have ears, then use them," he snaps back. "Taking Lucifer with us is dangerous—"

"Then you can stay behind. I never asked you to come with us."

For a brief, brief moment, I swear I see a flash of hurt in eyes that are normally apathetic. It's there and gone faster than a shooting bullet, and I half wonder if I imagined it to begin with. If I was, perhaps, projecting my own hurt and pain. Dimitri Gray doesn't have cracks in his unflappable mask. Hell, I'm not sure if the cold bastard even feels any emotions aside from bloodlust and anger.

He certainly doesn't feel *hurt*.

"Let me go arrange transport for our prisoner," he barks out, still glaring at me.

"Make that two prisoners," Mason adds, still seeming unsure of what he walked in on. When Dimitri whirls around to grant him the full force of his penetrating stare, Mason shuffles from foot to foot and absently tugs at his gray beanie.

"Two?" Dimitri asks.

"The necromancer arrived," Mason explains, shooting his eyes in my direction.

"Alex?" I frown. "Did Memphis arrive as well?"

"Who the fuck is Memphis?" Dimitri explodes. He tosses his arms into the air and begins to pace. "Another one of your harem members?"

"Fuck you, Dimitri," I hiss, baring my teeth at him. "And to answer your question, fuck no. He was just the one who broke me out of detention."

"How the fuck did he do that?"

"No idea." I shrug. "All I know is that he made me into a tiny bug, put me into his pocket, and walked right on out without a care in the world."

"Lucifer probably convinced the faculty that Memphis was your lawyer or some shit," Mason mumbles with a taut frown. "They wouldn't question him coming to visit you."

"He didn't talk to me about it," Dimitri seethes. Usually, Dimitri's anger reminds me of a cold frost permeating every available surface. Now, it resembles fire. Ravenous, scalding, untamable fire. "Why the fuck didn't he talk to me about it? I'm the damn headmaster!"

"You know why," Mason murmurs softly with a pointed look in my direction.

That only makes Dimitri's frown deepen, as if he doesn't like being reminded of my presence.

"And we actually need to plan for three prisoners!" I interject before Dimitri can go off on another one of his long-winded tangents.

"Three?" Frankie, Mason, and Dimitri all ask at once.

Suddenly, I find myself the sole focus of three very intense gazes.

I refuse to blush. "Balor's in the dungeon. Last I checked, both Alex and Lucifer have keys."

"Three." Dimitri releases a slightly hysterical—and definitely unhinged—laugh. "We have three prisoners. One of them is the King of Hell. The other is a murderous, vamp-hating psychopath. And the third is a powerful necromancer with known ties to both vampire hate groups *and*, apparently, the actual devil." He shakes his head rapidly, a strand of pure white hair falling out of his ponytail and into his eyes. "Do you want to know how I stayed alive for so many years, Violet Dracula?" He whirls around to face me so quickly, I stumble back a step. His abrupt change in topic causes my head to spin, but he forges on ahead before I can respond. "Do you want to know how I became the best assassin in the world?"

"Because you can travel through mirrors?" Frankie answers.

"Because you're super scary and most monsters would shit their pants if they saw you coming?" Mason adds.

"Because you like stabbing things?" I suggest.

That damn eye twitch Dimitri perfected begins again. "Because I was smart," he says, ignoring our guesses. "Because I never took any unnecessary risks."

"You don't have to help if you're so afraid," I bite out, my anger mounting before I can stop it.

Dimitri barks out a harsh laugh. "I'm not afraid for me, you stupid child." I bristle at his use of the word 'child,' especially after all of the things we've done together, but he continues on before I can interrupt and bitch-slap him silly with my words. "I'm afraid—"

"Dimitri." Mason's voice is a warning, a threat, and a promise all in one. "Go help Vin secure the prisoners. I'll stay with Violet."

Dimitri glares at the other man, no doubt hating being ordered around, but he doesn't protest as he shoves past him and storms out of the room. Mason watches our headmaster go with a weary sigh.

"Pinkie, I wouldn't be too hard on him if I were you…" He trails off when he notices my shocked expression.

"Not be too hard on him? Mase, he's an asshole! Did you hear what he said—?"

"He's scared," Mason confesses. "And not for himself, but for you. Don't you see that?"

I snort. "Why the fuck would he be scared for me? He hates me."

"That's not true, Violet," Frankie murmurs gently, stepping up behind me and once more placing his hand on my shoulder.

"Dimitri's in love with you," Mason states blandly. When I gape, wondering if I heard him wrong, he smiles sheepishly. "Don't give me that look, Pinkie. It's the truth. He's in love with you, and that terrifies him. He went from never giving a single shit about another living person to dedicating his entire life to protecting one. To protecting *you*."

"I… He doesn't… He wouldn't…"

"Come on, Vi." Frankie takes my hand and begins to lead me out of the room. "We need to get you to the safe house… before the citizens of Hell realize we kidnapped their king."

# CHAPTER 12

DIMITRI

Violet fucking Dracula is a complication I don't need in my life—an obstacle, a wayward storm, a swirling tornado that brings nothing but destruction—but she's also someone I can't let go of. She's a parasite that's slowly eating away at my brain, until everything that I am is consumed by her. I soak up the little rays of affection she offers me like a sunflower tilting towards the ball of light in the sky.

I hate it.

But I also love it.

The contradicting emotions pound against my defenses like a hurricane—a torrent of rainfall, high gusts of winds, and crackling thunder.

She's my greatest sin and my most desired salvation all in one.

The safe house I chose for us is more of a cabin than anything else. It rests on the outskirts of Edinburgh, Scotland, in a town that seems to be predominantly occupied by sheep and cattle. Everything is constructed out of varnished mahogany, giving the three-bedroom home a rustic feel. Ambient moonlight shines through the numerous windows, intermingling with the fairy lights strewn through the boards above. Aside from the three bedrooms, there are two bathrooms, though only one with a shower, a kitchen, a dining room, and a living room.

It's definitely not the type of home that can fit six hulking men, one teeny vampire, and three prisoners. Each of the bedrooms have been transformed into a makeshift prison cell, with our esteemed guests tied to chairs inside of them.

I suppose my father, Dorian Gray, is useful for something. He charmed Aphrodite, fucked her brains out, and then convinced the dim-witted goddess to provide him with god-blessed chains. They're supposed to be the toughest chains in all of existence, capable of locking away even a god.

And hopefully a devil.

My skin feels too itchy having all of these people in my space. Every time my shoulder accidentally brushes Vin, or I get a face full of Cal's wings, or Mason steps on my toe, or Frankie's impassive voice discusses his recent find...I lose a little bit more of my mind.

Don't even get me started on *her.*

Violet Dracula.

Her scent tickles my nose, taunting me, and her laugh is like the sweetest temptation. I yearn to hear that noise for the rest of my life...and also never to hear it again.

She doesn't acknowledge me.

Not once.

She doesn't even fucking *look* at me.

I try to keep my mask in place, try not to let any cracks show, but it's so hard when she's offering out affection like candy. A smile here, a laugh there, a kiss here. It's driving me mad.

I replay our recent conversation back in Lucifer's apartment and inwardly wince. I may have been too hard on her, but that's only because the infuriating woman confuses me. *Terrifies* me. The thought of anything happening to her makes me break out in a cold sweat in a way I haven't done since I was a boy, when I learned to compartmentalize my fear and not allow it to control me.

Somehow, Violet has found a way to slither beneath all of my defenses with nothing more than a tiny smile that carves away at me like a serrated blade. She's nothing but sharp edges, but maybe a part of me wants to be nicked by her.

I cannot deny the appeal of falling into bloodshed with Violet Dracula.

Cursing the direction of my thoughts, I focus on my phone once more. I've claimed a tiny corner of the living room as my own, and everyone knows not to disrupt me here. Though I can't say I would mind too much if a certain blonde-haired vampire joined me…

I shake my head vehemently and scroll through the messages I've received on my secured, untraceable line. Since Lucifer's revelation came to light, I made it my mission to research everything I could about the prophecy and Dracula's adoption of Violet.

If Lucifer's telling the truth, if someone's lying to me, then I'll be able to uncover it. The issue becomes finding which thread to pull and unravel. One might lead to answers; another might end with all of us getting caught.

I curse myself yet again for not uncovering this information sooner. For so long, I prided myself on being one step ahead of all my enemies. Now, I'm ten feet behind and have both my legs broken, making it impossible for me to catch up, let alone take the lead.

I've messaged my contacts in Olympus and also the ones in Hell. I even phoned King Tut back at Prodigium Academy to determine if he had any new information.

He didn't, except for what I already suspected—Violet's wanted by the entire monster council, and the warrant has changed from merely capturing her to killing her on sight.

The thought forms a tight fist in my throat, but I shove aside my pesky, irritating emotions to focus on what matters.

Deciphering the validity of Lucifer's words.

And to do that...

I pull up my most recent text chain with a nurse at the hospital near Prodigium Academy. With bated breath, I read her most recent message.

*He's awake.*

Vladimir Dracula is awake.

Scrubbing my hand through my pure white hair, I debate my next course of action.

It'll be quite easy for me to sneak away using one of the numerous mirrors located around the cabin. It's how we entered the safe house, actually—by portaling through the bathroom mirror in Lucifer's apartment.

I can leave and return before anyone even notices I'm gone. But...

Even as that thought flits through my mind, Violet's soft laughter drifts to me from the kitchen. My head snaps upwards instinctively, chasing the sound like a lovesick puppy, and I grit my teeth together hard enough to break a molar.

I told myself I wouldn't keep any more secrets from Violet. She would want to know that her dad's alive and awake. She deserves to be there to ask her questions.

The thoughts solidify in my head before my brain can truly catch up. Without conscious thought, I'm stalking across the room and into the kitchen, where Violet is giggling with Mason. I wrap my hand around her wrist—all without breaking stride—and practically drag her towards the nearest bathroom.

Fortunately, luck is on our side, and none of Violet's harem members are taking any shits, thank Zeus. I'm easily able to pull her inside and slam the door in Mason's furious face.

"Hey! What the fuck?" he demands, pounding on the wooden door.

I ignore him and focus my attention on a frowning Violet. "Dracula is awake." There's no point in beating around the proverbial bush. "Do you want to see him?"

Her perfect pink lips pop open before she snaps them shut and eyes me suspiciously. She folds her arms over her chest, her fingers tapping against her biceps. "Why are you telling me this?"

I blow out a breath at her obvious distrust.

Stupid, idiotic, *infuriating* female.

"Because I don't want to keep secrets from you," I intone blandly.

The pounding on the door is joined by a second pair of fists. Vin, if the angry snarl is any indication. It won't be long until the other idiots realize something's amiss and try to wrap Violet in bubble wrap.

When will they realize that our pretty vampire doesn't need to be protected? She may be a queen, but she's not the type to sit idly by while we defend her honor. No, our girl—I mean, *their* girl—is stronger than any of us give her credit for.

An untraditional warrior? Most definitely. But she's smarter and braver than she'll have the world believe.

Violet still seems unsure by my proposal, her teeth nibbling on her lower lip, and I blow out a breath of impatience.

"You're either coming with me, or I'm going by myself," I huff, already crossing to the mirror. "But you need to decide quickly before those...lovers of yours break the door down."

When Violet doesn't answer, I deduce she's made her decision. I can't ignore the strange throbbing sensation in my chest at the knowledge that she doesn't trust me enough to go with me. That she doesn't believe I can protect her.

It *will* be dangerous. The hospital is located in the heart of the monster community, only a few miles away from Prodigium. But the danger seems almost irrelevant to me, because I know I can protect her from any threat. No one will get by me unless I want them to.

I've just taken a step towards the mirror when a tiny hand grabs the back of my shirt. I freeze, my muscles locking tight, but Violet simply rests the palm of her hand against the bare skin of my lower back, where my black T-shirt has risen up.

"I'm coming," she whispers. "I...I need to see my father."

WE'RE PUKED OUT INTO A DEPRESSING, STERILE ROOM decorated in shades of teal and eggshell white. A single cot rests in the center of the room with a collection of machinery surrounding it. Opposite the bed are two doors—one that leads to the hospital's hallway, and another that exits into a tiny bathroom.

It's the bathroom door we both focus on as it creaks open, and out steps a tall, domineering man looking like death warmed over.

"Dad?" Violet's voice is practically a whisper as she stares up at the man who raised her.

His head snaps up, and shock widens his eyes.

Dracula, for a lack of a more eloquent description, looks like shit. His dark hair is wildly unkempt and greasy, as if he hasn't washed it in years, and his skin has taken on an unnatural pallor. It's so pasty and translucent, I can practically see the blood pumping through his veins. He seems to have lost weight as well in the weeks he's been in the hospital.

*This* is one of the most feared monsters in the entire world? I want to scoff at how ridiculous such a concept is. I imagine my damn pinkie finger could knock him over with the state he's in now.

"Vi?" A strange tenderness I've never seen before on the terrifying man splays across his face, and he's across the room before I can even blink.

Though he should know better than to try to get one up on an assassin.

Just as he reaches for Violet, I reach for *him*, resting the tip of my god-blessed dagger beneath his chin as I hover over his shoulder.

"I would step away from her if I were you, Vladimir." I keep my voice low and decidedly casual, not allowing a hint of my panic and fear at seeing a predator so close to Violet lace my words.

I know it doesn't work when Dracula shoots me a scathing—but knowing—glare over his shoulder.

"I wouldn't hurt her, Gray. You know that." And then he wraps her in his arms, placing his chin on the crown of her golden hair.

"You're alive," Violet cries into his chest as he holds her.

"Of course I am." He scoffs. "Your old man can't be taken down by a measly stab wound."

I suddenly feel painfully awkward, as if I'm intruding on a private moment I have no business being around for, and I shuffle back a few steps.

They're still in my line of sight, but I'm no longer breathing down their necks like a damn creep.

I don't lower my weapon, however, as I watch Violet and Dracula converse in low voices. She expresses her disbelief at seeing him alive and well, and he cockily claims that he always wanted a near-death experience.

Finally, I snap.

"Violet, we came here for a reason," I grit out, hating myself a little bit when she glowers at me. I work to soften my tone, if only to pacify the little demoness. "Ask your father your questions before we get discovered."

Dracula's dark brows furrow. "Discovered? What do you mean?"

"So, yeah, about that..." Violet lazily twirls a strand of golden hair around her finger, staring anywhere *but* at her father. "I sort of, maybe, possibly, probably murdered a bunch of vamp haters and got sent to detention to await my execution. Maybe. Possibly. Probably. It was totally an accident though."

For a long moment, Dracula just stares at her, apparently at a loss for words. I wait for him to berate her for her carelessness, maybe demand an explanation, but he surprises the shit out of me by...crying? And smiling? At the same time?

*What the fuck?*

I half wonder if I'm hallucinating things, but when the vampire hugs Violet once more, I realize...nope. This is reality. Stupid, idiotic, painful reality.

"I'm so, so proud of you, Violet. So proud," Dracula sobs into her hair.

My lips tug down. "You're proud of her...for committing mass murder?"

Did I step into a parallel dimension somehow? The Upside Down? Is a creepy bald girl going to come out of the woodwork with her telekinetic powers and put me down?

"You've become the monster I always knew you could be," Dracula praises Violet, pulling back just enough to see her face.

She blinks up at him owlishly, seemingly just as shocked

by his reaction as I am. Though I suppose it's in a different way than me.

For so long, Violet has struggled to meet Dracula's approval. She constantly tried to please him only to be told time and time again she wasn't good enough. So to have his explicit approval...

Tears burn her eyes, and Zeus help me, emotions I long thought buried tug at my soul like the ominous screech of a violin being tuned.

"There's so much I have to tell you, but I don't have a lot of time." Violet glances in my direction for a fraction of a second before focusing on her father once more. "If we're found here, they'll kill us. Do you understand?"

"What do you need to know?"

I have to hand it to Dracula. He's the only man I know who can switch from eccentric to deranged to caring in a span of minutes. I suppose it's one of the many things that make him so dangerous. His personality is tied to a switch, and you never know which direction it'll be flipped towards until the moment of.

"Lucifer—"

That's the only word Violet can get out of her mouth before screaming erupts from directly outside the hospital room.

# CHAPTER 13

I push up on my tiptoes to see out the tiny rectangular window and into the hallway beyond.

My heart propels itself up my throat and then catapults across the stark white room as I take in the sight before me.

It's a fucking *massacre*. Bodies are strewn across the hospital flooring, their heads disconnected from their bodies and lying in a pool of bright red blood. Doctors. Nurses. Patients. And emerging from every door, every window, every crevice are masked beasts. Monsters. Humans. Fuck if I know. I swear some have distinctly humanoid appearances, while others are nothing but gnarly legs and fur-covered torsos. The only thing that remains consistent from one to the next is the mask on their faces—a mask crafted out of an animal skull. I can't tell *what* animal, but if I had to hazard a guess, I would say a wolf with a long snout.

They carry machetes and swords. Bows and arrows. Guns.

As I watch, horrified, one of the masked figures rushes

towards a half-shifted werewolf doctor and slices off her head with his katana sword. The head rolls across the ground like a damn basketball, the doctor's face perpetually etched into an expression of absolute terror.

Dad sidles up beside me, his pupils blown wide. "Holy fuck." He places his palm against the now blood-soaked window. "I see…a charmingly handsome man with dark hair and pale skin. Who is he? What does he want?"

I pinch the bridge of my nose at his horribly timed dad joke. "That's your reflection, Dad."

Dimitri stares at us in horror. "How the fuck have you two survived all these years?" He seems to consider it for a moment and then changes his question. "How the fuck have you guys built up reputations of being fearsome monsters?"

Dad turns a glare onto my headmaster…slash boyfriend. Kind of. "Because I eat dumb boys like you for dinner and then use the remaining body parts—say, the flaccid micropenis—to wipe my mouth with."

Welp.

That escalated rather quickly.

"Let's just get out of here," I urge, imploring both Dimitri and my dad to listen to me. The last thing I want is to have my head cut off by these mask-wearing murderers because the two of them are too busy bickering. Without a head, I wouldn't be able to talk…and that would be a damn shame. A world without me talking is a world I don't think anyone wants to live in.

"All right." Dimitri cracks his neck from side to side as he focuses on the mirror we came out of.

Honestly, the damn thing looks out of place where it rests on top of a medical counter, and I half wonder if Dimitri had it installed for easy access to my father. And then I wonder if he did it for me or for himself. I can never say for certain with the handsome, aloof headmaster.

"Do we even know who these…*killers* are?" His upper lip curls away from his teeth in disgust.

Trust the scary assassin to be offended by a brutal mass murder. Dimitri's definitely more likely to stealthily snap your neck or slash a blade across your throat than murder you in broad daylight in front of a thousand witnesses. He's probably having heart palpitations right now with how messy this particular killing is.

My crazy, anal, OCD assassin.

Well…not *my* assassin. *An* assassin. An assassin I despise. He most definitely does not belong to me. Nope. Nada. Not at all. Not even a little, teeny, tiny—

"Violet!" Said assassin's sharp voice whips my head in his direction. His pale, slender hand is extended towards me as the furrow between his white brows deepens. "Are you even listening to me?"

"Most definitely." I nod my head erratically as, in the hall-way, someone screams in anguish. A second later, a blood-stained hand lands on the window.

Dad, Dimitri, and I all watch as the hand slowly—so fucking slowly, it conjures up images of molasses—falls from the window, smearing the splattered blood already present there. The limb makes a deafening squelching noise as it descends, but I don't look away.

"We're going to travel through the mirror portal again." Dimitri finally rips his gaze from the window, seemingly unfazed by the macabre display we all just witnessed. "So grab my hand and—"

His words cut off abruptly as two hands materialize from out of the mirror, their fingers sheathed in black leather gloves. His icy-blue eyes widen in surprise, but before he can get a single word out, before he can even open his mouth, he's tugged backwards into the mirror. His legs kick desperately before they, too, are swallowed up by the glimmering vortex.

"Dimitri!" I scream, lunging forward with my arms extended.

No! No! No!

I force some of my vampire speed into my legs—though perhaps I should be calling it demon speed, considering I have no vampire blood in my body—and lower my head like a charging bull. I need to reach him. I need to save him. I need to—

Pain splinters from where my forehead connects with the glass, causing the mirror to shatter. It rains down upon me and slices up my arms and cheeks.

"Owww." I bring my hand up to my forehead, where I'm sure there's a baseball-sized bump on my flesh. My palm catches on a shard of glass that has embedded itself in my skin, and I wrench it out with another moan of pain. "Holy fuckwits."

"Come on." Dad's voice is uncharacteristically grave as yanks me up and brushes a few more glass shards out of my blonde hair. "We need to go."

"But Dimitri…" I glance in dismay at the mirror my head-master disappeared in, and Dad shakes his head with a taut frown.

"We'll worry about him later. Right now, we need to get out of here."

I know he's right. Logically, I know that, but my heart still screams at me as I stare intently at the mirror. I don't have the power to create portals like Dimitri can, but I feel like I need to do something. Anything.

Time is slipping through my fingers like sand in an hourglass. And I have no idea what will happen when that precious time inevitably runs out.

I remind myself that Dimitri is a scary and powerful

assassin who can take care of himself, but my brain issues an ominous premonition. A warning.

Why do I feel in my gut as if I need to save him? As if I'm his only hope?

The thought of Dimitri being taken away from me—of ornery, combative, angry Dimitri no longer walking this world—is almost too much for me to bear. Fear burns through my stomach lining like a corrosive acid, and dark flecks manifest in my vision.

"Violet…" Dad's rumbling warning snaps my head in his direction.

I blink up at him myopically, but he doesn't give me a chance to piece my thoughts together. He simply grabs my wrist and begins to drag me towards the hallway…and directly into the midst of battle.

"Ummm…is this a good idea?" I babble, trying to dig my heels in. "Shouldn't we be moving in the opposite direction? Like, jumping out a window or something so we don't have to fight off masked monsters? We don't even know who these fuckers are. They could be monster hunters, vamp-haters, Lucifer's peeps, Hera's fighters… I have a lot of enemies, Dad. A fuck ton. And we don't know who these people are, and—oh my Zeus, you just bit his head off."

I continue to blink owlishly at my father as he straightens from where he was biting the neck off one of the masked monsters running at us with a machete.

Blood stains his teeth and cascades down his chin as, at his feet, the monster's head rolls across the floor. The bone mask slides off as well, revealing a face…

I've never seen before.

Honestly, I thought I would recognize the face of one of the monsters attacking us, but I don't. His hair is long and scraggly, indicating that he's probably a shifter of some sort, and when I bend slightly to get a closer look, I see his mouth is made up of two rows of serrated teeth.

"Do you know him?" Dad keeps his attention on the now-empty hallway, his body poised like he's ready to fight at a moment's notice. Screams reach my ears from farther down, though they're quickly silenced.

What the fuck is happening?

This reminds me of something out of a horror movie—bodies littering an already blood-covered ground, intestines dangling from the ceiling, and...oh yeah, the dumb blonde girl forced to fight her way out of who the fuck knows what while her ailing father relies on her for support.

Yup.

I'm dead.

So fucking dead.

I wonder who will become the new main character of my story. Cynthia, perhaps? I could see it. I always root for the underdogs when I watch movies or read books. She'd have an *Ugly Betty* sort of storyline. The best friend of the deceased heroine...who eventually wins over the dead girl's harem for herself. My mates will grieve me, of course, and some might even commit sacrificial suicides to bring me back to life, but eventually, they'll move on.

With Cynthia.

Fucking Cynthia.

If Cheryl were still alive, I would guess she would be the new main character. Who doesn't love the stories about the bad girl being redeemed? Maybe she'd turn her life around and win back Vin and Mason.

The thought of her putting her scaly, bitch-ass hands on my mates makes me seethe with rage. I'm so goddamn pissed right now, I feel as if I'm going to explode.

I don't even know why I'm pissed—I'm not dead, my mates haven't moved on without me, and I don't plan on dying anytime soon—but I'm feeling slightly irrational right now. I'm totally PMSing. Post-Mortem Syndrome. Thinking about life after your death and getting furious for no fucking reason.

As soon as I get back to the cabin, I'm going to tie my guys up and ride all of their dicks simultaneously just to show them who owns them.

Impossible? Scoff.

Trust me when I say…I'll find a way. Even if I have to tie all of their dicks together to make one super dick. I'm sure I can get my vagina to stretch—

"Violet!" Dad places his hands on my shoulders and gives me a shake. "For the love of all that is unholy. Stop. Zoning. Out." He narrows his shrewd eyes at me. "You're thinking about your harem, aren't you?"

I squeak involuntarily. "W-what? No!" Too much denial? I try to tone it down a couple dozen notches. "I mean, I don't have a harem. Who has harems nowadays? That's *so* last year."

"I just read a reverse harem the other day about a girl who attends a prep school while a supernatural war wipes out, like, half of the population. The guys are complete dicks to her at first, but she wins them over and becomes their queen." Dad taps a blood-soaked finger to his chin as he considers me. "So tell me, Violet, are those mates of yours treating you like a queen?"

"Why the fuck are you reading smutty romance novels?" I squeal, incredulous.

"Need to understand my baby girl's sex life," Dad responds seriously.

I wrinkle my nose. "That might be the most disgusting thing you've ever said in your life, and—Watch out!"

I shove at Dad's shoulder just as an ax embeds itself in the wall where he was once standing.

This killer appears to be smaller than the first male my dad killed. Feminine. I can clearly see her curves through the unassuming black T-shirt and cargo pants she wears.

She grunts as she attempts to wiggle the ax free of the plaster, low growls escaping her.

"All vampires must die," she hisses. "Violet Dracula must die."

Yeah…how about "no thank you."

Dad takes a few steps closer to the oblivious monster, his fangs extended, but something stops me from advancing as well. That voice…

It's familiar.

Before I can second-guess my decision, I race forward and jam my elbow into her face, unhooking the animal mask in the process. She grunts and whirls around, but I'm faster. I may not technically be a vampire, but I do have super speed.

As she reaches for me, I grab at her mask and rip it off completely.

"Holy fuck," I murmur dazedly, the animal skull crashing to the ground at my feet.

Crazed eyes peer back at me beneath a mane of pitch-black, greasy hair, the exact same shade as Vin's.

The last time I saw Vanessa, Vin's sister, she'd been vibrant and full of light, a perpetual smirk gracing my designated best friend's lips. But now, she's nearly unrecognizable. Her olive-green eyes, so much like Vin's, are hooded and feral. When she snarls, she doesn't even look human anymore but like a beast. A monster.

"Death to all vampires!" she roars, lunging at me with a deafening snarl. "Death to Violet Dracula!"

The moment her hands would've connected with my face —and trust me when I say, I would've let them connect, too stunned to defend myself—Dracula steps up behind her with his fangs bared.

"Dad, no!" I scream.

He glances at me, her lightly tan neck, and then me again. After a moment, he sighs, lifts a fist, and whacks her across the head.

She collapses at our feet like a bag of rocks.

"Do you know this girl?" Dracula asks, the derision in his tone clear.

I nod minutely, not trusting myself to speak.

"And what do you suppose we do with her? Violet, she tried to kill you."

"She wouldn't." My words are barely audible, lost to the sound of my own thumping heart. "I mean…she wouldn't. She *wouldn't*." That's all I'm capable of saying, all I'm capable of thinking. Those words repeat on a continuous loop in my brain, reminding me of a record being played over and over again until the music is nothing but background noise despite the volume remaining the same. "She's my friend."

"Obviously not." Dracula rolls his eyes.

"We need to take her with us. Vanessa… She wouldn't hurt me. Not on purpose. Not intentionally. Sh-she's not herself."

My gut is telling me to take Vanessa with us, to demand an explanation for why she would want me dead.

But my heart is weeping at her betrayal. I claimed her as my own—as my best friend—and the loss of her leaves me hollow and bereft. The pain is as keen as any blade to the chest would've been.

No, I can't kill her. Even if there weren't ulterior motives for her actions today, even if she truly betrayed me, I know her death will hurt Vin irreparably. He might not ever forgive me if harm comes to his beloved sister.

"We can't kill her," I repeat resolutely, and Dracula sighs, his features twisting with disgust, before he nods once.

"Come on." He bends down, scoops Vanessa up, and positions her across the width of his shoulders. I can see the strain it's having on him, but he doesn't protest as he jerks his chin towards a bloody hallway in the opposite direction of the screams, shouts, and growls still echoing through the hospital. "I know a back way. We can steal a car once we're out of this place."

This time, I don't hesitate to hurry along behind him.

# CHAPTER 14

Dad's easily able to steal and hotwire a car in the hospital parking lot, and we soon find ourselves zipping away from the hospital and onto the highway. When Dad takes a particularly sharp turn, releasing a whoop of triumph, I hear the audible bang of a body being tossed around in the trunk of the car.

I inwardly wince.

What the hell was Vanessa's problem back at the hospital? Why did she attack me the way she did? Even if we weren't designated best friends, which we totally are because I claimed her, I was still her sister by mating. She knows that. Obviously, she wasn't in her right mind, so it just begs the question… What happened to her? A spell? Compulsion? Something else entirely?

Questions swarm in my head, and that causes the butter-flies in my stomach to swarm as well. I place a hand on my belly to keep the contents firmly inside where they belong.

That doesn't help matters, though, when Dad takes

another turn, the side wheels scraping against the curb, causing the car to wobble precariously to the side.

Only when Dad manages to straighten out the vehicle do I say, "We need to get in contact with my guys."

The amusement on his face fades in the blink of an eye, replaced by a stone-cold frown that has gooseflesh pebbling on my skin. "Your guys," he repeats blandly. "Do you mean your harem?"

I roll my eyes. "Yes, Dad. My harem. My mates. Whatever." I try to wave away my words, but of course, Dear Old Dad won't let it go.

"Are they treating you good?"

"Treating you *well*, I think you mean," I correct like a smart-ass. When he quirks an eyebrow in my direction, I proudly state, "School made me smart." He continues to stare at me—so intently I'm honestly afraid he's going to crash the car—and I heave out a breath and relent. "Yeah. They're... They're honestly fucking incredible."

"Good." Dad's fingers tighten around the steering wheel as he reluctantly focuses his attention on the road once more. "Then I won't have to murder them and bury them in shallow graves for their grieving families to find." A cold, sardonic smirk tugs at his lips. "Of course, their families won't be able to recognize their bodies once I'm done with them. I know of ways of making men scream for days until they eventually pass out from the pain. But then I'll just wake them up and begin again. And again. And again. And again. I'll keep going until they're nothing but carcasses, husks of their former selves. And then, only then, will I grant them the peace they so desperately crave by the form of a knife embedded in their skulls." My dad's voice takes on a wistful, almost dreamy quality as he speaks, his eyes faraway and glazed.

I blink at him.

And then blink some more.

"...the fuck, Dad?"

Dad shakes his head abruptly, as if dragging himself out of a murky hole he happened to fall into, and then flicks on the blinker. He pulls the car off an exit and towards a tiny diner connected to a shady-looking gas station. "Let's get in contact with your harem, shall we?"

THANK FUCK DIMITRI TREATED HIDING OUT THE SAME WAY most guys treat anal for the first time—lots of preparation, lube, and easing.

Not only did he have a safe house prepared for us, but he also set up a number for us to call in case of an emergency. And *only* an emergency. He made that abundantly clear. Like, I think he repeated that ten times. Maybe eleven. Maybe thirty-two. But who's counting?

If my guys haven't left the cottage yet, then I should be able to get in contact with them.

I'm on pins and needles as I twist my head away from the waitress eyeing me with one gray brow raised. When I asked to use her cell phone, she understandably looked cautious and wary. But Dad—that fucking perv—put on the charm, and she handed over the phone after making me promise I wouldn't use it to call anyone international.

Sucks to be her.

But in my defense...I've had a really shitty day and almost had my head cut off by my designated best friend. One call to Scotland won't kill her.

The phone rings once, and then, "Violet?"

Mason's familiar, chirpy voice resonates down the line, and I feel my body sag in relief.

"Mase?" I want to sob at the emotions bombarding me

from every direction. One bitch-slaps me, and another sucker punches me in the gut. But instead of giving in to the intensity of my emotions, instead of falling apart, I put on my metaphorical big girl panties, take a deep breath, and focus on what's important.

"I'm here, Pinkie. What the fuck is going on? Where did Dimitri take you? I swear to Zeus that if he hurt you, I'll rip his tiny head off and—"

"I asked him to take me," I break in. "Well, he offered to take me, technically, but I didn't argue. But that's not important. What's important is that Dracula is awake."

Mason sucks in a sharp breath. "He's awake?"

I nod once, before remembering he can't see me. Duh. "Yes. And I'm hoping he'll be able to provide us answers, but if I'm going to be honest…he doesn't seem to know anything. He still believes the drivel Hera spewed when she asked him to take me in back when I was a baby."

"Because that could be the truth," Mason points out. "We can't trust Lucifer."

"And we can't trust Hera," I agree with a sigh.

I notice one of the restaurant patrons giving me a strange look—probably because of the nature of my conversation—and I inch a few steps farther away until she's no longer in eavesdropping distance. Nosy bitch.

She's probably named Felicia or something equally as pretentious.

*Byeee, Felicia.*

"When are you going to be home?" Mason demands. "We're all going out of our minds with worry."

"Is Dimitri with you guys?" My grip on the cell phone tightens, and I can barely hear Mason's answer over the blood sluicing between my ears, a metronome to counter my pounding heart.

"Dimitri?" Mason's confusion is the only answer I need,

and I squeeze my eyelids shut to ward off the pesky tears that want to escape. "Why would he be with us? Isn't he with you? Did he fucking leave you? I'll kill him. I'm not joking this time, Pinkie. I'll murder that asshole if he left you."

"No. Well, yes. But again, it's complicated." I quickly recount what happened at the hospital—from the strange attack, to Dimitri's disappearance, to Dracula and my escape. I conveniently leave out any and all information about Vanessa still, hopefully, passed out in the back of the car. That's something I need to tell Vin directly and in person, not through a game of telephone with Mason.

"Don't move, Pinkie. We'll come pick you up." There's silence for a second, the sound of shuffling paper, and then Cal's muffled voice from farther away. Mason responds, though I can't make out the words, and then Vin's deep baritone replies. Finally, Mason comes back onto the line. "We're coming. It'll take us a little bit because without Dimitri, we can't travel through mirror portals, but we'll be there as soon as we can."

"We'll probably get a hotel in town," I say.

"Wait there. Don't move." Mason pauses, and at first, I think he's hung up, but then his soft voice whispers, "I love you, Pinkie. More than anything."

"I love you too, Mase. More than...chocolate."

He chuckles. "More than chocolate? Don't let Hux hear you say that. He'll start putting me in his pocket instead of candy bars."

Hux...

The familiar ache that always accompanies thoughts of Hux and Jack starts up again, as incessant and persistent as always.

"Tell the others I love them too," I plead.

"I will." His warm voice batters at my defenses until I'm a puddle of mush at his feet. "Stay safe."

"You too." I hear the telltale sign of the call ending, and my entire body seems to sink in tandem, like a balloon being popped and slowly losing air. It's not an explosion of noise and then…boom. Instant deflation. It's an annoying wheezing sound as the balloon gradually sinks on itself, becoming smaller and smaller and smaller—

A hand on my shoulder makes me jump a foot in the air, and I spin, heart in my throat, to see Dad standing behind me.

He eyes me quizzically but doesn't comment on my reaction. Instead, he nods towards the phone still clenched tightly in my hand. "You get in contact with your lover boys?"

"For one, don't call them lover boys. And two, I did. They said they'll meet us at a hotel somewhere in town."

He slowly removes the phone from my suddenly numb fingers. "I'll start looking around for one. Why don't you take a seat and grab a bite to eat?"

"I…" Arguing seems useless, so I nod and slide onto a barstool.

Dad, meanwhile, returns the phone to the simpering waitress who blushes and pushes out her ample chest in an attempt to seduce. I roll my eyes and instead focus on the laminated menu.

The entire diner is what you get when you clash a seventies restaurant with modern-day trash—and I'm not saying that to be a bitch. They tried to replicate a stereotypical fifties diner but failed spectacularly. The gray and white checkered flooring is covered in grease and dirt stains, as if it hasn't been mopped in weeks. The booths, a gruesome shade of green, are ratty and riddled with holes. Even the tables— the only thing the staff seems to clean on the regular—have numerous syrup and ketchup stains, making them perpetually sticky. The counter, however, is notably cleaner, hence why both Dracula and I have chosen these seats.

"What can I get for ya'?" a waitress, different from the one Dad's still flirting with, questions.

After placing my order of waffles and bacon, I set the menu aside and begin stacking up coffee creamers as my mind runs rampant.

So obviously, Vanessa has been placed under a spell...or something. That's the only logical explanation. Whatever it is has made her insane and consumed by hatred for me and all other vampires.

Which is quite funny, considering I'm not even technically a vampire. I wonder how many of those vamp-haters will apologize once they realize they've been hating me for no reason.

And that brings about another question.

Was the hospital attacked because someone knew I was there? Were they after Dracula? Did they know he woke up? Was every monster there spelled to attack? Or only Vanessa?

Did we kill innocent monsters forced to fight us against their will?

The thought has a stone settling in my stomach and then sinking, sinking, sinking. I'm not sure I'll be able to take even a bite of my waffle without vomiting.

A pair of long, alabaster fingers enters my field of vision, and I frown as they add a toothpick to the top of my coffee-creamer creation. I turn slightly to stare at my dad, who frowns at me.

"I can see the wheels churning in your head, kid. What's the matter?"

"What isn't the matter?" I grumble, knowing I'm sounding like a petulant brat but no longer caring.

Fortunately, I'm saved from Dad responding by the waitress reappearing with two plates of waffles and bacon. She puts one in front of Dad and one in front of me.

Dad smirks. "We may not be related, but we sure are similar."

"Because you're my dad," I insist. "I don't care if we're blood related or not. You're my father, and that's that."

I swear Dad's eyes flash with pleasure and his chest puffs out. And, if I'm not mistaken, a hint of color enters his cheeks as well.

"Damn right, kid." He digs into his waffle, and I half wonder if it's not in part to hide his blush. "I'm not letting anyone take you from me. Not even one of your annoying, creepy lover boys." The last words are said as a grumble.

"Annoying, creepy lover boys?" I tease. "And what did I tell you about referring to them as lover boys?"

"So you don't consider one of them just staring at us through a window creepy?" Dad cocks an eyebrow at me, finally placing his fork down to grant me his full attention.

"Huh?"

Dad twists to stare over my shoulder, and I follow the direction of his gaze with my pulse skittering madly. But it's not one of my mates I see watching us through the window, shrouded in shadows like the devil himself.

It's Alex.

Who's supposed to be kept under lock and key in the safe house.

I jump to my feet immediately, and Dad's brows furrow as he volleys his gaze between me and the glowering necromancer, who's now stalking into the diner.

"Is he not one of your lover boys?" Dad whispers conspiratorially, seemingly unconcerned by Alex's presence. He simply digs back into his waffle as if he hasn't a care in the world.

"No," I growl. "He was actually a prisoner of ours. I don't know how he escaped."

Dad still seems unperturbed as he continues eating. The exaggerated munching sound he makes only serves to exacerbate my rage. "Interesting."

"Interesting?" I half whisper, half yell as Alex approaches us. "He's a threat."

"And I like wearing pink, sparkly eyeshadow." Dad rolls his eyes, and I raise a brow.

"You do like wearing pink, sparkly eyeshadow," I counter. "Remember that phase two years ago?"

Dad's saved from responding by Alex stopping directly in front of me, the piercing in his eyebrow glinting in the restaurant lighting.

Unable to remain sitting while he's standing, I jump to my feet and aim my fork at his chest. The piece of waffle still connected to the fork begins to slide off of it slowly before falling onto his shoes with a plop.

Alex doesn't react, and I don't either, keeping my fork lifted at his chest as if I plan to stab him with it.

"What are you doing here? How did you escape?" I demand.

"Do you know nothing of necromancers, Violet?" Dad sounds so incredibly disappointed in me, and he breathes out a heavy sigh. "They're able to travel through the bones of dead monsters and humans, sort of like…electricity traveling through cable wires. If Alex knows where you are, he just needs to connect his essence to the bones of someone in the area. And poof. He arrives."

Dad gives me jazz hands to emphasize his point, but I keep my glare firmly on Alex's stupid face. The muscles in his jaw begin to grind together, as if he's pissed at Dracula for giving away all of his dirty secrets, but he doesn't refute my dad's claim.

"I overheard Mason talking to the others," Alex says in a deep voice. "And I knew I could get here faster than them."

"And you came to...what? Finish the job your lackeys failed to do?" I'm fishing for answers at this point. But if the attack on the hospital was from Alex's vamp-hating friends, then he might have the information I need.

At that, the first genuine sign of confusion I've seen since Alex arrived materializes in his russet-black gaze. He frowns. "What the fuck are you going on about, woman?"

"The attack." I step forward until the syrupy prongs of my fork touch the material of his black T-shirt. I hate the way it snugly clings to his muscular body. Stupid Alex. And stupid T-shirt. Why couldn't it be a parachute or something that covered every inch of him? Why does it have to fit him so perfectly? Ugh. "You have something to do with it, don't you?"

"Why the fuck would you say that?" he growls out, his hands forming into fists by his sides.

I just take that as more proof that he's guilty. If he's not guilty, why does he look as if he wants to hit someone? Logic.

"Because you've been after me and my kind since you first arrived at the academy," I grit out.

"If I wanted you dead, you'd be dead," Alex practically spits.

"So you don't know anything about the attack on the hospital?" My voice betrays my incredulity. "I don't believe that."

"I do." Dracula stands gracefully and stalks out of the diner without a backwards glance. "Come. I want to show you something, necromancer."

Alex looks furious—no doubt at being bossed around by a vampire, and by Dracula at that—but I can tell he's curious as well. That perpetual crease between his eyes only deepens as he watches Dracula's retreating back. Before he can take a step to follow my father, however, I tug at his arm, forcing him to stop.

"Wait." Without removing my eyes from his, I lower my hand down his taut abs—ignoring his shocked intake of breath and the way he seems to freeze beneath my palm—and then into his pants pocket. I take out his wallet, grab a couple of twenties, and place them on the counter for the waitress.

"What the fuck?" Alex glares at me, as if he's only just now realized what I've done, and I toss him his wallet before sashaying out after my dad.

"Waitresses and waiters deserve to be tipped, you asshat."

"And why did *I* have to tip them?" Alex hurries after me into the rapidly cooling air.

The sun is still in the sky, painting everything in shades of orange and pink, but it's beginning to descend. Soon, it'll be just a dot on the horizon before the night will swallow it completely.

I don't respond to Alex as I move towards where Dad stands by our…um…borrowed car, the trunk popped open to reveal a tied-up and struggling Vanessa within.

"What are you doing, Dad?" I whisper as Alex moves to join us.

"Trust me," Dad responds conversationally, though I recognize that shrewd glint in his eyes. He doesn't trust Alex any more than I do.

"What the fuck is this?" Alex gapes at Vanessa in disbelief as she growls something incoherent, her words muffled by the gag in her mouth.

Her eyes flash with malice as she writhes in her bindings, shaking back and forth in a way that rocks the car.

"Vin's sister. Vanessa," I explain, though I know Alex

already knows who she is. "This isn't like her. She's my friend. She wouldn't… I mean…I don't think she would…"

"Is it possible she's been radicalized?" Alex asks, a taut frown pulling at his lips. "After you guys left, I mean. She's been a vampire hunter for years, and you did murder her father."

"After he tried to kill me!" I protest…though the words feel weak. I killed him in self-defense, yes, but the way he died was a fucking slaughter. I don't remember what, exactly, I did to him, but I know it wasn't a simple or painless death.

No, Stefan Van Helsing and the rest of his friends suffered for what they did to me and Cheryl Ness. The monster inside of me made sure of it.

"Wait…" Alex hesitantly reaches into the trunk, and I tense automatically.

I don't know why or even who my reaction is for. Am I worried Vanessa will hurt Alex? Or am I afraid Alex will hurt Vanessa? Neither of those things happen, though, as Alex gently removes a strand of Vanessa's sweaty, dark hair away from her neck.

"What the hell?" I murmur, squinting.

"It looks new," Dracula deduces as he leans forward to get a closer look.

On the side of Vanessa's neck is a tiny tattoo I've never seen before—half the size of my pinkie's nail. It appears to be a series of diminutive shapes interspersed with lines. Symbols, perhaps? Runes?

"What the hell is that?" I ask what we're all thinking, but for once, neither Dracula or Alex have an answer.

# CHAPTER 15

ALEX

I press my palm against the smooth shower wall as torrents of blistering hot water rain down from above. Steam permeates the stifling air, even with the fan circulating above.

Fucking hell.

What am I even doing here?

I don't mean *here*, as in the shitty-ass motel that Violet and Dracula found for the night. I mean here...with two people who, for all intents and purposes, should be my enemies. Yet, I willingly walked straight into the vipers' den and asked them nicely not to sink their fangs into me.

What the fuck am I thinking?

And why haven't I left yet?

I can leave. At any time. Even when those fuckers tied me up and shoved me in a spare bedroom, I knew escape was at my fingertips, just waiting for me to grab on and tug. And yet for some ridiculous reason, I remained their prisoner. I didn't throw up a single fuss until I heard Mason tell Vin, Cal, Frankie, and Barret what happened to Violet. It was like…a switch being flipped inside of my brain. I couldn't wait idly by, knowing Violet was in trouble.

So I closed my eyes, envisioned the name of the podunk town Violet and Dracula had found themselves in, and then chose the nearest dead body I could find. I landed on top of a graveyard, my scythe in hand, and made my way towards the diner. I don't know how I even knew where Violet was. It was like a sixth sense, an innate voice inside of me urging me towards her.

And then I saw her sitting at the counter, her golden hair cascading around her shoulders in sunlit curls. Even my anger and hatred towards Dracula couldn't eclipse the relief I felt at seeing her alive and unharmed.

I hate her. I fucking despise her.

So why am I still here? Why can't I leave? Why did I come running the moment there was an issue?

Violet and Dracula had "locked" me in one of the motel rooms, but we all know I can leave at the drop of a hat if the mood hits me. One blink of my eyes, and I'll be halfway across the world. There are dead bodies everywhere, underneath every surface, and I use them to transport myself from one place to the next. Dracula was right when he explained my power as electricity moving through wires. That's basically what I do…but instead of wires, I use dead bodies.

Violet Dracula.

Violet motherfucking Dracula.

My mind unwittingly snaps back to what I walked in on the other day in Lucifer's dungeon. Violet, riding that dark-haired fucker's cock, her head thrown backwards as he touched her perfect body. I couldn't see everything, not from where I stood, but her ass jiggling would forever be etched onto my eyelids, so when I close my eyes, it's all I can see. I had a glimpse of perfect pink pussy lips sheathing Hux/Jack/Balor's cock like a glove as he pounded into her. And then there was the profile of her tits, the pink nipples beaded as she bounced.

Fucking hell.

I bring my hand to my rock-hard cock and begin to play with the mushroom head, running the tip of my finger over the seam already leaking with precum. I try to stop myself, try to make my hand stop moving, but it seems to have a life of its own. Fuck, my balls feel heavy, as if they're made of cement, and my cock is so hard it's almost painful. It throbs when I touch it.

*"Alex..." Violet stares up at me with hooded eyes where she's lying sprawled on the bed, propped up by a few pillows. One of her hands lazily traces her areola while her other hand travels down her toned stomach and towards the treasure I know is hidden between her legs. "I want you to fuck me."*

*She traces her pussy lips with one finger, her eyes never leaving mine. Her other hand cups her heavy breast as her fingers tighten around her nipple. She begins to twist and pluck at the tiny bud as a single finger slowly enters her tight channel. Her lips part open, her eyes turning glazed with desire, and she moans.*

*"Oh, fuck!" she cries as she begins to move the finger in and out of her pussy. A second finger joins the first as she continues to fondle her own tit. As she arches her back to fuck herself faster with her fingers, her breasts bounce enticingly, those perfect pink nipples just demanding my mouth on them.*

*She adds a third finger and begins to move them even faster, the tiny digits disappearing into her wet heat as she plays with herself.*

*"I need you, Alex," she whimpers. "I need you."*

*I can't resist.*

*Before I'm aware of what I'm doing, I'm on my knees before her, pressing her breasts together and hungrily moving my lips between one and the other. Tasting her nipples. Sucking on them. Rolling the buds around my tongue. Flicking each nipple with my piercing. Grazing them with my teeth.*

*Tiny bumps erupt on her areolas, and her nipples harden.*

*"I want to fuck these breasts with my cock," I growl. "But you don't have time for that, do you, baby? You want to come now."*

*"Fuck, yes." Her fingers continue to move in and out of her pussy, and for a moment, I fixate on that. On the way her porcelain fingers disappear into her channel and then reemerge soaking wet.*

*"You're so close to coming, aren't you, baby?" I grab her wrists and pull them away from her cunt, eyeing her pussy like it's my next meal. I settle myself so I'm on my stomach between her legs. "All you need is a little touch."*

*"Alex..." she moans, her thighs tensing around my head.*

*I chuckle and reach up her body until I can cup one of her heavy breasts. With my other hand, I pull apart her pussy lips so I can see her better. And then, I bring the tip of my tongue and press the cold metal of my tongue ring against her clit.*

*It's like a detonation.*

*She screams, shaking and crying, as her body tightens around mine. And then I'm lapping at her juices, palming her breast, twisting her nipple...*

*Punishing her.*

*Punishing her because I want her so fucking badly.*

I come with a roar, shooting spurts of hot cum across the shower door. The fantasy was so vivid, so real...

I can practically taste Violet on my tongue.

Fuck. Fuck. Fuck!

She murdered my brother and had a hand to play in my father's death. I suspect that it was actually the cupid, Cal, who murdered him, but I know Violet was involved somehow as well.

I should hate her.

I *do* hate her.

But…

I slam my fist against the wall hard enough for it to crack. And then I rest my forehead against the smooth porcelain and squeeze my eyelids shut.

If my father were to see me now, he would hate the man I've become. Weak. Pathetic.

Caring for a girl who hates me.

Hating a girl who I simultaneously care for.

When did everything get so confusing?

I turn the water off, barely noticing that it had gotten ice-cold sometime during my wistful daydream, and then step out of the shower. There's a clean towel folded on the counter, and I dry my body and hair before wrapping it around my waist.

I step out of the bathroom…only to immediately freeze when I spot the figure perched on my bed.

Violet Dracula.

The object of every one of my most inner desires and all of my nightmares. She's temptation in the flesh, *my* temptation, but she's also the one sin I refuse to commit.

The one sin I *can't* commit, not if I'm going to survive this with my heart intact.

"What the fuck are you doing here?" I growl, stomping towards the bed and hovering over her. My towel is so short, she could probably see my balls if she decided to look, but she keeps her eyes firmly on my face.

Until they drift lower.

And lower.

And lower.

Those blue orbs of hers graze the width of my shoulders, then my chest with the two nipple piercings, and then the eight-pack of my abs covered in tattoos. Goddammit, but my traitorous cock enjoys her perusal more than I do. It begins to rise to attention, taking my towel with it and leaving no doubt to how excited it is.

One of Violet's brows quirks, and her eyes dance with amusement. And...intrigue, maybe? Lust? I wish I could read her better. I wish I could understand every expression that flicks across her face.

"We need to talk, Alex." She chooses her words carefully as she finally lifts her eyes from where they've been studying my body.

"Why the fuck do we need to talk?" I snap. This close, her presence is muddling my brain, causing the wires to cross and then explode.

"You know why," she retorts, casually uncrossing her legs and shoving her hands farther back on the bed. This new position eerily resembles the one from my fantasy, and I feel my cock grow even harder beneath the flimsy, thin towel.

I refuse to be embarrassed, though, as I meet her gaze levelly.

"I don't. Care to explain? Or, and I like this option a lot, get the fuck out of my room?" I clench my jaw as every dirty fantasy I've ever had concerning Violet Dracula plays on a loop in my head. Dropping my towel and forcing my cock between her plump, pink lips. Throwing her skirt over her stomach and feasting on her pussy. Grabbing her hair in my fist and—

*No!* I growl to myself as she shifts again on the bed. This time, her skirt slides farther up her creamy white thigh until I can see... Oh fuck. Is that a pair of pink panties? With bats on them?

Fuck. All I can think about is running my tongue over the tiny wet patch I can see at the bottom of her panties, the only hint that she's not as unaffected by me as she would want me to think.

I don't know if I hate that she's attracted to me or love it.

"We both know that you can leave here whenever you want to. So why the fuck are you here?" she growls out.

"Maybe I'm just doing my job," I respond casually, though I don't rip my gaze from that flash of pink and black panties.

"What the fuck does that mean?"

"You wanted to know how I knew Lucifer, and the truth is…he hired me." I wait for the bomb to fall squarely in her lap, for shock to splay across her face, before continuing on. I want her to hurt the same way I've been hurt time and time again. "To keep an eye on you, believe it or not. I don't think he knew you were his daughter, but he never knew Dracula to take any interest in his kids. You were an anomaly, one he wanted to study. And when those murders happened on campus…" I shrug.

I truly believe that Lucifer didn't know Violet was his biological kid until after she won the Roaring and met with him. But that didn't mean he wasn't aware of her existence. Lucifer never trusted Dracula, not truly, and Dracula's interest in Violet wasn't lost on any monster in the community. The vampire has…three or four hundred kids? Give or take? So why the interest in one insignificant daughter? What made Violet so special?

"He asked you to bully me." Violet sounds aghast.

Her legs shift a second time, concealing her panties once more. I half want to scream and half want to sag in relief, thanking the universe for sparing me.

"No." I smile sharply. "I did that just because I wanted to. Believe it or not, Violet Dracula, not every man on campus is wrapped around your pussy."

She snorts and places a hand on my chest, directly over my heart. I hate myself for it, I honestly do, but the damn organ speeds up at her proximity.

"You wish you were wrapped around my pussy," she

hisses, climbing to her knees and glaring at me as if she fantasizes about ripping my spleen out of my body.

"Fuck you."

"No, fuck you! Why the fuck do you hate me so much?" she demands.

"I never said I hate you," I point out, though my tone clearly states, "I most definitely do hate your guts."

"Answer me, coward."

"Don't call me a coward, bitch."

"Fucker."

"Whore."

"Dipshit!" she snarls. "What the fuck is your problem with me? I know you hate vampires, but I already explained what happened with your brother and—"

"My problem," I seethe, stepping even closer until my shins hit the bed, "is that you're so fucking perfect, and I *hate* you."

"No."

With her on her knees on the bed and me standing, I still tower about a foot above her. However, I don't feel like the big, scary man at all. I feel...small. Vulnerable. And when she continues speaking, jabbing a finger at my chest, that feeling only intensifies.

"You don't hate me."

"Yes, I do." My words are a whisper.

"You hate how much you want me," she counters, continuing to poke my damn skin. "You hate the way you respond to me."

She pokes me again, harder this time, and I stumble back a step instinctively. Not because she hurt me, but because I'm so overwhelmed by my own emotions that I can't think straight. Can't walk in a straight fucking line. I feel drunk.

Drunk on Violet Dracula.

And then the knot in my towel slips, and we both watch as it falls to the ground at my feet.

# CHAPTER 16

VIOLET

I want to say I immediately avert my eyes and look away. But that would be a lie.

I want to say that after taking a tiny peek, I divert my attention and focus on the fading wallpaper instead. Another lie.

Your girl ogled his dick shamelessly. I-is that drool on the corner of my lips?

Ugh. Curse Alex for being such a hot asshole.

"That looks…" I swallow. "Painful."

I don't know if I'm talking about his erection, which strains against his stomach, or the multiple piercings lining his penis.

A motherfucking Jacob's ladder.

Yup.

And that's a ladder I think I want to climb like a—

*No, Violet! No!* I forcefully shove the errant thought away with a scowl and force my attention back on Alex's face and that ticking jaw of his. He probably has stellar facial muscles with how often he seems to be working his.

Great. Now I'm thinking of things he can do with his face. Things that involve my suddenly wet pussy and—

"What do you want from me, Violet Dracula?" His words are an agonized growl that I can feel in my soul. In the foundations of my genetic makeup. They embed themselves beneath my fingernails like dirt I can't hope to remove or scrub clean. "You destroyed my life."

"I didn't—" My protest is cut off by him taking a step closer until he's between my slightly parted legs staring down at me. He's no longer glaring, but somehow, I find the anguish on his face even scarier. It tugs at something inside of me, something that feels suspiciously like…pity. Maybe empathy.

"What are you doing to me?" he whispers hoarsely.

A response is on the tip of my tongue, but I'm not sure it's capable of articulating every thought running rampant through my brain. I'm not sure anything is.

I'm saved from saying something idiotic by my motel room door being kicked open. Quite literally kicked—splintered wood and all.

Two figures stand in the doorway, highlighted by the swatch of moonlight dancing over their shoulders.

"Vin! Mason!" I cry, jumping to my feet and hurrying towards my mates.

I futilely attempt to wrap my arms around both of them at the same time, and they humor me, if only for a moment. In the next, Vin is shoving me firmly into Mason's arms and stalking towards Alex, his back muscles tensing with every step forward he takes.

"What the fuck did you do to her?" he rumbles out. "How the hell did you escape?"

There it is again. That damn jaw twitch that Alex seems

to have perfected, as if he's gritting his teeth in a bid not to say the thousands of insults he's so desperate to. His russet-black eyes are flinty as he levels an incandescent glare on first Vin and then Mason. He's still naked, his pierced cock on display, but he doesn't make a move to lift his towel as he chooses to focus his attention on Vin.

"My powers are none of your concern," he hisses. "And I didn't harm the idiotic girl."

"Okay, first!" I twist in Mason's arms so my back is to his chest, his arms steel bands around my waist. Instead of being constricting, they infuse me with a sense of warmth and comfort. I know that nothing and no one will be able to harm me now that he's holding me. "Don't call me idiotic, you…idiot." I know. Real smooth. But can you blame my insults for not being up to par? It's been a rough day, dammit. "Secondly,"—I twist to address Vin—"he's able to travel through the bones of dead things. Apparently, he could've left our makeshift prison days ago."

Alex gives me an incredulous, slightly betrayed look, as if he's pissed at me for revealing his top-secret superpowers. I just give him a bland, don't-fuck-with-me look that makes—you guessed it—his jaw clench.

Why the fuck does my mind picture tiny little body-builders inside of his jaw lifting weights with bulging muscles every time he does that facial tic?

*Probably because you're fucked in the head, Vi. Duh.*

"You're going to need to go see a dentist if you keep doing that," I point out wryly. "It can't be good for you."

Alex's hands clench and unclench by his sides. I wonder if he's imagining punching someone?

Huh.

I should probably rephrase my question.

I wonder if he's imagining punching *me*?

Wouldn't be the first time that happened. I've been told

that I have a very punchable face—all round and soft-look-ing. Perfect for a monster punching bag.

"Is he a threat?" Vin demands, and at first, I think he's asking the question to Mason or even Alex. But then I realize that despite his glare firmly on the necromancer, the words are directed at me.

"No," I say softly, somehow feeling the truth of that one word deep in the marrow of my bones.

I know it's true in the same way I know Vin and Mason are two of my many mates and that they love me. Don't ask me how I know it, only that I do. Alex, despite all his bluster and bravado, won't harm me.

I think.

I'm, like, ninety-nine percent sure, which is close enough to one hundred to give me confidence. A ninety-nine percent is still an A on most tests, so I'm gonna A-ssume Alex won't fuck me over. Get it? A-ssume? I crack myself up.

No wonder so many guys love me.

Alex looks as if he wants to retort. Hell, his mouth even opens before he immediately snaps his lips together—prob-ably because of his jaw muscles. I imagine those fuckers hurt from all the clenching they've been doing.

My jaw muscles are, unfortunately, still very much relaxed. I would much rather have them be stiff and hurting from swallowing a bunch of cocks—

*Focus, you horny bitch,* I scold myself, twisting in Mason's arms so I can loop my arms around his neck.

Feeling my eyes on him, he shifts his attention off of Alex and Vin and smiles languidly down at me.

"Hey, Pinkie," he says softly a second before his plush lips connect with my nose in a chaste, innocent kiss.

"You came for me."

Do I get butterflies in my stomach? Nah.

Do I get bats flying around erratically down there? Yup.

Bats are ten times better than butterflies, after all. They're bigger, stronger, and smarter. So anyone who claims they get butterflies obviously doesn't have as big of a crush on their man or woman as I do with all of my bats.

I probably don't make any sense, but ehhh. I blame it on the head injury from running face-first into a mirror.

"As if we'd leave you to fend for yourself." He kisses my nose again before leaning back and giving it a squeeze like a clown horn. "You tend to get into trouble when left to your own devices."

"I do not," I protest instinctively, and he quirks a brow at me, amusement shimmering in his blue-gray eyes.

"You went to detention and befriended two of the scariest monsters in existence," Vin deadpans from behind me. "And now you're mated to one of them, and the other one is desperately in love with you."

"In love?" I squeak, because Barret is most definitely *not* in love with me. We're just…friends. Good friends. Best friends. Who both happen to be sleeping with Cal.

"You somehow ended up in Mount Olympus with the supreme ruler, Zeus, and my mother," Mason adds, his voice betraying his amusement.

"You murdered, both intentionally and unintentionally, over a dozen people," Alex unhelpfully supplies, and I whirl around to glare at him.

"Keep out of this, buddy. It's mate business," I snap.

He simply matches my glare with one of his own.

"As if I'd want to be your stupid fucking mate." He scoffs as if he finds that idea appalling, but his dick twitches, something we all see.

Because how can we not see it? I'm not even looking, and that thing is still consuming my vision.

Not because it's big.

Of course not.

Eight inches is most definitely not big.

Like, it's not even an entire ruler, so ha.

"Nothing happened between us. Between Alex and me, I mean," I point out to both Vin and Mason.

I don't know why I didn't feel the need to defend myself earlier, when they first walked in on us in a compromising position. Maybe it's because I knew I hadn't done anything and wouldn't have without talking to my guys first?

Or maybe because I know in my soul that anything I do with Alex is fate—

Fucking hell. I half want to stab my fingers into my brain's ears and scream "la la la" at the top of my lungs.

Fate?

Alex?

Puh-lease.

I don't want Alex. At all.

Not stupid Alex and his stupid eight-inch cock and his stupid piercings that glint in the moonlight in a way that almost taunts me.

Mason grins down at me and once again kisses my nose. Does he have a nose fetish I don't know about?

Correction.

A nose fetish I don't nose about?

Ha.

"We know that, Pinkie," he replies softly.

"We trust you," Vin adds, though he doesn't divert his attention from Alex. "We know the only men you'll ever be with are your mates…both old and new."

"Not the only men," I pipe up, spinning around in Mase's arms to face the others once more. "I've been with a ton of men before I met you guys. Like Roberto? Fuck, the things that boy could do with his tongue—"

All three of the guys have stopped their stare off with each other to glare at me. Vin's eyes are molten with rage,

Alex's jaw is once again doing that weird clenching thing, and Mason? Well, I don't know what he's doing with my back towards him, but I feel his eyes searing a hole into my scalp.

"Roberto?" Vin asks through clenched teeth.

"We'll kill him," Mason agrees lazily. "Do you have a last name for us, Pinkie?"

"I can ask the spirits of the dead," Alex growls. "They can track him down, then we can rip him apart and—"

"Woah! Woah!" I place both my hands up in the air as if I can fend off their crazy. "Okay, so talking about my past boyfriends is a no," I muse more to myself than to them.

Vin's right eye begins to twitch. "Boyfriends? You had actual boyfriends? Not just random, senseless, meaningless hookups?"

"Are you serious right now?" I attempt to place my hand on my hip, but with Mason's arms suddenly wrapped around my waist, it proves to be impossible. Instead, I just settle for popping my hip to the side with all the sass I can muster. "You had a girlfriend…Cheryl. And I know for a fact all three of you have slept with her." I give all of them my best evil glare even as a tiny pang lights a fire in my heart at the thought of her death.

"I didn't sleep with her," Alex points out with a scowl.

"And I only slept with her once," Mason protests, his arms tightening around me almost imperceptibly. "And for me, it was a random, senseless, meaningless hookup."

"Yeah, I dated her," Vin growls out, "but the feelings I had for her are nothing compared to what I feel for you. Absolutely nothing."

"I'm not saying that," I quickly cut in. This time when I attempt to step forward, Mason immediately releases me, as if understanding I need to console Vin. "What we have is… well… It's fucking amazing. But we all have pasts, you know?

Like, I wouldn't be upset if you're grieving Cheryl. If you're mad at me—"

Vin cuts off my rambling with a bruising, searing kiss on my lips. It causes fireworks to explode in my bloodstream, shooting in all directions and filling my veins with fire. I gasp against his mouth, and he takes advantage by plunging his tongue between my parted lips.

When he pulls away, we're both breathing heavily and my nipples are hard diamonds through the tank top I'm wearing.

"You're right," Vin confesses. "I'm upset that Cheryl's dead. Not because I miss her or have feelings for her anymore, but because I truly believe she could've been saved. Redeemed. Whatever you want to call it." He lifts my knuckles to his lips and presses a chaste kiss against them, the same way Mason kissed my nose. "I'm upset that someone died saving the woman I love while I was…incapacitated by those damn hunters." His eyes flare with a venomous rage—those olive-green orbs alive with a banked, blistering heat that sets my skin ablaze. "I'm upset that my father's dead, but not because I grieve the man. He's a monster. I know that, you know that, Vanessa knows that." His mention of Vanessa conjures up images of the brunette still trapped in the trunk of the car. But before I can interject, Vin steals my attention with his next words. "I'm furious that you're to blame for a death that we all know was in self-defense."

"Vin," I interrupt softly. I don't want to say these next words, don't want to confess them. They have the capability of altering everything completely, and the prospect terrifies me. "You don't understand. I didn't just kill your father and the rest of those hunters. I obliterated them. I destroyed—"

"You did what you had to do," Vin cuts in vehemently, his eyes shining with sincerity. "They goddamn tortured you,

Violet. Nearly killed you. No one can blame you for defending yourself, even if it was in such a…gruesome way."

His lips curl downwards momentarily, and I wonder if he's seen the bodies. If he was the one who had to identify his father's remains.

The thought makes a huge-ass boulder drop down in my stomach, sluicing the contents around and causing the acid to rise up my throat.

Maybe that's why Vanessa hates me—because I killed her father.

Butchered him.

"I didn't want to have this conversation with you before," I confess in a whisper. "Not because I didn't think we needed to have it, but because I was—"

"Scared?" Vin finishes for me. His eyes are uncharacteristically soft as he cups my cheek, his calloused palm tickling my smooth skin. "You don't ever have to be scared of me, Violet. Ever."

"I'm scared of losing you," I confess. "All of you."

"That'll never happen," Vin vows.

"Never, Pinkie," Mason chimes in from behind me. "You're stuck with us for life."

His conviction brings a weary smile to my lips before it immediately slips away. All I can think about is Medusa's ominous prophecy, about how Dracula's daughter will be responsible for Mason's death.

I know, technically, I'm not Dracula's daughter by blood, but I'm still his daughter in all the ways that count. So is it possible that my love will kill my sweet Mase? No, I refuse to believe that. If he dies, I'll torture Alex until he agrees to bring him back to life—though I remember reading that isn't in the necromancer's job description. They can't reconnect souls to bodies, only control and manipulate vessels that are already dead.

"Hey." Vin presses the pad of his finger against my brows, where I'm sure there's a lake-sized furrow residing. "Stop worrying. We love you, and we won't ever leave you. There's nothing you can do that will scare us away."

"You say that now…" I murmur, once again thinking of Vanessa. Taking a deep, fortifying breath, I say, "Vin, I need to tell you something, but first…" I once again twist until I'm in Vin's arms facing Mason. I peer over my mate's broad shoulders and towards the door at his back. "Where are the others?"

"We made Cal, Barret, and Frankie stay behind to look after Lucifer and Balor," Mason confesses.

"And Dimitri?" I ask urgently. "Did he ever end up coming back?"

Mason's frown deepens. "No. We haven't seen him. Do you think something happened?"

He looks as concerned as I feel. God, my emotions are all over the place, a tumultuous storm inside of my stomach and mind. I feel lightheaded, sparks of lightning dancing across my eyelids in tandem to the booming of thunder in my skull.

"If you did something to Dimitri…" I point a finger at Alex, who appears stunned…and then a little pissed.

"I didn't touch the fucking headmaster," he hisses. "Now get that finger out of my face."

"Why?" I taunt. "Afraid I jabbed it in my pussy and now you'll get cooties or some shit?"

My words cause Alex's eyes to flare with a strange, electrifying heat, and he's suddenly staring at my finger in a new light…as if he wants to lean forward and suck the digit.

Ew.

Gross.

Extremely gross.

And…I *totally* inch my finger a little bit closer, in licking range. I blame it on my horny vagina. That bitch has a mind of her own, and that mind seems to constantly be screaming, "Fuck me." She wants to slide a pair of assless chaps on, bend over, and present her goods for the world at large.

"So Dimitri's missing." Mason's voice pulls me out of my reverie—nightmare, I mean—and I turn just in time to see him finger the edge of his gray beanie. "And what the fuck happened at the hospital? I don't understand."

"That's what I need to show you," I whisper, my fingernails digging into Vin's arms hard enough to draw blood.

What if he sees his sister and blames me?

Hates me?

Leaves me?

The thought has cold panic skating down my spine, but I force myself to push it away, to focus on what matters. I have to believe that my bond with both men—with *all* my men—is strong enough to withstand anything that life has to throw at us.

Including a deranged, evil sister trying to kill me.

"Come on." I pat Vin's arm once before detangling myself from his embrace. "I have to show you something."

And that's how we find ourselves standing around the trunk of Dracula's stolen car, staring down at the brown-haired, disheveled girl as she snarls and curses at us.

"You bloodsucking, stupid whore! I'm gonna kill you! I'm gonna skin you alive and then feed you to the—"

"Can we put her gag back in?" Alex deadpans from where he stands behind us, slightly apart from the group.

Vin is staring down at his sister in horror, his eyes wide and his mouth slightly agape.

"This can't be... This isn't... Vanessa?" He tentatively reaches down to touch his sister, but she snarls at him like a rabid dog, her teeth just barely missing his hand.

"That isn't Vanessa." Mason places a hand on Vin's shoulder, though his gaze doesn't waver from the inconsolable woman. "That's..." He shakes his head. "I don't even know what the fuck she is."

"I noticed this on her skin." As quick as I can, I reach down to push away some of her sweaty brown hair. The strange symbol I noticed before seems almost luminescent in the tiny crescent moon above, bathing us all in a silvery yellow light.

"What the...?" Mason leans forward, his eyes wide. "I think I know that symbol."

"You do?" Alex and I ask at the same time. And then we both immediately scowl at each other for being on the same wavelength.

Vin looks as if he's going to be sick, his naturally tan skin taking on a green hue. "Where, Mase? Where have you seen that symbol? It looks... Fuck, it looks like it's been tattooed on her skin!"

"Not tattooed." Mason's voice is as grim as I've ever heard it, and his lips are a red slash on his pale face. "Branded. It's a symbol common in Mount Olympus."

"Mount Olympus?" I whirl around to face him.

His lips compress even farther as he nods once. Stiffly. Reluctantly. "I think it's time I had a talk with my mother."

MASON

The night air whips around my face as I stand in an empty section of the parking lot, as far away from the motel as I possibly can get. Even though the sky is black as pitch, the muggy, tepid air hints that a storm is brewing. Any second now, the heavens will open up and release torrents of rainfall on my head.

The turmoil in my mind is almost a mimicry of the incoming storm.

I hear her before I see her—the deafening clack of her high heels against the asphalt as she strides forward. My mother never does something as mundane as walking or even strutting. No, the gorgon practically glides as she moves to stand in front of me.

She's wearing the familiar, starlit gown that I've seen her in before, one that offsets the nest of slithering, green, yellow, orange, and red snakes on the top of her head. Fuck, it almost appears as if all of those snakes are staring directly at me, burrowing themselves into my brain and uncovering all of my deepest, darkest secrets.

But this meeting isn't about uncovering my secrets. It's about digging up hers.

Medusa.

A muscle in her jaw ticks furiously as she glares down at me from her towering, impressive height, her naturally pasty skin bathed in moonlight, making her appear like a porcelain doll.

"Mason," she greets crisply, absently scrubbing a hand down her skin-tight gown and smoothing away imaginary wrinkles. "I don't appreciate being summoned like a common house dog."

Her upper lip curls in disgust, but I don't allow her ire to affect me. If I did, we wouldn't be able to have this long-overdue conversation. My mother is naturally an intimidating woman—no surprise, considering she's a goddess—but I've never allowed it to bother me.

No, I have perfected my mask over the years. She can never know how badly she rattles me.

"We need to talk."

State my intentions clearly.

No hesitation.

No backtracking.

No second-guessing.

Her upper lip curls even farther away from her teeth in an expression I would almost consider a snarl. She quickly works to smooth out her features, to eliminate the trenches between her eyes.

Heaven forbid the esteemed Medusa gets—shudder—face wrinkles.

"What the fuck is this?" I don't bother beating around the bush as I hold up my phone, displaying a photograph of Vanessa Van Helsing's neck. The symbol etched into her tan skin looks especially prominent in the light of my phone screen—brutal red slashes, slightly raised and puckered.

My mother's face cracks for a tenth of a second. Most people wouldn't have been able to see it, but I know my mother.

And I know her tells.

What maelstrom of hell did we find ourselves in now?

"You know what it is," I say. It's not a question, but my mother still treats it as one.

"I don't know what you're talking about," she huffs, the lie slipping from her lips like poisoned honey. "I've never seen that before in my life. Really, Mason, this is beginning to become ridiculous. That damn Dracula girl is making you act delusional and crazy—"

"Don't talk about her like that," I bite out, my temper flaring like a banked flame demanding release. I take a deep breath—one meant to calm—and curl my hands by my sides. Not into fists, though. For some reason, I find the repetitive motion of crooking my fingers and then immediately straightening them calming. Relaxing. It soothes the wrath traveling through my bloodstream like a corrosive acid.

"That *child* is going to kill you," my mom snaps vehemently, the first hint of true emotion seeping into her eyes. Her snakes, in response, begin to writhe and hiss on her head, their beady eyes focusing solely on me.

"That *woman*," I counter immediately, "is my mate."

"She's a monster!"

"We all are." I throw my hands up in the air with a huff of exasperation, and Medusa's eyes narrow on me. She doesn't have to say a word for me to see and recognize the rage brewing directly beneath the surface.

I'll never admit this to anyone—not to Vin, not to the other guys, and definitely not to Violet—but I'm terrified of what my mom will do in her quest to "save" me. But doesn't she realize that I'd rather be dead than live in a world that doesn't include Violet Dracula? If the price for loving that tiny vampire-who-isn't-truly-a-vampire is my death, then so be it. Better to love and lose my life than to have never loved at all.

Pretty sure Shakespeare said that. Somewhere. Maybe.

"This symbol is your doing, isn't it?" I press, practically shoving the phone into her face. She doesn't bother to look at the picture again, though, which is all the confirmation I need. My breath is thready, almost ragged, as I whisper, "Why? What did you do?"

"What I had to for my son! For my child!" she finally explodes, her eyes flashing with fury. "Something you don't seem to appreciate."

"You think I'd appreciate your attempt to assassinate my mate?" I demand, my voice rising in volume. I work to modulate it, though, not wanting to wake the entire motel— both humans and monsters alike. "That symbol… It's a spell, isn't it? A curse? It makes the wearer hate vampires and want to kill them."

"Vampires and Draculas," Mother corrects with a sneer.

And I wonder, briefly, if that distinction is what allowed Violet to be attacked in the first place. She's not technically a vampire, not if her parents are Lucifer and Hera, so the only way she would've been targeted is if Hera made sure her little army attacked both vampires *and* monsters with the last name of Dracula.

Does she know the truth about Violet? About what she is?

I dismiss that thought immediately, though a tiny sliver of doubt remains.

Still, if my mother doesn't know—and I have no reason to believe she does—then I need to be careful how I play my cards. I can't lay down my full house if she has a royal flush.

"So that sigil…" I swallow. "It makes normal monsters

want to hurt and kill vampires?" A metaphorical light bulb dings on in my head, and my rage grows exponentially. "Is that why there's been a war in the monster community? Because of *you*?"

My mate's life has been put on the line because of the unfounded hatred against vampires. And to know my own mother, my flesh and blood, is behind it…

Medusa laughs, the noise raw and gritty, conjuring up images of sand particles.

"You'll never understand the things a mother will do to protect her child. Parents…" Fierce anger distorts her beautiful face as her bony shoulders touch her ears. "Parents are supposed to love and protect their children, not cast them aside."

"This isn't loving or protecting me," I hiss. "Your damn spell is causing monsters and humans alike to hate vampires for no Zeus-damn reason! They carved words into my mate's arm! They tortured and tried to kill her—"

"Good riddance," Medusa cuts in snottily, tilting her chin up and sniffing the air. "That means they're doing their job."

I want to attack her. Kill her. Protect my mate.

But…

She's my mother. She's not warm and cuddly. She's not necessarily friendly…but she's the only mother I've ever known. I can't hurt her, no matter how much her words make me want to.

"Get out of my sight," I bite out, seething. "I don't want to even look at you right now."

"Mason…" She reaches a perfectly manicured hand out to touch my shoulder, but I stealthily move out of the way before it can connect.

I don't want her toxic touch anywhere near me, let alone Violet. I can't even imagine what she'll do if she discovers that Violet is in one of the motel rooms behind me.

"If you hurt Violet, I'll kill you, Mother," I vow, staring into her fathomless eyes and allowing her to see the promise and threat in mine.

Her face tightens, nostrils flaring, but she doesn't respond right away. She seems to be considering her next words carefully, picking and choosing like she's at an apple orchard trying to find the largest, juiciest piece of fruit to sink her teeth into.

"You don't understand," she decides on at last. "You're not a parent."

"And when I become one, Violet Dracula will be its mother. And I'll be a damn better parent than you are," I hiss, already twisting to give her my back. I can't stand to even look at her.

The few good memories I have of her—training how to utilize my snakes as a toddler, learning to ride a bike as a child, laughing over dinner as a dumb tween—are tainted by this version of my mother today. She's different than she was when I was a kid, and I imagine her love for Zeus has something to do with that change. It twisted her, changed her, until I barely recognize the person staring back at me.

That type of love is toxic. Demented.

Something grotesque masquerading as something beautiful.

And nothing like the love I share with Violet...and the love she, in turn, shares with me and her other mates.

"Don't you walk away from me, Mason!" Mom screeches at my retreating back, her shrill voice like razor blades piercing my skin.

I wince but continue walking.

"I'll protect my family, Mason!" she screams at me, and above my head, the storm crackles with thunder. "Even if that means getting my hands dirty."

CHAPTER 18

DIMITRI

My shoulders feel as if they're being ripped from my body.

That's quite possibly because they are.

My wrists are bound above my head, and only the tips of my feet are capable of brushing the cold linoleum ground. It's white, of course, making the blood smears across the surface even more visible. And the room itself must be magically enchanted to make time stand still, because I've been here for what feels like months without any sleep or food. I haven't died from it yet, but my body feels the effects. I'm tired, sluggish, and my mind is practically inconsolable with madness.

Every bone in my naked body aches fiercely, and my skin feels raw, as if someone has taken sandpaper to my arms, legs, and stomach. My head lolls forward, my chin touching the top of my chest, but I force myself to stay awake, to focus.

You never know when your captives will get complacent,

when they'll fuck up and leave an opening for you to weasel your way through.

Not that I have a lot of experience being held prisoner…

I don't get caught.

I was an assassin before I even knew how to ride a damn bike, and I've never, ever gotten caught before. Not once. I've lived a semi-existence for years where I hid in the shadows, my form coalesced from the darkness itself, and never interacted with the world more than I had to. You wouldn't know I was there unless I wanted you to.

However, a certain infuriating female entered my life like a shooting star providing light to an unrelenting darkness.

A shooting star, might I add, made of acid. Burning. Searing. Mutilating everything it comes into contact with.

Violet fucking Dracula.

And even as I try to muster up the familiar tendrils of anger, I find that I can't. Blind panic beats against my skull, throbbing in tandem to my racing heart.

What happened to Violet after I was pulled through that portal and into this hellhole? Is she okay? Did she make it out of the hospital in one piece?

The thought of anything happening to Violet, of harm befalling her, makes me clench up instinctively. I try once again to free my wrists from the shackles imprisoning them, but like the thousand times before, it proves to be futile.

Fuck.

"Well, well, well," a slimy voice coos, the noise punctuated by the slap of bare feet on the cold tile flooring. "Are you ready to talk now, Headmaster Gray?"

I quickly slip my mask back into place, not bothering to dignify such an asinine question with a response.

Too soon, one of my three captors steps in front of me with a hideous grin tugging up his lips.

"Dustin," I bite out, glaring at the minotaur who had once been a student at Prodigium Academy.

He's large, nearly as large as Barret, with a head that resembles a raging bull, complete with sharp, curled horns and beady black eyes. Two rings cut through his nostrils, and with every exhale he makes, they sway forward. His top half is distinctly masculine, though it's covered in a thick layer of pitch-black fur. The fur dissipates where it reaches large, tree-trunk-sized humanoid legs and the extremely large, semi-erect penis hanging between them. A tiny bit of fur—a single line, to be exact—covers the length of the cock as if he hasn't bothered to shave the entire damn appendage.

I imagine Violet would say something as crude as, "Woah! His penis has a mohawk!"

But even as I'm being tortured, I'll maintain some dignity.

"The silent treatment again, eh?" Dustin smirks at me as if my silence is exactly what he wants. And hell, maybe it is. I've always suspected he was a sadistic bastard when I had him in my class, but I never had any proof.

At least not until he sliced and diced me one hundred different ways.

As I watch, my face carefully devoid of any emotion, he brings the knife in his huge, furry hand down until it slashes through the center of my chest, joining the myriad of scars already present there. I don't wince, don't even blanch, as pain explodes throughout my body in ripping waves of heat.

"Tell us about Violet Dracula and the powers she possesses," the minotaur demands, bringing the blade down again, this time aiming it at my bicep.

Like before, I don't cry out or allow a single flicker of my discomfort to break through my meticulous mask. I just… take the pain, compartmentalizing it the way only I know how.

He tries everything he can think of to get me to talk—punching me, stabbing me, slicing my arm, cutting my face.

But I remain silent.

I'll always remain silent if the price of my acquisition is Violet's life.

Dustin has just stabbed a fifth dagger into my thigh—in a place dangerously close to my cock—when the door to the torture room opens and my other two torturers step inside. This time, they're not alone.

Dangling between them, his orange head bent forward, is one of the teachers at Prodigium Academy. Mr. Pumpkin, cleverly named after his large pumpkin head.

The two captors carrying him are also former students of mine, though it took me hours of torture to recall their names.

The woman, Persephone, has a slate of pitch-black hair that cascades around her shoulders. She has a face that's designed to lure men in—pouty pink lips, glimmering emerald eyes, and a perfect button nose—but one glance into her expression…and you'll see nothing but pure malice staring back at you. Even her body is a trap, one designed to trick and entice. She's naked, as she was when I first woke up in this version of hell, with supple breasts, tiny pink nipples, a toned stomach, and a splatter of black hair down below. Her right leg is made out of copper, however, and in most circumstances, that would only add to her ethereal and slightly unusual appearance. But all I need to do is look a little closer, pull the façade away just a teeny bit, and I see that her skin is tinted a vomit shade of green, her breasts are actually tiny skulls, and her pussy? It has teeth.

Her appearance is nothing but an illusion designed to lure young, stupid men in until she eats them alive.

Only men faithful to the woman or man they love are able to see past her illusion.

I don't even want to think about what that means for me —that dreaded L-word that twists my heart up.

Persephone, an empusa, sashays forward in a way that probably has more men than I care to count falling at her feet. But since her illusion doesn't work on me, all I see are two skulls jiggling and vagina teeth currently curling into a malevolent smile.

"Has our prisoner talked yet?" she coos, reaching out to run a hand down my naked chest.

I meet her stare with a deadened one of my own, a threat in my eyes.

*If you don't stop touching me, bound or not, I'll find a way to remove your hand from your body.*

"No," Dustin grunts, his eyes devouring Persephone with a hungry glint.

I half want him to fuck her here and now. As soon as her evil vagina eats him, I'll have one less person I'll need to kill when I inevitably escape.

"He's being a stubborn fuck." He taps the tip of his blade against my stomach with a chuckle. "But I'm sure we can get him to talk."

Persephone laughs giddily and flutters her oily lashes at me. "I'm sure *I* can get him to talk," she practically purrs.

Behind the two of them, the third monster stands silent. A sentry awaiting orders.

Trill is a sphynx, though you wouldn't be able to tell that by looking at him. From what I remember when he was a student, he's also half human and prefers that form. His shaggy brown hair constantly falls forward into his eyes, the shade almost metallic in color and the only indication he's anything but human. As I watch, he absently reaches a hand up to brush a few loose strands away, his fingers bumping his wire-framed glasses in the process.

Trill is shy and timid, the type of man to spend his days

reading a book instead of engaging in violent torture. He certainly wouldn't associate with students like Persephone and Dustin. So what the bloody hell is going on here?

I don't allow a single question to show on my face as Persephone turns her insidious attention onto Mr. Pumpkin. He's weeping, fat, chunky, yellow tears that slide down his carved-up face—a triangular nose, two oval eyes, and a square smile.

"Please. Don't hurt me," my coworker pleads, trembling.

My frown deepens.

"We just want you to answer a few questions about Violet Dracula," Persephone purrs, stalking closer until she's directly in front of him.

Trill presses down on Mr. Pumpkin's shoulders until he's forced to his knees, his eyes level with Persephone's pussy. I wince inwardly as those razor-sharp teeth begin to gnash down as if they're already tasting his pumpkin flesh. And is that…? Is that a tongue snaking out of her pussy lips? Fucking hell. I've seen some strange stuff in my years alive, but that takes the cake.

"Violet?" Mr. Pumpkin's strange lips curl downwards.

I'm pretty sure a relative of Mr. Pumpkin—perhaps a third distant cousin or something of the sort—attacked Violet in the maze of the Roaring. She killed him in self-defense. But Mr. Pumpkin? He's been nothing but supportive of her from day one.

"We know you were one of the professors to find Violet after she murdered all those people," Dustin snarls. "We want to know exactly what you saw. Do you know what she did? What powers she had?"

I have to will my body to remain calm, to not tense up the way it so desperately wants to.

When they turn their questions towards me, I know I can refuse to answer them. They may torture and beat and maim me, but I know my silence is my own. My lips are a steel vault that they can't hope of opening.

But Mr. Pumpkin? He's an enigma, one that I don't like. He has no loyalty to Violet Dracula aside from being her teacher. And if the choice is one unruly student accused of murder or torture or his own life? I don't need to have a molecular biology degree like Cal to know his answer.

"I-I don't know much." He flashes what I would almost describe as an apologetic frown my way before focusing on the three monsters surrounding him. *Motherfucker.* "J-just what I saw."

"And what was that, darling," Persephone coos, tilting her body in such a way that the teeth in her vagina are inches from the stem on the top of his head. I wonder what Mr. Pumpkin sees—a pussy or two rows of serrated teeth. I suppose it depends on how loyal he is to his wife. How much he loves her.

I swallow again at the thought that Persephone's illusion dissipated almost as soon as I set eyes on her because my heart remained loyal to the woman I love.

*The woman I love.*

*Fuck.*

"The room. Covered in blood. And body parts." Mr. Pumpkin has to swallow convulsively to get the words out, and I grit my teeth.

All of that information was stuff the three of them could've found by hacking the school's records, but I still feel my hackles lift at how freely Mr. Pumpkin gave away confidential information about my Violet.

Persephone's green-tinted lips twist in a scowl. "We already know that," she huffs.

"Do you have anything else to share?" Trill asks…rather fucking calmly for a psycho murderer. He once again fiddles with his glasses, his sleeve sliding down just enough for me to see a strange symbol branded onto the inside of his wrist. A tattoo, perhaps?

Before I can inspect it more closely, he lowers his hand and focuses on Mr. Pumpkin.

"Th-that's it," the teacher whispers breathily.

"Then I suppose you're useless." Persephone sighs, as if extremely put off by the fact, before she steps overtop of the trembling man.

Then, to my utmost horror, her vagina lips spread open until her mouth is the size of a basketball. Or a pumpkin. She then places her vagina directly over Mr. Pumpkin's head and clamps down. There's a sickening crush, a guttural squeal, and then the distinct chomping of teeth through crust and juice.

I never feel the need to use pointless expletives to describe my discomfort, but, as Violet would say, *holy fuck*.

I just watched a teacher get eaten by a female's literal vagina.

"Oh. Oh yeah. Right there. Oh!" Persephone groans in ecstasy, her head falling back and spilling her curtain of greasy black hair across the floor. She moans as she comes, blood squirting from her pussy and down her legs...and Mr. Pumpkin's corpse.

Again, as Violet would say...

Holy. Fuck.

"That was hot, baby," Dustin purrs, wrapping an arm around her waist and tugging her close. He doesn't seem to mind that his old professor's head is still fully inside his girlfriend's pussy.

"If you guys are going to fuck..." Trill's face twists in disgust as he steps over Mr. Pumpkin's corpse in my direction. "I'm going to see if I can get some more information out of our esteemed professor. Or...is it headmaster now, Professor Gray?"

~

"Dɪᴍɪᴛʀɪ."

Her voice reaches for me through a rippling sea of fathomless depths. Nothing but inky darkness surrounds me from every direction—clawing at me and dragging me deeper into the dark, watery pit of hell itself.

"Dimitri."

There it is again. Her low, husky murmur that sends bolts of heat straight to my cock in a way no woman has done before. Not any of my past lovers and certainly not the man-eating vagina Persephone.

"Violet," I murmur, blinking rapidly until her beautiful, heart-shaped face comes into view.

Her blonde hair appears especially radiant today as it cascades around her shoulders. Austere, fluorescent light illuminates her features as she steps forward—from the pucker of her lips, to the slash of her eyebrows, to the tears glimmering in her brilliant blue eyes.

"Violet," I repeat, loving the way her name tastes on my tongue.

"Oh, Dimitri," she whispers brokenly. "What have they done to you?""

Her voice caresses my ear like the hot, languid flick of a tongue. Fuck, I could listen to her speak to me all day.

Apparently, the continuous torture has lowered all of my defenses. My walls have crumbled down around me, reverted to nothing but fine particles of dust.

"You came for me," I whisper. My lashes feel like they've been coated in concrete, and I blink them rapidly, hating the way they scrape against my cheekbones like sandpaper.

"Of course I did, idiot." She rolls her eyes in a way that makes me want to spank her. "I'll always come for you."

"I didn't tell them anything about you," I slur as I attempt to focus on her…something that proves impossible to do with my eyes swollen shut. "I would never tell them anything about you."

"Don't talk." She presses a delicate finger to my lips. "Save your strength."

"I love you, Violet," I murmur as sleep reaches for me desperately. I fight against it. No, I don't just fight it. I bend that bastard over and fuck him in the ass with a sword.

When have my thoughts become so…uncouth? Is Violet rubbing off on me?

The thought makes me smile, but that twitch of my lips only intensifies the pain radiating down the length of my face.

"You love me?" Violet whispers.

Did I say that? Did I tell her I love her?

"Obviously," I drawl, still half delirious from the pain. "I wouldn't put up with torture for just anyone."

Do I love Violet? My mouth seems to be running away from my brain, but I can't find it within myself to take those words back. To refute my impromptu confession.

Because…I do love Violet Dracula. More than I ever thought possible.

"Then…" Violet leans in closer, her lips a breath away from my own. "You should tell her that when you see her again."

"I should tell her that when I see her again," I repeat drowsily, my eyelids slipping shut for a fraction of a second. I immediately snap them back open to see that I'm still in the painfully bright, white room…with no Violet. "Violet? Violet!?" My voice rises to a shout before I can stop myself, desperation clawing at my heart.

A cold chuckle echoes from the doorway where my captors disappeared hours ago. I slowly lift my head, pain splintering down my spine, as a familiar figure steps into view.

"I have heard that prolonged periods of torture, starvation, and sleep deprivation can bring about hallucinations, but I never tested that theory before. But don't worry, Mr. Gray. That person you saw may not have been the real Violet Dracula, but I can promise you'll see her again soon. After, of course, I cut her into tiny pieces."

# CHAPTER 19

VIOLET

"I'm going to kill that bitch," I growl, pacing the small expanse of the motel room. I then pause, frown, and toss a sheepish expression Mason's way. "No offense."

"None taken," he replies gruffly. He reaches up to finger the edge of his gray beanie, and I swear I see the hat moving as if his snakes are sharing in his agitation, as if the sensations coursing through us all are compounding into something volatile and ugly.

"Fuck, I don't know if I can take this." I fork my hand through my tangled golden hair, frowning when my fingers get caught in a particularly bad snarl.

"What do you mean, Violet?" Vin, who has been silent since Mason relayed the conversation he had with his mother, leans forward on the edge of the bed and frowns.

"The prophecy…" I continue to pace. No doubt, my bare feet are wearing holes into the carpeting, but I can't find it within me to stop, to slow down. I need to keep moving, keep walking, keep…doing something. I'm afraid of what will happen if I choose to stop. Will I shut down? Will my systems fail me? I spin around so I'm facing my lover leaning against the headboard of the queen-sized bed. "Mason, I'm fated to kill you."

"Correction," Alex cuts in. He's sitting apart from our group, on the lone leather chair in the corner of the room. He steeples his hands together and leans forward as well, almost mirroring Vin's position. "Dracula's daughter is supposed to kill him. That doesn't necessarily mean you. Technically, you're not even his blood—"

"He's still my damn father," I cut him off savagely. "Blood doesn't always mean family."

I should know that better than anyone. My birth parents are the devil himself and a cunt of a goddess who apparently wishes for me to be dead. I can't see them winning any parenting awards.

Alex rolls his eyes but wisely doesn't refute me. Instead, he settles back in the chair and watches me with keen, narrowed eyes. I give him the finger and focus on my two mates once more.

"If I were to hurt you, let alone kill you—" I begin, but Mason cuts me off by leaning forward.

"It'll be worth it, Pinkie." A tender smile adorns his painfully handsome face, even as the bulge beneath his beanie shakes again. "Because it means I had you, if only for a little bit."

"Don't say shit like that," I whisper, crawling on my hands and knees across the bed until I'm directly in front of him. The thought of something happening to Mason, to any of my men, really, tears me up inside like iron shears. A full body tremor reverberates through me, and I have to squeeze my eyelids shut to ward off the explosive, unimaginable agony even the thought brings. "Nothing will happen to you."

"But if it does,"—that warm smile never disappears from

his face—"it wouldn't be your fault, Pinkie, you understand? I'm a big boy who can make my own decisions, and I chose you. I'll continue to choose you time and time again."

"I'm not worth it," I say softly, brokenly, truthfully.

My mates should not have to lose their lives for loving me. That's not a future I'll even consider. Tentatively, I reach out and grab the edge of Mason's beanie, sliding it across his head.

His hand snakes upwards and captures my wrist, stopping me. "Don't," he warns breathlessly, his gaze lowering to my parted lips. "I don't want you to see me like that."

"Like what?" I lean closer instinctively as his hand tightens, his fingers biting into my skin hard enough to bruise.

But...

I like it.

"Like a monster." The words are a breathy exhale that caresses my face, and my lashes flutter shut instinctively.

"You're not a monster, Mase. You're beautiful." My eyes slowly open so they can collide with his, allowing him to see the sincerity of my words.

How could I ever think that Mason—funny, caring, jovial Mason—is a monster? It's almost laughable how ridiculous that sounds.

"What if my snakes hurt you," he continues, though he doesn't raise his voice above a whisper. Vin has gone quiet behind us. Watching the exchange. Cataloging both of our reactions with that penetrating stare of his.

"They won't." I know that in my bones, and he must know it too because when I remove the beanie completely, he doesn't stop me.

His snakes immediately rise to attention on the top of his head, their green scales shimmering in the ambient motel lighting. I'm awestruck. Speechless. I can't look away as the snakes curve around my wrist as if in greeting.

Their flesh feels cold beneath my fingers and smoother than a polished stone. I don't know what I expected, but it definitely wasn't this.

"I think they like me," I whisper as one of his snake's forked tongue licks at my fingers and another closes around my ring finger in a mockery of a hug.

"They love you," Mason replies, seeming just as surprised and awed by it as me.

I wonder how often he let his snakes come out to play. My guess is never. He's always been afraid he would accidentally turn someone to stone.

The thought that I'm the first one to see him like this, to run my fingers over the smooth skin of his snakes, buoys me up, fills my stomach with thousands of tiny bubbles that drift me towards the ceiling. It's a boneless, disembodied sensation, like I'm made out of nothing but air.

"And are they the only ones who love me?" I tease, leaning in close enough that my lips are a hair's breadth away from his. I can taste his cinnamon toothpaste on my tongue, despite the fact that I haven't yet breached the distance between us.

"Are you fishing for compliments, Pinkie?" Mason offers me a slow, salacious smirk, one that has his light-green eyes glimmering with a million untold promises.

"So what if I am?" I pantomime tossing a fishing line out and then reeling it back in.

"What did you catch?" His hands move to settle on my waist, his fingers digging into the smooth skin where my skirt has risen up.

"A compliment, of course." I wait patiently, and he simply blinks at me, still offering that infuriating, sexy smirk. "This is the part where you tell me I'm pretty."

"You're not pretty, Violet Dracula." The husky murmur comes from Vin who has moved onto the bed until he's directly behind me, his lips trailing down the side of my neck.

I arch my head to the side instinctively, granting him better access, and I can feel his smile against my skin.

"You're a goddess among mortals, my love."

Alex makes a choked, gasping noise in the back of his throat, but I ignore him.

I should send him away. I should tell him to leave and come back in, say, two hours. I should slam the door in his stupidly handsome, pierced face and lock it before he can get back in.

But I don't.

The thought of him watching me, watching *this*, has my panties dampening even more than Mason's and Vin's dirty words.

Alex can leave at any time, yet…he doesn't. He hasn't. I can feel his eyes on us as he sits rigid and taut in the leather chair, his fingers clenched around the armrests.

But this moment isn't about Alex and what may or may not—cough, definitely not, cough—be brewing between us. It's about me and Mason and Vin.

"I owe you an apology too." I tilt my head so my lips are able to whisper over Vin's, the softest caress. "If you hadn't been my mate, if Vanessa hadn't been my friend—"

Vin cuts me off with a bruising, possessive kiss, one I can feel in the marrow of my bones. "You had nothing to do with what happened to my sister. That's on Mason's mother and her alone. We're going to break the curse and free my sister. That's a damn promise. But…" He claims my lips once more, and I feel as if he's doing more than just kissing me. He's letting the world—aka Alex—see exactly who owns me. "The last thing I want to be talking about right now is my damn sister."

"Vin's right," Mason cuts in, his hands continuing to

smooth across the skin of my waist. "We're together now, and that's all that matters. The future? Eh." He waves a hand in the air dismissively. "We'll worry about that when it comes to it."

"I like worrying about the future." Fuck help me, the words are an embarrassing gasp of breath.

What can I say? It's hard to keep a straight head when you have one sexy-as-hell dude kissing your neck and another slowly caressing both of your sides, pulling your shirt up in the process.

Both men lean away slightly to allow me to tug the shirt over the top of my head. Now, I'm just in my black miniskirt and bright pink bra that shows the clear and hard points of my nipples.

"The past? I say let bygones be bygones. The present? I usually just do my own thing and pray I don't fall on my face. Or into a wall. I've fallen into a lot of walls in my time. Do you know that it hurts when you face-plant into cement? I know. Shocking. Anyway, back to what I was saying... The future. I like the future. Plans and all that shit. And I really like knowing which one of my mates will potentially die in the future, because...you know...death sucks. Death can kiss my sculpted ass and—"

My rant breaks off when Mason sucks on my nipple through the fabric of my bra. I gasp and arch my back against Vin's hard, naked chest.

Wait?!

Naked?!

When did he get his clothes off?!

"Stop talking, mistress," Vin growls in my ear, and Zeus help me, but a flood of heat crashes through my system at what he just called me.

I found early on in our...sexual relationship that Vin likes giving up control. He's so dominant and alpha in real life that he enjoys submitting himself to me in the bedroom. I'm not sure if it's a need for him or just a want, but tonight... Tonight, I don't want to be his mistress. I just want to be Violet feeling loved and cherished by two of her mates.

Vin must see that in my eyes, because he smiles softly and tugs at my hair, twisting my head even farther around to kiss me. His tongue doesn't just prod at my lips—no, it surges inside like he owns my mouth, tangling with my own tongue and taking everything I willingly offer him. His grip on my hair is almost painful, but I don't complain, not when it feels so damn good.

Mason pops my bra down just enough to free one of my breasts. He fondles the fleshy globe and then leans forward and blows air onto the hardened peak. It stiffens under his attention, and I, in turn, stiffen in my mates' arms.

"Look at that pretty, pink nipple," Mason purrs as he leans in close enough for me to feel the smooth curl of his snakes touching the top of my breast. It's a startling contrast to his warm mouth as it closes over my aching nub, his tongue curling out to lick at the peak. He pulls away just enough to whisper, "Do you want to see more?"

At first, I think his dirty words are directed at me, but when I reluctantly break my kiss with Vin, I see that Mason is focusing solely on the necromancer still seated in the corner of the room. He's gripping the armrests so tightly, I'm surprised the chair itself doesn't snap in half. That damn muscle in his jaw begins to twitch once more.

But he, yet again, doesn't leave.

He simply sits there, staring, his cock tenting the dark blue jeans he changed into after his shower and our... um...talk.

Mason reaches behind me to deftly unclasp my bra, and Vin grabs my arms and holds them behind my back, offering my breasts out as some sort of offering.

As Mason lowers his head to once more shower my tits with attention, Vin leans forward to whisper in my ear, "We can stop this at any time. We can kick Alex out if you don't feel comfortable with him watching. Just let us know."

"No." The word leaves my mouth before I can think better of it. What the hell am I even thinking?!

Yet allowing Alex to stay doesn't feel wrong.

Dirty, most definitely.

Sensual, hell yes.

My pussy practically jumps up and down for joy, shooting off confetti cannons and doing an entire gymnastics routine in her happiness.

Who knew I had such a voyeuristic kink?

No, I want the asshole to watch. To yearn. To desire. To want something he can never, ever have.

As if to prove to both Vin and Mason I mean it, I twist slightly so I'm facing Alex completely. I then crudely spread my legs, allowing him to see my pink panties beneath my dark skirt.

Mason continues to suck on one nipple while Vin fondles the other.

Alex…

Alex just watches, an almost pained expression on his face as if he can't decide if he wants to run away, beg to join in, or—

He unzips his jeans, almost as if the pressure is too much for him, and his hard, pierced cock springs free. My mouth waters as I stare at the rows of piercings running along the length of his shaft. There are so many questions I have in regards to that pretty dick.

One—did it hurt when he got it pierced? Alex seems like the type of man to laugh in the face of pain and tell it to get fucked. I can't imagine having a shit ton of piercings inserted into a penis could feel good. But what do I know?

Two—did he have to be hard or soft while he was getting it pierced? I really hope it's the latter. The thought of Alex getting himself hard to someone who isn't me fills me with an incandescent, burning, sweltering, all-consuming rage.

And finally…

What will it feel like inside of me?

In my pussy?

In my mouth?

I'm falling down the rabbit hole and straight into Wonderland, and honestly? I can't find it within me to give a single shit. Not when Wonderland is made up of tattooed, pierced men with dicks that have me smiling like the Cheshire cat.

"I think she likes what she sees, necromancer shit face," Mason points out conversationally, his eyes flicking to Alex's dick. "But my girl better not get a taste for piercings because of that thing. There ain't no way I'm allowing any person near my dick with a needle."

"Because you're a damn pussy," Alex grunts out, his fist doing a corkscrew motion around his cock.

Mason shrugs unapologetically as he slides away from me and pulls off his purple flannel shirt. He then tugs off the gray undershirt until his beautiful, slightly tan chest is unveiled to me. This time, it's me leaning forward, my breasts pressing against his stomach, to run my tongue around his nipple.

His hips jerk upwards instinctively as, behind me, Vin grabs a fistful of my hair so it's not in the way as I lick and suck at Mason's tiny pink nubs.

"I may be a pussy—which, might I add, is significantly more badass than a cock—but at least this pussy is able to taste Violet's pussy." Mason sounds so damn smug I don't have the heart to tell him he doesn't make a lick of sense.

Instead, I kiss down his stomach, pushing him onto his back in the process, until I'm able to slide down his jeans.

His cock immediately springs free, and I wrap my hand around it, the same way I see Alex doing. The necromancer stares at me, one pierced brow raised, and I simply smirk back.

When he brings his hands down the length of his shaft to fondle his balls, I do the same to Mason.

When he runs his thumb over the bead of precum on the tip, I do the same to Mase.

Alex licks his lips, his chest heaving, and Mason throws his head back with a groan.

"You're killing me, Pinkie," he all but whines.

I shrug. "Blame Alex. He's the one jerking you off right now."

Alex grins mischievously as his fist begins to move down his length even faster. I copy the motion on Mason before deciding…fuck it. I need to taste my sweet, handsome mate. I lower my lips until I'm able to slide his dick into my mouth, forgetting about Alex and the rest of the world. All that matters is my mate. I want to make him feel good.

This new position has my ass in the air, and I feel rather than see Vin slide my skirt and panties off until I'm bare. I want to feel self-conscious with both Vin and Alex staring at me intently, but I don't. Maybe it's because I'm done being scared, done hiding. I'm embracing my destiny…and whatever this thing is with all my mates. Well, my mates and Alex.

I still hate the sexy fucker.

"Look at this perfect pussy," Vin murmurs, and I feel his fingers against the sensitive skin of my lips, pulling them apart for his inspection…and Alex's. "Don't you want to taste it? To put your tongue between her sweet lips?"

Alex makes a strangled sound in the back of his throat but doesn't respond. His breathing, however, turns raspy and uneven, thready gasps that have my pussy clenching around air.

I release Mason's dick to moan, "Vin…"

"So greedy when you're not in charge," he teases a second before his tongue darts out to lick at the seam of my pussy lips.

"Oh, fuck." My hips buck towards his face instinctively.

"Violet." This time, it's Mason who's pleading, the snakes on the top of his head twisting and writhing as he stares up at me with hooded eyes.

"Yes, my love?" I slowly place my mouth over the head of his cock…just enough so my tongue can press against the slit on the top. It's not enough for him to feel me around his shaft, not really, but to tease him of what's to come.

"You're not being nice," he chastises.

Vin chuckles against my pussy lips, a sensation I feel all the way to my aching nipples. "If you're not going to be nice to Mason, then maybe I shouldn't be nice to you." As he speaks, he begins to move his lips away.

"Don't you dare," I growl, the words causing me to breathe against Mason's jerking cock, still shiny with my saliva.

"Tit for tat," Vin says lightly.

"Tit." Mason squeezes one of my breasts with a cheeky grin and then adds, "Tat," with a slap to my ass.

Alex groans—apparently, the kinky fucker likes it when I'm spanked—but I don't tear my attention off of Mason to acknowledge him.

"You want a blowjob, Mase?" I offer him a smile steeped in wickedness. Yeah. If I were him, I would run screaming for the hills. "Then so be it."

I open my mouth as far as it can go and suck the head of his cock, closing my lips just enough to graze his skin with my teeth. His hips jerk upwards, a moan escaping him, but if he thinks this is the worst, then he's sorely mistaken.

I've just begun.

Behind me, Vin has placed his lips back to my pussy lips, licking, sucking, and biting…but completely avoiding the tiny nub that demands his attention. Asshole.

I slide my mouth up and down Mason's shaft like a goddamn pro, and only when my nose is flush against his skin do I pause and hold him deep in my throat. And then I begin to hum.

The noise that comes out of his mouth? Fucking priceless.

It's not dignified or sexy or anything of the sort. It's positively guttural and feral and savage.

Heat travels up my spine, a blazing pathway of fire, as Mason grabs my hair, tugs my mouth off his dick, and then claims my lips in a sexy kiss. He can no doubt taste himself on me, on my tongue, but that only makes him more…ravenous.

I gasp against Mason's mouth as Vin finally—fucking finally—clamps down on the bundle of nerves as his fingers enter my channel, pistoning in and out fiercely. My body shakes madly, tremors radiating through my entire being, and my thighs clench around Vin's head.

And then I'm exploding.

Imploding.

Every type of "ploding" you can think of.

I don't even know who I am anymore as the foundations of my genetic makeup fall apart and then are reassembled back together again.

My entire body shakes as Vin roughly pulls me up against his chest and Mason slides his boxers and jeans the rest of the way down his toned legs, kicking them aside. Once he's fully naked, he grabs my hips and helps position me over his throbbing cock while he lies back on the bed.

"I need to be inside you, Pinkie. I need to feel your tight walls squeeze my cock in an iron vise. Do you want that, baby? Do you want my cock inside of you?"

Do lions eat gazelles?

Fuck yes.

Instead of answering Mason with words, I grab his cock in my fist and line it up with my sopping entrance. I use my heels for balance as I push myself up and then slowly lower myself onto his hard dick. Vin keeps his hands on my waist, holding me steady, as I adjust to the intrusion of Mason's massive girth.

"Oh…fuck yes," I moan as Mason tugs me to him so I'm practically draped over him.

"Think you can take both of us, Pinkie?" Mason groans, remaining perfectly still underneath me.

I slide my fingers over his chest and across his pebbled nipples as I wiggle my ass. "Yes. God, yes."

A moan lodges in my throat as I feel Vin's hand curl around the swell of my ass. Teasing. Kneading. Caressing. I expect him to touch me there, to breach that tight ring of muscles, but he doesn't.

Instead, the head of his dick pushes against my slick pussy, directly beside Mason's.

"You want this, baby girl?" Vin lowers his head to murmur the words directly in my ear. "Both of our big cocks inside of you, filling you up?"

Fuck yes.

Obviously, I know what DVP is—double vaginal penetration—but I never thought I'd be woman enough to do it myself. My pussy already feels so stretched, the pressure almost too intense, and I can't imagine adding another dick to the mix…especially one as large as Vin's.

But then I stare down into Mason's lust-filled eyes, the

snakes on his head caressing the arms I placed on either side of his head.

He wants this. They both do.

And I…I want this too.

I want to be filled by two of my men, their cocks touching inside of my pussy. That thought alone has my muscles clenching down on Mason's dick, and a low, thready moan escapes him.

Unbidden, my eyes slide to Alex where he still sits on the chair, his jaw clenched as he watches us. His hand continues to stroke his huge, pierced dick as he volleys his gaze from my breasts, to Mason's cock inside of me, and then to Vin over my shoulder.

The thought of him watching me, touching himself…

Of Mason and Vin's huge cocks rubbing against each other…

It's almost too much for me.

"Yes." I arch my back slightly, and Vin takes the opportunity to run his palm down the length of my spine. "I want both your cocks in my pussy. Together. Take me together."

Mason's hands grab my ass cheeks, and I don't quite know if he's holding on to me or spreading me for Vin. Either way, I begin to rock unconsciously against him, my fingers grazing down his chest before twisting his little nipples.

I lean forward even farther, my breasts practically in Mason's mouth at this point—something he takes advantage of as he wets one of my nipples with his tongue. He continues to hold my ass lewdly as Vin's cock pushes against my pussy lips, rubbing against Mason's. He does it slowly, giving me a second to adjust to his girth, and I almost scream at him to stop.

I'm too full.

It's too much.

It hurts too bad.

But when his balls brush my skin—and Mason's shaft—all of those worries fly out the window to be replaced by pleasure.

Holy fuck.

Mason stays still underneath me as Vin pistons in and out of my pussy. I can feel Vin's cock brushing against Mason's with every thrust of his tan hips, both of them stretching me more than I've ever been extended before. My hunter's face is etched in pleasure, his mouth parted and sweat dotting his perfect skin.

"Fuck, man," Mason moans, and I can tell remaining still is taking a lot out of him. "I can feel your balls hitting my dick."

I know he doesn't mean for his words to be dirty, but I cry out instinctively.

"Oh...fuck," Alex murmurs, claiming my attention. His hand fists his cock as he watches us with hooded eyes.

"Do you like this, fucker?" Mason asks crudely, twisting his head to stare at the necromancer. "Do you like watching us fuck our girl? Do you wish it was your cock stretching this perfect, tight pussy?"

Alex's teeth clench together, but he surprises me by answering. The one word is low and guttural, ripped from his throat in a way I imagine hurts. "Yes."

Mason smirks wickedly, and his dick pops out of me.

"Let's give the asshole a show, shall we?" He directs his question at Vin, and the next thing I know, my back is draped across Mason's stomach as he lies down and his cock is lined up with my entrance again. He plunges inside of me just as Vin climbs over my body and enters me from on top.

"Oh, fuck!" I scream as Vin begins to fuck me from above.

From this angle, I can see the way Vin enters me, his tan cock a startling contrast to Mason's paler one. The two dicks rub against each other as they both fuck me—Vin jerking his hips forward and Mason pushing his upwards.

My breasts bounce as I sit up slightly, placing one hand on the pillow for leverage and the other on the comforter. Mason reaches up to cup one tit from behind, plucking my nipple, while his other hand lowers to my clit. His fingers begin to rub against it and consequentially Vin's dick. At first, I think it's an accident, but when Mason cheekily runs the pad of his finger across the throbbing vein on Vin's shaft, I know it's not.

"You fucker," Vin growls out, his breathing ragged and his huge chest heaving.

Mason chuckles as he returns his focus to my clit.

"You love it, Vinny Poo," he taunts. He then adds, "You like this, Alex? Don't you? You love watching us fuck our girl. Look at her pretty breasts bounce." He squeezes one for emphasis, tugging at my nipple hard enough to hurt and then releasing it.

Alex groans as his hand moves faster around his cock. A bead of sweat cascades down his forehead, across his smooth jawline, and then disappears down the neckline of his back shirt.

I want to lick that bead of sweat.

I want to follow the path it just took with my tongue.

"I'm so close," I warn as Mason continues to pay attention to my clit and nipples.

"Me too." Vin's words are said through gritted teeth as he lifts my leg up and places it on his shoulder. This new position makes me see goddamn stars, and I feel my orgasm approaching.

No, not approaching.

It's goddamn happening, and I'm helpless to do anything but hold on.

My stomach lurches the way it does when you're click,

click, clicking up the first hill of a steep roller coaster. That slow, steady incline where your stomach bottoms out and you can't help but glance over your shoulder at the ground below you. And then you reach the top of the hill and there's a moment of serenity and peacefulness. But just a moment.

And then you're falling. Diving. Twisting. Turning.

Pleasure rockets through my body as teeny-tiny stars explode behind my closed eyelids.

When did I close my eyes?

"I'm gonna…" Mason doesn't get a chance to finish his sentence as his hips jerk upwards and he's showering both my pussy and Vin's cock in wave after wave of sticky cum.

That seems to set off a chain reaction. Vin gasps out my name, his fingers digging into my hips, and then roars as he comes.

I twist my head just in time to see Alex's pierced cock jerk in his hand as he, too, falls over the edge with a cry, his head falling back and his thick lashes feathering against his cheekbones.

Holy. Fuck.

Later on, there'll be a lot I'll have to unpack concerning this moment.

I had sex with Mason and Vin…together…at the same time…in my vagina…

Without condoms.

And Alex? The asshole necromancer who once made me shit my pants in the cafeteria? He watched and jerked off.

But as I fall into a sweaty heap against Mason's chest and Vin rolls onto his back beside us, I find that I don't mind what just occurred.

Not one fucking bit.

# CHAPTER 20

FRANKIE

I place both my pointer fingers against my lips as I peer at the anomaly sitting before me.

Balor...or Jack and Hux...watches me with narrowed eyes, his head tilted to the side and a sneer distorting his face. With his sweaty hair brushed behind both of his ears the way it currently is, I can clearly make out the scar curving through his cheek. Jack would hate to be on display this way, but Hux? He would wear it with pride.

Balor's lips remain fixed in a haughty scowl as he regards me with barely veiled dislike. I imagine I'm studying him in a similar manner, though I suspect my interest is more...analytical.

"So you're the scientist." Balor finally breaks the silence, his Irish accent an unwelcome lilt that fills the air.

I continue to eye him coldly, the way a scientist does a frog just before he dissects it. And that's all I am, after all. A scientist. And Balor? He's the frog I'm seconds from sticking a pair of tweezers into.

The guys may believe me to have developed human emotions like compassion and empathy after meeting Violet, but I'm not sure that's necessarily true. I do feel something… but only when I'm around my angel. Violet makes my artificial heart skip a dozen beats and activates my sweat glands. I feel like a child when I'm with her—young, carefree, and painfully innocent.

I know about the dangers plaguing our worlds—the horrors—but they all fade from my mind when I stare into her light-blue eyes, the exact shade of the Caribbean Sea. I swear I could drown in those glittering orbs, losing myself to the turbulent ocean waters that pull me under and then spit me back out.

"Did Frankenstein not insert a brain into that head of yours?" Balor cocks his head to the side with another humorless grin. "Or did he forget to give you a tongue?"

"I have a brain." My voice is soft, a breath of sound, but it straightens his spine where he sits tied in an office chair near the fluffy, queen-sized bed. I'm not sure how well these god-blessed chains will hold him, but it's the best we can come up with. And so far, he hasn't been able to escape. "And right now, this brain is working overtime to find a way to get rid of you."

"Get rid of me." He laughs snottily, once again doing that strange head tilt that makes a strand of inky-black hair fall forward into his fathomless eyes. "You can't get rid of me, Frankenstein."

I don't bother to correct him on my name as I fold my arms over my chest and wait him out.

"Not without hurting your precious Jack and Hux."

"Maybe. Maybe not." I shrug nonchalantly, my mind calculating all of the possibilities, sifting through my limited knowledge on souls and bodies. "But I have been developing a serum that's supposed to be able to separate Jack and Hux.

If I'm correct…well…I should be able to extract your soul from their body. And who knows what I'll do with it then?" The grin I offer him would be chilling to most monsters. "Maybe we'll stomp on you like the bug you are."

For a brief, brief moment, a multitude of emotions flash in Balor's eyes too quickly for me to read. I'm still not apt at deciphering nonsensical things such as emotions and feelings, at least not in people who aren't my Violet. However, I swear a flash of panic bleeds into his dark gaze before he adopts an indolent, nearly apathetic mask.

But he's not fooling me.

Emotions, to me, remind me of a book written entirely in a foreign language. No, not just a foreign language…a dead one. There are familiar shapes and even some letters, but the meaning constantly evades me, slipping through my fingers like water in a strainer. A splitting headache rips apart my brain as I force myself to continue reading, continue flipping page after page to put meaning to this dissonant world.

There's no meaning to be found, however. Only more questions.

And my current question?

What caused that momentary burst of panic on Balor's face? Is it the prospect of being separated from Jack and Hux, men who he seems, for all intents and purposes, rather fond of? In a sadistic, serial-killer type of way, of course.

Is it Violet? Is he worried that if he's separated from this body, he won't be able to remain near her?

Or is it simply the unknown that terrifies him, that has fear emanating off of him in waves I can almost feel like electrical currents? I imagine it must be terrifying to lose the one body that has been able to hold your soul in the thousands of years he's been around. Where would he go? Would he simply cease to exist? Would he wander this world as a bodiless Formorian?

The Wild Hunt.

When Violet told me what Balor said back in Lucifer's apartment, I nearly had a heart attack. I then proceeded to do all the research I could on the monsters that the world believed to be dead.

Balor was telling the truth, in part. The Wild Hunt were in charge of rounding up all the souls on the Earth plane and sending them to either Heaven or Hell. I don't necessarily know what happened to put them in prison, but I do know that Lucifer and Zeus took over the collection of souls with their monstrous minions as soon as the Formorians were locked away.

"I'm not the bad guy here," Balor grits out, his eyes spewing vitriol in my direction...vitriol that rolls off my shoulders like raindrops. "My people aren't the bad guys either. We were imprisoned for simply existing."

My heart twists at his words, mainly because they sound eerily familiar. Isn't that the same for Violet and the rest of the vampires? They exist and have a strength that surpasses other monsters. Immortality. Invincibility to some extent as well. My mind conjures up images of those vampire hunters carving up Violet's arm, and blinding rage cascades through me.

Then I think about Balor's behavior. The way he treated Violet and the other vampires.

I'm not used to this sensation—this rage that bubbles in my stomach like fizzing soda.

"If you know what it feels like to be a hated species, how could you treat Violet the way you have? The other vampires?" I place my hands on my knees and lean down so we're at eye level. His eyes are so dark, I feel as if I'm staring into black holes. Into endless, fathomless abysses.

"I admit"—he sounds as if he's speaking through gritted

teeth—"that I took my anger out on someone who might not have deserved it—"

"You're a monster, Balor. You may believe you're fighting for a noble cause, and maybe at the start, you were, but over time, you've become twisted and demented…exactly like the monsters you claim to hate."

I don't mean for my words to have the effect they do. Maybe it's because I'm speaking so matter-of-factly, without an ounce of emotion lacing my voice, but his back straightens imperceptibly and what looks like pain flashes across his face. And maybe…maybe guilt and regret too.

Whatever asinine response he was about to give me is interrupted by the door pushing open and Violet stepping inside. Both of our eyes immediately snap to her face, but she ignores our prisoner to focus on me.

"Frankie," she murmurs, hurrying forward so she can throw her arms around me. Her curves press against the soft planes of my chest as I plant a kiss to the crown of her head.

There it is again.

Those pesky emotions I once hated with the entirety of my being but now can't imagine an existence without. They're all-consuming, explosive, and the best damn things that have ever happened to me.

*She's* the best damn thing that's ever happened to me.

My fake heart feels too big for my chest, and it pounds incessantly in her presence, a rhythmic tempo that we can dance to.

And…

When did I turn so sappy that I can't help but envision waltzing her around a prisoner's bedroom, her tiny hand clasped with mine, my palm on her waist, her smile luminescent on her perfect face?

"I was so worried when you disappeared," I murmur, taking an immense deal of comfort in her safe return.

She's like a shooting star in a pitch-black sky, providing light to an unrelenting darkness. That inner light of hers is what demarcates her from every other person and monster in this world.

"*I* was worried when I disappeared," she jokes, twining her arms around my neck and fingering the dark hairs there. She bites down on her lower lip as lust darkens her expression and her eyes glimmer with a thousand things she wishes to do with me…and *to* me.

And that's another thing I love about her.

When Frankenstein created me, he didn't make me model-thin or muscular like the other guys. My body isn't a work of chiseled art. But Violet has never once stared at me as if I'm less than. She never once commented on my weight or appearance. No, she sees me for who I am and doesn't fault me for my flaws.

She finds me handsome.

Sexy, even.

I'm not sure anyone ever has before.

The grin she throws me now disarms me in a way that shouldn't be allowed. I desperately want to meld my lips to hers, to lose myself in the presence that is Violet Dracula.

But I can't.

Not with that fucker looking on, a lewd grin distorting his face.

"I'm happy you're safe," I tell Violet sincerely, reaching up to grab her hands and giving them a squeeze as I detangle them from my neck.

She allows me to with a soft exhale.

"I'm happy I'm safe too. Though…economy class all the way across the world? Not fun. Longest ten hours of my life." She cracks her back for emphasis. "But we all made it here safely. Me. Vin. Mason. Alex. Vanessa."

Vanessa?

"Dracula." She pauses then, and I can't help but pick up on the one name she didn't say.

"Dimitri?"

A shadow crosses over her expression even as she shakes her head minutely. "No. There's... There's a lot I need to tell you. A lot we discovered."

The vacant look in her eyes tells me all I need to know, and my brain immediately conjures up a dozen different things I can do to make her smile again. To put that familiar, blinding spark back in her eyes.

"I might have a way to remove Balor from Hux and Jack's body," I blurt out, unable to see that frown on her face a second longer.

Immediately, a brilliant smile curls up her lips, and that fire I've come to love so much flares to life in her gemstone eyes. "Really?"

"Don't sound so excited, love," Balor drawls.

"Eat shit, dickhead," she parries back, all without taking her attention off of me.

How the fuck does she do that?

How can she make me feel like the only man in the world, even when I know she's in love with multiple others?

"I...I still need to work out some kinks..." I hesitantly bring my hand up to ruffle my dark-brown hair. I don't want to give her false hope, but if my theory's correct, if I can separate Balor's soul from Jack's and Hux's...

"Don't doubt yourself, my love." Violet places her tiny palm on my cheek and cups my face, forcing me to stare into her cerulean eyes.

My heart skips a beat at the term of endearment, something that seems to be a new constant for me. The damn artificial organ remained still for who knows how many years, but now, it beats like I just ran one hundred miles in the sweltering summer sun.

"If anyone can do this, it's you."

"Your faith in him astonishes me," Balor lazily says, though I can hear a tightness in his voice that wasn't there before.

I wouldn't have been able to detect such a change in inflection before Violet, but I swear her presence is... changing me. Maybe not completely, but enough to make it noticeable.

Balor's smile is reminiscent of a shark as he grins up at us. "Are you sure you want to get rid of me, Violet Dracula? After all, I have a feeling you're going to need my help if you intend to win this war."

# CHAPTER 21

BARRET

I once heard the saying "I'm on pins and needles," and I never really understood it until now.

How can one *be* on pins and needles? Did someone accidentally knock over a container of sewing equipment? But why wouldn't you have stepped away as soon as you felt something pointy embed itself in the sole of your foot?

Now…

Now, I understand that saying. My skin feels…prickly, as if it's been stabbed a thousand times by those tiny little swords you often get with cocktails. I scratch absently at my bicep and then the back of my neck and then my upper chest, where the material of my button-up shirt clings to my skin. Why do I feel so itchy?

Do I need medical attention? An ointment?

"Relax, my friend." Cal materializes in the doorway of the room that once served as Alex's prison but now is simply an empty bedroom. His pink hair looks particularly tousled today, as if he hadn't found the time to style it the way he normally does, and his lips are pursed. Purple and black shadows mar the tan skin beneath both of his eyes, hinting at how little sleep he's gotten since Violet first disappeared with Dimitri Gray.

And then Mason got that damn phone call, Violet sounded frantic, even with her voice tinny and her words indecipherable, and Mason and Vin stormed away to play heroes.

Cal and I were left behind...again.

Why do I feel like I'm always on the outside looking in? That my face is pressed to the glass pane of a window and I'm watching Violet and her lovers like some creepy stalker and interloper? At least Cal has something with Violet that I don't—a mating bond. He stayed behind because he's one of the fiercest monsters, much better at keeping Lucifer and Balor contained than a simple hunter like Vin or a gorgon like Mason.

And me? I wasn't even offered a chance to go, a chance to ride in on a white horse and save Violet.

Though how I'll navigate a huge stallion through the maze of the hospital remains a mystery, but for Violet, I'll manage.

"I am relaxed," I huff out, my hands curling into fists by my sides.

My power brews just beneath the surface of my skin, this tangible, alive force that blows my green hair with an invisible breeze. Even Cal isn't entirely unaffected. His majestic, red and black wings begin to ruffle, as do the strands of his pink hair.

"You're nervous to see Violet, aren't you?" Cal's persistent voice has my stomach muscles tensing and then knotting into a tight ball.

I freeze like a deer in headlights but don't comment.

Maybe if I remain very, very still, he'll forget that I'm

here. I mean, I'm not exactly inconspicuous, standing at over six foot seven with muscles upon muscles. But maybe if I duck just a little bit…

"You want to know for sure that she's all right, but you don't feel as if it's your place," Cal continues.

"Are you reading my thoughts?" I blurt out, panic crashing through me in a tidal wave of feeling.

It breaks my vision into jagged, white lines. I've known the man for a long, long time, since we were first put into detention together, but I still don't know the extent of his powers. He's a cupid…but he's also a dark fae and an incubus. I know a few facts about him—like the smug bastard has no refractory period—but skills like mind reading? Fuck, that could explain how he knows exactly how to move his mouth over my cock to make me see stars.

"I don't read minds, Barret." Cal rolls his pretty eyes as he ruffles his wings. And then, because he just can't seem to help himself, he adds, "But my powers are pretty damn awesome, even without the mind reading."

"Yes…very awesome," I agree, knowing my only option in this situation is to placate my dear friend. He gets…well… He gets his feathers ruffled if he's not the most perfect specimen to walk this Earth. And I mean that literally.

At least, he used to think that until he met Violet. Now, I'm pretty sure even he can admit that she's the most perfect specimen to walk this Earth. A crazy, semi-unhinged, clumsy, beautiful, perfect creature.

Oh fuck.

I blink the cobwebs out of my eyes as I attempt to think about anyone or anything but Violet Dracula. Because I can't allow myself to care about her like that, like she's my lover as well.

I try to focus on Cal, on his glimmery white teeth shining in his golden skin and the way his skin usually feels as it glides against mine, before panic shoots off in my chest like a firework.

I can't think about Cal like that, either. He's Violet's, not mine.

Never mine.

"Stop overthinking things, Barret." In five quick strides, Cal's across the room and standing directly in front of me.

When I saw him with Violet, he had to stare down at her in order to press his lips against hers. But with me? His neck cranes to stare into my green orbs. His own are so blue, they remind me of two tranquil pools of water, devoid of any moss or dirt. Beautiful. Just like him.

"You're allowed to care about her the way you do. You're allowed to care about me the way you do. Don't you see? Don't you understand yet?"

Slowly, giving me the chance to pull away, he reaches up to grab at my neck and pull my lips down to his. With Violet, I imagine he'll tug on her long blonde strands, but with me, there's not a lot of hair to hold on to, minus the longer strands directly on the top of my head.

Fuck. Why does everything have to remind me of her? The woman I can never have?

When Cal's lips gently glide against mine, I know I should push him away, should put a stop to this, but I'm weak. Fuck, I'm so weak. I just want someone to care about me and love me, the way that Violet cares about and loves all her mates.

Everyone but me.

"Cal," I practically whimper against his lips as he grins widely.

"You think Violet would be upset by this, don't you?" His voice is a hushed murmur as he pulls away, our lips remaining connected by a strand of saliva.

My cock strains against my blue jeans, but I shove the reaction down. Lock it away. Beat it until it's black and blue.

Cal isn't mine.

*Violet* isn't mine.

The last revelation chokes me up, makes my insides feel as if they're made of a thousand tiny, keen knives and each one is slicing at something vital.

"How often do you think about kissing her, Bare?" Cal brings his lips to mine, and I'm helpless to resist as he kisses me once. Twice. Three times. On the fourth, his tongue traces the sensitive seam until I'm forced to open for him. His smooth skin is a startling contrast to the stubble on my chin, and I wonder if it itches when I rub against him.

"You're not mine anymore, Cal," I murmur, our lips still pressed together.

"Are you upset about that, my dear friend? Or are you upset that you're not *hers*?" His tongue parries with my own, making words impossible.

Thank fuck.

I don't necessarily know how to confess to my best friend that I'm in love with his mate.

That I want to be hers, just as I want her to be mine.

I'm not selfish. I don't want to covet her as my own. I'm fine with sharing her affections, her love. And Violet? She has a lot of love to give.

Cal once again pulls away, his teeth biting down on his plush lower lip as his eyes spark with mischief.

"What do you think her kiss tastes like? Her lips?" he asks me, his tone almost conversational.

"I don't know," I blurt instinctively. "I haven't had the chance to kiss her yet."

"But you want to," he points out, and twin flames lick my cheeks.

I desperately want to duck my head and hide from his probing, all-seeing gaze.

"She's not mine. Neither of you are." And the thought fills

me with such sadness that I feel as if I'm drowning beneath layers upon layers of sludge-like cement. Any second now, it's going to harden, leaving me trapped in a prison of my own making forever.

"You don't see what I see. Feel what I feel. I'm part incubus, remember?" Cal's cryptic words make my head reel, but that's nothing compared to the sensation that shoots through me like a lightning bolt when his deft, sure fingers begin to unbutton my shirt. The tips of his fingers graze my chest with each button he undoes.

I place my hands on his wrists to stop him. "I don't want you to cheat on your mate with me."

Just the thought of hurting Violet twists raw, self-directed anger through my insides. I'd rather stab myself with a knife than hurt a hair on her head.

Though hair can't actually *be* hurt…

At least, I don't think so.

Perhaps it's different for females.

Cal pulls away from me suddenly, and his eyes flash with pure fire. "Don't you ever suggest that I'll cheat on my mate," he growls vehemently. "Violet loves us both and already said—"

"She loves *you*." No one can miss the bitterness in my voice. "She… What's the opposite of love?"

"Hate?" Cal quirks a pink brow.

"I don't think she hates me…" Oh Zeus. What if she does?

"Of course she doesn't hate you!" Cal throws his hands up into the air in exasperation. "Neither of us hates you."

"But—"

Cal cuts off my words with another kiss that claims a tiny piece of my soul. Just a piece. The rest of it belongs firmly to a blonde-haired vampire-not-vampire who consumes my every waking thought. And dreaming dream. And waking dream? And dreaming wake thought? Is that a thing?

Fortunately, I'm saved from my own mental turmoil by Cal shoving my shirt off my shoulders.

Wait…when did he get the buttons undone?

I don't have time to think too hard on that, though, because Cal reaches over his shoulder, grabs a fistful of his own T-shirt, and tugs it over. It's a little difficult with his red and black wings, but Cal has had a lot of practice over the years. Usually with me.

I want to run my fingers over the membranes, the soft red feathers, the dark black ones…but it's not my place to touch him. Not like that. Not anymore.

Cal places his hands on my stomach and very gently pushes me onto the bed. He's usually so demanding in the bedroom that this…softness he's displaying takes me by surprise.

"I don't think you understand what's happening here, what's happening between the three of us," he whispers, and I know by "three of us," he means me, him, and Violet. Because for years, it's been only us two, and in a span of days, it became the three of us.

Cal and Violet.

And…me.

So is it the two of *them* now? It can't be the three of us. It can't. That's one fantasy I refuse to even indulge myself in.

"Stop thinking," Cal rumbles out. He rubs his palm down my chest, stopping it directly over the bulge in my jeans. "This erection… How'd you get it?"

"What?" Can you blame me if my voice rises in pitch?

"I know it's not just because of me," Cal continues as he crawls onto me and places one knee between my thighs and the other on the outside. "Who do you think about when you touch yourself? Whose face do you envision? Be honest."

The last words are a guttural growl that twitches my dick in my pants, demanding release.

I want to say him. After all, he's the one kissing me and touching me and making my insides turn to mush. But that's not the truth.

At least, not the whole truth.

"You, sometimes," I confess.

"But...?" He quirks an eyebrow, and another one of those irritating blushes heats my cheeks.

I was once told that my blushes came from a fire being lit beneath my skin. For years, whenever I flushed or felt heated, I would pour ice-cold water on my head in fear of starting myself on fire and being eaten alive from the flames.

Obviously, I know that's not true...*now*...but I suddenly wish I had a bucket of water somewhere. I need something, anything, to quell this gnawing, incessant heat within me.

"Violet." The confession hurts my throat coming out, like raw, gritty pieces of sand. "I think about Violet, okay? She consumes my thoughts."

I expect Cal to be furious with me. To hate me.

But his grin only widens like the cat that ate the canary.

"She's my world, Barret...but I think she's yours as well." His earnest, warm eyes ensnare my own, and I'm stunned once again by how handsome he is.

How beautiful. With his pink hair tousled, his red wings ruffling behind him, and his tan skin flushed, he looks like a work of art, an angelic portrait you would see in a mosaic.

"I...I..." Words evade me, as they often do.

"Imagine if she were here with us right now." Cal leans down to press an open-mouthed kiss on one of my lower abs. "What would she be doing?" He kisses another ab as I suck in a breath.

And...I can see the vision he's painting. It's so vivid and wonderful that I want to grab it and never let it go. I can't remember the last time my dick was so hard before.

"She would be here with us," I whisper as Cal continues

kissing up and down my stomach, the silence following my words punctuated by his lips on my skin.

"Doing what?" Cal demands, his tongue tracing the ridge of one ab.

"We would be worshiping her perfect body." I can't stop myself from speaking, from regaling him with tales of my deepest, darkest fantasy. "The way you're doing to me."

"What part of her body would you want to kiss first?" Cal keeps his voice light and airy as he rests his chin on my stomach, waiting for instruction.

My heart pounds.

"Her nipple," I decide on at last. "We would each take a nipple in our mouths."

"Good choice." Cal nods seriously as he presses a chaste kiss to first one of my nipples and then the other. He runs his tongue around one of the sensitive nubs, causing it to bead painfully, before lowering his lips back to my stomach and peppering kisses across my abs again. "What next?"

"Her stomach." I'm panting now, the thought of touching Violet like that almost too much for me to resist.

What would she look like as I kissed down her stomach? Would her eyes remain open or squeeze shut? Would she murmur my name or scream it? Would she beg me to go faster or slow down?

"You're so hard, Barret. You're so hard for our girl." Cal grabs my cock through the denim and gives it a squeeze. "Imagine it's her hand touching you. Her lips on your skin. Can you do that?"

I want to protest, want to remind him that she's his mate and not mine, but my body betrays me, as it always does when Cal gives me a command. My eyelashes flutter shut, and Cal rewards me by giving me a heated kiss on the lips.

"Good boy," he purrs as his fingers scrape against my hard nipples.

Only…it's not just him anymore. At least, not in the vision my brain conjures up for me.

Violet sits on my stomach, her bare breasts glistening in the stripes of moonlight streaking in through the curtains. Her hands pluck her tiny pink nipples as she bends down and begins to trail her lips down my neck.

Cal sits behind her, straddling my thighs, and runs his hand down the curve of her spine. She arches beautifully against his touch, bringing her nipple close to my mouth. I bite down instinctively, and a masculine gasp reaches my ears.

I don't dare open my eyes, though, too lost in the fantasy even though I know it's not Violet's nipple I'm sucking on. It's Cal's.

Violet tilts her head to kiss Cal over her shoulder, and my dick swells at seeing two of my favorite people share such a passionate moment.

I want to be a part of it too.

No, I *need* to be a part of it.

Violet breaks the kiss with Cal to flutter her lashes coyly at me. And then she's leaning down and kissing me while Cal brushes his lips over her shoulder. When Violet moves away, Cal's there, his lips hungry and possessive. The two of us grab Violet's golden head and drag her down until we're exchanging sloppy, messy, sinful three-way kisses. I don't even know whose lips I'm touching anymore.

The fantasy pops like a bubble when I feel my jeans and boxers being pulled down my ass, my huge cock springing free.

Cal grins where he now rests on his knees by the bed, my legs on either side of his tan body and my cock in the air before him.

There's no preamble or foreplay as he leans forward, hollows his cheeks, and takes me all the way into his mouth.

His head bobs as he takes my dick as far into his throat as he can—which is pretty damn far. I'm pretty sure the cupid doesn't have a gag reflex.

All I can hear is the slurping and sucking noises he makes as he takes me to the brink with his skilled mouth.

What would Violet say if she were watching this?

Once again, my brain plays tricks on me and conjures up an image of Violet kneeling above my head, her pink pussy lips glistening with her arousal. I grab her hips, tug her greedy cunt down to my mouth, and devour her pussy like a man possessed.

Cal releases my cock with a slurp but uses his own saliva as lubricant as he strokes me. The fantasy of Violet once again dissipates like a cloud of smoke, leaving me hard and wanting.

"What are you thinking about, my friend?" He shifts his fist so it's doing a corkscrew motion around my dick, and my hips jump upwards instinctively, chasing the pleasure.

"You, sucking my dick," I breathe as he continues to stroke me. "And me, eating Violet's pussy."

His grin widens as he leans forward and licks up the side of my shaft. "What do you think it tastes like?" he demands before he swallows the head into his mouth.

I place one huge, dark arm over my eyes as a groan lodges itself in my throat. "Fuck, I have no idea, but I want to know, Cal. I want to know what her cunt tastes like. Have you tried it yet?"

Cal releases me again and allows his hand to take up the job his mouth was just doing.

"I haven't yet, but you're right. We need to change that, pronto." His eyes glimmer. "If you suck her pussy, then I'll need to kiss you afterwards to taste her on your lips. I don't think there'll be anything sweeter."

My heart stutters. "I want to taste you after you come inside of her. I want to taste your cum mixing with hers."

Cal's eyes shine with a fierce possessiveness and yearning that makes me think I crossed some invisible barrier. Some unseen line.

What the fuck did I just do?

"Did you know that the dark fae inside of me wants to shove my cum back into her tight little pussy?" His voice is a rasp of air as his fist continues to work my shaft. "That I want to push it up her creamy white thighs and back into her cunt? There's something so sexy about knowing my cum is inside of her, you know? But can you imagine if it's *our* cum inside of her?" His eyes turn glazed, wistful, and the monster inside of me gives a roar at the image he's just painted.

I want that.

More than anything.

Suddenly, I can't take this anymore. As Cal continues to lick my dick from base to tip, I feel my tenuous control snap in half.

I need to touch someone. Need to bring them to ruin.

I'm off the bed before Cal can even blink. He stands, frowning, but I simply move to my knees in front of him and place my hands on his tight ass. He must've lost his jeans and boxers at some point because he's as naked as I am, his hard cock erect and waiting for my mouth.

We've been in this position before, Cal and I. Thousands and thousands of times.

But this feels…different. Maybe it's because we're both imagining a certain blonde-haired woman to be here with us.

I take Cal in my mouth as he puts one hand on my broad shoulder, holding me steady.

"Oh…fuck," he moans, his fingers digging into my skin.

I don't have the same gag reflex as him, but I do know

how to suck dick like a champ. I've had hundreds of years of practice.

I move my head up and down his length as he murmurs encouragement, his hand inching up my shoulder and fisting in my short green hair.

I allow one of my hands to travel up his toned, tan stomach, caressing his skin.

"Oh, yeah. Fuck, Barret. Fuck. Your lips around my dick is one of my favorite things," he praises.

I pull away from his cock with a smirk. "But I'm guessing Violet's pussy is your absolute favorite?"

He growls sharply, his eyes flashing black before he regains control of his dark self. "Fuck...yes. You need to try it, friend. You need to—"

I cut him off by lowering my head to suckle on his balls. I use one hand to hold them away from his body to allow me better access while my other hand continues to stroke his dick.

I don't want him to talk about Violet, not when I know I'll never have her for myself. Even this moment with Cal is fleeting, something I'm sure he'll regret later.

Yet I can't bring myself to stop.

I suck his balls into my mouth as my hand continues to work his length. He's not as thick as me, but he's longer—he really does have the perfect cock.

"I want to fuck you." Cal grabs my shoulders and pulls me up. I'm significantly bigger than him, but I allow him to drag me back to the bed and shove me onto my back. "I want to fuck your ass while you fuck Violet. I want to set the pace as we all fall apart together."

"That won't ever happen," I tell him as he grabs my huge thighs and hoists them over his arms.

Most men wouldn't be able to do that, not when I'm twice the size of the average male, but Cal... Cal is the exception.

"Won't it?" Cal's voice takes on a distinct teasing lilt as he uses his own saliva to lubricate me with his finger.

He pushes inside the rosette of my asshole as I hold perfectly still, struggling to adjust to his invasion. And that's just his damn finger.

I know his cock will fit—it has before—but I feel unusually tense today.

"Why don't you come in and enjoy the show, my love?" Cal calls out cheekily, and at first, I think he's talking to me.

But then I see that he's staring at someone to the right of us, and my breath catches.

Violet stands in the doorway, her mouth parted in shock as she watches her mate add another finger to my asshole.

"Oh, fuck!" I'm not sure if the curse is because of the additional finger…or because Violet Dracula is watching me. Watching us.

My cock twitches in a way that clearly seems to be saying, "Come join us!" If cocks can talk, of course. Mine can't.

"Look at how big his cock is, Vi," Cal continues as the tip of his cock touches my opening.

My cheeks flame yet again, and I half want to stab him… and half want him to continue, especially when Violet's gaze drops to my twitching dick.

Fear strangles me. Holds my airways hostage.

Is that disgust on her face at seeing me with her mate?

Hatred?

Anger?

*Please no. Please no. Please no.*

She takes a step into the room, her chest heaving, her eyes hooded with that indecipherable emotion, her gaze fixated on my cock…

But then the room erupts in chaos as the perimeter alarm Dimitri set up around the safe house begins to beep erratically.

# CHAPTER 22

Holy cheeseballs.

I did not know what I expected when I snuck into the spare bedroom to greet Cal and Barret…but it definitely wasn't this.

My mouth turns dry, and I swear all the water that once lived there now resides in my poor, weeping vagina. That thirsty ho just got double the dick only last night, but she's already craving more.

She's craving them.

Her mates.

*My* mates.

I swallow as my eyes take in Barret's strong, muscular body spread out on the bed, his thighs over Cal's forearms and his huge cock resting against his stomach.

Logically, I know that larger guys have larger dicks, but holy fucking dildo balls. That thing looks liable to rip me in half. I swear it'll enter my pussy and then immediately pop out of my mouth like I'm fucking him and giving him a blowjob at the same time.

I've never seen Barret naked before, and I know I should announce my presence or look away, but my eyes can't stop themselves from greedily lapping up every inch of exposed skin on display. He's so massive, he makes me look like a delicate flower in comparison. His broad shoulders surround an even broader chest of dark, smooth skin. His nipples are darker than Cal's light-pink buds, almost black, and I watch, hypnotized, as Barret begins to pluck at his own nipples almost absently. I'm not even sure he knows what he's doing.

My gaze continues to drag down his muscled stomach—is it possible for a man to have a twelve pack? Or does that only work for a pack of beers?—and then to that massive python resting above his belly button. A bead of precum rests on the tip, just begging for attention from my mouth.

And then there's Cal, my perfect cupid, my dark angel, with his tousled pink hair, sweat-soaked skin, and straining, hard cock lined up with Barret's asshole.

Oh fuck.

Oh fuck. Fuck. Fuck.

I want to watch Cal pound into him, watch Barret's cock bounce against his chest as his eyes flutter shut with plea-sure. And then I want to…I don't even know. Sit on Barret's face? Wrap my lips around the head of his dick?

Fuck Cal from behind with a strap-on?

My panties grow damp as I stare at the two gorgeous men, and I know, with unwavering certainty, that they both belong to me. They're mine.

Cal, the flirty, posh, arrogant cupid.

Barret, the kind, innocent, protective boogeyman.

They belong to me, and I belong to them.

That clarity hits me like…well…like a dick slapped across

my face. I've just been dick-slapped by the enormity of my feelings for these men. Cal, I already knew. But Barret?

I can't look away, and a tiny voice inside of my heart calls out to him, pleading with him to twist his head and look at me. Will he invite me to join them? Will he ask me to leave? The thought of being turned away has my heart hammering against my chest like sheets of rain crashing against the window. I want to be between the two of them, now and forever.

I want to feel their large, powerful bodies come apart for me, and me for them.

"Why don't you come in and enjoy the show, my love?" Cal's voice snaps me out of my reverie like a bucket of ice-cold water being poured over my head.

I know that saying is a goddamn cliché, but it's the truth. Being caught perving on my mate and his lover dampens my lust and makes me feel like a piece of shit.

But then his words register.

He wants me...to come in?

Is this the invitation I've been not-so-secretly waiting for?

My mouth pops open, lust surging through my veins, as Cal adds another finger to Barret's tight asshole, playing with the puckered hole.

"Oh, fuck!" Barret curses, twisting his head to the side to stare at me.

And then he just...stares. That dark, obsidian gaze of his doesn't turn away, even as his cock begins to twitch on his stomach.

What is he thinking? Does he want me to join in? To leave?

"Look at how big his cock is, Vi." Cal's dirty words make my knees go weak.

And when the head of his cock touches the rosette of Barret's ass?

I'm only one girl, people.

And a very weak one, at that.

I take a step closer, my hands sweating and heart racing. I can't pull my gaze away from Barret's cock. Would he want me to…touch it? Would he be angry if I did?

Why isn't there a manual for *How to Touch Your Mate's Lover's Dick, Who You May Have Feelings for as Well*? The man, I mean. Not the dick. Though…it's a pretty nice one, if I'm being completely honest.

My feet are whispers on the soft carpeting, barely audible, as I take another step closer. Do I look like a hungry whore? Probably. Do I have any shame? Nope.

Noise explodes from every direction, this repetitive beeping sound that has my hands coming upwards instinctively to cover my ears.

Cal and Barret are off the bed in a flash, as if they hadn't been mere seconds away from fucking. Their cocks still strain in a way that's probably painful, but that doesn't seem to bother them as they gather around me in a protective formation.

"What the fuck is that?" I demand, trying to make my voice audible over the blare of the siren.

"Someone tripped the protective wards around the house," Cal explains in a growl, reaching down to grab a pair of pants and tossing another pair to Barret.

"What?" My voice squeaks in a way that would embarrass me…if I wasn't freaking right the fuck out.

My lust cools instantly, almost as if it never existed to begin with, as I race out of the room with Cal and Barret on either side of me. I need to see my mates, to ensure with my own two eyes that they're alive and well.

The first thing I see is Vin's broad back as I stagger into the living room. Before I can take a step around him, though, he grabs my arm and tugs me right the fuck back until I'm sandwiched between Cal and Barret once more. Just a minute ago, I would've loved to be sandwiched between the two men, but now?

I attempt to see over Vin's broad shoulders, but he purposely moves with me, as if he can sense what I'm doing even with his back turned.

"I need to see my daughter!" a voice bellows. A feminine, familiar voice.

My theory of this intruder's identity is only confirmed when Vin's brutally shoved aside with a blast of power and a familiar goddess stares down at me.

"Hera?" I whisper, my throat feeling tight with some unnamed emotion.

How the fuck is she here? How did she find us?

Like the last time I saw her, she looks as if she just plopped out of a stained-glass window you would find hanging in a church. Yeah, we look kind of similar, but while she has a grace and elegance I couldn't even begin to emulate, I look like I fell out of the same stained-glass window thousands of feet in the air, tumbled down a steep ravine, and then landed in a mud puddle at the bottom of the hill. And then, to add to my misery, a bird took a shit on me.

The two of us? We may look alike, but we're most definitely *not* the same.

Golden curls cascade around a face that I imagine inspired numerous pieces of art over the years. Yeah, it's that pretty. Bitch. Her blue eyes are the exact same shade as my own, but they look somehow…better on her. I know, I know, I know. Way to be self-deprecating, huh? But it's the truth. Those perfect, oval orbs are framed by lashes so long and dark, they can't possibly be real.

Unlike the last time I saw her, however, she isn't wearing a shapeless white dress that seems befitting of a goddess in Olympus. Today, she's wearing a floral sundress with a low neckline, thin straps, and a slit up the thigh. It's modern, adorable, and instantly makes me jealous.

*This* is the person who tried to kill her newborn baby? This five-foot-nothing slip of a woman?

Lucifer…yeah, I could totally see him being a mass murderer into infanticide.

But her?

I tilt my head to the side as I study her petite frame.

Nope. Don't see it. She looks as if she's the type of woman to capture flies and let them roam free outside. Hell, she probably even gives them a tiny, fly-sized bag of money and a fly-sized home for them to live in until they can get their lives in order.

But as I watch, riveted, her pink lips curl into a horrible sneer that distorts her entire face. At first, I think she's directing all of that ire and vitriol at me, but then I realize it's aimed at the two men on either side of me.

Barret has grown to nearly twice the size of his human form, his head scraping against the wooden beams of the ceiling. He roars, and the noise has every hair on my body standing at attention. And yeah, maybe my pussy gets a little excited too. Just a little.

Sue me.

"Unhand my daughter!" Hera roars.

Suddenly, she doesn't look so sweet and innocent anymore. She reminds me of a tiger that isn't just out for the hunt, but for the kill. She's liable to maim, slice, and dice everyone she comes into contact with like some sort of… kitchen knife. Yeah. She's a goddamn kitchen knife.

"What the fuck are you doing here, Kitchen Knife?" I growl …and even I can admit that nickname sounded way better in my head. Perhaps I could call her KK? Nope. Not even going there.

Hera it is, I suppose.

"Violet." All at once, the rage dissipates from Hera's eyes, and her blue orbs begin to glimmer with glossy, unshed tears. "You're okay. I was so worried."

"The fuck you going on about?" I glance around at my mates for help.

Mason and Frankie are directly behind Hera, the former holding a—snort—kitchen knife in front of him as if he plans to stab her bumhole when she's not looking. The latter fingers a vial that he's tucked into his shirt on a silver string. Knowing Frankie the way I do, it's a poison of some sort. Maybe even a type of acid. Fuck only knows with my scientist.

Vin groggily lifts his head up from where he's still sprawled on the ground, a low groan tearing from his lips, as he focuses on my bio mom. He tenses, looking as if he's seconds away from jumping to his feet and attacking her if she tries something, but he never gets the chance.

Because in the next second, a cloud of smoke appears directly in front of me and then reforms into the solid shape of a man.

A very familiar man.

I suppose it's just a regular, old family reunion, huh?

"Lucifer," Hera hisses, crouching down with her arms raised as if she's about to start throwing down.

The visual… Yeah, it almost makes me start to laugh. It really, really shouldn't be funny, but my twisted brain doesn't see it like that. Hera is barely five foot and, as I said before, almost delicate in appearance.

Lucifer, on the other hand, towers over us all at six foot five and is a beast of rippling muscle and power.

Did I mention that he's also the literal devil? There's that too.

"I won't allow you to harm my daughter," Hera growls, her eyes flashing with an almost incandescent rage.

"You lost the right to call her your daughter the second you tried to have her murdered as a baby," Lucifer snaps.

Hera laughs haughtily, the noise eerily resembling twinkling bells. I hate that it's so pretty. Shouldn't villains have…I don't know…evil laughs?

"Is that what you've been telling her?" She curls her tiny, dainty hands into fists. "Have you been filling her head with such lies?"

Lucifer growls fiercely, and I swear I feel the noise rumbling through my bones. I lean against Barret instinctively, seeking comfort from the massive monster, and one of his huge arms settles protectively around my shoulders, pulling me against him.

"She's my daughter!" Lucifer roars.

"She's *mine*," Hera retorts viciously.

"No…" Dracula enters the room with a lazy, sardonic smirk tugging up his lips. Despite his nonchalant façade, I can see the barely contained violence shimmering just beneath the surface, demanding an outlet like lava that has been compressed for too long and is ready to burst. "Technically, she's *mine*. I have the adoption papers to prove it."

"Is this the part where they each grab one of my limbs and tug me in every direction until I break into tiny, Violet-sized pieces?" I whisper conspiratorially to Barret, and his eyes widen with horror.

"That would never happen, Violet," he assures me, and a warm swell of heat fills my belly. But then he continues. "There's only three of them, yet you have four limbs. Two arms. Two legs. You would need a fourth parent to materialize out of the woodwork to really pull you apart." He gives me a commiserating pat on the shoulder even as my mouth pops open.

Cal, despite never taking his attention off the Texas

standoff directly in front of us, rolls his pretty eyes. "That's not what she meant, Bare."

"Huh?" The huge man's brows furrow, but he's saved from responding by Lucifer chuckling darkly.

"Dracula. I didn't know beetles could get into the house."

His insult slides right off Dracula's shoulders. To be fair, it's not a very good one. Lucifer really needs to work on his trash talk.

"And I didn't know you could escape the god-blessed chains *my* daughter tied you up in." No one with ears can miss the emphasis Dracula places on "my," and Lucifer bristles.

"I could've left whenever I wanted to," he growls. "Did you really think mere chains could hold a god like me?"

"Demon, technically," I mumble under my breath, but they all ignore me.

I half expect them to whip out tiny guns and aim them at each other's chests. I suppose that would take care of all my problems, having them dead. Not that I want Dracula dead, of course.

Or the birth parent who *didn't* try to kill me.

The question is…which one is telling the truth? Hera, with her elfin face and soft voice, or Lucifer, with his domineering personality and murderous tendencies. The logical answer would be that Hera's telling the truth, but I've read enough mystery thrillers in my life to know that the person you least expect is usually the innocent one. So does that mean Lucifer's telling the truth?

Fuck.

I never get to see if three of the scariest monsters in existence have tiny little handguns they use to shoot at each other. Nope. Their standoff is interrupted by the siren blaring yet again and the door to the cabin pushing open, careening off the wooden wall with a heavy bang.

"Holy shit!" I scream as a bloody hand drags itself down the wood, leaving behind a trail of red liquid.

Dimitri's ice-blue eyes lock with mine through the myriad of bruises discoloring his face…

Before he promptly tilts to the side and passes out.

# CHAPTER 23

VIOLET

"Dimitri!" I scream, skirting around Lucifer and Hera until I'm able to kneel beside the fallen headmaster.

An uncomfortable silence settles behind me, but I don't pull my attention off of Dimitri's pasty, mutilated face to see what has happened now.

"Can you assholes put your dicks away and come help me?" I grit out, my hands hovering over his muscular body but not daring to touch any skin.

Yeah, I just told my two dads and mom to put their penises away, but worry for Dimitri supersedes all logic. I don't even care that my back is to the enemies, that any one of them could stab me and I'd be none the wiser. My focus is firmly on Dimitri. *Only* Dimitri.

*Fuck, I'm a goner for this man.*

*Fuck him.*

Ugh. Why did he have to go and make me care for him?

"Don't move a goddamn inch," Vin snarls from over my shoulder.

I don't bother to turn around, though. I trust him and my other mates to watch my back while I'm watching and protecting Dimitri's.

A second later, Cal and Barret kneel on either side of me, their faces creased with concern.

"What do you think happened to him? Is he going to be okay?" I attempt to smooth a strand of wayward white hair that has fallen forward to obscure Dimitri's closed eyelids.

He'd probably shit a brick at the thought of so many people seeing him disheveled. Dimitri Gray always has to be meticulously groomed, not a hair out of place or a wrinkle on his suit jacket. He would burst an ulcer at his current state.

"We'll bring him to the spare bedroom." Frankie moves to stand above me, one of his hands coming down to rest on my shoulder and give it a squeeze.

Barret and Cal drag Dimitri up, one of his arms slung over each of their shoulders, and then walk him down the hallway. Dimitri's bare feet drag against the wooden floors, leaving a trail of blood in their wake.

He's naked, another vulnerability I'm sure he'll despise if he were conscious, but I don't allow my eyes to wander over his smooth expanse of pale, bloody skin. Not now. Not when he's not awake to sneer at me or seduce me or do one of the thousand things Dimitri likes to do to fuck with my head.

"What the fuck are we gonna do about them?" Vin murmurs to Mason and Dracula.

"Don't worry, young Van Helsing." Lucifer's voice is as haughty as his appearance, though I can't see his face right now. My guess? It's twisted in his customary scowl that reminds me of a zebra giving birth. Not that I've ever seen a zebra give birth before… "I'll keep Hera in line. No harm will come to my daughter."

Hera snarls viciously. "I won't allow you to harm another hair on Violet's head, Lucifer Morningstar."

"Ohh. I'm so scared," Lucifer deadpans. "Are you going to strangle me with your mane of golden hair?"

Kind of a weird taunt, but okay.

"Are you gonna poke my eye out with your long, hard cock?" Hera quips.

Um…nope.

Gonna pretend I didn't hear that one. I already want to vomit just staring at Dimitri's bruised and bloody face. I don't need my gag reflex triggered a second time.

But…

I think both of my birth parents need to work on their taunts and jabs. Seriously.

"Don't worry, my peeps." This, of course, comes from Dracula. Apparently, he's "hip and cool" Dad today. As I said before, he changes personalities like a whore changes panties. Sometimes, he goes completely commando in the personality department. I believe the humans refer to it as a psychopath. Or maybe a sociopath. It's definitely a "path"…but not one I want to travel. "I'll keep an eye on D-dog and H-homie."

"Oh, Dracula…" Hera blows out a breath, and I wonder how well those two really know each other. Obviously, Hera trusted Dracula enough to raise me as his own daughter. At least, that's what Dracula told me.

I'm beginning to wonder if that entire story has been fabricated somehow.

"You gonna fuck him too until he gives you another baby for you to kill?" Lucifer scoffs.

"Fuck you, Lucifer."

"You did that already."

I'm saved from hearing any more of their childish bickering—are these seriously two of the most feared monsters in the entire world?—by entering the spare bedroom and allowing the door to slam shut behind us.

The last time I was here...

Heat burns hot in both of my cheeks as I stare intently at the bed where Barret and Cal were only a few minutes earlier. But any lust dampens in a maelstrom of fear as the two men heave Dimitri's body onto the mattress.

The headmaster flops onto his back, his head lolling to the side, and I feel as if all of the oxygen in the room has been sucked away. I suddenly can't breathe, can't do anything but stare at the man I hate and love in equal measure.

"Is he going to be okay?" I once again ask. Well, more like demand. I don't think I'll accept "no" as an answer.

Frankie's already opening up a black leather suitcase stocked full of strange jars and vials. He grabs a few at random and begins to apply a colorful cream on the worst of Dimitri's wounds.

"He should be fine," Frankie assures me after a few tense moments of silence. He rubs a green salve into a wound on Dimitri's chest, and immediately, the skin begins to stitch back together again until only a dim and jagged scar remains —puckered pink flesh on a canvas of porcelain skin.

"Do we know what did this to him? *Who* did this to him?" Violence heats my stomach lining like acid. My control feels...tenuous. A swarm of moths pulling apart an old, ratty blanket, leaving it riddled with holes. Any second now, that blanket is going to fall apart completely in a heap of yarn and stitching.

Just like my damn control.

"I might be able to help with that." Barret hesitantly runs his fingers through the light-green hair on the top of his head. He's still shirtless, his rich ebony skin on display in the austere light flickering in through the window blinds. When he catches me staring at him, he blushes and ducks his head. "I can enter his dreams, the way I did to Mason when he was recovering from his addiction. The way I did to you."

"Yes!" I rush forward and grab his arm, giving it a squeeze. It's so large, my hand can't even fit halfway around his bicep. "Please, Barret. I need to know... I need to know who did this to him."

"And we need to know if the threat has been neutralized," Cal agrees. His strong arms wrap around my waist, and I find myself perched comfortably on his lap. His red and black wings fan around us, providing a barrier against the outside world. His breath tickles the hairs on the top of my head a moment before his lips descend and kiss my crown.

How is it that I can have two penises in my vagina and not get even a little bit embarrassed, yet I blush like a damn schoolgirl at a chaste, innocent kiss from my mate?

Ugh. Stupid hormones. Stupid feelings.

Barret's jaw hardens to granite as he flicks his gaze between me and a sleeping Dimitri. After a moment, he nods once and extends a hand.

"I'll bring you into the dreamscape and leave you two alone to talk for a little bit. But, Cheese Curd?" His earnest, chocolate eyes ensnare my own. "Be quick. If there is an attack coming this way, we can't afford to have you trapped in Dimitri's head."

"I will." I give his hand a reassuring squeeze before focusing on my lover's slack, sleeping face. "Let's do this shit."

Of course the pompous dickhead would dream about his office at Prodigium Academy. I don't believe he has an ounce of imagination in that thick head of his.

Barret clears his throat as he stands in the waiting room just outside the headmaster's office.

"I'll wait here," he tells me with that magnanimous smile of his.

Now that I've kind of decided I want him as mine, butterflies erupt in my stomach.

Fuck, who am I kidding? Those butterflies have always been there, demanding my attention, and I was just too dumb to see them.

Wait…not butterflies.

*Bats.*

Lots and lots of bats.

"I'll be quick," I reassure him as I take a deep, steadying breath and place my hand on the office doorknob. I really don't know what men like Dimitri Gray dream about when they've been beaten to a bloody pulp. Grading papers? Doing finances? Stupid, boring adult stuff?

So when I push open the doorway and step inside his plush, elegant office, I'm surprised as fuck to see Dimitri on his knees eating out a girl's pussy.

What the hell?

Jealousy roars within me, heavy and fierce, as the bimbo cries out his name in an annoyingly high-pitched voice. God, I hate that voice. It makes me want to rip her vocal cords out and feed them to a pack of angry hyenas.

The door slams shut behind me, the sound almost deafening, as I stalk forward and prepare to murder the bitch where she stands…errr…lies. But when I come around the table, I see my own face staring back at me.

My eyes are half slitted in pleasure as I pluck my own nipples and roll around on the desk. Tiny mewls escape my lips as Dimitri continues to feast on my—her—pussy.

Dimitri's dreaming of…me? Is he remembering the time he had me in this exact same position, feasting on my pussy like a man starved? Because I'd be the first to admit that your girl here has relived that moment more times than she cares to count. Me. I'm the girl.

Thirsty bitches say what?

*What?*

Ha.

Another moan escapes the Dream Violet, and I crinkle my nose instinctively.

I don't sound like that, do I?

Note to self—be absolutely silent during sex. The noises I'm making now are atrocious.

"You taste so damn good, Violet," Dimitri murmurs against my doppelganger's cunt as he continues to lick and suck at her. "Fucking hell."

And…

I'm jealous again. That tiny green ball of emotion I thought dissipated at the revelation the bimbo is actually a dream version of me returns with a vengeance. I know, logically, I have no reason to be jealous. Dimitri is licking *my* pussy, for fuck's sake, but emotions are a fickle thing.

And this insidious emotion? It wants me to kill the bitch for touching what doesn't belong to her.

Before I can rethink my decision—because, really, who has time for that? It's much more fun to be spontaneous—I'm across the room, grabbing Dream's Violet's neck, and giving it a twist. Immediately, those Zeus-awful moans cut off and her blue eyes glaze over in death.

Oh. That's a little demented, even for me.

I never really imagined what I'd look like dead, but I have to say…I'm a really pretty dead person. Honestly, I have a great pair of tits too. If I were into girls, I would soooo tap my own ass. Ten out of ten, would recommend.

Dimitri immediately pulls away from Dream Violet's pussy, jumps to his feet, and has a blade pressed to my throat all before I'm able to blink. His eyes are wild and frantic, and he seems to be struggling to orient himself as his gaze flicks from me to the dead bitch and then back to me.

"Violet?" Confusion laces his tone, but I have to give him some credit—he's not a dumb man. It only takes his brain a few seconds to piece everything together, and the hand holding the knife to my throat slowly lowers. "I take I made it back to the safe house and, consequently, to you and your boogeyman?"

Your boogeyman.

Chills. Literal chills.

*Focus, Violet,* I chastise myself as I blink up at him repeatedly.

"I didn't know you dream about me," I blurt oh-so-tactfully.

His hand twitches by his side, as if he's debating holding my neck hostage with his blade once more. Ha. Joke's on him. I actually like being at his mercy. I'm a kinky bitch like that.

Besides, he can pretend to hate me all he wants, but I quite literally walked in on him eating out a dream version of myself. So...fuck him.

"You killed your dreamself," Dimitri muses.

Zeus help me, I narrow my eyes. Just a little. "I didn't like seeing you with her," I huff out. This is *so* not the time to be having this conversation, but I can't seem to help myself.

Dimitri's white brow begins to twitch sporadically as he stares at me with that cool, impassive façade I've come to expect from him. I now see it for what it truly is— a mask. An impeccable mask with not a single crack distorting it, but a mask all the same.

"You didn't like seeing me...with yourself," he repeats blandly. And I swear, his eyes burn a little brighter, the core of a blistering hot flame capable of scalding my flesh from my body. The blue may look pretty and unassuming, but it's damn more painful than any normal fire. "You were jealous."

Why does he sound so pleased by that prospect? Why does the erection I already see straining his dress pants get slightly bigger?

"I don't get jealous," I counter…knowing full well I'm lying to him and myself. "I get anti-jealous, actually. Like, you can fuck Dream Violet as many times as you want. I don't care. Go for it." I fold my arms over my chest with a scowl, and his lips twitch.

"You're jealous," he repeats.

"Totally not." Even as I say that, I scowl at the little slut lying dead on the desk. Seriously. The desk. Talk about a cliché.

Dimitri even had Dream Violet wear a skimpy school skirt and white blouse. I'm beginning to believe my headmaster has a serious professor/student kink. Not that I'm complaining. I could totally get behind fucking Dimitri on the top of his desk while wearing a short skirt, knee-high socks, and a white blouse with buttons he can rip open caveman-style.

"Do you always have to have such a sassy mouth?" His hot breath fans across my earlobe, eliciting full-body shivers down my spine.

"I'm one hundred and thirty pounds on my best days," I quip. "Sarcasm and sass are my only two defenses."

"And what do you need to defend yourself from, Ms. Dracula?" His voice is a low, salacious purr…and most definitely not something I would hear if he were awake and conscious. No, this Dimitri is different from the headmaster I've come to depush. That's despise and crush on, if you must know.

Depush.

A Violet original word, thank you very much.

"What *don't* I need to defend myself from, Headmaster Gray?" I mimic his tone, keeping my voice low and husky, and those icy blue orbs of his flare with a contrasting heat that tickles my skin.

But whatever moment we may or may not have been having dissipates as Dimitri's eyes suddenly widen with panic. In the next instant, I'm against the wall, his hands on my shoulders as he peers intently at my face.

"Everything we thought we knew about what happened to you is a lie," he begins earnestly.

As if it has a mind of its own, my right hand reaches out to play with the loose strands of white hair that have fallen free of his trademark ponytail. It feels incredibly soft beneath my fingers, like the fur of a cat.

"What do you mean? What happened to you?" I ask.

His jaw tightens as a multitude of memories flicker behind his irises—memories I'm not sure he even realizes he's reliving. A muscle in his jaw twitches before he can regain control of himself, before he can place his mask back on and hide behind it.

I don't want him to hide from me, though.

Not ever.

Now isn't the time to get into that, however, as I await his response with bated breath.

"I was kidnapped and placed inside of a spelled torture room." Shadows swarm across his face, darkening his features, before he forces himself to continue. "I have similar ones located across the globe. They're designed to stop time."

"Oh..." My heart crawls up my throat and becomes lodged there when I realize what he means.

Dimitri may have only been gone a couple of days, but for him, it felt like... Who the fuck even knows how long?

Anger ripples through me like brutal, vicious waves cresting the shoreline. My hands curl into claws that dig into

Dimitri's shoulders. I want to ask him how long he was there, what he experienced, but the words get caught in my throat like soggy toilet paper.

"As you can probably imagine, I was tortured." Dimitri says those words without a hint of inflection, but I notice a lump traveling down his throat as he swallows. "They wanted to know about you, Violet. About your powers. About what you are and what you can do. I didn't say anything, of course."

"Of course." Funnily enough, the thought that he gave me up never even crossed my mind. I know, logically, that he could've saved himself from what sounds like a shit ton of torture, but he didn't. For me.

"There were three of them, all former students of mine. A sphynx, a minotaur, and an empusa—"

"Wait." My frown deepens. "Aren't empusas usually naked women who charm and seduce men?"

Yup. I officially want to murder that bitch. Even the thought of her placing a hand on my—I mean, on Dimitri Gray makes me see red. And the thought of Dimitri giving in to her charms? Of sleeping with her? Bile rushes up my throat.

Dimitri grimaces. "Nasty creatures, empusas. I watched her eat a man's head off with her vagina—"

"You were staring at her vagina?" I interrupt. "Was it… prettier than mine?"

What the fuck am I even asking?

Dimitri's grin turns carnal—definitely not an expression he would ever wear if he were awake. "It had teeth, Violet. Big, serrated, bloody teeth. So no, her vagina was not prettier than yours."

"Did she…?" I don't know how to phrase my next question, so I decide to just spit it out, to rip the metaphorical bandage off, so to speak. "I know you would never… I mean, did she…? Did she touch you without your permission?" I can't swallow. It feels as if there's a huge piece of concrete lodged in my throat. "Because if she did, I'd cut her in a thousand different places and—"

Dimitri's lips are on mine before I can finish my threat. This kiss…

I don't know how to describe it.

It feels like sunshine is being poured directly into my veins, this warm, brilliant ball of light that disperses all of the shadows inside of me. My heart feels seconds from bursting in my chest as I lean into his kiss and twine my arms around his neck, pulling him even closer to me. All too soon, Dimitri pulls away from me and rests his forehead against mine.

Why did I think his blue eyes were icy?

Just now, they're pure fire.

"She didn't touch me. Not like that," he murmurs. "None of them did. They just…hurt me a little bit."

"A lot bit." My voice chokes up, but I don't allow my eyes to leave his. I want to bask in the heat that is Dimitri Gray. I want to burn in the fire he emanates until I'm nothing but ash.

His lips twitch in the beginnings of a smile I'm not sure will ever fully form. "A lot bit," he agrees. "But they got complacent. They didn't realize I was just biding my time, waiting until they lowered their guard." His long lashes flutter against his cheekbones as he takes a deep breath. "I killed them all and managed to escape. But Violet…I had these teenagers in my class before. They were good kids. Not murderers."

"Did you notice any strange markings on their skin? Like tattoos or brands?" I bring my hands up to his shoulders and begin to knead the muscles there, hoping that he'll relax. I hate how tense he is, like a rubber band pulled taut. He practically vibrates with suppressed violence.

"I…" His forehead creases. "I thought I saw a strange tattoo on Trill…the sphinx. Do you know what it means?"

"Medusa," I growl. "It's a spell or a curse or a rune or something designed to make the wearer hate vampires and Dracula to the point of being irrationally angry and stabby. She wants to get rid of me and the rest of the vampires."

"Not just Medusa." He leans slightly away from me and shakes his head. "I was visited by someone while I was being…interrogated."

Interrogated. Just a fun, fancy word for tortured.

I'm gonna *interrogate* the shit out of Medusa and her merry gang of assholes as soon as I get my hands on them.

"Who visited you?" I don't dare ask my question above a whisper.

"Zeus." Dimitri's eyes squeeze shut. "Zeus came to visit me."

# CHAPTER 24

CAL

I don't know who to aim my glower at.

Lucifer, who sits primly on the edge of one of the armchairs, his long legs folded over each other as he glares at Dracula and then Hera.

Hera, who stands apart from all the men—no doubt overwhelmed with the testosterone permeating the air—with a scowl on her pretty face and her hand clenched into a fist by her side.

Or Dracula, who reclines on the sofa with his legs dangling over the edge, completely at ease despite the bombshell that has just been dropped on all of our heads.

Zeus used some of Medusa's lackeys to kidnap Dimitri Gray and gather intel on Violet. Not only that, but the God of Gods threatened my mate.

When Violet emerged from Dimitri's head and told us all the news, I swear it was so silent you could've heard a pin drop. It was a tense type of silence, too. One that spoke of a dozen breaths being held collectively and our hearts momentarily skipping a beat. And then, like all tranquil things, chaos inevitably erupted.

Lucifer began to rage, Hera fumed quietly, Dracula snarled and barked orders. But Violet's mates? We simply exchanged glances as the truth of Dimitri's words settled over us all like a heavy, weighted blanket.

Zeus wants to see Violet dead, but why? And does this have something to do with the prophecy? Something to do with her attempted murder when she was just a baby?

Question after question swarms through my head like a contingent of angry, buzzing bees. It's rare for me not to understand something—after all, I'm the smartest person in the room—but just then, it feels as if I'm being offered a bunch of jagged pieces and then instructed to assemble them into something coherent.

I don't know who to trust aside from the men in this room—excluding Lucifer and even Dracula—but I do know that all of us will lay down our lives for Violet Dracula. She might hate us for that, but I'd rather she hate us and be alive than love us and be dead.

She hasn't left Headmaster Gray's side since we first brought him here. She remains vigilant, constantly wiping away the sweat peppering his brows and placing ice cubes on his face and neck when his fever gets bad. Frankie has done what he can for the strict professor, and now, all we can do is wait. Dimitri Gray's a tough bastard. If anyone will survive this, it's him. I'll give it a day before he returns to the land of the living, as imperious as always and barking orders at anyone who cares to listen.

Barret has stayed with Violet during this time, allowing her to enter Dimitri's dreams whenever the headmaster seems distressed or anxious in his sleep. She can't utilize Barret's gifts for too long—not when we need him at full strength for the battle to come—but she does it often enough that I know it's taking a toll on my friend.

Not that he'll admit it.

I blow out a breath and run my hand through my tousled, pink hair.

I'm a cupid, for fuck's sake—part dark fairy and part incubus. Not just any cupid, but *the* Cupid. I'm mother-fucking Cupid, and even I can't get my two favorite people to admit their feelings for each other.

Something has shifted between the two of them recently, but they're too irritatingly obtuse to figure it out for them-selves. Barret... Barret has been in love with Violet for months now, but Violet's emotions towards the boogeyman have only recently changed and distorted. I can sense the lust wafting off of her in tangible waves whenever he smiles in her direction, that timid, beguiling smile that he never shows anyone, not even me. I can see the way her eyes dilate, her chest rises and falls, her pulse skips a beat.

She cares for him, just as much as he cares for her.

But how to get them to see that...

Sometimes, when I look close enough, when I embed my sight with a little bit of my power, I can sense the bond thrumming between them. It's thin, barely the size of my pinkie finger, and almost translucent, but it's real and vibrant. Every interaction they have, every word they exchange, causes the bond to grow just a little bit more.

A mating bond.

The same mating bond that connects Violet to me...and all of her other mates.

It's the exact same mating bond I see thrumming between Lucifer and Hera, despite the caustic glares they throw at each other.

Sometimes, I debate interfering—confessing what I know to everyone. I could add my magic to the flimsy bonds and reinforce them. After all, it's what I did back in my village before the monster council took me away and threw me into detention. It's what I did for Cynthia, Violet's roommate, and Pete the Pumpkin.

But something stops me from doing the same for Violet and Barret, for Lucifer and Hera. For the former, I know my inactivity is because I want them to be together because *they* want to be, not because I force them to. I want their love to be mutual, not a product of a bond I amplified.

And for Lucifer and Hera? I don't trust them. At all. One of them lied about what happened the night Violet was born, and I'll be damned if I don't uncover the truth. For now, however…

I slowly push myself away from the wall, and Vin's eyes slide to me. He quirks one eyebrow that eloquently asks, "Violet duty?" I nod once, and he returns his attention to the three monsters in the room.

Mason has gone to get supplies at the local market, and Frankie is in the second spare room—and Lucifer's abandoned prison—to try and solve the Balor issue. With everyone occupied, I feel as if this is the perfect opportunity to talk to my sweet, perfect mate.

She might even be as perfect as I am.

Vanity has, and always will, run through my veins. I don't know if it's because of my incubus heritage or my dark fae one. Either way, Violet seems to accept me for who I am— minimal flaws and all. If you can even call being vain a flaw. Violet sure as fuck didn't seem to think so when I told her my dick was the longest she's ever seen…and then proved it to her by pounding her tight little cunt.

As if the mere memory of Violet's pussy is a switch to stir my dormant lust, my cock jumps to attention. I mentally chastise the damn organ, reminding it that our mission today is to comfort Violet…and maybe get her to confess her feelings for Barret.

Baby steps.

I knock on the wall beside the open bedroom door but don't wait for her to respond as I step inside. Like the last time I saw her, she's perched on the edge of Dimitri's bed, a washcloth in her hand as she wipes at Dimitri's sweaty face. Most of his bruises and lacerations have healed thanks to Frankie's potions —though I should be the one being thanked for carrying his heavy ass into the bedroom in the first place—and his face actually has a hint of color. Barret sits in the chair beside Violet, his eyes intent on her profile as she focuses on Dimitri.

"How's he doing?" I jab my chin in Dimitri's direction, as if she needs any clarification for who I'm talking about.

"Good." Biting her lower lip, Violet lifts a hand to tuck a strand of his white hair behind his ear. Her palm grazes Dimitri's cheek a second longer than necessary before she reluctantly drops her hand back to her lap. "He seems to be healing."

"That's good." I shift from foot to foot.

To be completely honest, this whole "empathy" thing is still pretty new to me. Remember when I said that my species is prone to being vain? Well, we're also prideful. And selfish. And assholes.

I'm not an asshole, of course, but everyone else is.

Anyway, before Violet barged into my life, I've only ever truly cared about Barret. Now, I have this spunky demon-goddess in my life and her harem of lovers who I need to learn to care for. Maybe a part of me already does. After all, they're not bad monsters, but my feelings for them are mere dots on a canvas compared to the enormity of my feelings for Violet and Bare.

But again, baby steps.

I don't want Dimitri Gray to actually die, at the very least, so I call that a win.

"I'll…um…leave you two alone to talk," Barret mumbles, already pushing up from the seat and hurrying out of the room.

He doesn't make eye contact with me. Then again, he hasn't made eye contact with me since Violet first walked in on us about to have sex.

Fuck.

Violet watches him go with a forlorn expression on her beautiful face. She glances down quickly, focusing on Dimitri. It's at that same second that Barret looks back at her, and his entire face seems to fall when he sees her attention elsewhere.

Fuck. Fuck. Fuck.

I'm going to need to up my game here. Up my cupid powers. No, I won't manipulate the bond between them—I refuse to—but I *will* do what I do best.

Spread love and lust.

Especially lust.

"Let's get you cleaned up, Vi." I gently move around the bed until I can touch her upper arm. I curl my fingers around her bicep and give it a playful tug. "You haven't showered since Dimitri arrived last night."

She sniffs but allows me to pull her to her feet. "Actually, I haven't showered since Dimitri kidnapped me through a mirror and brought me to a hospital full of psychopathic, cursed murderers. Or maybe before that. I can't remember the last time I showered." She lifts her arm up in the air, the one I'm not holding, and sniffs her armpit. Immediately, her nose wrinkles and her eyes begin to water. "Holy shit."

"So…is it shower time?"

"How can you stand to even be around me? I smell like…I

don't even know! I'm pretty sure this scent didn't exist until now."

I lead her out of the bedroom and into the bathroom as she continues to sniff her pits dramatically. "You don't smell…that bad."

"I smell like a piece of toast full of butter that has been left on the counter for over a year. And then a dog somehow jumped up, snagged the bread, and ate it. And then that dog took a shit in the front lawn, and lo and behold, the moldy toast was discovered in that pile of poop. Then, a skunk came strolling merrily along, lifted its tail, and wham-bammed that shit mountain. And finally, a poor, innocent kid came skipping through the front lawn, stopped in front of the shit, and keeled over dead. That's what I smell like."

As she talks, she moves to pull her clothing off. Her words become muffled as her face gets caught in the fabric of her shirt.

I chuckle as she flails about, and then I lean down to turn on the bathtub. Cold water immediately emerges from the faucet, and I twist the nozzle until smoke emits from the tub. I know my girl likes her baths scalding.

"I have a few questions," I begin conversationally as I open the bathroom cabinet and sift through the selection of shampoos and soaps Dimitri has stocked. I pour lavender-scented soap into the tub and then swirl my fingers through the water until bubbles emerge. "First, what happened to the owner of the dog?"

"Excuse me?" She pauses with her ass in the air as she attempts to pull down her panties.

I groan and subtly try to rearrange my junk.

Even smelling like moldy bread shitted out by a dog and sprayed by a skunk, she still makes me hard as rock.

"Obviously, the owner intended to eat this piece of toast. He went as far as to slather it with butter," I point out. "And he probably would've noticed if it had just been sitting out on the counter for over a year. So what happened to him?"

"First of all, it's a she," Violet corrects primly, unclasping her bra and allowing the material to slide to the floor. Her pink nipples are pebbled as she steps forward. "And…she died. In a house fire."

"So why wasn't the bread burned to a crisp?" I extend a hand to help her step into the tub, and she accepts it with a tiny flush on her cheeks.

She settles beneath the water, and I reach forward to turn off the tap. Immediately, the sound of sloshing water is replaced by the tranquil, almost melodic tune of it rippling around her naked body.

"Because she didn't die in her own house fire. Duh." Violet relaxes back against the tub, her eyelashes fluttering shut as she rests her head against the porcelain edge.

When did she last sleep?

We really need to be taking better care of her.

"Okay…so she died in a house fire. Then who was taking care of her dog?" I grab the shampoo bottle I picked out for her and squeeze a generous amount into my hand.

"Her will stated that her brother had to stop by every day to take care of the dog. But since the dog was in a separate portion of the house than the bread, he never noticed it," she says.

I smile. Trust Violet to construct an entire backstory concerning her stench. Crazy, silly, perfect girl.

"Duck beneath the water to get your hair wet, please."

She complies without complaint and then pushes herself back to the surface. Her breasts bob just above the water, appearing almost glossy with the beads of water dripping over them. I physically have to restrain myself from taking one of her nipples into my mouth.

Instead, I continue my line of questioning. "So how did the dog escape and eat the bread off the counter?"

I move to kneel behind her and then rub my hands together. Once the shampoo is foamy, I bring my palms to her head and begin to knead her scalp. She groans, a noise I feel carnally, but I don't take this further. I just…wash my mate. I want to focus on her. Take care of her. Please her. Love her.

Worship her.

I'm just a willing altar boy coming to his goddess's temple.

"The dog got rabies," she confesses. "He bit the brother, escaped from his cage, and immediately ate the bread."

"By jumping onto his hind legs?" I clarify, going along with her little story as my fingers move through her tangled blonde hair, applying the shampoo.

"Exactly." She nods once, but I stop the motion of her head by tugging on her golden strands.

"And then he got outside?"

"The brother left the front door open," she explains. "So the dog went outside, pooped, and then obediently traveled back to his cage."

"And it was at that point the skunk arrived?" I continue to massage her scalp as low, throaty, sexy-as-fuck moans escape her lips. I don't even think she realizes she's doing it.

"No. The poop stayed out in the sun for a few days. And then the skunk came by and sprayed it."

I reach around her to grab the showerhead, flip it on, and then place it over her head, extra careful not to accidentally drip soap in her eyes.

"And what was the child doing skipping through the front lawn?" I comb my fingers through her golden mane, attempting to untangle the worst of the snarls out.

"Isn't it obvious?" She lowers her voice to a conspiratorial whisper. "She was the one who started the house fire in the first place with the attempt to kill the dog's owner. She wanted the dog for herself and always intended to steal the pup one day."

"Ohhh…what a plot twist." I chuckle as I finally finish rinsing her hair, turn off the showerhead, and return it to where it was.

Violet giggles too, and it's a sound I swear reverberates through the marrow of my bones. My heart. My fucking soul.

"You know…" She spreads her fingers out and then moves her hands through the hot water, watching the tiny ripples. "You're pretty good at this."

"Pretty good at what?" I place my elbows on the rim of the tub, not caring when water sloshes my sweater, and peer down at her. From this angle, I can only see the back of her head and those damn, perky breasts that consume way too much of my attention.

"Taking care of me," she whispers.

Her words tug at something in my heart like a rope tethered to the most sacred, intimate part of me.

My pulse practically does palpitations.

"I've only ever done it with you, Violet," I confess softly. "I…I'm not the type of man to take care of people. *They* take care of *me* usually."

Something inside of me twists and tightens uncomfortably at my unwitting confession. I don't want her to look at me differently, but she needs to know the truth. She needs to know what type of monster I truly am.

"I don't know if I ever truly cared about someone before Barret. And I don't know if I ever truly loved someone before you." My chest suddenly feels too tight. Is this what dying feels like? If it is, then what a way to go.

"You loved your family," she points out, finally shifting in the tub to stare up at me.

She should look absolutely ridiculous right now—like a drowned cat—but somehow, she radiates an ethereal light most models could only pray to emulate. She's beauty personified, and every moment I stare into her glittering blue orbs, I notice something new, something I never noticed before.

Say...

That freckle directly below her right eye, a tiny brown dot that somehow accentuates her natural beauty.

"I loved them, yes." I rub my hand over my mouth as I consider my next words. "But I didn't really know what love was. I was just a kid then. A stupid, irresponsible kid who saw men and women as games to be played and beaten. Instruments to be plucked and used. I knew I was beautiful, and I used that beauty to have people do things for me. I was never the one to wash another person, Violet. I was always the one being washed."

I don't know if my words make a lick of sense, but her eyes soften, her pink lips forming a perfect O.

"You're a better man than you give yourself credit for, Cal," she whispers, leaning forward.

We're practically sharing the same breath now. I can taste her on my tongue, a decadent treat that reminds me of sin, temptation, and redemption all in one.

"Only for you, Violet. Only ever for you."

I lean forward at the same time she does, our lips meeting in a clash of teeth and tongues.

At the same moment, the door to the bathroom opens and Barret stands in the doorframe, holding a change of clothes in his huge hands. His cheeks instantly turn crimson when he sees our compromising position, and he ducks his head.

"I...I knocked," he murmurs. "I'm sorry. I shouldn't have... I didn't mean to..."

"Barret," Violet begins gently in a voice meant to coax a scared and injured animal.

It has the opposite effect on Barret, however.

"I'm sorry," he says helplessly. His eyes flick to my face before focusing entirely on Violet. "I'm sorry. I'll leave. I'll..." And then he's throwing the clothes onto the countertop and running out the door.

"Barret!" Violet calls after him.

This time when my heart begins to pound erratically, it's for an entirely different reason.

Why do the words "I'll leave" seem to have an entirely different meaning than just exiting the bathroom?

Barret isn't going to leave us...is he?

# CHAPTER 25

VIOLET

"**B**arret!" Water sluices around the sides of the claw-footed tub as I scramble to my feet and step out.

I fumble with the bathrobe hanging on the door and curse when I can't seem to figure out how to tie it. Obviously, I know how to tie a fucking knot, but my hands shake so badly that the simple task proves to be impossible.

"Here. Let me." Cal's voice is uncharacteristically grave as he steadies my trembling hands with his steady ones and gently closes the bathrobe across my chest.

I'm still dripping wet, my hair leaving puddles on the bathroom floor, but I can't find it within me to give a damn that I'm creating a horrible slipping hazard. My mind has been in turmoil since Barret first walked in on us, since I saw the anguish in his eyes. I need to...

Fuck if I know.

Reassure him?

Tell him that he means the world to me? To Cal?

I don't know if he'll want my brand of comfort—perhaps

the beast within him will only be soothed by Cal's presence—but just then, I feel selfish. I want to be the one to talk to Barret, to wrap him in my arms and assure him that everything will be all right. I feel in my soul that's where I'm supposed to be right now. With him.

Cal, surprisingly, doesn't protest as he gives my shoulders a reassuring squeeze and then twists me so I'm facing the still open bathroom door.

"Go. He needs you."

I don't need to be told twice.

My heart has practically crawled up my throat and now rests on the tip of my tongue as I race down the hallway towards the spare bedroom. I can't say for certain how I know that Barret's in there, only that I do. It's like an incessant tugging in the center of my chest, a rope that has been wrapped around my heart and the end of it rests in Barret's huge palm. All he needs to do is pull, and I'll be tripping over my own two feet to get to him.

Not that me tripping over my own two feet is necessarily an unusual thing for me...

Barret's sitting on the edge of the huge bed when I step inside, his head lowered so it rests in his hands. I've never noticed how large his hands actually are before. It's a weird thing to focus on now, that's for damn sure, but I can't seem to tear my eyes away. I imagine one single palm will engulf my entire face. I could probably suffocate just from him cupping my cheek.

Damn.

Why does that thought make me so hot?

*Because you have a breath-play kink, apparently, you slutty whore.*

I scold my horny vagina—reminding her that now isn't the time to get all weepy—and take a few steps farther into the room. I'm not sure if Barret just isn't aware of my arrival or if he's ignoring me, but he doesn't glance up as I step inside. If it's the latter… That tightness in my chest reminds me of Mason's snakes. Hissing, writhing, and constricting until I feel light-headed. My vision is broken apart by jagged black lines as I swallow heavily. But even swallowing doesn't allow any moisture to enter my mouth. It's as dry as a nun's vagina.

"Bare?"

His head snaps up as if he's been electrocuted, pain and panic—two P words I despise when they're not associated with sex—lancing across his handsome face. He scrubs a hand across his broad forehead as his gaze flicks to my feet, then to the bed, and finally to the window…anywhere but my eyes searing a hole into his scalp.

"I shouldn't have walked in on you in the bathtub," he blurts. His knee begins to bounce erratically, yet another thing hinting at the anxiety lurking just beneath his skin.

"I don't care about that," I insist, finally tugging up my metaphorical big-girl panties and walking farther into the room. "I care about *you*."

His features once again twist with pain—pain that I can't even begin to understand, let alone articulate. Why is he so damn hard to read? Am I just an idiot? Probably.

"Don't do that," he snaps abruptly, his voice rife with frustration.

"Don't do what?" I cock an eyebrow.

"Pretend to care about me."

My mouth drops open. "What in the devil's anus are you talking about, Barret? Of course I care about you."

He scrubs a huge hand down his face and blows out a breath. It's a weary sound, that one exhale of air, and it hints at the emotions percolating just beneath the surface of his semi-calm façade. "I know that. I… Look, it doesn't matter. I shouldn't have said anything."

"I don't want you to leave." I don't know how he can hear my voice. Heaven knows it's practically a croak, only a step or two above a complete whisper.

Yet his head snaps up as if I screamed at the top of my lungs and banged a drum just beside his ear.

His eyes widen, and the hair on the top of his head begins to twitch in agitation. "Leave?"

"Isn't that what you said to me and Cal? That you were going to leave?" Fuck, it feels as if my heart is breaking, as if someone has physically reached into my chest, grabbed either side of the sensitive organ, and then tore it in two. Can someone die of a broken heart? Because that's what this certainly feels like.

I always assumed I would die of something cool, like murder or a light stabbing. Not *this*. Fuck, anything but this.

He jumps to his feet and is across the room before I can even blink. He hovers his hands just above my shoulders, but he doesn't allow them to clamp down. Instead, he just… stands there, staring at me. Watching me. Piercing my skin with a gaze that may not be necessarily acute but sees way more than I would like him to.

Every inch of me is bared to this huge, towering man, and it's both terrifying and exhilarating at the same time.

"I would never, *ever* leave you, Violet Dracula," he rumbles, his powerful voice reverberating through me like rocks sliding down a ravine. "Not when you need me."

"I'll always need you," I assure him, and his lips twitch in the beginnings of a dry, humorless smile.

"I know, Cheese Curd. I'll always be your friend. Your *best* friend." He swallows once more, and that fissure cracking down the center of my heart expands until it's the size of a canyon. Holy fuck.

Did I just get…friend-zoned?

I don't know what I expected when I came here to

comfort Barret, but it wasn't this. Maybe it was stupid and naïve of me to believe that all of these sexy-as-hell men would have the same feelings for me as I have for them, but motherfucker. The pain tearing up my insides from his words is unimaginable, flaying me apart and twisting up my internal organs like a witch stirring the contents of her cauldron.

"Best friends…" I whisper numbly.

His eyes squeeze shut as if he's in physical pain before he forces them to reopen, to focus on me.

"That's what you want, isn't it?" His head tilts to the side in a way that almost reminds me of a golden retriever. It would be stinkin' adorable if I wasn't, oh you know, bleeding from the inside out.

"Is it what *you* want?"

"What I want is irrelevant." He crosses his bulging biceps over his chest.

A defense mechanism, I realize.

But what does he have to protect himself from?

*Me?*

The thought is practically laughable.

"It's not irrelevant," I insist, tilting my head up to stare into his hypnotic brown eyes.

Sometimes, they appear so black that I can't even see the pupils amongst the inky color of the irises. But other times, like now, they glow with an amber tint that lightens the mahogany into a color I would almost describe as umber. That's what they look like now, with the artificial light hitting them in such a way. Umber.

"Don't look at me like that, Cheese Curd." His words are practically a rasp, pulled from a closed throat.

"Like what?"

"Like I matter to you."

"You *do* matter to me."

"Not like you matter to me," he whispers, forking his fingers through that slightly longer green hair at the top of his head. "I can't keep doing this."

My heart, which has stopped beating altogether at his first confession, picks up speed at the anguish lining his face.

He can't keep doing what?

Being my friend?

Being around me?

Oh my god.

Realization dawns on me, and the intensity of it actually has me staggering backwards a few steps.

Does Barret...know about my crush on him? Does it make him uncomfortable? Is that what this entire thing is about?

Fucking dick turds.

My eyes begin to water, but I don't allow a single tear to fall. I know Barret can see the glossy sheen over my irises, though, and his own features twist and distort as if he's been stabbed in the gut.

"Don't cry, Violet," he begs hoarsely. "I can't stand to see you cry."

Violet. Not Cheese Curd.

The distinction has never felt so...glaringly obvious before. It has never hurt so badly before, either.

"I can just be your friend, Barret," I practically beg. "We don't have to be anything more."

His brows furrow, and he reaches for his chin, running his hand across the length of his stubbled jaw. "Friend," he repeats. And then again, "Just be your friend."

That damn, pesky tear I've been trying to hold back finally slips free. It trails down my cheek, the warm water a contrast to my suddenly cool skin, and lands on the edge of my lips. Barret watches it fall with a tortured expression.

"I just don't know what you want from me," he finally

manages to choke out, his hands curling into fists by his sides.

And then…he explodes.

That's the only word I can think to use, but even that doesn't begin to encapsulate Barret's reaction. It's like I'm staring at a completely different person. Night and day. My chest constricts as a deep ache builds there.

"Why can't you just leave me alone?" he bellows, and I flinch automatically.

Barret has never, ever yelled at me. Never raised his voice to me before. The sudden animosity saturating the air is almost as shocking as the rage twisting his lips into something ugly and unrecognizable.

"I will," I promise, even as those words tear at something already bleeding inside of me. Pretty soon, there won't be anything left to hurt, to maim, to break.

Because it'll already be irrevocably destroyed.

Barret towers above me, his huge chest heaving, and finally grabs my shoulders. Gently, though, as if even in his monster form, he knows not to hurt me. As if he knows he *can't* hurt me.

"Why can't you just love me the way that I love you?" he says between pants.

Love?

That one word bounces around in my head even as Barret tugs me forward and plants his lips onto mine.

Holy. Fuck.

Holy fuck.

Kissing Barret is like standing in the center of a field on the Fourth of July. In every direction, glorious, colorful fireworks light up the pitch-black sky and break up the monotony of darkness. Greens and oranges. Yellows and reds. Blues and whites. Colors and shapes are everywhere, each one more beautiful than the last.

He kisses me like he's starved for my touch, for my affection, and every scrap I offer him he accepts greedily. He kisses me like I'm the air he needs to breathe, like he'll quite literally keel over and die if I stop touching him. He kisses me like I'm the sun and he's the moon, forever fated to chase each other through the sky but never connecting, never knowing true harmony.

And his touch… Fuck, his touch…

His hands are everywhere, burning, searing, branding my skin. He tugs at the knot holding my robe shut, and the silky material falls over my shoulders and onto the floor.

He moans low against my throat as his hands find my breasts, kneading and pulling and basically unraveling me with every heated touch he grants me.

I match his kisses with desperate ones of my own until I can't figure out where he ends and I begin. I'm practically wrapped around the man as we stagger towards the bed, me on top and him falling onto his back. Still, we don't stop kissing, don't stop touching, don't stop teasing.

I run my hands over his broad shoulders, suddenly wishing he didn't have a shirt on. I want to feel his skin on mine.

As if he can hear my thoughts, he sits up just enough to tug his shirt off in that sexy, one-hand-over-the-shoulder way that guys do so well. Only when he's shirtless do we resume our relentless kissing.

What are we doing?

What does this mean?

I know I should take the time to consider the answer to those questions, the ramifications of our actions, but I can't get my brain to work again.

I begin to rock against the erection I can feel straining against his jeans as our tongues tangle. My naked breasts, still damp from my bath, brush against his chest, eliciting goose bumps across my entire body.

But as quickly as he began kissing me—began sucking the soul straight out of my body—he stops. Pushes me away. Stands up. Pants.

Terror lines his face as he breathes heavily, staring down at me as if he doesn't quite recognize the person in his bed.

"Barret..." I whisper, naked and needy and wanting him.

I can't remember the last time I felt such desperation. I desire all of my mates equally, but this thing with Barret feels new and foreign. Not strange, necessarily, but full of the giddiness and newness of two young kids falling in love for the first time.

Yes. That's what my relationship with Barret reminds me of—a first love. Sweet, innocent, and soul-consuming. You don't necessarily know how it's going to end, but you *do* know that you'll cherish the moments you have together until then.

But if I'm being completely honest, I don't want this to end. Ever. I want to love and care for Barret until we're both...well, we can't be wrinkly and gray, considering we're both immortal.

Is it weird to want him, as well as the rest of my mates, forever? Is it too soon to wish for that?

"We can't do this." Barret sounds pained, and he doesn't quite meet my eyes as he focuses on something just above my head. I sit up slightly, suddenly wishing I wasn't naked.

Which is totally a first for me. I *love* being naked—clothes are constricting as fuck, after all—but I feel too vulnerable right now. It's terrifying.

"You don't want me?"

"I don't... I can't... *You're not mine.*" The words are a roar, a cry, and a sob all at once. They scratch at my brain like a sword made of fire.

I move onto my knees and crawl towards him until I'm able to cradle his face between my palms.

"But what if I want *you* to be *mine*?" I whisper.

Shock splays across his face, and something akin to hope enters his dark eyes.

"You want me to be yours?" he rasps out.

Keeping my eyes trained on his, giving him the opportunity to pull away if he desires to, I lean forward and brush my lips against his. The touch is teasing in nature, almost a mockery of a kiss, but licks of flame travel down my spine where he caresses it with his hands.

He holds me as if I'm…precious. So incredibly precious. As if he's afraid that if he applies any sort of pressure whatsoever, he'll harm me irreparably. It's a startling change from our heated, passionate kisses from a few minutes earlier.

Just like before, he pushes me away, almost as if my lips against his physically burn him. He begins to shake his head vehemently as he continues to back away.

"I don't want your pity, Violet." The hoarse, broken words tug at my heartstrings. "I don't want you to—"

"No pity." I chew on my bottom lip, pulling it through my teeth and then releasing it. "Barret, I think…I think I'm in love with you."

He blinks at me.

Stares.

Blinks some more.

The big, scary, intimidating man is at a loss for words. I've quite literally struck him dumb.

I would find the deer-in-headlights look sort of cute if I wasn't freaking the fuck out.

Did I just say the L-word to Barret? And *mean* it? The bats in my stomach flutter their leathery wings as tears prick my eyes.

I don't know when it happened, but I do know *how*.

Barret has always been the type of guy, the type of monster, I felt comfortable talking to. Confiding in. Leaning on. He makes me feel safe, even when the rest of the world warned me against befriending him.

My beautiful, innocent, compassionate boogeyman.

Barret's in front of me in the span of a heartbeat, his dark eyes consuming my vision as he flicks them back and forth between my own. Searching for something.

My sincerity, perhaps?

"Say it again," he rasps, and the desperation in his tone is nearly my undoing.

"I lo—"

His lips smash to mine in a clash of teeth and tongues. I whimper against his mouth as I curl my body farther against him, my breasts pressing against his chest.

He moves his body against me until I'm lying back on the bed with his huge frame hovering over mine. Still, his lips never leave mine even as his palms press down on either side of me.

"Y-you want me?" He sounds stunned, breathless, though that flicker of hope and *love* never dissipates from his eyes.

"Don't you want me?" As I speak, I squeeze my hands between our bodies and begin to unbutton his dark jeans.

"More than anything." He begins to kiss me once more before he lowers his head to between my breasts, planting a chaste kiss on the skin there. He then captures my right nipple between his lips, tugging at the pert bud, as I gasp and arch my back.

My hands have given up their task of removing his jeans completely and instead wander over his muscular body. His dark hands capture my porcelain wrists, making the most striking contrast of skin color, as he moves his mouth to my left breast.

"You're so beautiful," he murmurs reverently, one of his

hands sneaking down my body to play with my cunt. "So perfect."

I reach between our bodies once more to unzip his pants and free his hard length from the denim prison.

"I didn't know how badly I wanted this," I whimper as I stroke him in tandem to his finger sliding in and out of me.

I'm already so damn wet he doesn't run into any resistance despite his fingers being absolutely massive. Not as massive as a cock, but definitely bigger than a lot of things I've put up my vagina before.

Not that I put strange things up my vagina, mind you. I'm weird but not *that* weird.

"I want to do everything with you, Cheese Curd." Barret's cheeks tint pink even as he continues to fuck me with his fingers. "Go to the movies. Go out for dinner. Sit at the beach. Travel to Europe or Australia. Fuck, even go to the grocery store. It doesn't matter…just as long as I'm with you."

Fuck.

Tears burn my eyes as I arch my neck to kiss him once more. And kiss, and kiss, and kiss…

"After this is over, I'm going to spoon the fuck out of you," I whisper.

His brows dip. "You want to turn me into a spoon?"

I don't know how I'm able to chuckle with his fingers in my pussy, but I manage. "I want to cuddle with you, silly. You know…spooning. And Barret?" I bite down on his earlobe, causing him to jerk. "I want to be the big spoon."

His eyes flare, almost as if the thought of me cuddling him is too much for him to handle, and then the pace of his fingers in my pussy increases.

I practically arch like a cat in heat—or a horny-ass demon-slash-goddess in heat, if we're being practical—until only my head and shoulders remain on the bed. The rest of my body is up in the air, held captive by Barret's strong hands as he fucks my pussy.

I reach to stroke his shaft, loving the contrast of hard muscle and velvet skin.

I won't tell this to any of my men—unless, of course, they piss me off—but Barret is by far the largest, both in width and length. I seriously have no idea how that...*thing* can fit inside of me. It's definitely not a normal cock.

It's a...get this...*monster* cock.

Ha.

He kisses down my body while simultaneously shucking off his jeans and boxers. Only when he's directly between my thighs does his tongue join the fingers still sliding in and out of me.

His nose brushes my blonde pubic hair as he tilts his head up to stare at me. The wonderment I've seen before is still there in his eyes, as if he can't quite believe this is real, alongside a shitload of lust. So much lust, I feel as if I'm drowning in it.

"Barret..." I push myself onto my elbows so I can see him better. "I want you."

He pulls his lips away from my pussy to adamantly declare, "You have me."

"No...I want your cock. Inside of me." I palm my own tit as his eyes flick from my slick heat to my face and then back to my pussy.

A tiny crease manifests between his eyes. "Are you sure you're ready for me, baby girl? You're awfully tiny, and I don't want to...errr..."

"Break me?" I finish for him.

That sexy-as-fuck blush of his returns. "I haven't ever... I mean...I haven't..."

Understanding dawns, and that knowledge is accompanied by an intense wave of pleasure and something almost primal.

"You've never been with a girl before, have you?" I whisper in awe and wonderment.

How could a man like Barret—exuding sex and violence and sin—still be a virgin?

His blush deepens. "I never wanted to before...before you." He ducks his head down to plant a soft kiss to my pubic bone. "But I don't want to hurt you. I don't want to break you, Violet."

"You won't break me." I grab his shoulders, urging him to crawl up my body, and he does so willingly. Heaven only knows I wouldn't have been able to move him unless he wanted me to. "I'm made for you, Barret, and you're made for me. Even that...python of a cock."

Those brown orbs of his widen in a way that would've been comical...if we weren't naked in bed together. "You think my penis is a *snake*?" He stares at me as if he's sincerely questioning my sanity, and I have to bite down on my lower lip to keep from smiling.

Ugh. Why does he have to be so flipping adorable all the damn time?

"Lie down, Barret," I murmur as I crawl to my knees, forcing him to take the position I just vacated. "I want to ride you."

I straddle his huge, muscular body—a feat by itself—and reach behind our bodies to palm his huge dick. I follow the pathway of my hand with my eyes and rub a tiny bit of his own precum down the length as lubricant before swiveling to face him once more.

"Are you sure?" I whisper, running my fingers through the green hair on the top of his head. It's so damn soft. Who would've thought?

"Yes." He stares up at me with love-filled eyes as I position his cock with my entrance. "I want to feel you around me, Violet. Squeezing my cock. But...but I don't want to hurt you..."

"I'm so fucking wet for you, Barret." I lean down to kiss him even as I slowly sink down onto his girth. "Oh! Fuck!" He's large, almost too large, and my walls constrict around him in a way that has him gasping and me moaning.

His dark hands land on my hips, his fingers digging into my tender flesh, as I lean forward. I watch his lips part on a breathless exhale as pleasure rakes across his stunning features. His long lashes flutter shut for a moment before he reopens his eyes and spears me with a smoldering look.

"Fuck, Violet..." he whispers.

"You feel so good, Bare. So good inside of me."

"Take what you need from me, Violet," he grits out. "Ride my cock."

I do as he says, bouncing on his length as his hands leave my waist to cup my breasts. His thumbs run over my pebbled nipples as his hips jerk up.

"You take my cock like such a good girl, don't you, Violet?" His dirty talk makes me ride him even faster, chasing down pleasure only he can provide me. "You like the way my cock feels in that tight little cunt of yours, don't you?"

"Barret!" I don't know if my gasp is one of pleasure or shock at his crude, primitive words. Who would've known that my sweet Boo Bear had this in him?

"I love watching those pretty tits bounce in my face. Just look at those pink nipples, desperate for my mouth."

"Yes, Barret, yes!" I throw my head back as he leans forward to roll his tongue around one of my beaded nipples.

"I dreamed about this moment. I dreamed about it every night from the day I met you in detention. Did you know that, Violet? Did you know I dreamed about slamming my cock into your sweet, perfect cunt and tasting your slick on my tongue?"

"Holy fuck," I breathe as I place my hands on his chest for balance and continue to ride him faster and faster.

"I still don't know if this is real or only a dream," he says between gasps.

"Real, Barret. Real. So, so real." I twist my hips so I can take his cock at a different angle. This new position makes him enter me even deeper, lighting up all of my nerve endings in the process.

"You know what would make this even better?" He nuzzles my breasts as I moan his name. "Your fangs in my neck as you sucked my blood. I want to feed you, Violet. I want my blood to be inside of you at the same time my cum is."

"Oh…oh fuck." A girl doesn't need to be told twice. Sex and food? Yes, please.

I roughly push Barret's head to the side and then slam my fangs into his neck. Immediately, his sweet, syrupy blood fills my mouth, and I moan low in my throat. Technically, I shouldn't need to feed on blood since I'm not a vampire, but there's a part of me that craves it. A part of me that will *always* crave it.

With Barret's blood in my mouth and his cock in my pussy, it's almost too much. And the second he begins to rub circles on my aching clit? Yup. It's all over.

My pussy clenches around Barret's massive cock as I come, my fangs still embedded in his corded neck even as I scream my release.

His dick pulsates inside of me, and then he's coming with a feral roar I imagine everyone across the ocean can hear. And it's perfect, this moment between Barret and me, and exactly what we needed to bridge that final gap in our relationship.

From strangers, to friends, to best friends, to lovers.

And when I fall asleep a few minutes later…

I'm the big spoon, my much smaller body curling around his in a way that's almost protective.

Because now that I've claimed Barret, I'm never, ever letting him go.

# CHAPTER 26

VIN

I lean forward in the wooden chair until my arms are able to freely dangle between my spread thighs. Then, I cock my head to the side as I study the screaming, inconsolable woman tied up before me.

"You betrayed our family!" Vanessa seethes, globs of spit forming on her lips. "If our parents could see you now—"

"Unfortunately," I drawl, reclining back and kicking my legs out, "our father is dead and our mother is in hiding, along with the rest of the Van Helsings."

She screams in absolute rage, attempting to break free of the chains restraining her. I know that her efforts will be futile. We're the closest things to human the monster community has. If not even Balor could escape, I don't have a lot of confidence in Vanessa's ability to break her way free.

"I don't know what to do, V." I lean forward once more and scrub a hand through my dark hair. "Everything is so fucked up. I feel as if we're all just living one big lie, you know? Like, I don't know what's the truth and what's fiction anymore."

"I'm going to break free of these chains and rip your head off!" Vanessa screams as she jerks forward. "And then, I'm going to find that pretty girlfriend of yours and slice her into tiny pieces. I've never eaten a vampire before, but it sure sounds tasty. Yum. Yum. Yum." She makes exaggerated chomping noises as I heave out a ragged breath.

"I just wish you were here, V. Truly here. I...I need to talk to my sister. I need to figure out how to protect my mate."

And isn't that the truth of it all? Fuck, I feel like a failure. First to my family and now to my mate. If I were a stronger man, a smarter one, I would've found a way already to free Vanessa of this damn curse. If I were a better man, I would already have a solution to all of Violet's problems and a way to save her from all of these lies and secrets that seem to be suffocating her.

But then again, maybe that's not my purpose as her mate. As her knight.

Maybe I don't need to tell the queen what to do. Maybe I just need to stand beside her, support her, and love her unconditionally. Violet may put up a front around others, but she's not an idiot. She's the type of woman to take life by the balls, give them a squeeze, and then declare life as her little bitch.

She'll make it out of this mess. Of that, I'm certain.

Will the rest of us?

My heart thunders in my chest at the prospect of not all of us surviving the battle to come. That dreaded prophecy plays on a continuous loop in my mind, and prickles of fear race down my spine.

Mason isn't fucking dying.

Violet isn't dying.

None of us are dying.

I ball my hands into tight fists—so tight, I can feel my nails embedding themselves into my palms—as I work to modulate my breathing. To inhale deeply and then blow out all of that excess air just as slowly.

We. Will. Survive. This.

We will.

"I can see the wheels in your head turning, brother." Vanessa snarls and leans as far forward as the chains will allow. A sweaty strand of dark hair falls out of her braid and touches her cheek as she cackles. "You may think I'm no longer your sister, but you're wrong. This is me. The new me. The woman who just finally had the veil lifted and is able to see Violet and the rest of the vampires for what they are. Monsters. And we're, my dear brother, monster hunters."

"We don't hunt the innocent," I growl.

I told myself when I first came to visit my deranged sister that I wouldn't rise to the bait, that I wouldn't allow her taunts to penetrate my defenses. But I can't seem to fucking stop myself. This is…wrong. Vanessa's wrong.

"Violet Dracula isn't innocent," she hisses. "She murdered our father."

"She defended herself!" I bellow, finally jumping to my feet with such force that the chair flips backwards.

Vanessa laughs mockingly, the noise so shrill and high-pitched that it grates at my skin in a way that it never has before. "You're just as disillusioned as the others, my dear brother. But you'll see. In time, you'll see." Her eyes sparkle with some indecipherable emotion, one that churns my stomach.

"This isn't you, V. This isn't you."

"You keep saying that." Another husky laugh escapes her as she throws her head back. "But I think… I think I've finally been liberated."

"Violet's your friend!" I roar.

I don't know why I'm trying to reason with her when she's obviously lost to that damn rune on her neck, but maybe a part of me hopes I can reach my sister. Maybe a part of me prays that I can say something, anything, to remove that scowl twisting up her lips and darkening her eyes.

"She's a harbinger of the damn apocalypse, brother." Vanessa's head lolls forward, almost as if she's too tired to keep it upright. "If you can't see that, then you're stupider than you look. The sooner Violet's taken care of, the safer we'll all be."

And then she begins to laugh, and the cold, malicious cackle scratches at my skin like talons. Only jagged, bloody lines remain in their wake.

She laughs, and laughs, and laughs, the sound never-ending and pounding at my skull. I bring my hands up to my hair and give the silky strands a tug.

"Vin." Frankie's voice is soft and soothing as his hand lands on my shoulder, giving it a squeeze. "Remember, that's not your sister."

"Ahhh. Frankie. Chubby, ugly Frankie," Vanessa taunts, and my friend stiffens beside me.

"Shut the fuck up," I snap at the imposter wearing my sister's face.

I tell myself that's not her, not truly. Sure, it may be her body, but the horrible things she's saying? The cruelness spewing from her lips? That's not Vanessa. She'll hate herself when she's free of her curse, that's for damn sure. The girl loves Violet like a sister, and she has even come to care for Frankie as a brother. Never in a million years would she hurt them like this.

Never.

"It's fine," Frankie bites out curtly, but the hint of compassion in his voice has dissipated.

When I glance over my shoulder at him, his eyes are flinty

orbs—not a single emotion peeking through his apathetic façade.

Violet once described him as a winter wonderland beginning to melt with the first hints of spring, but just then, I can't see it. At all. No, when I stare at him, all I see is a bitter storm crashing through the clearing and shrouding everything in layers of ice and snow. There are no flowers peeking through. No grass. Nothing living can survive such fierce, biting weather.

My sister did that to him.

Vanessa.

Guilt swarms in my lower belly like an army of gnats, but I shove aside the irrational emotion. I can't control the BS my sister says, even if I wish I could. Though perhaps Alex had merit when he mentioned the gag...

"Is there anything you can do for her?" I know I'm pleading, that I'm asking a question that has already been asked one thousand times, but I can't seem to stop myself. Frankie's the smartest man I know, and if anyone can discover a way to save her, it's him.

Sympathy radiates from his eyes like a tiny bud poking through a fluffy snow mound. "I'm sorry, Vin. I did all the research I could on runes and Mount Olympus curses, but I'm not overly familiar with their work. My father, on the other hand, might have more information, but—"

"But since we're not sure if we can trust him, there's no point in asking?" I finish for him.

He nods once, his jaw gritting and genuine regret flickering in his eyes. "I'm sorry."

"It's not your fault. It's Medusa's, and maybe Zeus's, and maybe Hera's, and maybe Lucifer's." I grab at my hair once more and give it a tug.

Fuck. Too many names on the suspect list and not enough

information to cross any of them out as being completely innocent.

"I actually came to talk to you about something," Frankie tells me.

"Did you find a way to enlarge your micro dick?" Vanessa taunts from over my shoulder. "Though...I'm not sure that you have a micro dick. After all, I can't see any other reason why Violet would love you. It's not like you have a winning personality, after all. You must have a big-ass dick to be able to win her over."

We both ignore her.

"What's up?" I ask.

"I think I finally found a way to remove Balor from Jack and Hux's body." Frankie's eyes gleam the way they always do when he solves a case, when he configures the exact measurements for a potion, when one of his experiments works. A begrudging smile twists up his lips. "But I need you to grab something for me. The final piece of this puzzle."

"Do you have a magic penis?" Vanessa muses contemplatively from behind me, and I inwardly wince. I really, really don't like hearing my sister talk about a man's dick. Fucking gross. "Is that what Violet sees in you? This is why I prefer the clamshells, if you know what I mean. I don't need to have a magic dick when I can do the exact same thing with my fist. Like, you should hear the way the women scream for me when I shove it up their cunts and—"

"I'm going to be sick." I place my hand over my mouth.

Even Frankie looks queasy, his cheeks turning green. "Me too."

The two of us quickly exit the room and lock the door behind us, blocking off Vanessa's incessant chatter.

"So what do you need?" I ask, once we're alone in the hall. "What's this final piece of the puzzle you want me to grab?" I cock an eyebrow.

Frankie's smile is sharper than any blade I've ever wielded.

And that, my friends, is how I find myself covered in dirt and sweat as I dig up the grave of a recently deceased college student.

The things this knight will do for his motherfucking queen, I swear.

# CHAPTER 27

VIOLET

I draw lazy circles on Barret's shoulder as I hold him to my body.

His head is nestled on my right breast, almost as if it's his own personal pillow—a titlow, if you must know—and his legs tangle with my own beneath the thick blanket. The air conditioning unit roars from above us, providing a monotonous background noise for this peaceful moment.

And that's what I feel—peace. I can't remember the last time I felt that before.

"What does this mean?" Barret's rough, baritone voice breaks me out of my reverie, and I tilt my chin down to stare at him.

I travel one of my fingers upwards to trace the contours of his handsome face, loving the contradicting textures of his jawline and cheek. Rough and painfully smooth.

"What do you want this to mean?" I whisper.

For some reason, this silence feels…tranquil, almost. Serene. I'm almost too afraid to speak, as if any word I'll make will disrupt the quietness that has settled over us both like a second blanket.

I don't want to ruin this moment between us.

This perfect, beautiful moment.

Barret shifts his head so he's able to place his chin directly on top of my breast and peer up at me. His dark-brown eyes radiate an inner light as he smiles up at me—a sheepish, hopeful, beguiling smile that makes the bats in my stomach do motherfucking cartwheels. Seriously. They should star in their own circus show at this point.

"I want this to mean you're mine," he confesses. "You can be the others' too, but…I need you to be mine as well."

Turtle jam and jelly donuts.

My heart…

It stops.

Quite literally stops beating.

"I'll be yours if you'll be mine," I say softly, continuing to memorize his facial features through touch. The smooth slope of his cheekbone. His broad forehead. That stubble dusting his chiseled jawline.

Barret truly is a work of masculine perfection, and maybe, just maybe, he's mine.

He seems confused by my request, his head canting to the side in a way that once again conjures up images of puppies. "But, Violet…I've always been yours. Always. Even when you weren't mine. You don't need to ask that of me." He blinks up at me with guileless brown eyes as my throat tightens up and my vision turns blurry.

"Why do you have to go and say cute shit like that?" I demand, tugging at his cheeks until his lips touch mine.

Barret lets out a contented, happy sound as he deepens the kiss. The huge-ass dick on my stomach begins to throb, jerking to attention, and liquid heat pools in my lower belly.

"Ready for round two, aren't you, big boy?" I tease as my hand sneaks beneath the blanket to wrap around his girth.

But unfortunately for me and my eager-beaver vagina, we don't get to play out one of my many explicit fantasies concerning the boogeyman. Before I can do more than graze my fingers down the length of his shaft, the door to the bedroom opens and Cal rushes inside with a shit-eating grin on his face. That smile only broadens when he takes in the two of us naked on the bed.

"This is the best day ever!" he whoops enthusiastically, running forward and belly flopping onto the bed.

"Cal!" I squeal, laughing, as his muscular body lands on top of us.

"Cal, I love you, but if you hurt my cheese curd, I'll rip your dick off," Barret says seriously, though his eyes sparkle with amusement.

Cal nuzzles against the two of us like a cat demanding pets before planting a kiss to first my lips and then Barret's.

"I'm just…" Another kiss, this one to the top of my breast. "So fucking happy."

"Finally able to reenact all of your dirty daydreams about the two of us?" I tease as I run my fingers over the feathers of his wings.

They jerk beneath my touch, even as Cal lets out a groan of pleasure.

"Fuck yes! I have sooo many positions I want to try. First, I want to have Violet on her back while I'm pounding into her tight cunt and Barret is feeding her his dick. That's a little tamer than the rest of them, but I figured we'll start easy. Besides, I look absolutely fucking marvelous fucking a girl from above. I mean, have you seen my abs? Perfection. Then, we'll have to try Violet on her knees with me in front and Barret—"

"Wait! Wait! Wait!" I cut Cal off with a laugh, and he turns towards me with a pout pushing out his full bottom lip. "Cal!"

"Ugh. Fine. We can totally do boring vanilla sex. I'm honestly good with anything…just as long as my cock is in your pussy." He says all of that with a completely straight face, and I know he doesn't mean for the words to sound so dirty…but fuck me with a dildo and name that dildo Cal, because I. Am. Here. For. It.

"You know, not all of these fantasies have to include me." I suddenly feel awkward, unsure of how to broach this topic of conversation.

Seriously, Violet? Now you're feeling self-conscious? You've fucked both of them and watched them almost fuck each other. Stop being a little bitch and woman up.

"What do you mean, Cheese Curd?" Barret tugs on my hair until my attention is once again on him.

I know he doesn't mean for the moment to be kinky, but all I can think about is him tugging my hair a little harder and guiding my face towards his rock-hard cock still pressed against me. Taunting me.

Huh. Another kink to put on the list—hair pulling.

"I mean, I'm fine if the two of you want to…you know… be together. Without me." My cheeks fill with flames, and suddenly, it's impossible to meet their eyes. I find myself focusing on the pillow instead, twisting my head to the side slightly.

But then Cal's there, and he's forcing my eyes back to him with a soft smile stretching up his lips. "Sweetheart, I appreciate you giving us permission, but—"

"We like being with you," Barret interrupts. When I glance at him in surprise, his cheeks turn even a brighter shade of red than my own probably are. "Yeah, we like to play together, and yeah, we care about each other a lot, but—"

"We like making you the cheese in our sandwich," Cal finishes, waggling his eyebrows suggestively.

I giggle and toss a half-hearted punch at his bicep. "I'm being serious, Cal. I wouldn't be upset if you guys ever wanted to do something when I wasn't around. This dynamic is new for all of us, and I don't quite know where we stand—"

"You're our mate," Cal says simply, as if that's the answer to all of the world's problems. "Now and forever." He once again leans forward to peck me on the lips, almost as if he can't help himself. As if he constantly needs to be touching me, kissing me, caressing me. "I appreciate you giving us permission, but how about we play this day by day? See where this relationship leads us?"

Relief droops my shoulders as I snuggle farther against Barret, planting a kiss on the top of his head. "I care about you both so much, and I don't want to do anything that will screw it up," I confess in a whisper.

Cal's eyes soften as he runs the palm of his hand down the length of my spine, leaving a trail of goose bumps in its wake.

"You could never screw things up, Violet. Not for us." His grin turns devious, mischievous, and then he's rolling on the bed until I'm straddling his hips.

Barret remains on the bed beside him, though he does twist until he's on his side resting on his elbow. Watching us.

Fuck.

"Now...I'm beginning to feel a little left out and jealous." Cal once again pushes his plump bottom lip out in a mockery of a pout, and I lean forward to tug on it with my teeth, nibbling the sensitive flesh.

"Oh, really?"

"Yes, really." His hands give my hips a squeeze. "So I think the only option here is to make me feel better."

I laugh as I place my hands on his chest.

"You're such a buttface, Cal," I say with a smile.

"Buttface?" Barret frowns. "He has a handsome face. I don't think it looks like a butt at all." He then leans forward to plant a chaste kiss on Cal's nipple.

"Maybe not a butt." I pretend to think about it for a long moment. "But perhaps a dick."

"Violet." Cal's voice rumbles with a warning as the pad of Barret's tongue begins to flick the cupid's nipple back and forth. Pushing down the tiny nub and then allowing it to pop back up again.

"Yes, baby?" I taunt, scratching my fingernails down his chest.

But it's not Cal who answers me.

"As much as I love everything I'm seeing—and trust me, I love this so fucking much, my dick is about to cut through my jeans like a damn drill—I'm gonna have to ask you to put these activities on hold." Mason's amused voice cuts through the lust-filled air.

I groan and twist my head around to glare at him. "Pussy blocker."

"Ouch." He grabs his chest dramatically and staggers back a few steps. "Shots fired, Pinkie."

"But not in my vagina," I grumble irritatedly.

"I'll make it up to you with a good deep dicking later on. How does that sound?" Mason offers.

This time, Cal and Barret are the ones who groan.

"So we get interrupted…and you get the benefits of said interruption?" Cal's wings ruffle with annoyance. "Please explain the logic in that."

"I don't need logic when I'm the favorite mate," Mason teases, grabbing my discarded bathrobe off the ground and handing it to me.

I reluctantly climb off of Cal, pad across the bedroom on bare feet, and take the offered robe from my gorgon mate.

"You guys are all my favorites," I grumble as I shove the robe back on and tie it tight.

"That's what a parent would say when she has an obvious favorite but doesn't want to hurt her other kids' feelings," Mason points out.

I gape at him. "Parents don't have favorites."

He cocks an eyebrow. "So you're saying Dracula didn't have a favorite kid...aka, you?"

"I... No! What?" I sputter...because he's totally right. Dracula has spawned hundreds of kids over his years alive and has only ever shown an interest in me. I even believe the sadistic bastard loves me in his own brutal type of way.

Mason winks, shoots me with his finger gun, and then offers his arm for me to take. "Now, come on. I'll let you stop by your room to get dressed, but then we'll need to get to the living room."

Behind me, I hear the sound of Barret and Cal climbing out of bed and throwing their clothes back on. Well, at least Barret does. Cal didn't come in with a shirt, so I imagine he's not planning on wearing one today.

Stupid, sexy cupid.

He's probably just doing that to drive me and my hormones crazy.

Mason's words suddenly register as we stop at the closet where all of us have been storing our spare clothes.

"What's going on in the living room?" I ask.

"Frankie believes he has found a way to separate Balor from Jack and Hux. But he'll need your help."

"Are we sure this will work?" I ask for the one-millionth time as I eye the glittering blue potion in Frankie's hand.

My scientist mate grants me a "will you just trust me and stop talking" type of look before moving towards a tied-up Balor in the center of the living room.

The Formorian hurls daggers with his eyes at Frankie, then at an intently watching Lucifer, and finally at me.

"You don't want to do this." His Irish accent is even more pronounced than usual as he struggles against his bindings. Genuine fear flashes in his eyes, and a tiny part of me feels sorry for him.

I can't imagine what it would be like to lose everyone he loves in a span of seconds. To then be forced to roam the earth as nothing but a sentient blob of energy, unable to find a host strong enough to contain him. And then, once he finds a host, being forcefully removed from it.

But even my pity isn't strong enough to change my mind. I want—no, I *need* Jack and Hux back. And if that means getting rid of Balor to do it, then so be it.

"You're not even dying, you little fucker," Dracula drawls lazily from where he's lying on the couch.

He seems utterly unconcerned with everything currently transpiring, but I know my father. And that twitch in his right eye is one of the only indications he's not as calm as he would like us all to believe.

"No, you'll just be…transferred." Frankie directs his gaze at the dead body lying on the floor near his feet.

My nose wrinkles instinctively as the pungent scent of rot and decay briefly overwhelms my senses. I know they needed to find a dead body—a body without a soul already attached to it—but did they have to pick one that smelled so awful? Yuck.

At least the body they chose is somewhat good-looking. For a dead guy, at least. Wavy blond hair. Sun-bleached tan skin. Muscular body. I imagine this boy was a looker before death claimed him. A car accident, according to Frankie. Shame.

"You don't think I tried jumping into a dead body?" Balor demands, furious. An ugly red tint darkens his cheeks as he volleys his gaze between everyone present in the room. "I was always kicked out. The body can't contain me."

"It probably couldn't." Frankie shrugs nonchalantly. "But you didn't have a necromancer on hand when you tried before, did you?"

All of us turn towards Alex who has been standing silently in the corner of the room, his face shrouded in shadow and his eyes guarded. When he notices the attention aimed his way, he scowls, pushes away from the wall, and stalks out of the room.

Drama queen.

"I had Alex pour some of his magic into poor Dustin's dead body there. It should be able to contain you. Hopefully. Maybe. Probably." Frankie shrugs his shoulders. "Now… Violet…if you will…" He gestures for me to step forward, and I do so hesitantly.

Balor's eyes immediately snap to my face, and everyone around me tenses. Vin's hand fondles the pommel of his sword, Mason steps closer, and Cal and Barret move to flank me, one on either side. Even Dracula, Lucifer, and Hera are no longer pretending not to be interested. The latter is studying Balor as if he's a bug squashed beneath a glass pane and then placed underneath a microscope.

"What do you need me to do?" I whisper, staring into the eyes of the man who looks so much like my mates…but isn't truly them. At all.

Frankie offers me a gentle smile and grabs my wrist, forcing my hand to land on Balor's knee. Balor jerks at the connection, his eyes widening with unbridled panic and fear, but I shove the swelling pity back down. He doesn't deserve an ounce of it, not after everything he did.

"Please, Violet," he practically begs. "Please don't do this."

I ignore him, though it's one of the hardest things I've ever had to do.

"I'm going to feed Balor this potion," Frankie explains, shaking the glass vial and causing the sparkly blue liquid to swirl. "While I'm doing that, Barret..." The hulking boogeyman places a hand on my shoulder, and Frankie nods once in approval. "Barret is going to form a connection between you and Hux and Jack. Well, their body, technically. I'm not sure if Barret will be able to find them specifically. That will have to be your job. You'll need to find the mate bond and follow it until you can find your mates. Then you'll bring them back to the surface at the same time that I'll place Balor's soul in Dustin's body. Does that make sense?"

"No," I confess. "But that's probably because I'm just dumb."

"Truth," Balor snarls.

"You're not dumb," Frankie assures me, ignoring Balor's interruption. "All you need to do is concentrate on your mates. Pull them forward. Can you do that? We'll take care of the rest."

"I... Yeah." I nod once. For Hux and Jack, I'll do just about anything. "I can do it."

"You ready, Cheese Curd?" Barret gives my shoulder a squeeze before he reaches towards a squirming Balor.

"Let's do this." I grind my teeth together as I meet Balor's fearful, penetrating gaze. "Let's get my mates back."

# CHAPTER 28

JACK

"**W**hat the *heck* are you doing?" I stare at my brother where he perches on the edge of his twin-sized bed, a guitar in his hands as he croons softly.

"Why, I'm writing a love song for my precious treasure, of course." Hux blinks owlishly at me, as if that answer should be obvious, and I attempt to fend off another growing headache.

Who would've thought it'd be possible to get multiple headaches while you're quite literally trapped inside of your body's head? Yeah. Even my mind can't wrap around all of that.

After our time with Violet in that strange dungeon, Balor reclaimed control and kicked us back into the far, forgotten crevice of our shared mind. Only…he didn't leave us stranded in an abyss of darkness this time.

Instead, we appear to be in some sort of bedroom. Two twin beds rest on either side of the spacious room, the blankets a dark shade of navy for Hux and a forest green for me.

Boyish colors, if I'm being completely honest. There's a bookshelf nearest my bed and a wall of weapons beside Hux's.

Aside from that, the room is sparse, devoid of any personal objects or memorabilia.

There's no bathroom, no kitchen. But then again, we don't need to eat, drink, or…um…bodily discharge as figments of a shared subconscious.

Instead, the two of us simply exist in this horrible, in-between space, never knowing what's happening in the outside world. We can feel through our bond with Violet that she's alive and well, but besides that? Nothing. Her absence leaves me feeling bereft and empty, like I'm only half a man without her here.

Errrr. One-third of a man.

Hux's Zeus-awful song drifts to me as he *attempts* to play the guitar and sing. And I'm saying "attempts" to be gener-ous. What he's doing shouldn't be legal. I'm not even techni-cally corporeal, and it feels as if my ears are bleeding.

"*Precious Treasure!*" He jams his fingers down the strings, and this horrible, screeching sound fills the large room. "*You're my pleasure! Because you're a precious treasure! Oh yeah! Precious!*"

He pauses, considers something very carefully, and then bobs his head decisively. He then grabs a pencil from where he positioned it behind his ear and leans forward to scribble the next lyric on the notebook in front of him.

To say Hux has gone insane while separated from Violet is like saying the Sahara is hot during the day. Insanity doesn't even *begin* to describe my psychopathic brother.

The first thing he did when we found ourselves trapped in this strange doorless and windowless room was pound his fists against the walls and threaten bodily harm on everyone and their mother. He then began to laugh erratically, placing a hand to his stomach and doubling over. Then, he sat in the center of the room, utterly silent and stone-faced. This phase lasted for what felt like *days*. During that time, he didn't say a single word. Didn't even seem to notice my existence.

Now?

He's on the wooing stage. The walls are decorated with his messy scrawl as he comes up with one thousand different things to do to win Violet's love—despite the fact he already has it. My brother seems to believe that we'll arrive home and she'll have moved on.

The thought makes my heart lurch in my chest, but I remind myself, as I have one hundred times already, that she loves us. That she needs us. That she's our mate, gifted to us by the fates themselves.

I slide my gaze to the right wall where the majority of his scribbles are.

**Idea one—deliver Balor's head to her on a silver platter. But since that's technically my head as well...**

That idea has been crossed off.

**Idea two—deliver Balor's hand to her on a silver platter. Jack and I can easily go without a hand.**

I argued against that one, and Hux, reluctantly, crossed it out.

**Idea three—buy every chocolate bar from every store in the town. No, every chocolate bar in the country. No, every chocolate bar in the world. CHOCOLATE.**

This last word he wrote in all capital letters, underlined three times, and then circled for emphasis. He seemed pretty pleased with that particular idea.

**Idea four—world domination. My WAP needs an empire to rule.**

I'm not sure Hux knows what WAP truly means yet, but I'm too much of a chicken to tell him it *doesn't* mean Woman I Adore and Protect.

Stupid Mason and his pranks.

His newest idea—idea number nine hundred and eighty-six—is to write Violet a song declaring his unwavering devotion and love and then sing it to her while a fountain sprays the blood of her enemies nearby. I had to remind him that it isn't practical to have a fountain that only emits blood, but he's a stubborn a-hole when he wants to be.

If it's a blood fountain his precious treasure wants, it's a blood fountain she'll get.

Thoughts of Violet have heat racing to my cock and dread pulsating through my veins. The contradicting emotions actually make me feel light-headed, golden speckles obscuring my vision.

On one hand, the memory of our coupling plays on a continuous loop in my head. The way she allowed me to take control, to be rough and abrasive...

But on the other hand, worry for her consumes me. It's all I can think about, all I can focus on. I know she's alive and relatively safe, but for how long? What if something happens to her and we're unable to protect her because we're trapped away?

It hurts to swallow around the tightness in my throat, so instead, I focus on my brother's newest lyrics.

"*Your titties look like mitties...and I want to put my hands in them,*" he sings.

My brows furrow. "Mitties? As in...mittens?"

He stops playing almost immediately and levels me with what I call his crazy stare—one full of ice and dripping with violence. Most people would know to immediately stop talking, but I've never been afraid of my brother before.

Well, not *completely* afraid.

I know he won't hurt me, at the very least, so there's that.

"What about mittens?" Hux doesn't remove his eyes from

me as he brings his hand down the strings, a horrible screech emitting from the instrument.

"Well…you can't put your hands in, um, titties." A blush rises in my cheeks as I fiddle with my glasses. "Only, um, on them."

"You can if you're removing her heart from her chest," Hux points out seriously, and I balk.

"You want to remove Violet's heart from her chest?" I demand, incredulous.

He stares at me as if I just insulted his entire family with one sentence. His mouth quite literally pops open as shock splays across his face. "I would never hurt my precious treasure!" he practically roars, his arm muscles going positively rigid.

A venomous snarl rearranges his features as his grip around the guitar…errr….head? Is that the term? Well, his grip around it tightens until a deafening crack reverberates through the room.

Is he going through another stage of grief and denial?

Maybe rage this time?

But then…all of those emotions accumulating in his eyes diminish to be replaced by wonderment. He tilts his head to the side, his silky black hair falling across his shoulder, and asks, "Do you hear that?"

"That horrible song you call music?" I ask dryly, but I stop to consider his question. What I hear is…

Nothing. Absolutely nothing. It's an unnatural kind of silence that always makes my hackles rise. No air conditioning unit whirring above. No fan attempting to circulate the air. No subdued chatter. No crickets or birds. Nothing.

But then I hear a soft, melodic voice, and it's like my world stops. Everything inside of me stops as well—my heart, my lungs, even my freaking mind. I can scarcely believe what I'm hearing, and I half wonder if this is one of Balor's tricks.

"Jack? Hux?"

Sweet. Tentative. Unsure. Lyrical.

Violet.

"PRECIOUS TREASURE!" Hux throws himself at the wall where her voice is coming from and begins to pound his fists against the plaster. His face is twisted with rage and a desperate, soul-consuming need to get to her.

"Violet! Is that you, sweetheart?" I raise my voice to be heard, though it sounds distant compared to the rapid thumping of my heart. I swear that organ is all I can hear as it takes up residence in my skull.

*Ba-dum. Ba-dum. Ba-dum.*

"Oh, thank fuck!" Violet's voice sounds directly on the other side of the wall where, if this were a normal room in a normal house, there'll be a doorway. "We need to leave! Now!"

Hux continues to throw his entire body against the wall, almost as if he believes he's the Kool-Aid Man who can break through the impenetrable material with little effort, materialize in front of Violet, and bellow, "Oh yeah!"

He can't, by the way. He already tried.

But I leave him be, knowing that he'll quite literally rip my head off if I attempt to stop him.

"We can't get out, sweetheart!" I call, moving forward until my hand can touch the wall. I imagine Violet directly on the other side, her own hand separated from mine by only plaster. The thought has my pulse skittering. "There's no doorway!"

"Fuck," she bites out. "You guys need to imagine a door, then, okay? Imagine a door, open it, and then come to me."

Hux roars in fury. Not at Violet's words, of course, but at his own inability to break free and get to her. The same desperation lining his face courses through my own veins and steals the breath from my lungs.

We need to get to her.

Now.

"We tried that already," I tell Violet, attempting to ignore Hux's ferocious snarls and growls. Frick. He's going to lose his darn mind if we can't get out of here.

"I'm right here, my loves. Right on the other side of the wall. I need you to concentrate. I need you to open up the damn door and come to me." Her voice is laced with steel and desperation and maybe a little bit of fear too.

It's that fear that stills my heart and floods insidious terror through my awareness.

For Violet, I'll try anything.

Even something as simple as closing my eyes and envisioning a doorway.

"For Violet," I murmur as my eyelids flutter shut.

I can still hear Hux's ragged breathing from the other side of me, but I know he's doing the same as me. He'll do anything for her, just as I would.

I focus on my connection to Violet Dracula and the way she makes me feel like the only man alive. When I'm with her, the rest of the world fades away like a spotlight has descended from the heavens to illuminate her beautiful, heart-shaped face. Her laughter and smile turn my palms clammy with this desperate, irresistible urge to please her. To hear that sound again and see that smile a second time.

Everything that I am belongs to her...including my mind.

As I think of her, a doorway begins to form behind my closed eyelids.

Violet's dorm room.

I focus as hard as I can on my need to get to her, to see her, to hold her...and when my eyes snap open, a nondescript wooden door now resides in the center of the wall.

"Precious Treasure!" Hux is already running forward, pulling the door open, and hurrying out of the room.

I'm only a few steps behind him, my mind consumed by Violet.

As soon as my foot exits the makeshift bedroom, my stomach gives a painful lurch and stars explode across my vision.

*Hux!* I try to yell his name, but I have no control of my body.

Is this a trick? Balor?

Terror squeezes my heart as I tumble through a sea of unending darkness.

And then…

And then I wake up, and the room is bathed in light.

I FEEL GROGGY, AS IF MY HEAD HAS BEEN PACKED FULL OF cotton balls, and I find myself blinking obsessively as a familiar, tear-stained face comes into view.

"What…?" I moan, attempting to clutch at my head before discovering my arms are restrained by thick metal chains.

"Get his chains off! Now!" Violet demands, and someone —I can't see who—hurries forward to do as she bids.

*Precious Treasure!* Hux roars in my mind, battling against our shared awareness.

An unfamiliar, low moan echoes through the room, and I hear Vin snap, "Tie the fucker up," but I can't look away from Violet to see who he's talking about.

"Is-is this real?" My voice cracks, and I find myself clearing my throat excessively, just to give myself something to do.

A single tear spills down Violet's cheek, and I hear Hux snarl in my head at the sight of it.

"It's real. You guys are safe. Both of you." She throws herself at me at the same moment the last chain clatters to the ground.

As soon as her soft curves are pressed against me, I give in to the incessant prodding of Hux and allow him to slip into the proverbial driver's seat.

"Precious Treasure," he rasps as I watch through our shared eyes, scarcely able to believe that this is real life. That she's truly here.

"Hux! Jack!" She begins to sob as she kisses us passionately.

I can taste the salt from her tears as they cascade across her lips.

"Where's Balor?" Hux snarls, pulling his head away from Violet to search the room.

I see a sea of familiar faces—Violet's other mates—as well as a few sort-of-familiar men and one woman. Is that Dracula? But who is that woman glaring at us? Who is that man scowling? Their names rest on the tip of my tongue…

Another low moan draws my attention to a blond man lying on the ground at Frankie's feet, a collection of chains wrapped around his muscular form.

"Who's that?" Hux demands, echoing my own confusion.

Before anyone can respond, there's a deafening boom that rattles the house.

Instantly, Hux has his arms around Violet in a protective embrace, and he roars his fury as he scans the room for threats.

Everyone, including the three strangers, are alert and moving to surround us in a defensive position.

Violet's fingers tighten in my—*our* black hair as her body shakes with tremors.

"What the hell?" she whispers as Hux continues to hold her protectively up against him.

He leans down to inhale her berry scent, rifling through her blonde hair with the tip of his nose. It's almost as if he can't help himself, as if the time we've been away from her has corrupted something fundamental in his coding. He can't seem to stop touching and sniffing her, even with the impending threat.

Not that I'm complaining.

I would happily keep Violet in my arms for the rest of my immortal life if I could.

But unfortunately, fate has other plans for us, as it always seems to. And those other plans take the form of two huge, towering deities that I know we'll need to fight and kill if we want to save Violet's life.

My heart pounds as Hux snarls fiercely, shifting Violet so she's now behind him.

Zeus and Medusa stand in the entryway, matching smirks on their faces. And as I watch, horrified, Zeus points one huge finger in Violet's direction and hisses, "It's time for the abomination to finally fucking die."

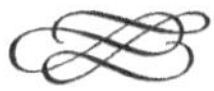

# CHAPTER 29

VIOLET

W hat in the hairy balls is even happening right now?

I try to peer around Hux's broad body, but he simply tightens his grip on me, turning us both so he's in front of me. Fierce indignation and anger ripple through me at the fact that these motherfucking assholes dared to interrupt my reunion with my mates. Just who do they think they are?

*Oh, just the god of everything.*

No biggie.

I half want to giggle hysterically, but one look into Zeus's vitriol-filled eyes drains away any mirth and amusement. In their place is fear.

Because that glint in his gaze…

The way he so intently focuses on me…

Chills erupt on my skin, and I have the irresistible urge to wrap my arms around myself in an attempt to ward off the coldness. My death is a promise in his eyes, but I'll be damned if I accept it with open arms.

"What's the meaning of this, husband?" Hera gasps, pulling herself away from the rest of the group to garner his attention.

His beady eyes caress her in a way that isn't loving or even affectionate—it's assessing and critical. "My darling wife. It's lovely to see you here." He smiles, but it's not the type of grin a doting husband would give the love of his life.

It's the smile a serial killer would offer his latest victim a second before he plunges a knife into her chest.

Zeus looks almost exactly the same now as he did when I last saw him, from the unruly black hair cascading around his face in waves, the scruffy beard lining his jaw, and those dark, penetrating eyes of his. He even wears the same ruby-red robe that clings to his muscular arms and just barely fits around his torso. But while before he exuded a childlike energy and playfulness, now, he reminds me of a python tensing just before it strikes to kill.

And I'm the tasty little piece of meat he's aiming for.

Oh god.

I'm gonna be eaten by the head honcho of Olympus, aren't I?

My name on the menu? Violet Dracul-yuma.

Yup. You heard it here first.

"You…" Lucifer's voice is rife with accusation as he takes a step forward, his pointer finger raised and trembling as he levels it at the god's thick chest. "It was you, wasn't it?"

Huh?

I feel as if I missed an entire conversation—or a train of thought—but no one else interrupts to demand an explanation, so I just nod my head and pretend I know exactly what they're talking about. It is my motto, after all.

Fake it till you make it.

Actually, my motto is, "When performing anal, make sure to use lots of lube, especially if you're using your fist."

But semantics.

I glower at Zeus and Medusa. "It was them," I say confidently. "I fucking knew it."

Actually, I don't know jack squat, but again…faking it.

Zeus's cruel lips curve into a malicious sneer as he gives me a slow, unimpressed once-over. "I suppose you're not as stupid as I thought, Miss Dracula," he muses.

"Of course I'm not fucking stupid," I snap. "I know exactly what you are and what you did." I point a finger in his direction, just as Lucifer's still doing, and growl, "Don't even try to lie to me."

Vin casts me a quick, dubious glance—probably the only one in this room who knows I have no idea what the fuck is going on—but he doesn't call me out on my bullshit. Instead, he flicks his attention back to the two bigger threats in the room, lowering his stance with his sword extended.

I notice that Mason must've grabbed Dimitri at some point, probably when we first heard the explosion, and is now positioning the still unconscious man protectively behind his body. My heart swells with love for my mate at his consideration. He knew we might need to leave in a hurry, but he also knew I would never, ever leave Dimitri behind.

Now, if only the damn headmaster would wake up…

"I sometimes wish my plan had worked," Zeus begins lazily. The idiotic man-child from before is nowhere to be seen. In his place is a fierce predator, his eyes homed in on the impending kill.

Me.

I'm the impending kill.

"Don't we all?" I sneer at him. "But guess what, Zeus? You're a fuckup."

Yeah. I have no idea what plan he's talking about, but

maybe if I can get him to talk, he'll reveal all of his deep, dark, dirty secrets.

Hera looks as if she's going to be sick, even as her body continues to tremor with barely contained fury. It's strange to see on her elfin, angelic face. Unnatural, almost. It paints deep crevices where there was once nothing but smooth, unblemished skin. Her eyes seem to spark with power and raw, incandescent rage.

"You tried to kill my daughter as a baby, didn't you?" she demands, her tone breaking as betrayal momentarily flitters across her beautiful face.

Ohhhh.

That's what they're talking about.

*Oh...*

Oh shit.

Zeus is the one who tried to have me killed? That makes no sense. Lucifer claimed it was Hera, and Hera insisted she saw Lucifer—

"It's amazing what an illusion spell can do." Zeus smirks cruelly as his skin ripples and distorts.

A second later, I'm no longer staring into Zeus's icy, all-consuming eyes. Instead, my gaze lands on Lucifer's face, his features still warped into a demented smile. I blink, and Zeus changes his appearance yet again until he's shrunk in height and delicate, golden curls cascade around his shoulders. Hera.

"No," Lucifer breathes in horror as Zeus grows exponentially, rising to his full, impressive height that towers over us all.

"I'm the King of Gods, my dear brother," Zeus taunts. "Did you really think I wouldn't be able to do something as simple as an illusion spell?" He twists his head to glare at my birth mother, who meets his gaze without an ounce of fear in her eyes, only fury. "That night your precious baby was attacked, you believed the assailant to be Lucifer." He flicks his gaze in Lucifer's direction. "And you believed your lovely Hera—my cheating whore of a wife—to be the killer."

"Is that what this is about?" Lucifer demands fiercely. "My affair with Hera?"

Zeus throws his head back and cackles. The noise is… eerie, to put it mildly. Goose bumps skirt up and down my arms at the cold, insidious sound. It scratches at my skin like talons, leaving behind jagged, bloody wounds that I know will never quite heal properly.

"Do you think I give a damn what my bitch of a wife does with her pussy?" He cants his head to the side mockingly.

"This is about the prophecy, isn't it?" Dracula asks softly.

He's been mostly silent since this entire confrontation began, but no one with eyes can mistake his quietness for duplicity. He's as wound tight as the rest of the men—and women—in this room, just waiting for the opportunity to pounce.

"No one"—Zeus's eyes zero in on my face, and the rage emanating from those orbs is almost palpable—"will take my throne from me."

"Why didn't you just finish the job when I was a child?" I demand, attempting to step around Hux once more.

Like before, he grabs me and tugs me tight against his body, shielding me as best as he can as if he's afraid Zeus will lob a fireball at us or something. Honestly, I wouldn't put it past the deranged bastard.

"I considered it," Zeus answers truthfully, shrugging his broad shoulders. "But then I had a taste of your power, Violet. Even as a baby, it was…" His eyes roll into the back of his head as if he's in the midst of an orgasm, and I feel my nose wrinkle in disgust. "Delicious. I decided to wait until you were all grown up, until you've grown into your powers, to kill you."

"Y-you want to take my powers?" I whisper, hearing everything he didn't say.

Horror inflates my veins like helium in a balloon, and I take a step backwards instinctively. Zeus watches that miniscule retreat with a wicked gleam in his eyes.

"I want to digest them," he corrects...as if there's really a fucking difference. Take, eat, digest. What's next? Shit out? "The same way I've been digesting powers for centuries."

"The souls." The shocked murmur, surprisingly, doesn't come from one of my guys or my parents. It's Balor who speaks, his body still restrained by chains and his face devoid of any color. He leans forward where he sits on the floor, and a strand of golden hair falls forward to obscure his eye from view.

"Balor." Zeus's eyes widen in recognition.

"Is that why you've locked my people away?" Balor demands, his Irish accent deepening in response to his mounting anger. He tries to stand up, but the chains prohibit him from doing more than wiggling around like a fish flopping on dry land. "Because you wanted control of the souls? Not to protect them...but to fucking *digest* them?"

"Wait..." My mind travels back to Mount Olympus the last time I visited it. How empty it felt. It reminded me of one of those post-apocalyptic movies where a radio broadcast declares the end of the world as we know it and everyone rushes home, forgetting that they've been in the middle of doing something. I remembered it had struck me as odd, but since Medusa didn't seem worried about it, I wasn't either.

"The souls." Hera gasps. "You said that the balance has just been tipped in Hell's favor, but that wasn't the truth, was it? You've been..." She looks as if she's going to be sick. "You've been eating the souls fated to live out their eternity in Mount Olympus?"

"*Digesting*," Zeus, once again, feels the need to correct.

"There's really no fucking difference, dude," I murmur under my breath, and Hux hushes me, his strong body rippling with tension.

"For once in your life, Precious Treasure, can you stop painting a target on your back? Please? For me?" he practically begs, his words a harsh rasp in my ear.

I blow out a breath. "Fine," I huff.

"Mother." Mason steps away from Dimitri, who's still lying unconscious on the ground, and Barret goes to take his place, standing protectively in front of my fallen mate.

Medusa licks her lower lip, but she doesn't meet her son's probing gaze even as he steps closer to her.

"Why are you doing this?" he continues in a calm, placating tone. He raises both hands in the air as if he's trying to show her that he's not armed, that he won't hurt her. "Is it because of the other prophecy? The one about me? About my death? You know that what Zeus is doing is wrong. You know that. You're a good woman—"

Medusa's twinkling laugh fills the room. Slowly, she reaches a hand up to cup my lover's cheek, her eyes growing tender. "I'm not a good woman, my dear Mason." Her thumb traces lazy circles on his cheekbone as her eyes fill with unshed tears. "But I have come to love you as my own son. It's a shame, really. A true shame. I'm sorry, my boy, but I always knew it would come to this. The only way to kill Violet is to kill everyone she loves. We need to break her, my dear child, and the prophecy told us exactly how to do that."

"What...?" Mason's face scrunches in confusion. He doesn't pull his gaze away from his mother's.

It's because of that he doesn't see the god-blessed dagger glinting ominously in Medusa's hand. It's because of that he doesn't see her bringing her free arm back, her gaze never leaving his. It's because of that he's only aware of the danger when my scream rips apart the very foundations of reality and pain lances my chest.

His eyes grow wide as the dagger impales itself in his chest, directly where his heart should be.

"No!" I scream, thrashing against Hux's arms, trying to break free. "NO!" It's an anguished cry torn from my lips, and it tastes like bile coming out.

This can't be happening. This can't be fucking happening.

"Mason!" Vin roars, attempting to lunge forward as well.

Lucifer, surprisingly, is the one who stops him, his hand fisting in the back of Vin's shirt until he's able to grab my inconsolable mate in a choke hold.

But all I can see is my sweet, funny, perfect mate falling to the ground, blood forming on the edges of his lips. All I can hear is the strange choking sound he makes as he topples forward and the whispered, "Violet," that shatters all of my defenses.

And then the jovial light I've come to love so much diminishes from Mason's eyes as he dies.

No! No! No!

Mason's name is torn in a hiccupping sob as tears run freely down my cheeks.

*This is just a nightmare.*

*Just a nightmare.*

*Not real. Not real. Not real.*

Medusa's face distorts the same way Zeus's did when he changed appearance and turned into my bio parents. One second, I'm staring at Medusa's elegant features, and the next, the sharp angles of her face turn softer as a familiar woman peers back at me. Brown, curly hair. Eyes that I once thought were bright and compassionate but are now twisted in malice. Lips curled into a hideous sneer.

"I'm sorry, my dear boy." Even her voice is different now that she's not disguised as Medusa—light and airy, like broken wind chimes rattling around in my brain. "I really did come to love you, even if your true mother has been dead for over ten years." Her eyes momentarily flash with sorrow and grief. "But I can't allow you to get in the way of our plans. You had to die, you see? We had to break Violet."

I suppose the prophecy was right after all. Mason *was* killed by Dracula's daughter...just not by me.

No, the person staring down at Mason's body with a forlorn expression is none other than Diedre Stevens, the teacher I killed months ago after she framed me for murder.

*Killed Mason.*

*Killed mate.*

*Killed...*

*Dead...*

*He's dead.*

*Dead.*

*Dead.*

*Dead.*

And...I shatter.

# CHAPTER 30

VIOLET

I don't even recognize the sounds leaving my mouth. They're not screams or sobs. Not really. They're just… noise. Terrible, horrible, hideous bursts of sound that have my ears ringing.

Mason. Not my sweet Mason.

Grief sweeps over me in a tidal wave of sensation—in emotions and feelings I can't even begin to untangle let alone put a name to. I'm crying, but then I'm screaming, and then I'm making that same, eerie noise from before. It may even be laughter. Fuck if I know anymore.

The part inside of me where Mason always resided, the piece of my heart and soul that belonged solely to him, is no longer there. It's like his death has taken a piece of me with him.

I'll no longer be able to hear his laugh as he tells a stupid joke. I'll no longer see his cunning smirk or the way his eyes twinkle when he smiles. I'll no longer hear him say, "Pinkie," in such a reverent way that my heart flutters and my skin comes alive with goose bumps.

He's dead.

Gone.

Because they took him from me.

I try to lunge forward, try to destroy the threat directly in front of me before they can harm anyone else I love, but strong arms grab me from behind.

Not one of my mates.

Dracula.

"Are you trying to get yourself killed?" he growls in my ear, but I'm too lost in my rage and pain to acknowledge him.

If getting killed means sparing my men, then so be it. I'll willingly rip my own heart from my chest if it means having Mason back.

"Mason!" I scream, unable to tear my eyes away from my sweet mate's face. It's so still in death. So slack. I would almost say he looks peaceful if his mouth weren't slightly open, blood drizzling down his chin. And then…I'm sobbing. Horrible, aching sobs that tear from my throat and make me light-headed and dizzy. I would've fallen if Dracula's arms hadn't tightened around me, holding me up.

"We always suspected that Medusa's son would be involved in the prophecy." Diedre Stevens—my mother-fucking teacher who died months ago—stares down at Mason's prone form with deadened eyes. Her lips tug into a frown. "What are the odds that the seer would give us two prophecies back-to-back and not have them related?" She laughs lightly, but the noise is devoid of any humor. "Zeus asked me to keep an eye on Mason, so…"

"So you murdered Medusa and took her place?" Hera fills in, and she sounds absolutely furious. More than furious—enraged. She glares at Diedre as if she imagines plucking every hair off of her perfect head.

"I did what I had to do for the man I love," Diedre insists, flashing doe eyes in Zeus's direction.

I hear their conversation. I do, but I'm not comprehending a word they say. It's like everything enters one ear and then immediately slides out the other, dissipating in the wind blowing through the doorway they exploded.

"Diedre." Dracula sounds stunned as he stares at his blood daughter.

"Hi, Daddy." She waves her fingers at him, even as her eyes darken, something truly menacing crossing her face. "Funny how you acknowledge me only because you know I'm about to kill your favorite daughter." Her lips curl. "A daughter, might I add, that isn't even technically yours."

"So you pretended to be Medusa to keep an eye on Mason when he was younger, believing him to play a part in the prophecy of Violet taking the throne," Lucifer deduces.

Mason.

Mason.

Mason.

His name reverberates through my head like a ball made of poison-tipped nails. Scratching. Slicing. *Burning.*

Oh god. It burns. It fucking burns.

"And then, when Violet got admitted to Prodigium Academy, you followed her there to keep an eye on her," Dracula continues, his tone assessing and slightly disbelieving. "You murdered all of those students, but not because you wanted Violet to be a martyr. You wanted to fuel anti-vampire and anti-Dracula sentiments."

"You're dead." Frankie points a trembling finger in Diedre's direction, tears streaming down his cheeks. "You're supposed to be dead. Violet killed you. I saw your body."

Diedre's plush red lips push out into a pout, even as her hands wrap around Zeus's arm and give it a squeeze. "I would've been dead, yes, if Zeus baby hadn't brought me back to life." She blinks coyly up at him, and that...

That breaks me.

"YOU KILLED MASON!" I scream, once again attempting to lunge at her.

I'll claw her eyes out. I'll burn her flesh from her bones.

Power, the same power I only experienced once before, ricochets through me. And I know that this ball of darkness in the center of my chest, this anger and rage and fury, is the same dark magic that murdered all of those hunters when they attacked me.

Will this strange, malevolent magic kill Zeus and Diedre? Or will it also harm my mates? Will it be able to decipher friend from foe or will it kill indiscriminately?

*No. I can't take that chance.*

*I can't lose another one of my men.*

I attempt to reel the dark power back in even as black spots erupt across my vision. My hands curl into fists by my sides, and I swear I feel claws embed themselves in my palms.

I want to scream, to roar. To hunt and maim. To bleed and kill.

"I wouldn't do that if I were you, Miss Dracula." Zeus releases a throaty chuckle. "Because you see, I didn't come here unprepared. Before I left Olympus, I digested hundreds and hundreds of delicious souls." He licks his slimy lips in euphoria. "Their powers are coursing through my veins right now, fueling me."

"You sick bastard—" I begin, but my words are cut off when Zeus smiles savagely, raises both of his hands into the air, and a wave of power ripples across the room.

At first, I don't feel anything. Not even an itch to signify he used his creepy, stolen magic on me or anyone else, for that matter.

But then my mates all roar in agony, clutching their

biceps. Even Dimitri begins to convulse on the ground, as if he's attempting to escape some phantom pain I can't see.

"What the fuck?" Vin breathes in horror, pulling up his black T-shirt until his bronze skin is bared.

"No…" I whisper. My eyes are glued to the symbol burned onto his flesh.

The rune.

The same one Vanessa wears on her neck, making her insane with rage.

I begin to shake my head adamantly, as if that can make me unsee it, but no matter what I do, the mark remains.

"Violet," Frankie says, terrified.

And then, as one, all of my men stiffen, becoming as still as statues. Even Dimitri ambles to his feet, though his body remains limp and unresponsive.

A puppet held up by strings.

"This mark doesn't just fuel rage, Miss Dracula," Zeus says with a cocksure smirk. "It also allows me to… How can I say this? Influence my victims. They'll have no choice but to obey me, even if it goes against every one of their instincts."

"No." I shake my head again as Lucifer, Dracula, and Hera all form a tight circle around me.

They're the only three who don't seem to be impacted by Zeus's spell. No doubt, they're too powerful for him to control like that.

I desperately glance from one of my mates to the next, praying I'll see some sort of recognition in their impassive gazes, some sort of emotion. But all I see are blank canvases.

Hux. Jack. Frankie. Vin. Cal. Barret. Dimitri.

They're all lost to me.

And Mason…

Another anguished sob escapes me as I fall to my knees amongst my circle of protectors.

No. No. No.

Balor struggles against the chains confining him. Apparently he, too, wasn't impacted by Zeus's spell.

His eyes are clouded with rage as he glares at the King of Gods. "I'm going to kill you for what you did to my people. You mark my fucking words," he hisses, venom spewing from his pores.

Zeus laughs haughtily. "Did you know that I tried to take the power of the Formorians at first? They're who gave me the idea, after all. A species of monsters who ride through the spiritual plane, collecting souls as they go." He leans down until he's at eye level with a seething, raging Balor. "It didn't work. I wasn't able to take their power, but my experiments *did* kill them. Not all of them, of course. I don't kill monsters and humans senselessly, only when I need something from them. When I discovered that I couldn't digest the Formorians' powers, I locked them back in their little prison to live out the rest of their sad, pathetic, miserable existence." He pats Balor's cheek in a way that I would almost describe as condescending. Balor jerks away as if his touch burned. "No matter. With the Formorians locked away, and my people now in charge of the collection of souls, I have more than enough to digest. Each soul has power, you see, regardless if they're human or monster. And the second I digest that soul? That power becomes *mine*."

"You're insane." My voice cracks, but it has the desired effect—Zeus's attention snaps to me.

"Maybe." He shrugs. "Or maybe I'm just a king who loves his throne. And when someone tries to threaten that throne..." He tsks his tongue and shakes his head as Diedre cackles. "She'll pay." He snaps his fingers, and all of my mates turn their attention on me, clarity momentarily entering their eyes. "Kill Violet's protectors but bring the girl to me. I want to kill her myself so I can digest her sweet, delicious power."

His eyes sparkle with glee as pained, tortured expressions mar my men's faces.

"I can't control it," Vin barks out through gritted teeth.

"Precious Treasure, get out of here!" Hux bellows.

And then they're charging. My mates, my loves, my entire world… They're running at me, and I know, I just know, they won't be able to stop until my parents are dead and I'm in Zeus's arms.

I wrap my arms around myself as I sob, just sob, distantly aware of a fight erupting all around me.

Barret roars as he throws a meaty fist at Dracula's head, but my father ducks out of the way with a burst of his vampire speed and then jumps onto the boogeyman's back. My mate bucks, attempting to dislodge him, but Dracula wraps an arm around Barret's throat, cutting off his air supply.

But then Cal's there, his eyes completely black, and he's ripping Dracula's arm off of Barret with a deafening, cracking sound.

Vin and Frankie have surrounded Hera, who's fighting like her life depends on it. Or…like *my* life depends on it. I notice, though, that she never goes for the killing blow, even when Frankie leaves a clear opening for her to stab him in the chest.

They're trying not to kill my mates.

But it won't be enough.

"Mase…" I whimper, crawling between the throng of fighting bodies until I'm overtop of my fallen gorgon. I sob as I bring his head to my lap and caress his cold cheeks. "Mason, I'm so sorry. I'm so, so sorry. I love you so much. I'm sorry." I don't even know what I'm saying anymore as I rest my forehead against his, sobbing into his skin. "I love you. I love you. I love you."

"GET HER OUT OF HERE!" Dracula bellows, and at

first, I think he's talking to me. Honestly, I have no idea who he's addressing, my attention consumed by my dead mate.

I killed him.

Me.

My fault.

And then I feel a hand on my arm, tugging me away, and I scream, "Don't take me from him!"

"Dammit, Violet! We need to go!" Alex's sharp voice cuts through the grief devouring me just enough to snap my head up, my eyes blurring with tears. He stands with his jaw clenched, his muscles trembling with barely suppressed fury, as, behind him, my mates and parents continue to fight.

I watch Vin rush at Lucifer with his sword raised, but my birth dad swats him away as if he's nothing but a pesky fly. Vin sails through the air, but before he can make contact with the wall, he expertly flips himself so he lands in a crouched position instead. And then he's running back into the fray, all without even breaking a sweat.

"Your parents are trying their fucking hardest not to kill your mates, but they won't hesitate to eliminate them if it means protecting you. So if you want to save your mates, we need to get you the fuck out of here!" Alex growls, grabbing at my arm again.

"But Mason…" I sob, clutching my dead mate to my chest.

The necromancer's eyes shadow. "Violet, I'm sorry."

"No—" My protest is cut off as Alex's hand clamps down on my upper arm, and then the world is fading away in a flash of images—graveyards and bones and decaying corpses. My stomach tightens as if it's been filled with cement when we're spit out into the middle of a cemetery, directly over a freshly dug grave.

"NO!" I scream as I realize what Alex just did.

Who he took me from.

Mason. Vin. Frankie. Dimitri. Hux. Jack. Barret. Cal.

My mates.

He took me from them.

And just like before, grief rips me apart from the inside out until I'm falling, falling, falling…

Then darkness.

# CHAPTER 31

Violet's cry of grief and rage will haunt me until the day I die.

But that sound is nothing compared to the tumultuous emotions inside of my chest as I think about everything that has just transpired in the last few minutes.

Being forced to attack my mate, the love of my life.

And…

Mason's death.

Grief strangles me, rips me apart, but outwardly, I know my expression to be apathetic, just like the others'. Impassive. The control Zeus has on us is ironclad.

As soon as Violet disappeared with the necromancer, Zeus bellowed in rage, screaming obscenities into the air. But inwardly, I was so fucking relieved that my girl had gotten herself out of there. I would have to kiss Alex's feet when I saw him next in gratitude.

From there, everything happened rather quickly.

Lucifer, Hera, and Dracula all stopped fighting, as if now

that Violet was gone, they had no reason to. And since they were no longer putting up a fight, Zeus had no reason to utilize us. He simply snapped his fingers, and all of us went utterly still, our bodies puppets for him to use and discard.

But our minds?

Our minds are still our own.

The way Zeus had me freeze puts me directly in front of Mason's body.

Mason...

My best friend...

He's all I can see, all I'm aware of, my attention utterly consumed by his corpse. If I had control of my body, I imagine I'll be sobbing right about now as grief tears me in two. My heart's a restless bird fluttering in its cage, but it's not the good type of flutter. No, it's the type that makes it feel as if you're free falling, diving headfirst off a steep cliff and praying that your death will be quick and painless. However, before your body can hit the rapid waters far below, you veer slightly to the right, where jagged, gray rocks protrude from the outcropping. All you can manage is a strangled cry of fear and agony before you're speared on a particular sharp one jutting higher above the rest.

Death.

Agony.

"What do we do with them?" Diedre Stevens jerks her chin to encompass the group of us surrounding Lucifer, Hera, and Dracula.

Unwilling slaves.

Victims.

Puppets.

Anger thrums through me like an electrical current, but with Zeus's spell in place, all I manage to do is grit my teeth together.

My gaze sweeps over the room, taking inventory of the

men who have become like brothers to me. Well, as close to brothers as we can be, considering we all fuck the same girl. I wouldn't want to see my actual brother's dick, if you know what I mean.

Hux and Jack's body is a picture of turmoil and anguish. One half of his face twists in anger—his upper lip curls away from his teeth in a snarl, his eye is molten with fury, and his hand is clenched into a fist he can't lift. The other half, however, is despondent—this eye droops slightly, tears glimmering in its dark depths, his hand is somewhat relaxed by his side, and his teeth nibble on his lower lip anxiously.

Hux and Jack...the perfect dichotomy. One as wild and savage as the ocean which drags your miserable soul away, and the other as steadfast and lethal as the rock which spears you. Both incredibly deadly, but for entirely different reasons.

I imagine all of Jack's pacifist policies will fly out the window the second he gets free of this.

I move only my eyes to focus on Frankie next. His features are slack and his eyes could best be described as docile, but I could never mistake him as being anything but calculating. Even with his expression carefully impassive, I know his mind will be sifting through every way we can get out of this mess and kill Zeus and Diedre for what they did. If anyone can come up with a solution, it'll be him.

Barret and Cal stand shoulder to shoulder on the opposite side of Frankie. Barret's light-green hair sways in the invisible breeze brought about by his impressive, but currently leashed, power, the only outward sign of his distress, and Cal's red and black feathers begin to ruffle in agitation. Both men hurl daggers with their eyes at an oblivious Diedre, still swooning and moaning over Zeus.

That bitch should wish she remained dead. The second we get our hands on her...

I force myself to take a deep breath, to not think about my best friend, and instead turn my attention to the last member of this ragtag group.

Dimitri Gray looks like death warmed over. He's still unconscious, a fact made obvious by the way his head droops forward despite his body hanging suspended in the air. His feet feather against the ground, but I'm not sure if they ever actually touch. After all, he's just a life-sized marionette for the gods to do their bidding with. Well, one god in particular.

That familiar burst of anger rages inside of me, demanding an outlet, a release. My fingers begin to twitch by my sides, and a thrill of hope surges through me.

If I can move my body…

If I can get to them…

If I can end this…

"Your quest for power, my dear husband, will get you killed." Hera's smooth, lyrical voice brushes past my ears as she confidently struts forward and stops when she's only a few feet away. "I'll be your willing prisoner, but you must know how this will end for you."

"And you, my darling wife…" He matches her five brisk steps with a huge one of his own. He's so much taller than the gorgeous, petite woman that she needs to crane her neck back to maintain eye contact, something she does without an ounce of hesitation. He tenderly places a hand on her cheek, cupping her porcelain skin, and her lashes flutter shut with something resembling pain.

Lucifer releases a guttural growl, but Dracula's hand on the devil's shoulder stops him.

"Your love for your daughter will get you killed," Zeus continues.

"I'll die a thousand times over for her." Hera's eyes snap open, filled with a fire I'm all too familiar with. A fire I've seen time and time again in her daughter's eyes. "Violet

Dracula is the true ruler of Olympus and Hell…and the only one who can fix what you broke. When she comes for you—and mark my words, she will—I hope she makes your death long and painful. I hope you suffer." She says the last words as a hiss of air and then punctuates the statement by spitting on Zeus's bare feet.

Shock momentarily splays across his face before he surprises us all by throwing his head back with a booming laugh. Hera continues to stand before him, defiant and unfazed, as Zeus guffaws.

As abruptly as his amusement arrived, it fades, and he pulls his arm back to backhand her across the face.

Lucifer growls again as Hera falls to her knees, but this time, it's Hera who stops the devil from attacking by raising one palm in his direction.

"It's okay," she says, slowly ambling to her feet. "If you attack him, you know he'll make Violet's mates attack us. She'll never forgive you if something happens to the men she loves."

Wait…

The three most powerful monsters in existence aren't attacking and killing Zeus and his side bitch…because they don't want to kill us? Violet's mates?

A realization dawns on me, and I feel like a fucking idiot for not seeing it sooner.

Lucifer, Hera, and Dracula love Violet. They truly love her the way a parent loves their child.

The revelation closes my throat up as my eyes flick to Mason's prone form.

If only Medusa, or Diedre, had loved Mason that much. Maybe he wouldn't be decomposing right before my eyes.

Grief tears a hole in my chest as a scream works its way up my throat. It crawls at my skin, demanding release, and all I want to do is give in. Diedre is distracted, her attention solely on Zeus, her eyes wide and guileless. She chose her love for that monstrous man over the child she raised. She may not have been Mason's biological mom, but I truly believe a twisted, demented part of her cared for him. I saw the grief in her eyes when she stabbed him with the blade. No person can fake that.

As if she can hear my screaming thoughts, she turns her attention towards Mason once more, and grief distorts her expression. That only amplifies my fury, sending it shooting through me in white-hot, rippling waves. What right does she have to cry for him? To grieve him? She motherfucking killed him.

Murdered him in cold blood, all because she believed his death would break Violet.

"We need to give him a burial," she whispers, slowly lowering to her knees so she can place a palm on his pale white cheek.

*Don't touch him! No!*

That scream continues to build, but it doesn't travel all the way up. Instead, it gets lodged somewhere in the middle of my throat, applying just enough pressure to my windpipe for the breath to be knocked out of me.

"Leave him," Zeus says dismissively, not bothering to turn his attention off of a still glowering Hera. "We have Lucifer, Hera, and Dracula contained and Violet's other mates under control. It won't be long until she returns and we can finish what we started."

He means to kill Violet. Steal her power.

No. No. No.

The arrow hits its target as though shot by an expert marksman. Rage explodes within me, and my heart somersaults straight into my stomach. The thought of these two despicable monsters hurting my mate the way they hurt Mason...

My scream can't be contained.

The roar tears its way past my closed lips, and both Diedre and Zeus turn to stare at me in surprise. But I'm already running, already sweeping my hand down to grab the dagger out of Mason's chest, already lunging at the bitch who should've been dead by Violet's hands months ago.

But maybe I can be Violet's hand of death. Maybe I can be the grim reaper sneaking through the shadows at night and collecting unsuspecting victims. And maybe, just maybe, Diedre Stevens will be the first on that list.

After all, she was supposed to be dead once before. Zeus brought her back in a way that defied the natural order of things. I'm only setting the world right.

A life for a life.

Diedre doesn't have time to do more than gape at me before the god-blessed dagger is in her chest, puncturing her heart.

"This is for Mason," I whisper in a choked voice as I twist my wrist.

Her eyes widen, fear bleeding into her irises, and a tiny whimper escapes her. I keep a hold of the pummel as she falls to the floor, me kneeling beside her so I can maintain eye contact.

I want my eyes to be the last thing she sees.

I want her to know that she died by my hand…and she'll die again and again and again if I have anything to say about it.

She tries to tear her gaze away and focus on Zeus, but I give the dagger another twist to reclaim her attention.

Behind me, the room is silent—too silent. It's like every single monster is collectively holding their breaths.

And then Zeus begins to laugh, the noise laced with amusement and disbelief, as the life fades from Diedre's eyes and she goes slack in my arms. I have no idea if the bitch will stay dead, but if she comes back to life, she'll be haunted by a goddamn demon.

By *me*.

I scream again—the husky noise physically pulled straight from my soul—as Zeus begins to laugh harder.

"Well...that sure made things interesting," he exclaims with another chuckle. "I suppose I'll have to find her soul in Hell and digest it. After all, I could never touch those souls with Lucifer in charge. But now that he's here...it'll be like a fucking buffet."

I don't bother to pull my attention off the dead bitch as he laughs again. And again. And again.

"I brought her back to life once before, but to be honest? She's way too clingy for my tastes." He shudders audibly. "No, I think this time, I'm going to...savor her. I imagine the power she's wielded over the years will be quite decadent."

"You can bring people back to life," I whisper hoarsely, my head lowered, my back muscles tensed, my hand still wrapped around the dagger in her chest.

"Of course I can." Zeus moves to stand above me, and a second later, his hand slams down on my shoulder. "I am a god, after all." He kneels until he's at eye level with me, though I still don't look away from Diedre's dead body. I can't. "You want to know if I can bring your friend back, don't you?"

I can't breathe.

Can't move.

Frozen.

I'm not even sure if it's the spell he placed on me...or if my body has decided to fail me once and for all.

"What if I say I can help you, my dear boy?" It's those words that have my head slowly turning to stare at him, to take in his grizzled black beard and cutting eyes. He smiles, and chills of unease race down my spine at the sight of it. "A life for a life. You help me track down and destroy Violet Dracula…and I'll bring your best friend back to life. But if you don't help me…" His smile broadens, even as the hand biting into my shoulder tightens to the point of pain. "I'll digest Mason's soul, the way I do all of them that have passed. There'll be no second chance for the gorgon. No afterlife. No eternity in paradise. He'll simply cease to exist. So what do you say? Do we have a deal?"

# CHAPTER 32

Grief is a funny, fickle thing that takes you off guard when you're least expecting it. Sometimes, that pain tears you up inside—removes your heart straight from your chest, throws it onto the ground, and then stomps on it with the heel of a stiletto.

Other times, it sneaks up on you when you're not paying any attention. You can be perfectly fine, enjoying your day, and the grief hits you out of nowhere like rainfall on a sunny day. There's no rhyme or reason for it. No explanation. Grief just *is*, and that's more terrifying than any monster I could ever face.

Right now, my grief has transformed into an icy numbness that freezes my heart, body, and mind all with one fatal swoop. I can barely think through the crushing sound of icicles rubbing against one another in my head.

Mason's dead.

My men are gone, lost to me by Zeus's curse.

My parents are captives.

I'm alone.

So, so alone.

"Violet." Alex's gruff voice barely registers through the mind-numbing pain. The agony…

It barrages me from every direction, trapping me in an inescapable box.

I feel as if I've been stripped naked and strapped down onto a table. The clank of wheels accompanies a cart being pushed into the small, drab, gray room. On that table is every torture device imaginable, from pliers, to garden shears, to knives, to flame throwers. And…all I can do is accept the pain, to not let it consume me the way it so desperately wants to. As the first slash of the whip rains down on my bare skin, I'm forced to take it like a good little demon-goddess, to not flinch away. Every cut, burn, slice, tug… It doesn't make me stronger the way the songs and books would have you believe.

It destroys me.

"Please fix it," I whimper, tears creating tracks down my cheeks. "Please bring Mason back. Please, please. You're a necromancer—"

"I can't do that, baby," Alex replies sadly. "You know my powers don't work like that. I can control bodies, but I have no power over the souls of the dead. Fuck, I don't even know where Mason's soul *is*. Maybe if we found the soul, I could do what I did to Balor's body to Mason's and make it livable again, but… Fuck, I'm rambling. I just don't know if I can help you. I want to, Violet, I swear. But…"

"Fuck!" I run my fist into the nearest wall, spin on my heel, and then kick at a chair blocking my path. "Fuck! Fuck! Fuck!"

"Violet." Alex frames my face with his huge hands, the black rings on his fingers a cold contrast to his warm palms. His russet-obsidian eyes ensnare my own as the furrow between his brows deepens. "Violet, you need to look at me."

"Zeus took everything from me," I whisper hoarsely. "And I'm going to repay him in kind."

"Violet, you need to think about this—"

I push myself out of his embrace, not bothering to pay attention to my surroundings as I stalk away from Alex and towards the nearest window. We appear to be in a hotel of some sort, but I don't know where. Not that I want to ask. The location is irrelevant at the moment.

"And to do that, I'll need an army." I absently bring my finger to the window and trail my finger through the condensation present there. The squiggly line reminds me immediately of a snake, and pain wiggles its way through the numb barrier I've attempted to erect around myself.

With a scowl, I rub my hand through the image and turn towards Alex who's currently staring at me with wide, fear-filled eyes.

"Violet…" he begins, his voice a plea.

There's something else in his voice as well, something I can't name in my current state. An emotion, perhaps, that I never thought I would see in the grumpy necromancer.

But I don't pay it any mind.

"I'll visit the monster council," I continue, my brain five steps ahead of my mouth as it concocts a plan. "Tell them about what Zeus has been doing. His plans. They believe that they'll be free in death…but they're wrong. So, so wrong."

I think of all the people who have died. I assumed their souls have been going to paradise or damnation, but what if that's not the truth? What if they've just been eliminated completely because of Zeus's desperate grab for more power?

He's been eating—excuse me, *digesting* souls for who knows how long. Every pure soul that has gone to Mount

Olympus…has been destroyed. By him. By the god who was supposed to protect them all.

"They'll kill you," Alex whispers brokenly. "If they have the same spell on them that Vanessa has—that your mates all have—then they'll kill you before they allow you to speak."

"Maybe so." I stare at him blankly. "But I'm going to need their help if I'm going to destroy Zeus."

His eyes narrow with suspicion as he takes a step towards me. "What else are you planning, Violet?"

Numb. So, so numb.

The old me might've responded to him with a quip or retort. Might've told him to mind his own business.

But the new me? She doesn't give a shit anymore.

"Isn't it obvious, Alex?" I cant my head to the side, and he flinches at whatever he sees on my face. Is it my deadened eyes that make him look so sick? My unnaturally pale skin? Something else? I don't have enough strength to ask.

"What's obvious?" he manages to bite out, his tone scathing.

"After I get the monsters on my side, I'm going to seek the help of the one species of monsters who have already lost everything. Who have more reason than anyone to hate Zeus and his followers." A cold grin stretches up my lips, and Alex seems to pale even further, a feat I didn't think was possible.

He swallows heavily, and that twitching muscle in his jaw once again commandeers my attention. It always seems to flex whenever he's upset or anxious or scared. Which one is he now?

"The Formorians," Alex whispers breathlessly. "You want to free the Formorians from Hell."

"What do you say, necromancer?" The smile slips from my face. I just don't have the energy to hold it a second longer. "Do you want to help me gather an army, kill a god, claim a throne I have no idea how to hold, and then find a way to bring the dead back to life?"

Alex stares at me, assessing my words. One of his hands inches upwards to fiddle with the piercing in his lip, running his thumb across the bulb as he fidgets.

Then, slowly, he nods his head once.

Just like that, this queen has her first general in the war to come.

And what a bloody war it's going to be...

*To be continued in the explosive finale, Blood, coming soon!*

# AFTERWORD

Did you think that was the end? Well, I'm sorry to say you were wrong. So, so wrong.

Book five, tentatively titled Blood, should be releasing early 2023!

Thank you for reading the next book in Violet's journey.

# ACKNOWLEDGMENTS

There are so many people I need to thank when it comes to this book.

First, I would like to give a shout-out to my big sister, who convinced me to split the finale into two books instead of one. You were right, as always.

Second, I would like to thank my incredible alphas for your valuable advice and feedback. A special thank you to Ash for reading over books one, two, and three and sending me notes. That helped tremendously!

I would like to thank my incredible editor, Lindsey, for polishing up the manuscript. And of course, my cover designer, Logan, for bringing my vision to life.

And last but not least, I would like to thank you, the reader, for loving this series as much as I do. Violet is one of my favorite characters to write, and this world

# ABOUT THE AUTHOR

Katie May is a reverse harem author, a KDP All-Star winner, and an *USA Today* Bestselling Author. She lives in West Michigan with her family, cat, and adorable puppy. When not writing, she can be found reading a good book, listening to broadway musicals, or playing games. Join Katie's Gang to stay updated on all her releases! And did you know she has a TikTok? Yeah, me neither. Follow her here! But be warned... she's an awkward noodle.

Together We Fall (Apocalyptic Reverse Harem, COMPLETED)

1. The Darkness We Crave

2. The Light We Seek

3. The Storm We Face

4. The Monsters We Hunt

Beyond the Shadows (Horror Reverse Harem, COMPLETED)

1. Gangs and Ghosts

2. Guns and Graveyards

3. Gallows and Ghouls

Out of Sight (Prison Reverse Harem, COMPLETED)

1. Blindly Indicted

2. Blindly Acquitted

Kingdom of Wolves (Shifter Reverse Harem Duet, COMPLETED)

1. Torn to Bits

2. Ripped to Shreds

The Damning (Fantasy Paranormal Reverse Harem)

1. Greed

2. Envy

3. Gluttony

4. Sloth

5. Pride

Prodigium Academy (Horror Comedy Academy Reverse Harem)

1. Monsters

2. Roaring

3. Venom

Tory's School for the Trouble (Bully Horror Academy Reverse Harem)

1. Between

2. Beyond

3. Beneath

Kings of Grove Academy (Contemporary Academy Reverse Harem)

1. Mania

2. Psychotic

3. Pandemonium

Supernaturalette (Interactive Reverse Harem)

1. Introductions

2. First Dates

3. Group Outing

4. Game Night

5. Exes

6. Truth or Dare

7. Scavenger Hunt

## CO-WRITES

Afterworld Academy with Loxley Savage (Academy Fantasy Reverse Harem, COMPLETED)

1. Dearly Departed

2. Darkness Deceives

3. Defying Destiny

Darkest Flames with Ann Denton (Paranormal Reverse Harem, COMPLETED)

1. Demon Kissed

1.5. Demon Stalked

2. Demon Loved

3. Demon Sworn

Darkest Queen with Ann Denton (Paranormal Reverse Harem)

1. For Whom the Bell Tolls

Fae Revealed with Quinn Arthurs (Paranormal Reverse Harem)

1. Courting Darkness

2. Seducing Shadows

STAND-ALONES

Toxicity (Contemporary Reverse Harem)

Not All Heroes Wear Capes (Just Dresses) (Short Comedic Reverse Harem)

Charming Devils (Bully/Revenge Reverse Harem)

Goddess of Pain (Fantasy Reverse Harem)

Demon's Joy (Holiday Reverse Harem)

Broken Howl (Wolf Shifter Reverse Harem)

BOXSETS

Together We Fall